Wembley Tewkes on the Edges of Time

Book One:
Imperfections on the Edge

by
C. Michael Perry

Leicester Bay BOOKS

Newport, Maine

Paperbound Edition(CS) 2013 by Leicester Bay Books --
ISBN-13: 978-0615907253
ISBN-10: 0615907253
Paperback Edition 2014
KINDLE Edition 2016

BISAC: Fiction / Fantasy / Epic --
Adventure -- Coming of Age

Leicester Bay Books
PO Box 536, Newport Maine 04953-0536

Cover art and layout by Brook Bowen
of Bowen Design Works, Salt Lake City, Utah

Visit us at: **www.wembleytewkes.com**

For my parents, Maurice & Maryan --
because of the world I gained through their love of reading,
and their ability to pass it on to me

Imperfections on the Edge

Contents

CHAPTER ONE
Swimming Through The Blue

Why was he standing naked on what appeared to be the ocean floor while the hair from his head and body, some of it just recently arrived, unraveled pore by pore, follicle by follicle, from his skin as if someone else, somewhere, had grabbed a hold of the single thread from his body's carpet and didn't want to stop until the unraveling of it was complete? Well -- it was complete!

Why was he where he was?

He was a perfectly normal boy with a father and a mother, but no siblings, yet oodles of aunts and uncles and dozens of cousins. He had plenty of friends of both genders. His teachers loved him. His Scout troop hung on his every word. The entire town, in fact, doted on the kind, gentle, intelligent and capable lad known to them all as Wembley Tewkes. Well, almost the entire town. There was Evie, who unfortunately seemed to pop up in every one of his classes at Yarmouth High School -- except for Boy's P.E. -- thank heavens.

He had never had anything lower than a B+ on his report card. He had earned 118 of the 121 merit badges available and the Scouting organization had run out of Eagle Palm combinations to award him. He had won the most promising award, or its equivalent, from the FBLA, the FFA, The Junior Kiwanis, The International Thespian Society, Swim USA, The Junior ROTC, Junior Tennis League and still he was too young by far, almost a year shy, to get a learner's permit. He already knew how to drive, but there were these pesky little irritations called laws.

So many things lay in his future: happenings, events, experiences, too many to even dare imagine. They were all waiting for the luck-born, sun-kissed, poster child that spoke to all parents everywhere saying 'don't you wish he was yours?' He inspired confidence and trust. It was just a part of him, somehow.

As Wembley looked around him under that clear, turquoise water it all seemed to be one long giant hair as it coiled and swerved and kinked and floated around him in the darkening water. The hair was blocking the light; making him wonder if anyone else could see him in his vulnerable nakedness.

Wherever he was!

Even his mother had never seen him naked; at least not since he was old enough to bathe himself. Since he always wrapped himself up in a towel and changed in the bathroom stalls during gym class no one else had seen him either. The thought of all that flesh exposed, his or anyone else's, really unnerved him. He even showered at home since gym class was the last class of his school day.

All these thoughts that had flowed through his mind since he had found himself submerged and staring at his floating hair, paled in comparison with the next of his sudden realizations. It stopped him cold. It brought him up short as his hands waved in front of him to help him maintain his place in the gentle currents eddying under the water: how was he breathing?

He didn't know. But he was! Breathing. He had to be! Unless he was dead. Was death this calm? Was death without hair? He couldn't be dead. He felt too alive! Enervated. Exposed. Excited. Elated. Enhanced.

Ensnared?

No, that was just his hair -- that one long hair that used to be his, anyway -- wafting around him, but teasingly no longer a part of him.

He freed his mind from the sudden panic that had possessed it and managed to move his hands over his skin.

No hair anywhere! It must be his hair that was in the water! And his hands were moving so he must be alive.

He felt like reaching out, taking a hold of the coil and wrapping it back around his body. It did belong to him after all! It *was* his! Why was it in the water around him instead?

Coming down off of his bald head his hands found something else that had never been there before. There were funny little slits on his neck. Did he cut himself? Is that how he died? He wasn't dead! The slits were opening and closing in time with the rhythm of the movement of his chest as his lungs were expanding and contracting.

When did he grow gills? Were they gills? They had to be. There were six of them; three on either side of his neck.

How was this possible? His life of superior normalcy, of advanced conformity, of uncountable but measured interests, could not have prepared him for the next engulfing moment in time. He could not fathom this so out-of-his-experience experience.

What about Brindi?

This wasn't the pool! There was sand here. The pool had a concrete bottom. He had been there, hadn't he? It's funny that he should think of Brindi now! He certainly did not want his girlfriend to see him in his present state!

Or was this just the start of another of those disturbing dreams that troubled all adolescent boys? That's it! He was just asleep!

He waited, breathing through his gills. *Cool!* he thought.

He pinched his hip.

Ow!

He pressed the tender sole of his foot against the sharp coral nearby.

He shouldn't have done that! It hurt! The pain sure felt real. His foot was starting to bleed. Also, as he inspected his current condition, trying to think rationally, a little red welt appeared on his hip where he had pinched himself to see if he was awake or asleep. The blood from the cut on his foot began to swirl away in a tiny crimson ribbon. Maybe it would go off and join the hair?

What about sharks? He thought: *They have gills, too! The blood could draw them to me!*

He reached down and pressed his fingers over the small foot wound as he tried to push the blood back into his body. He stopped the bleeding. Direct pressure. First Aid merit badge!

Unfortunately, while his focus was shifted to his foot, his one, single, solitary, more-than-a-mile-long-hair drifted away from him and disappeared.

Oh, no!

Out of reach.

Out of sight.

Out of his mind!

What was he thinking? He folded his hands over his chest and breathed in. Then out. What worked for him in the air worked for him here, under the water.

He would not get depressed. But he missed his hair already. He had liked it that one time when Brindi had run her fingers through the moderately long, dark curls that used to cover his skull. It had been a playful gesture of their friendship. But a welcome one. She would never dare touch his bald egghead!

His depression returned, beginning to overwhelm him to the point of irrationality. He supposed he'd have to join a skinhead group. It would be the only place for him, now.

That was enough to turn his thoughts again. What a dumb thought!

He liked everybody. (Well, maybe Evie Griffith was the exception there. It's not that he didn't want to like her. She just gave him -- or anyone else at school -- no opportunity. She was pretty, though. But not as attractive as Brindi!) He felt that everybody had something about them, something good, nice, or attractive; something to like; at least as far as he was concerned. (Even Evie! He just had to find it.) He mentally thunked his forehead. How could he have thought of joining a group based on the hatred of others? He had not felt hate a day in his life.

He couldn't hate! He couldn't join. Join what?

He tried to calm himself. He breathed deeply -- through his gills!

This had to be a dream! It was too absolutely weird to be really happening.

But it was happening! No, he had not yet awakened! That was the answer. What answer?

But he couldn't remember ever getting home from the pool where he and Brindi spent most of every summer day. Dreams didn't last this long! Or did they?

He pushed off from the sea floor and reached toward the golden glow that was far above him. His arms and legs cut through the water, propelling him toward the surface.

His hands, then arms, then face, followed by his lithe, strong body broke through the horizon of the water, launching him into the warm, moist air like a dolphin breaching. He was not ready for what he found there, in the air. There, of course, was nothing to hold him up. So he merely belly-flopped back against the water's surface. The landing almost took his breath away with its forceful impact.

Soon, he was easily treading water, looking around, seeing nothing but an island a little less than a mile away. He eased into an Australian Crawl, his tan and pink body slicing through the warm turquoise waters heading for the little yellow and green island. The windmill of his arms; the fan-like flutter of his legs and feet; the rhythmic breathing every two strokes, even with the presence of gills; all told him that this was not normally where or how someone would find him. He wondered if there was a sicko sorcerer around somewhere. He'd seen too many movies. While he was still pondering who, where and what he was, his feet touched down on the sloping sands in the bay of a little island.

His head and shoulders rose out of the water to see -- naked people. A whole beach full. Not one stitch of clothing on as far as he could see.

And I thought gym class was bad!

Where was he? Some nudist colony in the Caribbean? Without a towel!

Then there was something even more different, more disturbing. All the brown bodies, tanned to perfection, were entirely hairless; just like he had become. He could tell there were men, women, boys and girls -- but certainly not by their haircuts. He quickly looked down at the water; he tried to keep his eyes focused anywhere but at those persons on the beach that had begun to move as if to greet him.

He suddenly knew where he was: on a planet without puberty!

He looked up again. The people were glancing in his direction. He dared to look at them; uncomfortable as it was to do so. They smiled at him. He stared back. Then several of those nearest to him, motioned for him to join them. One spoke.

"Come on out -- the sun is fine!" Was that an adult? Or a kid? He couldn't tell.

Was that English?

He was frozen. Memories of 7th Grade gym class, the cruelty and insensitivity of the kids back home -- for he was certainly not at home -- rushed back to his mind and he froze. He continued to stare, open-mouthed and dumbfounded, as if he were rooted to the sand like some transplanted variety of seaweed. He was half in and half out of the water. What else could he do but stand still?

"You're new here, aren't you?" A kid, this time?

Wembley continued to stare but managed to nod slightly.

"It's no matter. Come on out." That was an adult -- at least he was as tall as Wembley.

The adults seemed to lag behind as a group of seemingly younger beings flooded into the water around him. They took hold of his arms, all saying things, welcoming him, reassuring him. After much convincing he slowly walked up the shore -- being guided out of the water. Why? He didn't know! The water got lower and lower. His hands got higher and higher -- which was difficult to do with all those other hands gripping his arms -- but he managed to move his hands to the fig-leaf position as his midsection cleared the surface. He braced for the taunting and teasing.

But there were no comments. No remarks. No suspicious eyes. No laughing smirks. No snickers or guffaws. He soon realized that he was no different from anyone else here. Just a hairless cueball like all those smiling back at him now.

"Where am I?"

"You'll find out soon enough."

"You'll like it here."

The greetings and reassurances continued until, "It's a nice place to be from."

"But I'm not *from* here." That stopped the queries and the seemingly false sentiments of comfort.

This small group of youths, who all seemed to be close to him in age, dragged him down the beach as they chattered away at him as if they had known him all their lives.

He had to be out of his own world and in a place where he felt no judgments from anyone. He sensed no need to have to prove himself here, like he sometimes had to do back home. Although proving himself had never been particularly difficult for Wembley, it was still a nuisance. For what was excellent came naturally to him. It was the everyday that sometimes troubled him or tripped him up. Literally. Soon, the group of youths had drawn Wembley into a sand volleyball game. Wembley was introduced to Fiona, Allison, Jared, Elisha, Lisa, Peter, Shane, Briony, Colin, Sharon and Vivi, who was also dragged, somewhat unwillingly, into the game

"It's a good thing you came along. Up to now we've always played short handed," Vivi laughed. The others looked at her a little strangely -- and Wem noticed their reactions -- for she had only arrived yesterday, or so Jared had said. Vivi had especially green eyes. All through the game, she never stopped watching Wem. Her smile also unnerved him. There was something so familiar about her that it was difficult for him to take his eyes away from hers. Besides she was pretty -- even without hair! At first, Wem felt like he ought to cover up, but it was a little difficult to do that and play volleyball, too. He looked around for a tablecloth or a towel he could steal. No towels at all and every tablecloth was spread out with food and people on top. Thoughts of Vivi, and her piercing eyes, as well as her physical presence, gradually melted into the background as Wem let the game and the environment take him over. It's kind of funny what we are able to do once we find we cannot avoid doing it.

As a natural athlete, Wembley fell into the rhythms of the match. He enjoyed serving the ball. But he loved to be on the front line even more because he was tall and could spike the ball really well.

They played all afternoon. Wembley was amazed. Every effort of each teammate was applauded -- by both sides. Except for Vivi. Every few games they would mix up the players so that everyone got a chance to play on everyone else's team. Vivi was the last one picked. Every time. Wembley thought that was a strange thing among these non-judgmental kids but no answers came to him.

He had never had an experience like this. There were no fights; no arguments. His friends back home, as much as he loved them, were sometimes contentious as they played. Here each point was made and accepted. If it was in bounds it was in, out was out! No debating. Wembley began to think that he had to be dead; that he was in Heaven because only Heaven could be this good.

No, he was alive. He could feel the sun warming him, and the air cooling him at the same time. These were living people in front of him; not some long dead or recently deceased spirits. He sure hoped he wasn't dead.

He wasn't sure that this was Earth -- at least it wasn't his Earth. Besides, the others were sweating too much to be dead. Their bodies glistened in the sun as they reached and dove and slapped at the ball. The sand stuck to their moist bodies in sheets and cakes. Every so often they would all run into the water to rinse off; like a flock of birds or a school of fish; all in the same mind at the same time. Except for Vivi. Then they would return to the neverending game of volleyball enjoying each minute of it as if it was the first -- while Wembley tried not to just stand there, watching while he played.

Wem sadly shook his head. It couldn't be Heaven. It wasn't quite perfect. But it was so close.

These kids made him feel at ease. Except for Vivi. She was kind of freaky. Always watching him. These kids were so unlike some of the other kids he knew, at his High School, whose minds were centered on the carnal; on crudeness; on depravity. On themselves. Like Evie. What they would do with this current situation would be mind-bogglingly sick. Thankfully, there didn't seem to be any of that here. It certainly could be heaven-like.

He had so long yearned for a place like this one, where those silly things of the world seemed not to matter -- even to the adolescents that had gathered around him. Neither did they seem to matter to any of the adults he had been introduced to over the course of the afternoon -- parents of his new friends -- and others. He studied each one, searching for some warning sign, some way of identifying how he had arrived here. But each one of them, adult or child, accepted him as a matter of course; almost to the point of ignoring him. How could they not notice him?

Acceptance was the norm here.

Later that afternoon, he joined his friends, and their mostly very large families, at a communal picnic. He really liked Shane and Briony. He seemed to fit with them the most. But every time he talked to them, or joked, or laughed, or even when he was sitting between them, eating a sandwich, he felt the heavy eyes of Vivi on him. He sensed that she did not like him talking to anyone but her. He remembered her strange comments during the volleyball game and the other's reactions to her. She seemed like an outsider where everyone else seemed like an insider.

Wem was drawn back to the party by a joke from Briony. He didn't remember ever enjoying himself so thoroughly. The food tasted like the food at home, but better. The games were the same, but more fun. The sun was warmer and the water more refreshing. At home he lived in the sun and water, too. But not like this. Where was Brindi, anyway? The people looked the same -- except for their lack of hair and clothing, which he thought should be bothering him, but it really wasn't anymore.

He hadn't noticed it until now but everyone here had little gills on their necks. It was a thought that made him sit up and reflect. There was something else that struck him strangely: while the children were playing, freely, in and around the water, the adults seemed to shy away from it, rarely even letting the waves touch their feet.

He came to the conclusion that what was different here was the attitude. The relationships between people were simple and unaffected. While at home, even though love was omnipresent, there were fights, disagreements, disillusionments, too many varied opinions; rudeness; murders, lusts and other undesirables that seemed not to be able to intrude upon this idyllic place; or have any effect on this uncomplicated people.

He figured that he could call this planet, or wherever it was, Eden. Vivi seemed to be the only snake in the world. She just didn't fit. She was glaring at him again as he laughed with Briony.

The warm yellow sun had begun to pull the shade of night over the purpling window of the sky as it slowly, peacefully, sank into the green-blue sea. Though he was almost completely accustomed to the nakedness by now -- which was a strange thought for the shy and modest Wembley Tewkes -- it surprised him that as it got slightly cooler, but not yet really cold, no one put anything on.

All they did was pack up their picnic packs and blankets and other trappings and head away from the sea; across a road to a community of small, neat, well-trimmed, well-appointed, similar-to-each-other houses, facing the beach, glistening white in the last ray or two of the sinking sun.

As the darkness fell, and it fell fairly quickly and suddenly, every door of each perfect little house closed with a click leaving Wembley alone on the beach. He loved the beach of his own Broad Cove, in Maine, at night, even though it wasn't as sandy as this one. He was content in his own solitude there, but he wondered why he was suddenly all alone, here. Had it all been just a sham? The friendship? The camaraderie? The well-meaning intentions from each adult and youth he had met seemed to have evaporated now with the loss of the sun.

He heard a rustle coming off the water. He turned to see the great waves, that had occasionally crashed against the warm sand and surrounded and delighted him and his new friends all afternoon, grow calm, flatten and trickle in tiny washes only then to become merely a pulse that traveled a short twelve to eighteen inches onto and off of the sand in a rhythm like a heartbeat.

As the sand dried out, it shifted, popped and exploded close to the water's edge. Little crab-like creatures leaped from their day-long confinement in the hot sands as if some conduit was spewing them out, evicting them from some crab hotel deep below the beach. First one or two appeared, then ten, then fifty, hundreds, thousands. Soon the beach was covered. Moving. Writhing.

Wembley heard a click and a creak from across the road. As he turned to investigate those sounds a voice sped to him out of the darkness: "Wembley! Get in here!"

Why? he thought. He looked back over the roiling beach. *It's just nature. Nothing alarming,* came into his mind. Then barks and squeaks rattled his hearing. Huge black and white bodies lunged their way out of the dark waters and onto the unquiet sands; mouths open, crab-things disappearing by the gulp.

Caws and screeches reached him from overhead as white wings flapped in a stormy flurry while yellow feet padded the shifting sands and sharp beaks sliced through exo-skeletons. Sharp beaks began to attack Wembley's sensitive skin. Then he felt hands grab him and pull him away. Shane and Briony were tugging at him. They ran from the beaks as he and his new friends rushed to and through their door.

Safe!

"What was that all about?"

"They don't intend to harm us. They just need to feed. In their frenzy we are as good to eat as anything else," explained Briony.

"We've learned to stay off the beach at night." Shane hung his head a little.

"A little warning would have been nice." It was a little loud, a little harsh, but Wembley was more than a little perturbed as he daubed at the tiny flows of blood from his legs. But as he looked up into the sheepish faces of his newest friends he could not be angry with them.

"Sorry." Shane, slightly older than Wembley, truly was sorry.

"Me too!" Briony insisted.

"This place is so different from where I live."

"How different?"

"We wear clothes."

"What?"

"You're kidding? Aren't you? You know -- clothing? Shirts ... pants ... socks ... underwear ..."

Blank looks of complete ignorance met Wembley's eyes.

"You know, things that cover up your body?"

Briony and Shane exchanged a glance. "Why?"

Wembley caught himself before speaking. Even in his moment of exasperation he realized that he didn't want to hurt anyone's feelings. After all, how they lived was pure normalcy to them.

"It's just something that's ... necessary where I live." There, the excuse had been made. "It's not warm there like it is here." He paused. Sighed. "And

I miss my hair." His hands roamed over his bald head.

"Your what?"

Wembley's eyes just about popped out of their sockets. "Never mind." He realized that it would be like trying to describe a sunny day to a blind person. There was no possible frame of reference. At least, Wembley hadn't seen one, yet. "So, what do we do now?"

"We play some games, have a light supper; watch the telly."

Wembley laughed.

"What's so funny?"

"Nothing, really. I've just never heard anyone my age use that word."

"What word?"

"Telly. My Grans use it, they're from the UK, but my friends don't use it."

"We're not your friends?" There was a mock hurt in the question.

"Of course you are. I meant my friends back home."

"Where is it?"

He shrugged his shoulders. "I really don't know. Across the ocean, somewhere, I guess."

Briony's mom entered. "Just like the place where most of us came from at one time or another."

"What do you mean?" Wembley was confused.

"Most of us came out of the sea, like you did today, Wembley, and got together and formed families."

"You're saying that you didn't give birth to your children?"

Wembley's question was met with more stares of complete incomprehension.

Briony's excitement cut through Wembley's reflection.

"So, it looks like you are a new member of our family!"

Wembley smiled. Shane and Briony smiled back in return. This wasn't a bad home. But Wembley wanted his own house. The old sea captain's house on what had become 'his' hobby farm. He needed Mom and Dad, his room overlooking the field with Broad Cove in the distance, Brindi and his other friends -- the people he'd grown up with.

But he was here now, however he got here, so he decided to make the best of the situation. He plopped himself prone onto the couch. "What's on the telly?" He sort of giggled.

Shane smilingly plopped down across the backs of Wembley's feet. Briony eased herself down next to Wembley's head. He tried to ignore her body that was so close to his. Did these people have no sense of personal space? But there it was. She picked up the remote and clicked it on. Laughter issued forth from the telly's speakers. As the image faded in, it was that of a department store -- a sales floor just off the elevator platform. 'Ba-duh-bup-pah-pah" played as a simple music transition while naked, hairless actors crossed the screen. Familiar words and accents spewed out of their mouths. More laughter from an unseen audience percolated and popped from the little viewing screen.

"I think I've seen this show!" Wembley was surprised.

"Yeah, great, isn't it?" Briony answered.

"You've seen it, too?"

"It's the only show on at this hour."

Wembley hadn't noticed but he looked now and saw that the television set had no controls for changing channels. Just volume and on and off. One channel?!

"Sandwiches!" announced Mother Stella as the kids sat up and she placed plates in their hands.

Stella and her 'husband', Ralph, took their places in their own chairs with their own sandwiches, leaving the couch to the kids. Little Gerald, about seven or eight, ran in and plopped right between Briony and Wembley. As the boy wiggled his bare little body into place Wembley felt a little safer, more removed from the temptation -- that only he seemed to feel -- that had been sitting right next to him. He felt more at ease with Gerald there.

Stella handed her youngest 'son' his own plate and he munched and laughed happily between his sister and their new brother. Laughter continued to resound out of the telly and from the little 'family' gathered to watch it.

The telly's screen was dark. The room was almost black. Wembley was alone on the couch, a pillow under his head. The house was silent. He got up. It was still so warm. He crossed to the open window, standing in front of the shrouded incoming light, warm breeze, and pulled back the curtain.

The beach and the sea beyond it were flat and empty. The silence was only aggravated by the shush of the water across the sand. The moons were full and shimmered in their reflections off the calm surface of the water. Wait! Moons?

Not Earth. Definitely!

A big moon hung in the sky with its little brother or sister just hanging on to its eternal hand as if they were on an adventure together. Where was he? He crossed to the door and looked around. He opened it and stood there revealed in the moonslight, his body caressed softly by the breeze.

The air smelled fresh and clean. Almost like after a rain. He breathed deeply. He loved the smell of the sea. He pushed the door all the way back against the wall and leaned his shoulder against the jamb. The moonslight enshrouded him, casting a blue mantle over his own tan and pink. That would be one thing he could feel good about losing here -- his tan lines.

It was very pretty out. Wembley was strangely content. But he did have that other life; that other family -- somehow, only half-remembered, now. He was sure that he was not from here! He had to be from somewhere else! He longed to see the people he was barely remembering. He wondered if he ever would. He knew that this was no mere dream. Not even a terribly long and wonderfully weird dream. It couldn't be. It was far too real. And even though it was weird, it had an order to it. Dreams were all discombobulated. A mish-mash of images, and these were no mere illusions.

As his thoughts drifted back and forth from his own world to this one, he lost himself in the possibilities and the perplexities, the ideas that swarmed over him; whether here or at home. He was accepted here, but yet, he felt that he wasn't really a part of it all -- only an observer. Briony and Shane didn't remember anything else before this existence. Had they come to this place just like he had? If they had then why could he remember where he came from and they could not?

To distract himself, he reviewed his day -- today -- his warm, whacky, wild, and wayward day. He felt a hand on his upper arm. It was warm, too, as it laid against his biceps. He was surprised that the contact didn't startle him. He turned slightly to see Briony illuminated in the soft glow of the moons. He put his arm across her back and placed his hand on her opposite shoulder. She did the same to him. They stood there taking in the beauty and the silence of a night that was beyond beautiful now; what with the absence of the noisy beach feeders.

Briony was very attractive. She had told him that she, too, was fourteen. Wembley thought that she was maybe a little too attractive -- especially for a 'sister.'

He then felt strong fingers in a gentle pressure, grasp the back of his neck and squeeze it a little. It was Shane. A greeting. They all stepped out the door, sat on the bench that was under the window to the door's left. (All of the houses, all the way down the row, had doors with windows and benches on their left.) But this particular bench was the only one occupied at the moment. Wembley sensed that among all this apparent sameness, there were sparks and moments of individualness.

The three youths leaned back against the now cooler stucco of the house and watched the night as it continued to unfold. The moons traveled their separate arcs, beam in beam. Stars twinkled. A few fell or shot across the carpet of darkest blue above. The three youths marveled, internally and externally. It was so like home to Wembley. But it was not home! But he had brothers and a sister here. It was like the fulfillment of his fondest wish. But dreams don't come true. That's what his teachers, the unimaginative ones at least, told him at school. They told him that he had to work for everything he wanted. Nothing was going to be handed to him. Which is pretty close to the truth; but it was still nice to be able to dream. Dream or reality; he was here now. It all left Wembley wondering how he had gotten here -- and why?

Had he come through a door to a different world? Was he only somewhere else on his own Earth? Nope. Two moons. If not, this was somewhere that the 'moral majority' back home had not yet ruined with its stamp of disapproval. It was simple and free -- and almost comforting. The conservatives and the liberals never stopped arguing back home. What would they do here, in this environment? Here everything was conservative at the same time that it was liberal. It wasn't perfection -- there was that no clothing and no hair thing -- but it was peaceful, pleasing, placid. (He loved aliteratives!) So unlike his Earth.

Was it a dream, after all?

A fracture of reality? An alternate?

Whose reality was this?

It must be somebody's reality. But, sadly, it didn't seem like his own. He couldn't accept it. He sighed, audibly.

The silence around him had changed. He felt watched. He looked to each side of him; to Briony on his left and Shane on his right. He smiled as he realized that his new 'brother' and 'sister' had lapsed into the soft, shallow breathing of sleep. They had come out here just to be with him. But he felt that there was some...thing else watching. It made him a little uncomfortable, but he neither saw nor heard anything that could confirm his uneasy feeling.

Had it happened to them like it had to Wembley? Had they come through the portal of the sea to a new existence in the same way he had; ripped from a complicated life of somewhere else to this Eden? Did they know? Did they remember? Were they here now only because someone had been there for them? Or could they only remember their lives from their last few moments in the sea before they emerged into what Aldous Huxley and Shakespeare had called a brave new world?

He had never had a brother or a sister before. His family's flight from Wales had been too stressful on his Mother, Marged, and she lost his little brother in a miscarriage. His parents were never able to conceive again. So there was a benefit to this place! Only one. Everything else seemed to jostle his senses and distract him into a lull, as if he were under some sort of spell cast by some pervert of an enchanter.

Even without siblings, he had never been lonely. His parents had made sure that he was always surrounded by people or things to do. Even if it was to be alone or to read a book. If that was his choice, they supported him.

The sheep he raised on their hobby farm; enrollment in Scouting, Kiwanis, Junior ROTC, and other school clubs like FBLA, FFA, Thespian Society, all kept him busy. Being on the beach here all day -- every day? -- that was not being busy. It was even something that was kind of empty. His parents had paid for piano lessons, tennis lessons, Little League and swim lessons at the local club. He was a fish. He touched the gills on his neck. Hey, he *was* a fish! There were no lessons here. Just activities. *No learning,* he thought, *does that mean no progress as well?*

His fingers lingered over the hair that wasn't on his head. Briony and Shane and the contentment of the night began to fade from his consciousness.

No! Don't go!

All was suddenly bright blue around Wembley Tewkes.

CHAPTER TWO
When Is A House Not A Home?

He was underwater again! The ground beneath his feet was solid, not shifting like the sands of that otherwhere ocean. He looked down. He was wearing board shorts! His hands went to his head. His long, dark curls were back!

There was a tug on the waistband of his shorts. He turned. It was Brindi! She was even pretty underwater. Maybe even more-so than usual as the sunlight streaming through the water played off her cheeks and hair! She pointed up, frantically.

He flexed his knees and pushed off the bottom. As he breached the surface -- as he had done only so recently, it seemed -- he realized that he had been holding his breath for a relatively long time. His lungs ached as he gasped for air. He felt his neck. His gills were gone! What was going on? Then he heard it!

"Cannonball!"

The water exploded around him. He and Brindi coughed and spluttered as they tried to seize their assailant. They caught up with him at the ladder, still wiping their eyes, and hastily reached up to topple him back into the water. All they got a hold of, briefly, was cloth. The boy was not in their hands. All they saw, again briefly, were two round globes of flesh. All they heard was the scream as the cloth was ripped back out of their hands. All they witnessed was Brindi's younger brother, Russel, dashing to the dressing room, clasping his shorts to his waist in front and back to keep them up and himself covered.

Whistles were blowing but the child would not stop running.

Wembley and Brindi smiled sheepishly at one another. Then at the lifeguard.

Then they were interrupted by a red haired girl in a black, one piece suit. "So, you abuse little children now, huh Tewkes?"

It was Evie Griffith. She was soundly ignored by both Brindi and Wembley as Wem left the side of the pool.

"I'd better go see what I can do."

"Thanks, Wem."

"Be back in a sec."

Evie walked away, smiling, either used to or unaware of the snub; probably seeing someone else she could insult. Nobody liked her at school. She didn't even have the usual coterie of fawning friends that most bullies did. She was a total loner. A total loser as far as Brindi was concerned. Wembley actually felt sorry for her. It still bothered him, a little, the way she was always hanging around wherever he was.

When Wembley arrived in the locker room it was empty except for the sound of sobbing and the sobber himself.

"Russ?"

"Go away!"

"I'm really sorry. We didn't mean for that to happen."

"Everybody saw my butt!"

"Is that all?"

"Geez -- I hope so!"

"That's not what I meant. I'm sure that's all anyone saw. I meant that it's really no big deal."

"So you did see!"

"No -- ach, you're taking this all wrong, Russ."

Russ was not convinced. A bare butt in a public pool seemed like a big deal to the almost ten-year-old. Especially when it was his own.

He sat there, considering his friend, Wembley Tewkes. "You sure?" finally emerged from Russ' lips, but he was still doubtful.

Wembley nodded. "We didn't intend to pants you. We grabbed for your legs and missed."

"Get better aim!"

"Our eyes were kind of full of chlorinated water at the time, if you'll remember."

"Oh, yeah." Russel giggled. "Got ya good, huh?"

"Sure did! How can a little thing like you make such a big splash?"

Russel shrugged and faced Wembley with the widest of grins. His mood had passed. Wembley made a suggestion.

"Let's swim."

"Can't."

"Why not?"

"Drawstring's broke. I'd just end up goin' skinnydippin' again."

"Ah -- well -- I can fix that."

"Ya can?"

Wembley nodded and went to his locker, opened it, and tossed a large multi-colored beach towel to Russ. "Wrap that around you and give me your suit."

"Will I get it back?"

"Even if you didn't you could wear the towel home. But yes, you'll get it back."

Russ thought for a few seconds. "Okay."

The suit was tossed to Wembley. There were two strings. Both were supposed to be anchored at the back of the waistband and then run around the sides to be tied off in front. One of them was no longer anchored. Wem ripped a little hole over the string that was still attached. He rethreaded the loose string through its side-channel in the waistband. He then tied the loose string through the hole and around the end of the already anchored one. He tied a knot at the front end of the reanchored string and then tied both together in a bow. He held the shorts out to Russ.

The boy's eyes were wide. "Whoa! How'd you do that?"

Wem tossed the shorts back to Russ and, after careful examination, the boy slipped them on and tossed the towel back to Wem.

"Dunno. Just did. Come on!"

They walked out of the locker room, Wem's hand resting on Russ' shoulder. He wished he had a little brother. Or a sister. Either would be great. This was one of the few ways in which Wembley Tewkes had not been lucky or blessed -- except on Eden.

"You in Webelos yet?"

"No. Next year. Gotta be ten. But I got my Tiger, Bear, and Wolf."

"Good for you!"

Praise from Wembley was always welcome in Russ' life. Most of the younger kids in town sought for Wembley's attention and kind words. Mostly because Wembley was always sure to provide them. Wembley didn't know it, but he had a lot of little brothers and sisters.

"Is it true that you've earned every merit badge there is?"

"All but ... four." Wem smiled. Actually he had earned 118 out of the 121 possible.

"Which?"

" Basketry, Truck Transportation, American Labor, and torturing nine-year-old almost-Webelos who ask too many questions!"

Wem picked Russ up over his head. Russ screamed and laughed with glee because he knew what was coming. A whistle sounded, but it was too late! Russ sailed through the air and landed on the water with a splat. Brindi was there to roughhouse with him while Wem dove in to join them. As their splashing calmed down, Wembley asked another question.

"How long have we been here today?"

"All day."

"I've been with you all the time?"

Brother and sister nodded.

"Yesterday?"

"All day too. Why?"

"Must've been a dream, then. Weird. I hoped somehow it was real. At least I think I do."

"What was real?"

"Tell. Tell!"

"You might be a little young to hear some of it."

"Am not!"

Brindi gave Russel a strong look. Russel folded his arms across his chest in a formidable nine-year-old pout. Wem glanced at Brindi. "There are other things in it that I should never reveal to a lady, either."

Brindi looked shocked.

Russel laughed in a long, machine-gun type blast. "That good, huh, Wem?"

"Good! Who've you been talking to? I fixed your shorts and I can unfix them ... or remove them!" Wem reached playfully for Russel's waist.

"I'll be good! I'll be good! I'll be good!"

Russel was in the air again, laughing and sailing to another part of the pool. He scrambled to the ladder nearest him, got out and turned back to the older pair. "Not!" He waggled his now covered butt at them in defiance.

His machine-gun laugh came again as he ran over to the waterslide area. One thing he did know was when to make a retreat. He also knew when his sister and friend needed to talk. (That's two things!)

Out of their laughter Brindi and Wem turned to face each other and let their laughter die away into an uncomfortable silence.

"Perverted dreams? You?"

"Not perverted -- just well, really, really weird."

He told her.

She blushed, and laughed, and sucked her teeth at him. Then they were silent again.

"It was so real."

"But ..."

"So -- real. Like I was physically there."

There was a slight pause as she looked at him, trying to figure out how to help him. "Briony, huh?" She arched her eyebrows at him.

"At least it starts with a 'B.' He waggled his eyebrows at her.

She kissed his nose. "You're here now. It's all right." She drew her hand across his cheek. "Should we join the munchkin?"

"Why not! I'm in the mood for a slide."

They waited at the bottom of the slide, in the splashdown pool, to ambush Russel. He loved it! Then they all ran to the top and went down in a train. Definitely against the rules but hey -- you only live once! (Or do you?)

That night at dinner, which Wembley's Welsh parents unfailingly called 'suppa', he asked them a really strange question. His father, Dylan Tewkes, was in the middle of a mouthful of bangers and mash. (Wem's favorite -- Dylan's too!) His mother, Marged, had just wiped her mouth.

"Do we know anyone who lives in the Caribbean?"

The formerly unalterable silence had been broken. His father stopped chewing. His mother hurriedly popped some potatoes into her mouth and started chewing. No answer was forthcoming from either of them.

"Do we?" Wem persisted.

Slack-jawed looks passed between the parents. Chewing stopped and resumed again.

"How about nudists? We know any of those?"

All chewing stopped abruptly as the adults almost choked. The butts of their knives and forks banged the table as each parent's hands came down a little too forcefully on the table top. Shocked faces turned to stern looks that pierced the silence like a crack of doom.

"I'll take that as a no." Wembley looked down at his own favorite food.

Chewing went back to normal as Wembley pushed himself away from the table, his dinner untouched.

"G'night, Ma -- night, Da."

He trudged up the stairs of their classic old sea-captain's home. He made his way to his room leaving his parents to set their tableware down and continue to stare at each other. Not in anger, but maybe there was a little fear and bewilderment present.

"Caribbean nudists?"

"Hardly like the Wembley we know and love."

"Where is he getting it?"

"I'll call Da. Mebbe he can make some sense of it."

"It skipped you, didn't it?"

"Da was the one with the over-active imagination." Dylan looked toward the stairs. "Poor lad. Hoped another generation'd be spared, I did. But it looks like it caught him square."

"Why now?"

"Why not now?"

"Puberty!"

"Has ta be, Marged. As if it isn't bad enough on its own."

"I'll take him his plate."

"Good idea. I'll go call Da."

Marged grabbed the place setting, kissed the top of her husband's balding head and passed up the staircase.

The light in Wembley's room was occluded by heavy drapes and shades at the wide, turreted windows in each of the two outer corners. It was not dark but it was dim as Wem opened his door, stepped through, turned to close the door, then turned again to face the darkness but suddenly faced a totally bright but empty room.

It *was* his room. Sort of.

But there was no furniture. No shading on the windows. It had all been there before he turned around. He was sure of it! He had seen it! Hadn't he? Now, none of his knick-knacks, trophies or memorabilia hung on the walls. The painting of Winslow Homer's *The Reaper* was missing! The wall paper looked old. Different. Faded. Peeling. His lovely braided rug, made by his Ma's ma -- his Gran Adelaide -- was no longer under his feet. He walked into the turret on his left and kneeled to look out the window. There were no cars outside. The trees were not the same. Smaller ... and different. The road going by was gravel not macadam. There were no telephone poles or power lines. He turned to look at the wall by the door. There was no light switch! He ran to the door. He paused with his hand on the knob. It would not turn. He could not open it. There was no exit for him this way. He pulled his hand off the knob and went to the right-hand turret.

He threw open the sash there and began to climb out. He suddenly felt like he was being squeezed like a piece of paper through the rollers of a computer printer. He thought he almost heard a little 'pop.' But soon he was balanced on the sill. When he was at last able to turn over, his feet found the downspout mounts. He grabbed a-hold and slid down the copper pipe.

His feet sank into the muddy grass which should have been his Ma's flower beds. He shook his feet off and ran away from the house, across the road and out into the field across the way. If he had kept going he would have reached the shore of Broad Cove in about half a mile. But he stopped halfway across the field. He realized that he didn't know where he was going or why. But he knew this rock -- the one he was standing by! It had defied removal by various farmers for over hundreds of years as they tried to improve their field.

It was one of his thinking spots. He sat.

For the first time he looked down at himself, taking inventory; almost afraid what he would find. He was still clothed. That was a relief. But these were not the clothes that he had put on this morning. A pair of black slacks, almost dressy but not quite casual. Suspenders were buttoned to the inside of the waistband. There was no belt. He wore a white, or was it a creme-colored, long-sleeved collarless shirt. His shoes were black, high lace-up types -- brogans, his mother had once called them. His socks were black, too. They itched. He pulled out the waistband of his slacks. His Calvin Kleins were not Calvin Kleins! They were like a loose-fitting, long-legged jockey brief. These were definitely not his clothes. Yet, they were on his body. How?

He continued to sit on his thinking rock and ponder the total opposites of the last two days. Yesterday -- was it yesterday? -- he was somewhere without clothes. (Or hair!) Today, he looked like a picture of his great-great-grandfather, Ivor Tewkes, who was born in 1889 in Glamorgan, Wales, dressed and almost ready to go to church.

Plus -- he had just 'not eaten' dinner. He always ate -- everything his Ma cooked. He loved his Ma's cooking! He had gone to his room to go to sleep! Was he asleep? Was this another dream?

He felt the warmth of the sun on his face as it rose in the sky to another bright Maine-summer day. He hoped it was summer! He hoped it was Maine!

It had to be. He had just left his own house. Was it his? He looked back towards it; just to make sure. It was his house, all right. A different color on the trim. The paint was fresher. But it was his house.

But where were the houses of his neighbors? The land he saw around him now was nothing but open farms with only an occasional, far-off farm house. Just a few of the dwellings he had come to know as his neighbors' houses. But he <u>was</u> sitting on <u>his</u> rock. Yet, everything around him looked only somewhat familiar; like it was almost right but not quite.

It was a lot closer to the familiar than the place where he had met Shane and Briony. A lot closer! But it still wasn't exactly the same as his old sea captain's home near Yarmouth, Maine, where he lived with his father and mother.

He looked up again. Yep, there it was. It appeared much newer, somehow, but the sturdy brick edifice hadn't been new since the 1820s. However, the copper flashing, gutters and downspouts were already only slightly tarnished with the green verdigris of time.

The far off rat-tat-a-tat-tat-tat of a martial drum interrupted his reverie. Then he heard the tinny blat of a bugle call. It was coming from the direction of town; past the other side of his home, towards the northwest.

He got up off the rock and ran towards town. What he didn't notice was the shimmer in the air -- the one that he ran right through.

As his shoes crunched along the gravel road, taking him closer to town, he heard the cheering of a crowd. He redoubled his efforts and forced his feet to fly down the road. After all, he was one of the better freshman runners on the Yarmouth High School track team last year. He had the ribbons hanging on his wall to prove it. Well, at least in his time they were there. He must be 'out of time.' Again.

As he rounded the curve of the road, past where the High School should have been, but wasn't, just to where it turned to join Main Street, he stopped. Cold. A crowd was indeed lining both sides of the street. But where were all the familiar buildings? There was one! The old school house, town hall in his own time. Whenever this was, and it was a new 'when' not a new 'where', the buildings had not changed much from this time (whenever it was) to his own time. There were more of them when he lived and they were closer together. But most of the buildings he was seeing now were still there in his time. He must be in the past! His past? No. The town's past.

Everybody was dressed in clothes out of a sepia-tone photograph. Main Street was still mud and dirt -- not concrete. He rushed up to a kid in the crowd.

"What's goin' on?"

The kid, whom he didn't know, looked at him like he was from outer space or something. "It's the Maine Volunteers, dummy, marchin' away ta fight the Rebs! Where you been, Africa?"

"The Maine Vol-"

"Sheesh! Don't ya know nuthin'?"

Wembley ignored the boy and passed on through the crowd of cheering and waving celebrants. It was kind of exciting, even though it was a bit bewildering. He had studied the Maine Volunteers' contribution to the Civil War in Freshman history class. Was he really here living it? If he was it would be called the "War of Rebellion." So, he'd better be careful and not mention it.

"Wish I was old enough to join," said another young man who looked pretty close to Wembley's age.

"It's cool, huh?" Wembley replied. Trying to blend in.

"Cool? It's a hot day!"

"Oh, sorry." Wembley racked his brain but all he could come up with was: "I meant great. I'd like to join up, too!"

The youth eyed him suspiciously. "I ain't seen you around these parts. What's yer name?"

"Wembley?"

The youth startled. *What an odd name!* he must've thought.

"Wembley Tewkes."

"Can't say as I've heard of ya. Don't go ta my school?"

Well, as the high school Wembley knew hadn't even been built yet ... "Nope. Down from Augusta on a visit." Stretchers came much more easily to him, now, since he had read <u>Huckleberry Finn</u>.

"Can't place yer accent."

"I was born in Wales."

"England?"

"No. Wales! I'm no Brit." It was a sore spot with Wembley, like it was with all Welshmen.

"Calm down, now. Didn't mean no insult. It's just that the Brits are tryin' ta help the South against us."

"So I heard. Still tryin' ta get even with us for the revolution."

"Ayuh. That Victoria's an interestin' piece o' work."

"I'd never call her my Queen." Wembley spoke in defiance over the proud, history-filled legacy of Welsh resistance to England felt by all Welsh of all times and in all places. "She's just a big bully."

The other youth smiled and nodded.

An old codger confronted the two young men. "Why ain't you two marchin' along?"

"Not old enough, sir," was the new boy's reply

"You the Lathrop boy?"

"Yes, sir. I'm only fifteen; just turned. And everyone knows it." Wembley could see that his new companion was quite miserable. "But I'd go now if they'd let me."

"And you?"

"I'm only fourteen," Wembley was startled into saying.

"He's from Augusta."

"Ayuh. Damn shame what them Reb's is tryin' ta do ta this great country. Damn shame. Well, Johnny Lathrop, time comes and you don't sign up -- I'll skin ya alive, if yer father don't do it first!"

The old man laughed and went on his way shouting encouragements at the passing parade of volunteers; it was evident that he wished he was young enough to be going with them.

As Wembley watched him cross the street and move down the block, he caught sight of red hair and green eyes. It was just a flash; a woman -- a young one. She had smiled ever so briefly as her eyes had met Wembley's, and then disappeared into one of the stores. Wem was tempted to go over and investigate but Johnny muttered something that demanded Wem's attention.

"I'm tired of bein' too young fer everthin'. My gran'father fought in the Revolution and he was only thirteen."

"A little bit different. We were under attack then."

"You a Reb-lover?"

"Nope. It's just that Maine isn't under attack today. Everyone was conscripted then. We're goin' off to defend the Northern Cause. Just a different situation."

"You must be from Augusta or Wales 'cause you sure talk funny fer a boy."

"The old man thought I wasn't a boy!"

"Well, you ain't a man," maintained Johnny.

Wembley stopped and stared at Johnny. A broad smile overcame his pensive, pursed lips. "Nope. But he thought so. We both could be."

Johnny suddenly put his hand out. Wembley firmly clasped it in his own. "Good ta meet ya, Mr. Wembley Tewkes."

"You, too, Mr. Johnny Lathrop."

"I wonder ... if we was to wander down inta Massachusetts, if they'd take us fer sixteen? What do ya think, Wembley?"

"I don't see why they wouldn't. You're tall enough." Wembley was, too.

Had the fever of the day taken hold of and dispensed with Wembley's brain?! He was thinking of signing up for a war that had been fought and won over a hundred and forty years before he was born! Maybe he was just encouraging Johnny to follow his heart. He'd heard hundreds of stories of boys, who were not quite old enough, signing up for military duty. But Wembley himself certainly couldn't -- wouldn't -- do anything so foolish.

"Do ya need to get anything at home 'fore we head south?" Johnny's face was hopeful. Pleading.

Wembley's eyes were drawn down the street to all of the far-too-young-boys who were chanting, screaming and running alongside the column of soldiers on their way south. Boys of all ages had always dreamed of the noble art of war. Even himself, from the enlightened twenty-first century, had occasionally drifted into thoughts of glory and battle. He was, after all, a Lt. Commander in his Jr. ROTC brigade with the local National Guard. He went on maneuvers for one weekend every three months. He was already a soldier! Why not go with Johnny as far as this dream -- or whatever it was -- took him?

"There's nothin' I need there. Let's just go."

"Do ya have any money?"

Wembley reached into his pocket and drew out his wallet. He found a couple of ones, a five and two tens. But they were crisp, new twenty-first century bills. Why couldn't his wallet have made the same change that the rest of his clothes had?

"Nothin'." He lied ... but not really.

"We better stop by my place. I sure hope my Ma ain't home."

Ma wasn't home. The whole family was still on Main Street for the parade. The boys scrabbled together enough money -- ten whole dollars, (like a hundred dollars today) -- then they found a rucksack and filled it with bread, apples and some dried meat.

Actually, Johnny did most of the procuring.

Wembley's attention was diverted from the procurement because there was something all too familiar about Johnny's house. It had nearly paralyzed Wembley as he entered the front door. Wembley had seen it before. He was sure of it! It was just so different in this era of oil and kerosene lamps and heat by a fireplace. No electricity. No fridges, dishwashers (except the ones at the ends of your arms), radios, dryers, televisions, telephones, computers, cars. Suddenly Wembley blurted out:

"What's your town address here?"

"Twenty-four York Street."

Wembley sat down in the nearest chair, silent and stunned. Like pieces of a puzzle tumbling out of a box and linking themselves together, the information on the tabletop of Wembley's mind had suddenly sorted itself out. He had made a connection. Several of them, actually.

Brindi Williams -- his closest friend, well, girlfriend -- was a member of one of the oldest families in town. Her family had lived in the same house, with additions and alterations and renovations, for over two hundred years. Wembley had been to her house at twenty-four York Street dozens of times. He'd seen the photos on the walls. He knew many of the family histories.

Two great-great-grandfathers, maternal and paternal, had enlisted too young in the Massachusetts Volunteers to fight in the Civil War. They had been photographed in uniform. Each photo of the young-looking recruits had hung on the wall above the desk in the living room since it was developed. Brindi had always thought the two men had looked funny; old-fashioned.

Only one of those grandfathers returned from the war. But which one? Wembley couldn't remember.

"Ever had your photo taken in uniform?"

"Photo?"

"Photograph."

"Oh. How could I? Not old enough."

Wembley nodded weakly.

"You look like you've seen a spirit, Wembley."

"I think I have." *I think I am seeing one* is what he was really thinking.

They had skirted through the edges of town avoiding contact with as many people as possible. The fewer people met -- the fewer the explanations that had to be made. They had traveled south happily; joking and in high spirits until they reached the town of Lynnfield, just passed the borders of New Hampshire and into Massachusetts. They even passed by a town called Tewkesbury. Wembley was astonished. Some ancestors may have preceded his family to this country.

It had taken them all day, all night and half the next day to travel by foot with an occasional hitch in a farmer's southbound wagon.

Lynnfield was a farming community much like Yarmouth where the boys were from. Lynnfield's commercial district was growing and expanding like most of small town America in the middle 1800s.

The town Sheriff, ever watchful, approached the boys as they wandered into the outskirts of the towne centre, as those in Massachusetts would call it.

"What brings you two rascals to my towne?"

Wembley thought up a whopper -- easy as pie. (Thanks again, Huck!) It kind of unnerved him that he could be so good at lying. He never had been before. He was an actor in the High School plays. He loved improvising! So, this was improvisation, not lying!

"The March of the Maine Volunteers came through our little village in New Hampshire. Since New Hampshire ain't signin' no one up yet we thought we'd come here and sign up. We heard Massachusetts had a great regiment."

"We got sixty or so great regiments!" The Sheriff was then silent for a moment. "How old are you two?"

"Just sixteen, Sir."

"Anyone to vouch fer that?"

Their faces fell.

"We hadn't thought about that."

"No letter -- no nuthin'?"

"No. We just got the idea into our heads and came down."

Now, these were not the kinds of stretchers that Huck Finn would soon be telling to the citizens of America and the world, but Wembley was pretty inventive.

The Sheriff considered a moment. "Well, I won't stop ya. Ya look old enough. Way I'm lookin' at it -- if yer capable o' gettin' here, yer good enough and old enough ta fight. Maybe even die." The Sheriff waited for that to sink in, and watched for the boys' reaction.

The boys were silent for a moment. The Sheriff could see that they were thinking.

"I was hopin' ya'd kinda already figgered that inta it."

"We had, Sir. It just kinda spoils the dream," was Wembley's considered reply.

"Ain't no dream I ever heard o' that has a bad endin'."

"No, sir."

"If ya still want, ya can sign up at the Court House down the end o' the street, there."

Wembley watched where the Sheriff pointed. "Thank you, Sheriff."

The boys walked off a little more somber, thoughtful -- at least Johnny was. The joking that had begun the trip was gone. Wembley had always been able to see all sides of any issue. That was just his way. That's how he avoided the usual trouble that trapped most others his age. But he could sense that Johnny had suddenly changed a little; at least in thought. He seemed more sober. More real.

Romantic notions are fine and well and good; even beneficial, most times. But where reality and unbridled romance met -- that place could become a wasteland of shattered dreams, broken hopes, unimagined stress and victory-less conquests. A battleground, as potent as that in any war, that is littered with the rotting corpses of our naive imaginings; and most times our youthful zeal would end up festering there as well. Something Johnny had not considered. Acting like a grownup, pretending, lying about it -- those things don't make you a grownup. Adulthood is hard enough when it comes crashing down on you and removes you from your childhood. Better to not start that too early. Better to always temper our romance, adult or youthful, with a little reality beforehand. A wise sheriff.

Besides, Wembley knew that one of Brindi's grandfathers had died. Something that Johnny was not aware of. But what Wembley could not figure out -- which one was Johnny?

The courthouse was busy, but not overly so. The voices of those present bounced lightly around the colonnaded hall mingling with the clack of the boys' shoes on the polished granite floor. There was a line of young men trailing out a door into the main hallway.

"This the line fer the Massachusetts Volunteers?"

"Yup."

Wembley and Johnny got in line. They looked in through the doorway to find that they were only about twelfth in line. The line shifted forward. They were now tenth in line. Soon they were standing at the table.

"Name. Age. Home address."

The person asking for the information didn't even look up until no answer came from his queries.

"Name. Age. Home address."

Suddenly the boys woke up.

"Wembley Tewkes."

"Johnny Lathrop."

"Sixteen."

"Sixteen."

"24 York Street, Manchester, New Hampshire."

"Tewkes Farm, Old Follett Road. Manchester, New Hampshire. And it's T-e-w-k-e-s not T-o-o-k-s."

The secretary scowled but made the appropriate changes in his more than legible hand.

"Raise your right hand and repeat after me. Put your own names in after you say 'I'."

"I,"

"Johnny Lathrop"

"Wembley Tewkes"

"swear to be true to the United States of America, and to serve them honestly and faithfully against all their enemies and opposers whatsoever; and to observe and obey the orders of the Continental Congress, and the orders of the Generals and officers set over me by them."

"I so swear."

"I so swear."

"Sign Here."

Both boys grasped a pen and dipped it in the ink. Wembley signed in a loopy, sprawling, masterfully legible hand. Johnny kind of scratched his name across the paper. You could still read it; even tiny and close together, it was still quite legible.

"You are now Massachusetts Volunteers. Go with Sgt. Porter."

They were taken into a little room were the two youths who were in line before them stood naked and shivering. Wembley and Johnny were ordered to strip. Wembley was shaking a little as their bodies were searched for pests and diseases. In this case, none, of course, were found. A cold bucket of water was dumped over each of their heads and they were handed a cake of lye soap and a scrub-brush. They soaped up and scrubbed, then faced another bucket of cold water.

The other youths had now received a pair of long-johns. Wembley was doubtful as to the state of their cleanliness. He wondered why he had bothered washing, as they looked a little dingy. But the other youths had put them on and exited the room. Johnny and Wembley tried not to watch while two more recruits stripped, were searched and then washed up. Johnny's and Wembley's long-johns arrived and our boys moved on to the next room.

They were fit into their muslin shirt; indigo fatigue blouse and sky blue trousers, wool of course; grey sox, also wool; and a pair of Jefferson brogans -- not wool. They topped it off with an indigo forage cap with a visor. They were each handed a musket and a shot pouch with powderhorn. They were pointed out another door where they were then guided across an open grassy area to a tented camp where hundreds of other uniformed men, young and old, were milling around.

On their way across the grass Wembley whispered into Johnny's ear. "Too bad we're not with the Maine Volunteers."

'Yeah, but we're in."

"Yeah, we're in." Wembley mused a little about what he had gotten himself into.

They arrived at a rail fence gate. Another sergeant asked their names.

"Tewkes and Lathrop," Wembley replied.

"Sounds like a couple o' barristers," the Sergeant laughed at his own joke.

Wembley joked back. "Maybe someday, sir."

"Maybe, son, maybe. Tent nine-a. Muster at noon for your first drill. The mess tent is in the center. You'll find it by the smell. Eat -- if you can. Rest and be sharp at noon on the parade ground behind you."

"Yes, sir."

Both boys were a little over-eager. The sergeant chuckled and waved them on.

The rows of camp tents started at one-a. One-b was behind it flanked by about fifteen others. Two-a next to one-a. They found nine-a. They entered. Two vacant cots. Two empty footlockers made of wood. Two stuffed haversacks with other equipment lay at the end of each cot. A boy of about twelve, in a snappy but too big uniform, knocked on their tent post. Johnny pulled back the tent flap to admit him.

"Here's your pack, sir."

The boy thrust it through to Johnny as he entered. Johnny took it. The boy sensed something; almost said something, but left the tent without further words.

Johnny tossed the forgotten but returned pack on his bunk.

"Hungry?"

"Starved!"

"Race you!"

Johnny was out through the tent flap leaving Wembley behind. As Wembley pulled back the tent flap he called out Johnny's name and felt a sudden pull, like he was being squeezed through that narrow passage again. Like birth all over; at least what he imagined birth had been like.

"Wembley! Not so loud! I've brought your suppa. And who's Johnny?"

Wembley just stood there with his hand on the door knob. The tent flap and every other remnant of the camp had vanished. His mother edged in passed him as he looked down at his Nikes, jeans and t-shirt emblazoned with 'All the way F-B-L-A.'

He went over to his bed -- which had returned between the turrets -- and sat down slowly while his Ma placed his suppa on his desk. Then she came over to feel his forehead.

"You feeling all right?"

"I don't know, Ma. It happened again."

"What happened again?"

Wembley looked up into the clear, yet worried, eyes of his mother.

"Nothin', Ma -- never mind."

"Just eat yer suppa ..." And she was headed out the door.

One of the age old remedies that mothers have for everything.

"I'll eat my supper."

The bangers and mash just stared back at him as he held his fork, toying with the bangers while he looked out the windows wondering what it was that had just happened.

His mother popped her head back in. "Don't forget tomorrow."

"What's tomorrow, Ma?

"National Guard -- bright and early!"

Wembley fell back on his bed with a groan almost skewering his pillow with his fork.

"Are your boots polished?"

"Ma?! Can't a guy eat in peace?"

"But you're not eating," she laughed.

"I will! I will! And my boots are polished."

He looked at his fork. His Ma popped back out. He looked at a sausage on the plate and thought, *When did I polish my boots?*

CHAPTER THREE
The Lamb's Clubs

Last Saturday and Sunday had found Wembley in his camos and polished boots tramping over an old logging road in Sunrise County, Maine -- east of the town of Brewer. Old Highway 9 had changed since he had been born -- widened -- improved. But his outfit always managed to find the muddiest parts of any field or road. *So, why polish the boots?* he thought.

Nothing weird or even remotely travel-related came at him on this maneuver. It was just a weekend with the Guard. Saturday was wet. Sunday was nice. His feet were sore, despite the polished boots, and he was tired when he arrived home late on Sunday evening. But his Ma had his 'suppa' ready. He ate as she sat with him. She studied the young man in front of her. He was no longer her little boy. At 14, almost 15, he towered over both his parents. She appreciated the man he was becoming. He had made a good start. She just hoped that this strange foolishness that had come upon him so suddenly, was something he could overcome. Wembley caught her staring.

"What, Ma?"

"Nothin', Wem. Just proud of ya."

"Mo-om!" It always made him uncomfortable, the unending praise from his mother. He really felt that he didn't deserve it. He was quite unable to realize how different he was from most of the others his age. Something for which his mother was very grateful.

"Thanks."

"For what, Son?"

"Just thanks."

He left his boots in the mudroom and tromped upstairs. He was half afraid to open his door. Where would he go this time?

But there were no experiences awaiting him -- except for the experience of a soft pillow and a warm and comfortable bed. He managed to get his uniform off before he fell into it to sleep, undisturbed, all night long.

The following Monday was a day alone. ROTC was over for the next three months. No friends available today. Not even an inkling of a vision or a dream. But it gave him time to think. He spent most of the day -- after his chores -- on his rock, reading a book: <u>All things Bright and Beautiful</u> by James Herriott. The sun was warm. He sat on his blanket with his back against the rock, bolstered by a cushion from his desk chair upstairs, occasionally taking his eyes off the page and looking out towards the sea. At the end of each chapter he would contemplate, but not over the chapter he had just read. There were no mysteries there. It was thoughts about a planet with no clothes and a Civil War he had never fought in that blinked and shuttered themselves across the visual interface of his mind. He thought it might be nice if he could trash the files; but there was no chance of that. He had been there. He had seen what he had seen, met whom he had met, done the things that were there in his memory. They were not dreams. He could find no way into them or out of them that associated them with anything close to 'dreaming'.

He smiled as he named them 'DreamTravels', but what did they mean? He was unsure of that, also. But they had to mean something. He would never have experiences like that in today's world unless he was a professional-nudist-civil-war-reenacter-swimmer. And that wasn't likely. But that planet had taught him something about relationships and tolerance, and being thrust into a new situation, and having to adapt -- quickly. His next trip to the club or school locker room would be a breeze. No dressing in the stall. Not necessary anymore.

Adaptation to a hundred year time difference was also a startling concept. But the chance to have seen history being lived -- especially his ability to remember it before it came alive, and then again after -- was the strangest of sensations. Then, to have the history already be a part of his memory from someone he was close to? That thought led him directly back to Brindi. He folded his book in his lap. He leaned back and stretched, head down touching the rock with his eyes to the sky. He smiled at the pleasant thoughts of his relationship with Brindi -- and Russel -- and their great-great-grandfathers. The thoughts of his home before it was his home -- empty for a while -- almost a relic before it was antique. He sat up and looked over at his house. He loved it. It was big and old -- plenty of history, tradition, stories now to be discovered. He wanted to discover them all. Like his real home -- Wales.

Then the thought came to him -- how would he be aided in discovering those stories? Had he been thinking about something that had led him to another planet? Had he been overcome by his fascination for the Civil War, and his impending Jr. Guard maneuvers so much that it had led him to experience it in an altered sense of reality? He was fascinated by a lot of things. What was next? Was there even something next? He thought there would be. Why should it end here? He had so many interests and he quested for knowledge. But then -- were these just dreams about what he had read and studied? They couldn't be! A memory cannot come from a dream.

After all the cogitation over things that were seemingly beyond his control, he decided to take the attitude of his Granda Gwyllym: 'don't get yerself bunched up over the t'ings that ya have no control in.' He even heard it in his Granda's thick Welsh dialect. He missed Granda Gwyllym and his Gran Bronwyn. But then he couldn't really remember living there. A few experiences, that's all. His DreamTravels were more complete than were his memories of Wales. Mostly he remembered the visits he and his parents had made at Christmas and other times of the year since they'd left; the wonderful Welsh summers where the rocks and rills and hills and valleys came alive ...

He was glad to live in America. It was a better life; maybe not richer in lore and story, tradition and history, because the Welsh went back about as far as you could go; but he didn't have England to deal with! The Welsh were Celts closely related to the Irish. They weren't Angles or Saxons, although they could be a little bit Pict, or even Viking! That was fascinating to Wembley. The Welsh accepted those separate heritages while they rejected, steadfastly, anything from England -- Angleterre, as the French call it -- land of the Angles (or Anglos). The land of Prydain, to the ancient Celts.

He thought of the Bible. The big one on the shelf in the study. It had written generations back into the early 1700s on its endpapers. And there were pages and pages of ancestors tucked into the back of it that took him back to the time of the domination of the Welsh under Henry VIII and even earlier. His Ma had searched it all out, along with his Grans. There were some Lairds in the bunch whose land and property were seized by the English throne. There were also lines that did more than hint of their Celtic and Pictish origins. The names in his immediate family solidified that claim, if nothing else did. The very fact that his Grans spoke the languages of their origin as well as English, authenticated the family's long history. The Tewkes name went back to the Roman times. He missed the Celtic languages of the Welsh and Irish. They had a musicality, a lilt that he loved to listen to. He also understood them a little. It was all that his Tewkes Grans spoke to him when he was with them. The same could be said of his Pictish Scots -- the Fitzroys.

The ruminations on the family he was missing were interrupted by his mother's call in to dinner. Already? He had just arrived at the rock to read! But he could smell the sausage and dumplings stewing in the sweet vinegar. The sausage available to them was a little bit too American -- bland -- at times, but he loved the traditional dishes of his homeland. He picked himself, his blanket and cushion, and his book up and ran across the field into the house where the familiar aromas overwhelmed him and drew him to the table where his Da was already waiting, fork in hand. Talk centered around how his lambs were coming along and would they be ready for the Fair by the weekend. Suspiciously absent was any talk or even question about naked people or Civil War reenactments.

Tuesday was a day with Brindi and Russel. Wembley didn't dread the locker room but he did dread the water of the pool. That was a new one: 'Fish' Tewkes afraid of the water? He endured the dread as the three splashed and swam and slid, gradually wearing down Wembley's publicly unadmitted trepidation. Nothing odd happened at all! Not even a whistle from a guard.

The Dairy King was the place for their after swim lunch. They sat there contentedly munching on burgers and fries and shakes, talking and laughing about what little information Wembley had told them of his strange happenings. Then she appeared.

"Tewkes, you're a real strange one. Only psychos and weirdos dream the stupid stuff you do." She laughed derisively.

If she thought it would get a reaction, she was correct. But it didn't come from Wembley.

"What a ho!"

"Russel!" was spit through his sister's clenched teeth.

"Well, she is. She doesn't know anything about anybody. Even I can see that!"

Wem just looked up at Evie. "My story is my own and I make no excuses for it. Do you?" He didn't understand the girl. He had tried, but nobody really knew her. She had just been there, in the shadows, since they were little. The story was that she was adopted. Nobody really knew for sure because she never let anyone get near her.

Evie's eyes flashed. She never could get the best of Wembley Tewkes. His always calm, non-judgmental demeanor seemed to smoothe over every situation she tried to create; every episode she tried to invent. She walked away as the three friends snickered. For even though Wembley was not a reactionary, he enjoyed the results of his 'non-reactions.'

They finished their lunch and threw their refuse away in the cans. Then they wound their way down the block and arrived back at the pool for their afternoon swim.

Russel, then Brindi, presented their passes and they were allowed through the turnstyle. Wembley showed his and the gatekeeper, a friend from school, looked uneasily over at the office. The blinds went down. Which meant that someone in there had been watching, waiting for Wembley.

"What's the matter, Jim?"

"Can't say, Wem. Just wait a sec."

Well, it was more than a 'sec' before an older man emerged from the now blind-drawn office with a paper in his hands.

"What's the problem, Mr. Wilcox?"

"Ah! Well, Wembley, uh -- it seems we have had some complaints about you and your conduct in our pool."

"Surely you don't think that Wembley ..."

"Brindi -- let me handle it. Please. Exactly what is the complaint?"

"Well, I don't know if I should reveal ... I mean, maybe it's not the time or the place ..." nodding towards Brindi and Russel.

"No better time or place."

"It is rather an indelicate matter."

Russ leaned into his sister. "What's indelicate?"

She stage-whispered back to him, "Dirty, which is impossible in Wembley's case."

Mr. Wilcox overheard Brindi's pointed remarks. He coughed into his next comment, because normally he would agree that this was something way beyond the possibility of Wembley Tewkes.

"We've had reports of ... um, well, of, erm, sexual harrassment by you, Wembley. It is totally out of character, I know. I've known you for a long time, but the complainant is adamant that you are guilty."

Wembley bowed his head and took a breath. He raised his head again and his eyes met with Mr. Wilcox's directly. "Let me guess. The complaint came from Evie Griffith."

"Well, now I can't reveal that ..."

"In this country," his Welsh accent coming out now that he was a little agitated, "the accused has the right to face 'is accuser, does 'e not?"

"Yes, normally, but in the matter of these complaints ..."

"So what are you doing about it?"

"I am required to suspend your pass priviledges, pending an investigation."

"What's this about, Wem?" asked a worried Russel.

"I think it has to do with Brindi and I grabbing for you the other day and your suit coming down."

"Oh, that! Mr. Wilcox -- that was an accident. Wem's no weirdo. Even if Evie says he is."

"Yes, Mr. Wilcox, consider the source," added Brindi with a pointed look toward the office. "Who is usually at the center of any trouble -- Wem or Evie?"

"Well, up to this point I would have to say Evie."

"Exactly."

"But our regulations allow me no variance to the rules. A complaint must be followed up. Come by tomorrow and I'll probably have it all sorted out."

Russel and Brindi made their way back through the entrance. Wembley joined them and the three of them silently walked away from Mr. Wilcox.

Jim spoke up, "If you want my opinion, Mr. Wilcox, Evie's the problem."

Mr. Wilcox stopped. "Sure?"

"Couldn't be surer if I was a Democrat on election day in Massachusetts!"

Mr. Wilcox returned to the office and the slam of the door disturbed the blinds. Jim just laughed. Evie was in for it now! Jim laughed again, later, as Evie screamed her way out of the office, rushing past him.

The damage had been done, and that was all that was intended in the first place.

It was a silent walk for the three until Wem piped up. "Sorry I spoiled our day."

"You didn't do nuthin'. It's that Evie ho!"

"Russel, you really need to not use that word."

"But, Sis ..."

"She's right, Russ." And Wembley ruffled Russel's hair.

"Why don't you hate her, Wem?"

"It's not in me to hate anyone. I really don't know much about her. How can I make a judgment about someone I know nothing about?

"Aww! You always make it make sense. It's not fair. If I wanna be pissed at someone, why can'tcha let me?"

"Because I'm supposed to be a good example for you." He leaned into Russ' ear. "Besides, if I wasn't, Brindi'd never kiss me."

Russel giggled and looked back and forth between Wem and his sister. "I knew it!" Smug chuckles continued from the little brother as Brindi poked Wem playfully with her elbow. She had overheard his comment to her brother; something Wembley had intended for her to hear.

Wednesday came and Wem was not allowed into the pool. Evie had begun to file all sorts of complaints and Mr. Wilcox had to follow each one up. He got so tired of it that he fixed her wagon. After a well-placed phone call, he canceled her membership in the club. Which was a very difficult thing for Evie to deal with -- to be separated from water, for she was born to it -- and she was a star of the swim team; just like Wembley. Kind of like a 'Lady of the Pool': well deserved for her talent, but she was someone who could not begin to act like a lady. Since she would not apologize or retract her false statements, Mr. Wilcox had no choice but to expel her. By that time Wembley had had some more adventures, that didn't include the club or the pool.

It was now Thursday and he was dressed in his favorite jeans and a yellow F.F.A. t-shirt, wearing boots that weren't his polished army blacks. They were his barn boots; with bits of pig, cow and sheep all over them.

He was at the Cumberland County Fair showing his lambs. They were clean and fat and sassy as they skipped around the enclosure in the sheep tent. As he leaned on the metal railing enclosing them he jolted a little. He had picked up a wood sliver in the fleshy part of his forearm. He looked at his forearm and the 'plank' that protruded from it. After he extracted the sliver, he noticed that the lambs weren't lambs but a single ewe. The fence wasn't a metal rail but a wooden rail and post fence, and he was no longer in a tent. He looked around almost afraid to find out where he could be this time.

He was outside a barn. He saw that much for sure. Low rock walls ran along and around dividing the barnyard and fields. His barn boots were gone. He was wearing black galoshes; Wellingtons, his Grans had called them. He still wore jeans -- but they were really old-fashioned. Old fashioned?! They were bib-overalls. His yellow t-shirt was now red and black plaid flannel. One sleeve was rolled up and an orangey liquid coated his exposed arm from fingertips to biceps.

"Well -- go'n. She's not gonna wait all night."

"Go on what?" Wembley asked fearfully.

"Are ya dreamin' again, Will? (Wembley wished he was!) That lamb's gotta be turned or it'll die and take the ewe with it. Now, Reilly Johnson wouldn't like that, would he, Will?"

A quandary passed over Wembley. *I'm Will?* he thought. *I'm Will!* Then he was there -- in the dream or whatever it was. "No, sir!" *Who's Will?*

Another improvisation? This time with a character he had to fit into and discover.

Wembley quickly hopped the fence. He grabbed the ewe, found its birth canal and inserted his orange-coated arm. Another thought came to him. *What? Am I nuts?*

No. His reason took over. If reason it was that allowed him to be somewhere else other than at the county fair. *It has to be done.* He'd read about it dozens of times in the books of James Herriott.

An old farmer in his own galoshes came out of the barn with a blanket in his hands.

"Well, Mr. Herriott -- how're we comin'?"

Wembley's, or was it Will's, jaw dropped to the ground.

"Looks like we're goin' to be fine, Mr. Johnson. Will's got a hand in it now."

Both men chuckled.

"Not his first time?" Reilly was a little worried.

"Not by a long shot, no. Right, Will?"

"Right!" *This is gross! I have my hand inside a ... eeewe!*

Well, yes -- he did. It was soft and gushy and ... "Ow!!!" *Was that a contraction?* "That hurts!" Wem mumbled.

"Right after that contraction finishes, find two legs, Will."

"Yeah!"

"Hurts, huh?"

"Yeah." His arm was trapped. The contraction passed. "Got 'em!"

"Then pull!"

Will/Wembley did so. Two little cloven hooves followed by a head, a body and two more perfect legs slid out into Wembley's -- Will's -- hands. He picked up the red, placenta-covered lamb and began to massage it while the ewe began to lick the placenta off of its offspring. He was all smiles as he lifted it into the blanketed arms of Reilly Johnson.

He felt a surge of dizziness. He was certain that he was not going to throw up. He was standing straight, just a little woozy. There was still a moderate weight in his arms.

But he'd given the lamb to the farmer, hadn't he?

He heard applause. He began to see a crowd around him. In that crowd was red hair, green eyes, just a glimpse. A velcroed Blue Ribbon was pressed into his lamb's clean, white fleece. Wembley tried to smile. He'd won but he couldn't remember how or why. All he saw in his mind's eye was his right arm coated in orange, wriggling around inside the birth canal of a sheep. It's funny that all he could smell was sheep. There was one in his arms, after all! Then a flash went off and blinded him. His mind's eye went white as well. When his vision cleared a woman who looked like his Ma was smiling at him from behind a camera.

Wembley found himself absent-mindedly tracing the outline of the little lamb as he pressed his fingers against the plastic, protective sleeve into which the photo had been slipped that afternoon. His mother loved the one hour photo store! Wait a minute! He'd just been holding a lamb! Hadn't he? Which lamb was this? His own prize-winner? The one he helped birth? Did he? Was he there? Here? Had he really been James Herriott's assistant, all those years ago? Just a few hours ago? For just those few minutes? In a dream? Or had he been there for real? He was so confused. Just when he thought he'd be getting a handle on it, it changed course and knocked him for a loop.

Then two arms, and the scent of a perfume he was really beginning to like, wrapped around him. Two familiar and welcome lips pecked him on the cheek.

"Congrats! Sorry, I couldn't be there."

"Where? When?"

"This morning at the fair. I had to go to Russel's ball game."

"Did he win?"

"Doesn't he always! Just like you!"

"If I didn't have this ribbon," he fingered the ribbon that was laying on the coffee table, "I wouldn't be sure that I was there."

"What do you mean?

He took her by the hands and sat her next to him on the couch. He placed the picture album next to the ribbon on the table and again lifted her hands in his. He looked deeply into those green eyes that had never been disappointed in him; had always understood him since the early days of elementary school.

He mumbled. "It happened again. Twice."

"Out of time stuff?"

Wembley nodded. His eyes went to brimful. He was worried that he was losing it. Brindi squeezed his hands.

He told her about being in her house one hundred and forty years ago. Brindi, fascinated, confirmed the name, Johnny Lathrop, the one who lived. The story was right. She was astonished. Then he mentioned the fair, the lamb, James Herriott and the farmer.

She went from astonished to bewildered. She began, in some small way, to share in and understand Wembley's frame of mind; his concerns.

"It all happens in the blink of an eye. So fast, it's like it never could have happened at all. But I know it did. It had to. No time passes here and now. But yet in the -- whatever it is -- days can pass. When I return here it's like not even a second has ticked away."

He bit his lip wondering if Brindi thought he was crazy; if she would ever talk to him; see him again. She only squeezed his hands again, never shifting the gaze of her eyes from his tearful ones.

"Am I nuts?"

"No -- never!"

Brindi pulled him close.

She's not going to leave me, was the thought of relief that slowly crept into his mind and heart.

She stroked his back and the back of his head and hair. This had never happened before! But it felt good. It felt right. He leaned his head on her shoulder and let out a huge, almost shuddering, sigh. The two friends stayed that way for a good while, feeling very comfortable in their friendship.

Once Wembley began to feel better, he pulled away, really wanting to stay where he was comfortable; where he felt safe, but he knew it was time. Brindi released him. The moment had been special. She had felt it, too. He could see it in her eyes. But now she was feeling awkward; embarrassed.

"Wanna go scrounge up a doubles match?" Brindi asked. "Take your mind off it?"

"That sounds great!"

The moment had indeed passed. His first 'opportunity.' He felt a little sad. It was time to move forward.

A game of tennis would do him good.

CHAPTER FOUR
When a Lob Isn't Just a Lob

Thwomp!

The ball careened off the racquet and flew over the net.

The sweat poured off of Wembley's head, pasting his mop of hair to his scalp, also soaking his white headband. It was designed to keep the sweat out of his eyes. It's so nice when something does what it was designed to do. Because in this game he needed to see!

Wembley and Brindi did not have to wait long for the ball to come back to them.

Thwomp!

Sam had managed to return Wembley's serve. Sam's partner, Jenny, smiled at her partner's prowess. But there was not sufficient time to exult in his success as Brindi backhanded the ball, aiming it straight at Jenny. (Nothing personal!)

Thwomp!

Jenny managed to get a piece of it with her racquet. A ball hit by string and metal combined does not make for the straightest of shots.

The ball arced widely off to the left.

"Out!" called Wembley.

"Good try, Jen!" Sam encouraged her. She was good but sometimes cracked under pressure. For her there was usually no stress in a match unless she was facing either Wembley Tewkes or Brindi Williams. Today she faced them both. Not as enemies but as friendly opponents. Still -- it unnerved her. Why had she said yes? Because she loved the game and any opportunity to play it. And being paired with Sam -- well, that was just an even bigger bonus!

"30-15" Wembley 'dug' a little bit. He didn't like ego in others. Why did he tolerate it in himself? He didn't. He apologized.

Besides, Sam and Jenny knew the score well. They had just managed to tie it all up and Brindi had now taken the tie away. Again.

Thwomp!

Wembley served again. A back court backhand, for Sam was a lefty, sailed the ball to Brindi who chopped at it giving it just enough backspin to bounce strangely near Jen's feet. Jen swooped her racquet and the ball was thrust high into the air. Before the ball even touched the court, Wembley with an easy-arching swing, slammed the ball past Jen, past Sam, where it touched just inside the baseline.

"In."

Sam was surprisingly disheartened at Wembley's call. He had never been able to best his younger opponent, even with the inspiration of Jen playing as his partner.

"45-15 -- Match Point."

Wembley bounced the ball against the surface of the court and caught it. Again. Trying to find the right grip in his fingers. It had to feel just right before he would serve it. He twirled his racquet, also searching for that perfect hand position. He found them both and the ball was in the air.

Thwomp!

It was on its way over the net.

Sam returned it with a strong forehand. Brindi shot it back. Jen squashed it. It bounced over Brindi's head and lobbed in Wembley's direction.

He prepared. He watched. He waited. (Not long.) His racquet went back, merely an extension of his arm. His swing was high overhead. His racquet connected with the ball and sent it racing ...

... until it splatted in a pasty mess against the stone wall across the road.

There was yelling. Cursing. Rotten potatoes and rocks were flying in all directions arching over the road. Wembley ducked.

"Y'almost got 'im, Liam!"

"Willem! Watch yer left!"

He lobbed another rotten potato that missed its intended target and knocked the sign at the Butcher's Shop askew.

"Next time. Yu'll get the Limey pig!"

Then the boys were running. Wembley was running, too. What had Willem called him? Liam? *Here I go again,* Wembley thought.

It seems that Liam/Wembley, Willem and a small group of other neighborhood boys had been hiding behind the low wall waiting for the small British Patrol to pass by. The boys had waited most of the morning, but the boys hadn't grown impatient. They were entertained by the thought that other boys in other towns along the patrol's march had, in a similar manner, delayed the arrival of the patrol in Glendalough.

So, the boys sat in keen anticipation with rocks and/or potatoes in their hands and small piles of the projectiles near the feet of each one of them.

Liam was 7. Willem was 10. Wembley was confused. Again. He was Liam -- Or at least he was supposed to be. But who was Liam? In most of his other 'travels' he had usually been able to make up a person; an identity -- an extension of himself. Here he already had a name and a set of relationships.

"Willem, where're we goin'?"

"Home, ya dummy. Mam's a-waitin'."

Wembley/Liam concentrated as he ran. Who were Liam and Willem? Were they anything special to him? Some relation, perhaps? This felt like Ireland. It sounded like Ireland -- the way the words were coming out of his own mouth ...

As they rounded a low rock wall into a yard of mud with some grass Willem ducked down and pulled Liam down after him.

They heard other, lighter footsteps go by. Must be some of the other boys, running home. They heard a shot. Then a scream. A body had collapsed right outside their yard. Liam started to move.

Willem restrained his over-eager younger brother and shook his head. "We'll see wot it is when they leave," while he put his index finger to his lips.

The footsteps of big people in boots were heard marching up to where the body lay near Willem's and Liam's yard. The person, whomever it was, had been still on the road since the bullet hit. The boys heard the words *'dead'* and *'forget 'im'* and *'let's move on.'*

Liam looked into his older brother's face. His own was streaming with silent tears -- great sobs were held in check by Willem's facial expression. Then Willem wrapped his arms about his little brother and clasped his hand over Liam's/Wembley's mouth hoping to help suppress the sobs that he knew would increase in volume. He held him tightly but not harshly. Liam's eyes were wide and full of fear. Willem managed, but only just barely, to keep his own sobs and tears in check.

The booted crunch of the patrol began to fade away. Willem peeked around the wall having released his hold on Liam. He crawled low through the open gate and into the road. Liam followed. They inched closer to the youthful body that was lying, stilled, near the other side of the road, opposite their gate.

Willem and Liam looked around and then down the road. The British patrol was gone. They stood and crept over to their compatriot.

"It's Billy McPhee!" Liam groaned and collapsed, calling Billy's name aloud again and shaking the boy's body. Liam hadn't noticed the large blood stain high on Billy's right shoulder, but Willem had.

The boys had known the twelve year old all of their lives. He couldn't be dead!

A groan issued deep from within Billy's form. Liam stopped shaking him. Willem knelt down.

"We'll get ya home, Billy. Can ya walk?"

Billy groaned again but pulled his feet up a little. "I t'ink so."

Willem sat Billy upright and Liam helped his brother get Billy to his feet. Willem supported the boy on his left and Liam tugged up on Billy's waistband, valiantly trying to keep him standing. It was only a hundred yards to Billy's gate. He had almost been home when he was shot down.

The boys slumped through the gate and limped up the stone path to the house. Willem knocked and opened the door. No one was home. Billy's Da was off digging coal in Wales. His Mam was diggin' what potatoes there were for the local lord along with Billy's older brother and sister.

"I'll go and get Mam!" Willem said as he rushed out the door. He didn't go out the gate and around. He leapt for the low spot on the rock wall that separated the Connell's property from the McPhee's. He scaled over and bolted for the door, yelling, "Ma! Ma!"

His mother Mary, a McGill from County Armaugh, in the North, swung the door wide. His Da was also in the coal fields of Wales. The potato famine had hit hard for a long time. But the crops were beginning to rebound a little.

"What is it, Willem? All that racket!"

"Billy's been shot. Come on, Ma!"

Willem did his best to help his Ma over the wall. It may have been quicker to go around. Mary Connell was still a spry woman in her early thirties. She triumphed. Willem smiled broadly as he realized that even though she maybe thought she couldn't, his Mam could do things that other boys' Mams weren't able to do.

Liam/Wembley had seated Billy in a chair at the table. Between Liam and Billy they had managed to get Billy's shirt off. Liam was washing out the puckered wound with cold, clear water.

"And just where'd ya learn ta do that, Liam?" Mary asked.

"I ... I dunno, Ma. Just seemed right."

Liam couldn't reveal that, for the moment, he was not only Liam but Wembley as well. If Liam wasn't aware of it, Wembley certainly was. Wembley's teenage, twenty-first century American consciousness had somehow mingled with that of Liam Connell's nineteenth century Irish seven-year-old persona. Wembley saw that now. He was both people. It was ... strange.

Wembley had somehow overwhelmed the younger Liam and enhanced the child's knowledge through Wembley's greater experience. He was sure that Liam was there still. He could sense memories of both his and Liam's lives. What a mix, a jumble! Wembley suddenly realized that there was something he needed to learn from his third-great-grandfather -- his father's father's father's mother's father. He knew them now. It was all clicking inside his still somewhat confuddled head. That Bible. He was glad he had read it!

This is weird! Is this what possession is like? Wembley hoped that his presence would not harm his ancestor.

While Wembley's mind was racing, Mary had taken over the cleaning of the wound.

"Willem -- heat that knife of yours up on the stove. Get it good and hot and then don't touch the tip. I'll need it to dig the shot out o' Billy. Liam find a bottle of whiskey. I'll need to sterilize the wound and Billy's gonna need a drink. Willem's and Liam's faces got impish grins on them in a hurry.

"Ya can wash out the wound, Ma Connell. But I won't be takin' any alcohol inside me."

"Are ya sure now, Billy?"

"Dead sure."

The whiskey poured and bubbled in and around the gaping hole. Willem and Liam now stood in shock and awe. Their faces were full of revulsion as their Ma dug into Billy's wound. Their stomachs started to churn a little. The wounded boy's own face tightened in a grimace, but no sound escaped him.

"Willem -- Liam -- hold Billy ta the chair. I've got ta go deeper."

The boys grasped Billy from behind and held him as tight as they could around the chest and waist. Ma Connell began to dig again. Every sinew in Billy's youthful frame tightened and strained, expanding against the restraint of the boys as the knife point probed deeply into the hollow below his shoulder knob.

"There it is!"

Billy groaned as the rounded shot was pried out with the probing knife. The groan was one of relief, not of pain. Billy tried to look behind him and ended up speaking over his shoulder to his friends, who were still holding him tightly, eyes closed. "Ya can let go, now!"

Willem and Liam released him and stood to Billy's right, looking at the gaping bloody flesh. Mary was daubing up the blood with clean towels. Liam picked the bullet up off of the table and examined it.

"Here it is, Billy."

Billy took the shot in his left hand as it was far too painful to lift his right.

"Cor -- wot a story this'll make -- eh?"

"Willem -- heat up the knife again."

"Wot fer, Ma Connell?" Billy's eyes widened a little.

"I've got ta sear the wound and close it up so it'll stop bleedin'."

Willem obeyed. Billy looked pale.

"Ya havta?"

"It's best."

Liam placed his hand on Billy's left shoulder. He squeezed his support into his friend. Billy looked up at him; fear in his eyes.

"Don't know 'f I can ... stand it again."

"Ya did it the first time, Billy. I never saw the like! I didn't know a boy could be brave like that."

Was that Liam or Wembley speaking? Did it matter? The memories of this moment would stay with all four boys for as long as they lived.

Billy smiled.

"Connells? Hold him."

The boys obeyed.

This time the knife blade was hot. Ma Connell held the handle in one hand and the towel in the other. She hovered over the wound. Billy's eyes grew bigger and rounder the longer she hovered. His torso was stained with the now streaming blood disappearing behind the waist band of his trousers, since the removal of the shot had released what flow the ball had partially blocked earlier. It was the only way.

"Close yer eyes, boy!"

Billy did. But Willem's and Liam's eyes were riveted to the knife in their Mam's hand. At least what they could see of it. But when they felt Billy's body go tight again; when they could smell the odor of burning flesh; they looked away, closed their eyes against the sight -- not to keep the sight out but the tears in. This was Billy -- their best mate.

To all three boys (well, four) the knife against the flesh seemed to last forever. But as the knife was withdrawn and the wet cloth pressed against the seared wound, Billy screamed, letting all of the pent up pain, fear and frustration out of his young body. Ma Connell daubed the remainder of the blood off Billy's torso, throwing the old and bloody towels into the fire.

"Ya'd better keep that wound covered up in case the British come pokin' around."

Billy grabbed his bloody shirt and the boys began to help him on with it.

"Not that one! With the hole and the blood the Brits'll spot ya fer sure."

"But it's me only shirt, Ma Connell."

"I'm sure yer Da won't mind if ya wear one of his older ones. It should come close ta fittin' the fine man yer turnin' inta."

The Connell boys stifled a laugh, which was only to cover their own envy, not because it wasn't true. There are some places in the world where boys leave their childhood behind them far too early. Ireland in the 1850's was one of those places. Billy would soon be expected to take the part of a man. He would be up to it when the time came. Just as Liam and Willem would be when it was their turn, at around twelve or thirteen.

"Me Da's?" Billy smiled. His Da wasn't a big man physically but he was an adult. Billy walked to the armoire and took his Da's oldest, smallest shirt. The boys helped him on with it. It was almost not too big!

"Toss the other'n in the fire."

Billy did. "Can I keep the bullet?"

Ma Connell nodded. Boys and their morbid fascinations! "Clean it off first. Then hide it."

Billy rinsed it in the dish of red colored water that was on the table. It left the water a little redder when he pulled it out. A few bits of flesh were also now floating in the murk.

"Ya'd better come over with us until yer Ma gets home."

The boys were all smiles and wonder as they walked around, through the gates this time, leading Ma Connell back to the Connell home. With Liam and Willem out in front Billy put his good arm around Ma Connell's waist and muttered a "Thank you."

Mary ran her hands through the boy's hair. "Yer welcome. But a habit be ye not a-makin' out of it. Around I may not always be."

Billy looked up. Mary was smiling. He let out a single blast of a laugh. The other boys had overheard -- and approved. Billy and the other McPhees were almost family anyway. The Connell boys joined their 'brother' in his laugh.

"Wot about the blood under me trousers?"

"I'd say that three boys needed a washup in the creek, that's wot I'd say!"

Three smiles, well, four, preceded a rush to the back door, where clothes were shed, then back across the yard, over the wall and into the nearby river. A smile from Ma Connell, holding Billy's bloody trousers, followed three bare bums over the wall before they disappeared from her sight.

Dinner was a simple one that night: a little bit of chicken and some cabbage with fresh milk. Billy's Ma hadn't come home yet and Ma Connell knew the boy needed nourishment as well as doctorin'. As the three (well, four) boys helped with the cleanup of the dishes there was a pounding on the door. Ma Connell went to answer it. There was an officer of the British Patrol standing there.

"We're lookin' fer the boy that was shot out dere in the road this mornin'."

"No shot boys around here, Sir."

The soldier peeked in and saw the three youths. They were all busy with kitchen work.

"I guess not -- just a bunch o' girls in this house."

Billy and Willem tensed at the insult. Ma Connell looked over at them and they calmed and nodded. The soldier waited for a reaction. There was none. Then he turned and spoke over his shoulder.

"Yep, nothin' but women here, me boys!" and with a laugh he walked away.

Billy and Willem ran to the shut door and looked for something they could throw at the man. Ma Connell placed a hand on one shoulder of each of the boys. She felt the anger, the hate, in the tension of their muscles. She almost cried for her sons and their friend, having to play the part of a man at such a young age and not even able to take any of the credit for it when it was well-deserved. The boys calmed. Liam/Wembley came over and gave Willem a hug.

"Don't do anythin' stupid, now, Will. I'm not lookin' ta say goodbye ta me brother. Or ta me best mate." He looked at Billy on that one.

Willem reached out and ruffled Liam's hair. Wembley loved it, because he didn't have a big brother to do that to him. Billy gave him a punch in the arm -- with his good arm. Ma led the boys back to the hearth, where she sat in the rocker. The boys sat around her. They knew it was time to be read to. Liam/Wembley stood up next to Ma and looked over her shoulder as she opened the big family Bible. He held her hands still as the endpapers, where the family genealogy was written down, came into view. He traced his fingers across the familiar names there. This was his family. Right now he was his own great-great-great-grandfather -- at least for the moment. He knew his line. He had known of it since he was Liam's age. He had learned it from this very Bible, because it was the one on their shelf in their home in Maine. As Liam's fingers touched the familiar names -- familiar to both boys -- Wembley felt that strange stirring in his stomach again.

The room started to blur and spin and soon he was once more staring across the net at a bright yellow tennis ball headed straight for him. He managed, he didn't know how, to backhand it right at Sam's feet. Sam swooped his racket and got a piece of the ball but sent it sailing high over Wembley's head and out of bounds. The match belonged to Wem and Brindi.

Wem hung his head. It just seemed that this DreamTravel stuff was not something he would ever get used to. Was he supposed to get used to it?

"Wonderboy looks a little winded, eh?" was Sam's remark. Then he saw that Wem didn't even react to it. He was standing there like someone had just shot his prize lamb and cooked it for supper. "Hey, cheer up -- it's us who lost!"

Wem startled as Sam and Jenny came over to pat him on the back.

"Whoa, easy there, Wem."

"Sorry. It's just been a weird day."

"Nothing so weird. You always win," said Jenny cheerfully.

"Yeah, you'd think that my backhand would have improved after all this practice." Sam laughed, along with Jenny and Brindi. Wembley only smiled.

"How about a shake at the Dairy King?"

Brindi grabbed Wem's hand and said, "I'm up for it! Come on, Wem."

Wembley nodded and allowed himself to be led to the gate. As he went through the door, he hesitated and leaned on the doorpost, looking back into the tennis court. He sighed, removed his headband and shook his head. He ran his hand through his long, dark curls. Then he felt Brindi's hand squeeze his and pull him onward. He chuffed a Wembley type of chuff and ran with Brindi to catch up to Sam and Jenny.

They walked the block to the Dairy King and ordered their shakes. Mint Chocolate Chip for Brindi, Cookie Dough for Sam and Jenny, Peanut Butter Cup for Wembley. They sat at a picnic table outside the Drive-in. All but Wembley dug into their shakes. He kind of played with it; separating the 'cups' from the ice cream. Brindi reached in with her spoon and stole a 'cup' out of the cup. There was no reaction from Wembley. Sam tried to make light of it all.

"I didn't know it was so tough to be a winner!"

Out of nowhere a voice interrupted them, "No winner's here."

Brindi looked up. It was Evie Griffith with the ever-present Griffith-smirk. She looked at Wembley, who was acting like he hadn't even heard the remark. Then she looked up and stared at Evie. Sam and Jenny stared at Evie, too.

"Present company included?" shot out of Brindi's mouth.

Evie's smile melted into a frown and she flounced off in a red-headed huff.

"How does she always manage to say just the wrong thing at just the right time?" Sam voiced the question that was on everybody's mind.

"Practice!" came from Wembley.

They all laughed, looking at their friend, worried and concerned, but glad that he was finally laughing and able to pay attention. Wembley spooned some ice cream into his mouth, picked up a 'cup' and tossed it at Brindi, who opened her mouth and caught it on her tongue. Her reaction was so quick that before she or Wembley knew it her ice cold lips had met with his warm and worried ones. She was just so grateful to have him back -- so to speak. He smiled and touched his lips. That was their first kiss -- on the lips. Wembley shifted over close to Brindi. Sam followed suit and squeezed over to Jenny.

"Don't you get any ideas!" Jenny cautioned.

Sam's shoulders and spirits sank a little. "Never ideas -- my life is only full of impossible possibilities!"

Sam held out a spoon full of Cookie Dough and Jenny snapped at it and devoured it. No kiss came. Sam knew better than to try one. His dad had always told him that the girl must make the first move. Then it would be his decision to follow up. Sam was getting tired of not being given the chance to make that decision, but he knew it was for the best. There was no one like Jenny. He knew also that Wembley felt the same way about Brindi. The two of them were huddled close together, eating their ice cream. Jenny scooted over and offered up a spoonful from her cup. Sam took the bowl of the ice-cream-filled-spoon in his mouth and let the ice cream melt off of it. Jenny smiled -- with a little bit of a twinkle in her eye.

Sam choked, he had been sucking too hard to get the ice cream off the spoon and the remainder of it shot down his throat. They all laughed again.

All was right with the world. Everything was back in its place. At least for the moment.

CHAPTER FIVE
Clamming Up

The beaches of Broad Cove were a little wider because of the very low tides at this particular time of year. Many of the mud flats in the tidal river, and sand bars further out, were exposed -- just in time for the Yarmouth Clam Festival. The beaches themselves weren't particularly sandy; more of a pebble type beach linked to a rocky coastline mixed with sand, but the clam-digging was spectacular. Hundreds of townies were out with their shovels during the whole week before the festival prising thousands of clams from their watery holes so that the throngs of celebrants could be fed on Saturday night at the Clambake.

Wembley and his friends were there, wellingtons on their feet and shovels and buckets in hand, waiting for the geysers to announce the location of a clam. Once found, the clam was pursued by furious digging so as to not let it get too deep and escape. Wembley's and Russel's buckets were almost full.

Brindi, Sam and Jenny were about halfway full and Bryce was already toting his first bucket back to the truck that would haul them all to the cooler at the oldest grocery store in town.

As Bryce lifted his bucket into the truck a soft yet snarly voice announced the weight of the contents of the bucket and wrote the poundage on a little chart. The digger of the most weight in clams got a free meal. The competition was by age group so there were plenty of free meals to be given out. Wembley had won in the teen male category last year and Bryce was determined to beat him this year. Just a friendly rivalry between the boys, not like the one that existed between almost every young digger and this year's weigher -- Evie Griffith.

She disdained or dismissed nearly every bucket, but there was an adult at her elbow to make sure the weight was recorded fairly, and to help her to dump the clams into the bed of the truck. She couldn't really cheat, which upset her a little, for she wanted to foul up the records; but she was foiled, maybe because even the officials of the Yarmouth Clam Festival knew of her reputation, but yet wanted to accept her offer of 'help,' allowing her to serve. Maybe they knew that service is what she needed. Maybe they thought they were helping her. Yeah, right -- and bleach tastes good on pancakes! She was still as obnoxious as the Devil to each one of the young participants, yet sweet as pie to all the adults.

Bryce had heard what she had said to the older man who unloaded his bucket just before him.

"Well, Mr. Tupper (Sam's dad) another big bucket!"

But when it came to Bryce, "Well, Bruce, got any clams, or are they all rocks? We can't eat rocks!"

Bryce glared at her because he knew that she was just trying to be difficult. It was who Evie was. It certainly didn't win her any friends. Then the bucket was dumped. "Oh, my mistake -- not a rock in the bucket!" came with her derisive laugh. Bryce just walked away and the man at Evie's side just shook his head.

Bryce returned to his group of friends as Wem and Russ were on their way to the weigh in. "With the hundreds of acres of beach available, you'd think they could put out more than one weigh station."

"Who's the recorder this year, Bryce?"

"Someone who's never done it before. She's never done anything before! Why does she bother?"

"Evie, huh?"

"You got it!"

"Well, Russ, do you think we ought to hurry and get the punishment over with so we can get back to the fun?"

Russ chuckled and nodded and they trudged off. Wembley watched his young friend struggle under the very heavy weight of his bucket of clams -- most topped out at around 25-30 pounds -- but Wem saw that Russ was determined to do it on his own. So, he walked along, easily, next to Brindi's little brother -- who was turning out to be more of a man than Evie would ever be!

When they arrived at the truck, there were a few in line ahead of them so Russ set down his bucket. Wembley just had to say something. "Russ, when I was your age it always took my Da and me to get my bucket to the truck. I've never seen anything like it. None of the other elementary kids can do what you can do."

Russel smiled that, 'I-got-a-compliment-from-Wembley-Tewkes' kind of smile.

Just then Sam came up with his own bucket in his right hand, and a shared bucket with his little brother, Asher, in his left hand. His little brother was huffing and puffing, but he was holding his own and Sam complimented him. Sam, although a little older than Wembley, was one who was quick to see the good in all the examples around him. He knew deep down that he was who he was partly because of his parents, yes, but also partly because he had one of the greatest friends another boy could have -- and that would be Wembley.

Wem leaned over to Russ and said, "Look at Asher. See what I mean?"

Russ looked at Sam's little brother, just a year ahead of him in school, and saw the smile on his face from his brother's compliment. He knew how Asher felt. It was the best feeling in the world.

Then there was Evie. All too soon her ascerbic tongue lashed out at Wembley, then Russel, then Sam and Asher.

Sam just couldn't stand her attitude. She was one of the only persons in the town who could get under his skin. All he came up with as he and the other three boys walked away was, "Why do you even try?"

Wem looked quickly over at Evie and saw that the barb had actually stung her. She quickly regained her composure, sloughed it off and was ready to insult the next youth. You could see the man beside her was just about ready to bean her with one of the empty buckets, but even he withstood the urge.

The two teens and their two charges jabbered on as they returned to the clamfields.

"Where do all the clams come from? Will we ever run out?" was Asher's question.

"You'd think so, huh, Asher. But they continue to come in at night and bury themselves just waiting for us to dig them up."

"And eat 'em!" added Russ.

Asher looked nervously up at Sam. Sam nodded. Asher smiled and spoke.

"Russ, do the Marlins need anymore forwards?"

"You wanna play?"

"Yeah."

"Cool! I'll talk to coach. I'm sure we could use you, Ash."

Asher smiled again. Sam gave him a brotherly punch on the shoulder and nodded. Asher thought his big brother was just about as cool, even more cool, than Wembley Tewkes -- mainly because his big brother was his! Ash loved soccer. But he never had the courage to tryout for any team. He just played by himself, kicking the ball against the marked goal on the fence in his backyard. Russel's absolute welcome sort of knocked him for a loop. He hadn't expected to be so readily accepted.

Russ was smiling at him and had seen the interchange between the two brothers. He knew that was something that he shared with Brindi and with Wembley. He also thought that Asher could be more than just a schoolmate. Yeah, they played together on the playground and raced around at recess. But he always thought Asher Tupper too shy to be comfortable as the friend of noisy, always busy Russel Williams. But now he was rethinking that one, because he liked Asher a lot. He liked Sam. 'Two peas in a pod' was what Wembley had called the brothers -- in the nicest way.

They passed Jenny and Brindi who were on their way in. Asher and Russ giggled as their older friends made 'googoo eyes' at the girls and talked quietly for a moment. Asher leaned in to his budding friend and whispered, "I'm never gonna act like that around a girl. How embarrassing!" Russ nodded and giggled, but he still knew something that the older Asher did not know. All teenaged boys lose their brains around girls. It was like a shift in the universe happened when that silly thing called 'love' came into your life. Russ knew about it, because of his experience with his sister and their best friend, but he preferred to agree with Asher. Besides it was more fun to have fun at the lovers' expense.

He kidded his sister about Wembley all the time, but she took it as it was meant -- a chiding between a big sister and her little brother about a boy who was special to both of them. Brindi had often confided to Russ, in a friendly, joking, yet hopeful, love-sick manner, that Wembley might make Russel an uncle someday. Russel remembered that conversation, there on the beach, and automatically recoiled at the thought of ... well, that! "Totally embarrassing! I'm with you, Ash! No girls!"

It was time for Wembley and Sam to snicker. "Just wait!" They managed to say at the same time, followed by a belly laugh.

"You'll eat those words -- and soon!" added Sam.

"Not a chance," assured Russel.

"Yeah!" was Asher's comment.

Then their shovels returned to the hunt for clams as their buckets began to fill again.

There is nothing like a Maine Clambake. It is not just a meal -- it is an experience. There are fried clams, boiled clams, baked clams, stewed clams, (sautéed and broiled clams for those from Boston) clam chowder, corn on the cob, hot dogs and hamburgers (for those who really don't like clams -- mostly young children) and plenty of whatever brew or soda you want to drink. Then there is the music, the games -- and the parade. It's an all-day event.

The morning started off with fund-raising breakfasts that were held all over town for this charity or that organization with flapjacks as the primary fare. There were always enough locals and tourists to fill the halls and threaten the food supply of every single group. Wembley himself, belonged to four groups that were holding breakfasts. The FFA, Thespian Society, Junior Kiwanis and the Youth Center.

At six in the morning Wembley was mixing what seemed like cauldrons of pancake batter for the Thespian Breakfast in the kitchen of one of the local churches. His apron was decorated with little plips and plops of batter that had escaped from the deep bowl as he stirred. He had to make sure that each tub of batter was lump-free. No one liked biting into a dry lump of flour in the middle of a delicious pancake, dripping with Maine's own maple syrup. After he finished preparing six gigantic tubs of batter he put down his spoon and took off his apron, said his goodbyes to his friends and headed to the next breakfast. The FFA used the kitchen at the fairgrounds. He donned another apron and flipped flapjacks for the next hour, filling the stomachs of hundreds of people.

At eight o'clock he was at the Youth Center, on the serving line, scooping hashbrowns and eggs onto every $6 plate. Brindi, Sam, Bryce and Jenny were at his side, scooping, serving, loading the all you can eat platters. It's funny but Evie was one of the people who passed by, having her plate filled by those who were almost, but not, her friends. They didn't spare the food until she said, "No bacon, please." Then, "No eggs. I can't eat them. I love them but ..." She looked into the eyes of the bacon and eggs servers -- Bryce and Jenny -- and turned away quickly. Wembley watched her as she moved, awkwardly through the hall looking for a seat. He saw her pass by many empty seats and exit the doors. He looked over at Brindi. She had seen it, too. There was an unvoiced question in both pairs of eyes as they regarded each other. Maybe a little sadness, also.

At nine o'clock most of the breakfasts were closing down because the parade started at ten on Main Street. Wem again hung up his apron and ran across the street to the Kiwanis Hall to help with the clean up. He put away chairs and folded tables. He was lugging a cart of chairs to their storage room when one of his sponsors asked him, "You et yet, Wem?"

"No. But I ..."

"Ya gotta eat."

"I know -- but I gotta get in uniform for the parade. Thanks anyway, Mr. Sellars!" And he left the man with a full plate in his hands.

The bands were playing, the onlookers were cheering and waving. Wem loved parades. His whole platoon looked sharp in their dress uniforms. They marched with the precision of a well-drilled corps. They executed several intricate marching patterns on Main Street to the applause of the crowds. The parade route was just about a mile from the towne center and the parking lot of the Academy, out and along Main Street, around the library square, and then down Elm to the high school.

Wem saw his friends on the north side of Main, near the Williams house, as he passed by. They were cheering and waving as madly as the rest of the town. He also saw the flash of red hair behind his friends. Then there was an open spot where the crowd thinned a little and he saw Evie. She was not smiling as she leaned against a telephone pole, in a casual yet judgmental pose. He couldn't rid his mind of the image of red hair and green eyes, even after he looked back to the front and called for the next formation to begin to be executed by the corps. They marched, the crowds appreciated and the town was -- well, what a town should be: celebratory. As the parade participants emptied out into the high school parking lot Wembley was suddenly surrounded by his friends.

"How'd you get here so fast?"

Bryce pointed to the far end of the parking lot. "Got Mom's car. We thought you might need a ride home."

"Love it. But I gotta eat!"

"No one at home?"

"Ma and Da are at the FFA, still helping out."

"You can't cook?"

"Been cooking all morning."

His friends chuckled. Brindi said, "How about Dairy King?"

Wem said, "How about Sizzler!" He needed a steak. He was tired and he didn't want to miss the rest of the festivities. So they all piled into Bryce's mom's car and headed back uptown to the Sizzler. Good thing it was a minivan. Bryce, Wem, Brindi, Sam, Jenny, Russ and Asher were piled in. Asher had claimed shotgun! As they drove up Elm they passed Evie. Bryce slowed the van down, at Wem's insistence, and the door slid open. Wem asked, "Need a ride?"

Evie just looked at them and continued on.

"Okay. Have it your way."

They were off again leaving Evie to herself. She deserved herself sometimes -- most times. Wem was wondering why she had left the Youth Center with a full plate of food. Had she eaten it? Where? What the heck was wrong with this girl? What was going on in her life that she couldn't be even the least bit friendly when all the overtures in the world were being made to her? Wem shook his head and slid the door shut.

"You tried, Wem."

"Try. That's all we can do. I'm going to find a way to crack her shell."

Bryce said, "With that knife she just stuck in your back, you could open her like a clam."

"Not funny, Bryce."

"I know, but -- geez, Wem -- we're all frustrated with her! Maybe if we just leave her alone."

"That, I think, is part of the problem. She is alone. Her parents are never around."

"Her real parents are dead."

There was silence as all looked at Jenny.

"That's what I heard from Julie who lives next door to them."

"Holy cow. So, she is an orphan."

"Yeah."

"Sad, huh?"

"More than sad."

The van was quiet for the remainder of the trip to Sizzler, where Wembley glutted himself on steak, seafood and salad -- all for $10.95 in the nearly empty restaurant. Everyone else had eaten breakfast, but they all got a soda.

It was now afternoon and Wembley was able to finally have some time for himself with his friends at the festival. While their parents spent a pleasant afternoon traipsing through town visiting all the crafts, and arts exhibits, the kids were at the pool. The pool was packed but they found some space. They splashed and tagged and dunked each other. The slides were busy, but they didn't care. They stood in the lines, laughing and joking, teens and pre-teens together. They even ran into Talon Waters.

"Hey, Tal."

Talon loved it when Wembley called him that and he smiled. The mute boy hugged his older friend. Wem hugged back.

"Who you with today?"

Talon pointed at his mom and little brother, age five.

"How about you coming to the pool with us next Wednesday?"

Mom was there and reaching out to pull Talon back into the comfort of her protection. "I don't think that would be a good idea." It was probably more comfortable for her than it was for Talon.

Wem was disappointed but he persisted. "See you at Big Brother, Big Sisters?"

Talon nodded, without looking at his mother.

She smiled. "He'll be there."

The little family walked off to the kiddie pool as the group of older kids inched up the line to the start of the slide.

The line didn't take long, but every minute out of the water during the summer was wasted time to a kid of any age. Most kids preferred to waste time in more productive ways -- like not taking out the trash, or not cleaning their room. Things like that were badges of honor for some time-wasters. Standing in a line -- boring! But the slide was worth it. Russ was the last one down. He always chose to be the last because he knew what would be waiting for him at the base. As he slipped out of the mouth of the slide he plunged to the bottom of the shallow pool. He waited and then surfaced. No one was there. He moved toward the steps and another body splashed down behind him. Then the water erupted as his friends jumped in and hauled him out and over to the larger pool where they threw him in. He would have laughed except that he didn't want to drown!

CHAPTER SIX
Two Trips For The Price Of One

July passed into August, Wembley's birth month. He'd be fifteen on the 29th. Brindi was planning something -- Wembley knew it -- but he couldn't get a morsel of information out of her. Sam and Jenny were as tight-lipped as Brindi was. Wem's parents were stoically close-mouthed. Getting anything out of them was like a Brit asking a Welshman for directions to the loo!

But there was one thing, that was not his birthday, which he knew everything about -- his second favorite trip of the year was coming up: a drive to Prouts Neck. It would happen on the fifteenth, kind of a pre-birthday present every year. The beach at Scarborough State Park had some of the warmest waters in Maine. He loved the area, small, secluded -- wealthy, but also quaint. He loved quaint -- it equated with simple, uncomplicated, time with Mom and Dad away from all the distractions of life. The Black Point Inn was one of his favorite places to stay. Then there was the studio -- Winslow Homer's studio. Being a Maine boy -- and Welsh into the bargain -- Wembley loved the sea and life on the coast. Winslow Homer managed to capture that in his paintings. Wembley never got tired of looking at the people and places that were living within the frames of the paintings at Prouts Neck, whether originals or prints. They were windows to a welcome world. He had romantic visions of being a seafarer. Or of having fun, or working hard -- something Winslow Homer had managed to grasp, wrestle with and throw onto the canvas.

But that was a little over two weeks away. He still had time to wheedle things out of Brindi. (Fat chance!) Or Russel!

Today they ignored the pool. Evie was nowhere to be seen there, anymore. Rumor had it that when her 'parents' heard what she had done to Wembley they put her on restriction until school started. Life was good. For everyone but Evie.

Today was a day to follow the haunts of old Yarmouth. A favorite of Wem's was the single cataract of falls on the Royal River, just east of downtown, near the old mill. It was pleasant to wade across the falls when no one was looking. Then do it again at the bottom of the falls, getting all sorts of wet. He and Brindi, with Russel tagging along as usual, met each other there.

Brindi and Russel lived just a few blocks away.

It was a day for t-shirts and cut-off shorts. A warm end of August day, that was getting a little hot and muggy by the time that ten in the morning rolled around. The water was too cold any earlier to brave the falls.

In addition to the Williams kids, Bryce Hauer was meeting them there. He was taller than Wem, longer legs and quite a fast runner; on the track team with Wembley. He was just a year older, in his Junior year; slender but wiry-strong. Wem, Brindi and Russel were sitting on the bank by the falls when they saw this dark mop of hair come up through the tall grasses and weeds on the other side and wave at them. They all laughed because you could only see him from the shoulders up. He looked like a 'bust' among the wheat. His well-tanned, lean and lanky frame, unadorned by a t-shirt, broke through the edges of the grass first. The rest of him quickly followed, clad only in his shorts and what he called his wading shoes -- an old pair of Converse. Wem and Russel were similarly attired -- the boys having individualy yet collectively decided that even a t-shirt was too warm for today. Brindi, however, stuck with the dress code: t-shirt and shorts over a twopiece with her wading shoes firmly tied on her feet. She had been poked and scratched before by the rocks under the water.

They started with their customary walk across the falls to pick up Bryce, then the four of them walked back to the south side together, tossing rocks into the ocean-bound current. This was a tidal river where the falls marked the upwards extent of the tide. Russ found a flat rock and sliced it out and over the water. It skipped about four times and Russ moaned.

"That was a good one. It's hard to skip on fast moving water."

Russel smiled at the praise.

Bryce reached the south side first, where the bank was less sloped, and he barged down it and into the water. He got as close to the falls as possible, standing there, back to the dam, his head just above the top of the force. He leaned back and the water rushed over his shoulders as he hunkered against the strong current, the water spraying around him. Wem joined him in trying to hold the water back. Brindi and Russ were not quite as strong so they stood in front of the two taller youth, still getting a good soaking from the cool, coursing water. It felt so good as it washed the sweat off their bodies. Russ felt like he was a car at the local car wash getting a power scrub!

Wem's foot slipped under the pressure from the water and he bumped into Russ, who flailed his arms and knocked Bryce back into the water, up against the wall of the dam. His head went under and it took him down to the river bottom. Wembley and Russel quickly reached down and grasped Bryce's flailing arms and yanked him to the surface.

As Bryce sputtered and choked a little, Russ started to whine, "Sorry! Sorry, Bryce!"

"Not yer fault, Russ. I'm okay."

Then Brindi screamed.

There was red streaming down Bryce's torso and right arm.

Wem examined him quickly and found that his chest, stomach and back were all right. It was the back of his arm. Something on the dam must have sliced it open -- it was gushing, but at least it wasn't spurting. Wem grabbed a-hold with both hands.

He hadn't seen so much blood since he had held his friend Billy McPhee in his Irish DreamTravel while his 'ma' cut out the bullet. He paused for a moment as he waited to be transported somewhere. But it seemed like he was destined to stay here today. Good thing. Bryce needed him.

Bryce had a lot of blood dripping from the back of his arm, even with the direct pressure on it. It was a pretty good slice. Wem was wishing that someone had worn a t-shirt. As he held his hands tightly over the gash, he smiled. There could be humor in anything, and he was the one to find it, so, since Bryce's life was not in danger, he decided to joke around.

"Russel -- I need something to tie off around Bryce's arm. Gimme your shorts!"

"No way!"

"I'm serious."

"Not a chance!"

"Why not -- It's not like we haven't seen it before!"

"Wembley!" Russ' painful face betrayed his anger. "Take off your own shorts!"

"I'm busy!"

"I'll hold his arm, then."

"Your hands are too small!"

"But --" Russ inched up to Wem's ear. "I'm not wearing any unders," was a fierce whisper.

Both Brindi and Bryce busted up. Wem finally cracked. Brindi took off her t-shirt and started ripping it up. "Here, Wem. Guess my little brother needs to learn a lot more about being prepared?"

They laughed again as Russ fumed.

"I don't see anybody else wearing a t-shirt -- even Mr. Eagle Scout!" He continued to mutter. "Be prepared?! Be a jerk!"

"Russ -- cool it -- it was just a joke. I planned on using Brindi's shirt all along." Russ settled down a little, looking at them with a look of incredulity. Wem nodded. "Wad that piece of shirt up into a pad, about five inches long, will ya, Russ?"

"Sure," came out a little sulkily.

He did, very efficiently, and handed it to Wem, who shook his head.

"Wait. Slip it under my hands and press it into the cut. Brin, I need you to tie it off with those strips you have."

Russ held the pad, Brin tied the strips. Wem took one larger piece and wrapped it around the whole makeshift bandage and tied that off tightly. Now everyone's hands were out of the way and they helped Bryce up the south bank and headed for the Medical Clinic downtown.

"I'm okay -- just lemme go home," protested Bryce.

"Can't -- it's gonna need stitches -- now!"

"Mom'll kill me!"

"No, she won't. She never has."

"There's always a first time!"

"Shut up ya big wimp!" Wem chided him, smiling.

Bryce was silent -- stubbornly so -- but Wem held onto his good arm with Russ pushing him along and Brin guiding him. Wem knew what the problem was. He had grown up with Bryce, knowing about Bryce's phobia.

"I hate needles!" was said under his breath.

"I know. But you won't feel a thing. I promise."

Russ snickered. He had not grown up with Bryce.

"Russ?" Russ looked at Wem. Wem bore down into the boy's eyes. "Shorts?"

Russ shut up.

As they climbed up the grass and hit the road into the downtown district, Wem was looking for cars. What he saw was a head full of long, red hair that disappeared behind a nearby building. He felt that he had been seeing that same hair everywhere he went. Even in a couple of his DreamTravels. He didn't even like her; he merely tolerated her presence -- sometimes.

"Did you see Evie?" Wem asked the little group.

Brindi looked around frantically. "Where?"

"I thought I saw her go behind that house," Wem pointed.

Russel chimed in. "I thought she was grounded."

"Her mom and dad both work. How can they possibly keep tabs on her? She doesn't have what it takes to obey them." Brindi was snide and full of 'tude,' a behavior that only Evie seemed to be able to bring out in her.

They continued to walk on to the clinic. "I guess you're right. I don't know why she does what she does. Nobody's ever done anything to her."

"I guess some people don't need a reason to be nasty."

Bryce chirped up for the first time, "She certainly qualifies as 'some people'."

They laughed as they rounded the corner of the house and ran smack into Evie. She was crying. Wembley thought, immediately, *She heard us!*

She had. Many of Evie's little pranks backfired on her in the exact same way. This one was no exception. She stared at them with the hate of a cobra for a pack of mongoose. Then, with a tear-streaked face, she ran across the bridge that took her to her part of town.

Wembley sighed. "I don't know what it is about her, but ... there's something that no one knows about -- yet."

"Maybe. But she never lets anyone get close enough. She's all needles and burrs and porcupine quills."

"She sure has her eye on you, though, Wem," offered Bryce.

"Where'd that come from?" Wem was astonished.

"I see her looking at you all the time. She's in most of our classes. I watch her. While you're lookin' at the teacher, she's starin' at you."

"No way."

"Yes way."

"Evie has a crush on Wembley?" was voiced by a dumbfounded Brindi. "I can't see why!" She laughed, never able to hold out long if she was teasing him.

"She must really like you, Wem."

Russ had been out of the conversation of the older kids for a while now, but he found his way back in. "If that's what likin' someone is like, what a crush is like -- I don't, like, wanna ever have one!"

Russel's hair was mussed and his shoulder punched and his upper body hugged as everyone giggled at that one.

Wembley looked back to where Evie had disappeared, wondering, bewildered. There was something that neither he nor anyone else was seeing about Evie Griffith. She was an enigma, but she existed. She was not benign like Charlie Brown's little red-headed girl. There was some malice -- spite -- present in every cell of her body. She was living and breathing. Who was she really? Why did she do the strange things she did?

The waiting room of the clinic smelled like any other area that contained doctors and their equipment. Too sterile. The ionizers were busy in the corners, purifying the air. The air conditioning was on full blast. The cool had hit the four friends as they entered about an hour ago. Now, Bryce was still behind the walls, in the exam rooms, while Wem, Brin and Russ waited. They hadn't had much to do. <u>Children's Highlights</u> has lost its appeal, even to Russ, a long time ago, but there were fish. A beautiful triangular aquarium about six feet long and three feet high poked out into the room.

"That thing holds more water than our hot tub," said Russel.

"The fish sure are pretty."

"Yep. I like the clown fish!" Russ offered.

"I like the angel fish," was Brindi's preference.

"I like the anemones on the reef. They clean it up and protect a lot of the other fish -- at least the ones they don't eat." Just like Wem to give a scientific and detailed opinion. It just came naturally to him as did the learning itself.

The three stared at the fish for a while. Wem kind of zoned out. The fish swam around the central piece of coral. When they reappeared Wem felt wet. He looked up -- blue. He looked around, all the way around -- no one but him in an ocean of blue. He looked down -- naked again. His hands went to his head -- hairless. He touched his neck. Gills!

He did not want to surface, although it was only a few yards above his head. He decided to watch the fish. That's what he had been doing before he had been diverted. Relocated.

Well, at least Brindi and Russel were not in the same state next to him! That would have been too much to handle. The fish were gorgeous. They looked no different than the ones he had so recently been looking at in the aquarium. Just bigger, is all; and more of them. He settled himself to the bottom and sat there as the fish schooled around him. He reached out and, as a single unit, they altered their course. Not one of them touched his skin. It was amazing. He had watched birds in the sky do the same thing and marveled at their abilities.

Humans can't act like that -- even at their worst, in the mob mentality -- humans did not have the knack. *Nor do they need it*, figured Wem. Humanity is strongest in its individuality. Each individual acting as part of a greater whole, contributing and bringing reason and talents to the community. These creatures were controlled by the whole. What one did, everyone did. No variance. No uniqueness. They even all looked the same. Humans may resemble one another but it was not very often that you had two who were exactly alike; even in the case of twins.

Wem smiled as he watched the beauty of the ocean in front of him. He pushed off the sea floor. He pushed too hard and broke through the surface. It was as bright up above as it was under the water. He was closer this time to the little island. It called to him. But he could not bring himself to go there. It was an idyllic place, one that had called to him since his first experience with it. But he knew where he belonged. His home was in Yarmouth, Maine -- friends there, and family related by blood, not by the simple acknowledgment of friendship, kinned to each other through mere words. His ties were the ties of an ancient bloodline -- eons of commonality, not just the washing up of a few people on a beach who would then organize themselves into families. His was a real family. Still he found it odd and wonderful that in this divergent, yet similar society, families were the most important thing to belong to. Kinship was sought after, even without the needful ties of blood. It only served to prove to him that he lived in, 'The best of all possible worlds,' as Dr. Pangloss had said to Candide -- one of the novels he had recently finished for his Literature class. Wembley believed it before he ever heard it from Voltaire: 'Life is happiness indeed.'

It wasn't perfect -- as he was somewhere else now -- but it was interesting and fulfilling.

As he stepped up the sandy slope to the island's beach -- he had been drawn there despite his best intentions -- he felt himself being dragged back down into the water. He fought against it and turned around. No one was there. He felt it again. He was being tugged at. He turned. Empty water in front of him.

Again!

His hands swept the water and grabbed hold of an arm. He sure hoped that it was human. It was. But it was not Briony. It was Vivi. Her green eyes were accentuated in the blue water. She smiled. She dragged him toward the beach. He resisted. She pulled harder and seemed to be able to lift him off the sands and not allow his feet to touch down, so forceful was her guidance. He looked around and where her feet had been, was now the fluke of a fish, powerful in its stroke through the water. No wonder he had so little ability to resist her. The water got really shallow and suddenly her feet were back. She had pulled him up onto the beach away from the crowded and noisy section where he had first surfaced. The teens were all the way at the other end of the beach, running about on their legs. She tugged him again.

Her grip was so tight that he could not pry her fingers away from his arm. When she got to a place where rocks invaded the beach, she shrunk down behind them, dragging Wembley to the sand with her. She stared at him. Even sitting, he was terribly uncomfortable and kept his knees together. She was silent. Wem saw no need to speak. He knew her, surely, but he had not seen this side of her before. She would not take her eyes from his. It was almost as if she was hypnotising him. He did not pull away; was not able to. He was much stronger than she was, physically, so why couldn't he just rip his arm out of her grasp?

Suddenly he felt safe. Strangely unthreatened. He settled down as she relaxed her grip on his arm. He felt he had to stay. He saw nothing but her eyes. She couldn't see anything else, which relieved him, because she never took her eyes away from his. She scrutinized his face. It was a good face. Her expression was almost pleasing.

Wembly thought, "*Vivi's pretty. As pretty as Briony -- maybe even as beautiful as Brindi.*" There. He'd thought it. He suddenly longed for Brindi. Vivi was not Brindi. But there were those green eyes. Brindi had green eyes -- deeper than Vivi's were; pool-ish when you gazed into them. Wem startled. He tried to imagine hair on Vivi. No luck. He felt himself standing, then being pulled back into the water, Vivi's eyes filling with tears. She reached for him as he was tumbled by a wave as it crashed over him, taking him down under. He reached out and caught the water with his strong arms as he pulled himself along under it. He felt a hand on his shoulder.

"Bryce's done."

"What?"

"Bryce is ready to go. Let's go. Wembley? What's wrong?"

Wembley shook himself. He got that look that Brindi was beginning to recognize. She gently put her arm through his and assisted him to a standing position in front of the aquarium.

"Hey, Wem. Doc said you did a great job. The stitches were easy because of you. Thanks. But then I knew it all along."

Wem just nodded.

"Wem, did ya hear me?"

"Yeah, Bryce. I'm glad it all worked out."

They walked across the street to the convenience store and bought a soda and a candy bar. They sat on the bench out in front of the store. They nibbled and sipped together.

"Shouldn't we get you home?" Wem asked.

"Naw. I got all day. Mom's in Portland for the day and Dad's across the country."

Wem nodded and nibbled.

Russ spoke up. He usually only said something to compete with the others, or because he really needed to say something. "Wem, d'you suppose I'll ever be as cool as you?"

Wem laughed.

"Don't laugh. It wasn't a joke."

"I'm sorry, Russ. I wasn't laughing at you or at a joke. It's just a little odd that all this stuff just happens to me."

"It's a good thing it happens to you. The other guys around here would be clueless," added Bryce.

"See, I'm not the only one that feels that way!" and Russ elbowed his older friend in the ribs.

Wem gave him a side hug. "I think it would be better though, Russ, if you just became someone as cool as you."

Russ actually blushed.

Brindi smiled. *Just one more thing to add to the long list of why I should like Wembley Tewkes.*

He was running. He was sweating like a pig. (Do pigs really sweat?) The leaves and branches were whipping at his face and arms. It was dark and all he could hear in addition to his own footfall was the sussuration of the wind through the trees. He didn't know why he was running. Then green eyes suddenly stopped him in his tracks. They were there in the path, staring at him not attached to anyone. They just hung there, boring into him. Again he couldn't move. He was held, spellbound, by some power behind or beyond those eyes. He smiled as he imagined Brindi's face forming around green eyes. He envisioned Brindi's body and legs taking shape beneath her heavenly face. As he looked back up into the bewitching eyes, it was red hair that topped Brindi's head not brown. Wem closed his eyes and looked again. Evie was standing in front of him. At this realization, Wem awakened and sat up in bed. His neck and chest were wet with sweat. It was August in Maine. The tears rolled down Wem's cheeks and mingled with the sweat from his own cheeks and forehead.

He got up and went over to the window. He opened up the sash and stood there in his pajama bottoms letting the cooler night air rush past his sweaty body. He brushed the unwanted, unearned, tears away from his cheeks, then banged the fleshy part of his fist on the moulding between the windows. He did it again and sank to the floor splaying out his arms and resting his chin on the backs of his crossed hands, which in turn rested on the windowsill. He looked passed his thinking rock to the waters of Broad Cove, out there somewhere past the darkness. He suddenly found that he was lowering himself out the window and down the spout to the turned earth of his mother's flower garden. Then he ran. Across the field, passed the rock, through the fields of grass and crops to the rocky shore of the cove. The breeze was better here. It dried his body; took away the tears that had flowed down his face.

He paused. He shucked his pajama bottoms and dove into the cooler waters of the cove. He swam out to a little island, really only a bar of sand,

and hauled himself out to sit there in the breezy darkness. It was quiet, peaceful; he could think. Thoughts of 'DreamTravels' began to return in a muddle of memories. He saw the Island World, Ireland, Civil War times, he heard James Herriott's voice. Images flashed and repeated themselves. As his thoughts coalesced, his attention was drawn back across the water to where his house was, to the porch light just barely visible through the darkness. He thought of home and Ma and Da; of his room with the new blue ribbon for his lamb hanging on the wall next to his dresser; of all the things that convinced him, again, that he was indeed alive; of his pillow and his blanket and his warm bed. He felt the goose-pimples rumpling his skin and he stood and dove back into the waters of the cove.

He crawled across the surface, cutting through the small whitecaps as he neared the shore. He got out and looked for his pajama bottoms. He couldn't find them. He waited to hear laughter, to see red hair or green eyes, but none of those were present. He scoured the bushes and found nothing. Figuring that it had been the wind -- the wind had stolen away his pajamas -- he started running again. The tall grasses flailed his body, as a penance for his nakedness. He reached home and climbed up the downspout, went to his dresser and grabbed a pair of sweatpants, slipped into them and fell onto his bed, spent, breathing hard, frustrated at, maybe even a little afraid of all the things that had tumbled into his life lately. He was exhausted. Sleep claimed him quickly.

No green eyes, no red hair.

Just the gentle shaking of his mother's hand as she said, "Time to get up. We need to leave for Prouts Neck."

She hadn't noticed the leaves and twigs on her son's back. She just came in and shook him awake, like she had had to do too many times lately. She smiled as she saw him rouse up and slide his feet onto the floor. Then she went down to fix a good breakfast. Once Wembley was up he was up. She had no worries there.

Wembley felt like he hadn't slept at all. What had he done last night? Oh! Yeah. Well. It was no more weird than anything else that had happened to him lately. The swimming and the running had been fun at least -- full of a release of some sort. He picked off little leaves of grass and their thin stalks of green from his body. He went to the bathroom and showered and dressed. Then he went downstairs, the smell of sausage and hotcakes luring him on, until he sat down with his Ma and Da at the table.

His home. His parents. His food. He wolfed down breakfast and his mother had more ready for him as she refilled his plate three times before he pushed himself away from the table.

His Da looked over at him.

"Haven't seen you eat like that in months."

"Just hungry, Da."

"'ts a good thing! Beginnin' ta think you were not really you anymore."

"No worries there. I'll always be Wembley. I'm kinda stuck with it."

His father laughed and clapped his son on the shoulder. "We leave as soon as we get the kitchen cleaned and the van loaded."

They cleared the table as Mother loaded the dishwasher and switched it on. They grabbed the picnic basket and whisked it out to the car. His father had, as usual, filled the car the night before with everything else that would ever be needed -- ever. Dylan Tewkes was not one to be caught unprepared in any situation. Wem was surprised that there was room for him in the back seat -- more than room -- leg room. He was no longer small enough to curl up in a corner of the seat. He realized that his Da knew that. He smiled as he climbed into his seat and buckled up.

Wem was excited. He loved the little-longer-than-an-hour drive down the coast. He never got tired of it. There was always something to see. The fishing boats, the trawlers, the sleek sloops out for a joyride, the titanic tanker ships as you got closer to Portland, the flocks of birds, the waves cresting on the horizon, the bridges up and over the little inlets, the license plates from New York, Massachusetts, and Canada, the beaches -- the girls in swimsuits.

The beach at Scarborough State Park was fabulous, especially in the warm month of August. It boasted the warmest waters in Maine. Without question. Not that any waters around Maine were truly warm. Maine was not Florida. Yet, it was almost as relaxing to swim there as it was at the pool in Yarmouth. Before entering the water Wem double-checked his board shorts to make sure they were one: there, and two: securely attached. His Da and Ma joined him as they splashed around in the waters of Saco Bay. Prouts Neck could be seen across the shimmering waters as it stuck out into the bay. They would go there after lunch. But for now, a beautiful Maine summer morning was to be spent in the ocean waters.

It was different here from what it had been on that little island in his 'DreamTravel'. Here, parents and their children frolicked in the waters together. There the parents didn't go in or even near the water. But their children flocked to it -- or should I say schooled to it like fish? He was very grateful that this place and these people were his reality. Is that what it was? Wem hoped so. It had occupied so many of his thoughts lately; much of his time, also. Were these other places and peoples just another reality? Was it that simple; if anything like that can really be simple. Or were they, sometimes, another time and place as well? Or were they both? He had come to no specific conclusions about it all; just that it was happening.

No matter. He was here, now, with his parents. They were enjoying themselves like they used to when he was little, in the becks, abers, tarns and lochs of Wales; some of the handful of memories of his past that had not dimmed. It was also like activites they had at this spot each year for the last eleven years, since coming to the States. Maybe that's why they liked this part of Maine so much -- because it reminded them of their ancient home. Wales exerts a strange call on those who were born to it. Even on those who traveled there, or were descended from its ancient blood, or came there to live, there was a fascination for the place.

He hadn't left his parents, even for a second. His hair and clothes hadn't abandoned his body. He had had no unusual experiences; except for the one last night. Yes, today, in the daylight, it had left him alone. Whatever 'it' was.

The little family ate a late picnic lunch and then took a leisurely drive down Black Point Road where they passed the 'neck' onto the small peninsula, and arrived at the Black Point Inn. They passed that, as well, even though that is where they had rooms. They went for their traditional drive around the loop. Older homes gave way to new homes on the beaches. As they neared the southwest they slowed down as they passed the Winslow Homer Studio. Everything was in its place and they would return as soon as they checked in.

They were known by the Innkeepers. After warm greetings Wembley practically flew to his room -- the same room he had stayed in for years. He passed the key into the lock -- it was an actual key, not a card -- and he swung the door wide open. There was 'his' fedderdecked bed all ready for him. No electronics in the room, except for a digital alarm clock, but even it was disguised as a sailing ship. The whole room was nautical. He ran his fingers over the ancient anchor mounted on the wall. There was even a print of Winslow Homer's "Breezing Up" hanging by the anchor. He ran his fingers across the image in front of him and closed his eyes. He imagined himself smelling the salt air as he steered the little ketch from the tiller at the stern. He opened his eyes. The painting was still in front of him and there was no sea spray around him or tiller in his hand. *Whew!*

He turned around, though, and saw his parents looking at him in that strange manner that they had adopted recently. It seemed to say to Wembley that his parents were not entirely sure that he was their son, but they would love him, whoever he was. His mother smiled. "Put your things away and be coming down soon. We're all stowed already."

"'kay, Ma."

How did they get settled in so fast? Have I been standing in front of that painting longer than I thought?

Wem took out his toiletries and placed them on his night stand, hung his Sunday suit in the armoire and dropped his clothes in the drawers. He stashed his bag in the bottom of the armoire and closed it up. He grabbed his key -- he had to remember that, solely because of the one time he hadn't and he had to have the Innkeepers unlock his room for him. It had been embarrassing. But he was only ten at the time. He shut the door and locked it and put the key in his pocket, patting it to make sure it was really there. He raced down the stairs where his parents were talking with the clerk at the desk, obviously waiting for him. As he landed with a thump they turned to him with another of those strange looks. He thought he would ignore it, this time, and raced out to the car. His parents followed.

"What's got ya goin', son?"

Wembley shrugged, smiling, and buckled his seat belt. His parents buckled themselves in and then they were off. It took no more than a minute or two to get to the museum. Wem's belt was off and the door of the van was opening even before the engine had been turned off. The lady at the front desk, one of the curators, greeted Wembley by name and he politely stopped his rush into the building to say hello. Duty done, he continued on his way to the exhibits he was most interested in. He had wanted to be blessed with an artistic talent -- painting, sculpting, something -- but no. He could play the guitar, sing and act but as for the talent of canvas or stone, he possessed none. He stood in front of the display of easel, palette, brushes and paints, imagining that he had created some of his favorite art in all the world. He watched as another worker at the museum applied oil to canvas, the colors mixing, the body of the paint itself making little hills and valleys across the canvas, in simulation of the master of sea and surf.

This little building had been Homer's studio. He had painted some of his major paintings in here and around the peninsula. Many were displayed -- not all originals, sadly -- but there was one original painting that fascinated Wembley: *Shooting the Rapids, Saguenay River*. Homer was painting it in 1910 when he died and it had remained here on display in its unfinished state ever since. Wembley imagined how he would fill out the canvas and imbue it with the life that Homer had only begun. Which colors, which strokes would he use? He tried to see it through Homer's eyes, for Wembley loved the sea, the sand, the shores, the people of Homer's paintings. He longed to be able to expand on Homer's vision -- to finish for Homer what he had not been allowed to finish for himself.

His parents had not entered the temple, yet. He turned and saw them sitting outside the converted carriage house of Winslow Homer's family estate. He didn't know what had drawn him away from his study of the unfinished painting, but there they were. Then *Snap the Whip* caught his eye. It had always been one of his favorites. The children in it looked like his friends, with different clothes. They played the same games in today's Yarmouth as these immortalized children did. He and Brindi and the others had played endless hours of snap the whip, red rover, kick the can, freeze tag -- all the classic games. Sometimes, though older now, they would still get together on a summer night and resurrect their childhood delights in an old fashioned game.

The boy in the middle of the pack of boys snapping their whip always drew his attention. He was bigger than the other boys, like Wembley was. He had a long stride and a square, sturdy build. There was also something about his face.

Wem was breathing hard.

"Again!" came the command from a way off. The boys reformed their line and ran around the pivot, a strong bull of a boy, named Elmer, was the anchor of the line. Wembley found himself dressed in brown pants, a white blousey shirt, with a grey jacket and a tan felt hat perched on his head. He was barefoot! As the boys wound up for another release there was a man furiously swathing paint on a canvas just a little way from them and their play. He would look up occasionally as the boys repeated their whip. Wembley and the others never seemed to get tired of it. It was a bright warm day, the flowers were out and the breeze was light and smelled of a mixture of heather and sea salt.

With the next round of the whip, Wembley noticed that the painter was no longer looking up. As some of the boys at the end of the whip tumbled, laughing into the grass, the line dissolved for a moment. Many of the boys, breathing heavily, collapsed to the long grass of the meadow as some of the other, older boys, crowded around behind the man with the brush. What they saw there was little bits of themselves appearing on the canvas. A foot here. A pair of clasped hands there. Brown and grey pants without torsos yet, romped across the canvas. There was a red building behind the boys. There were others across the meadow, nearer to the barn.

"I don't get it."

"Yeah. How does he do it?" Elmer asked.

Wembley spoke up. "He paints what he sees."

"Yeah, but look at Jimmy crawling there, Bill. It's like he's in two places at once -- over there on the grass -- for real -- and right there on that canvas."

"That's the magic, isn't it, Mr. Homer?"

"Yes, Bill, it certainly is. I'm astonished at it sometimes, myself."

"Elmer, look at yourself. You're the only one who could anchor us."

"And you're the only one who can run so far and so fast."

"That's right. And Mr. Homer is the only one who can paint it like this -- like he sees it."

Winslow put down his brush for a minute. He told Bill/Wembley to hold still for a moment; to turn his head toward the sun. He picked up a piece of paper and a charcoal pen and sketched the details of Bill's face, in profile, telling Bill again to hold still. It was a strong, handsome face. Wembley as Bill, knew now why that face had always drawn him to that character in the painting. It was Wembley's face -- always had been. Wembley and Bill were like twins: over a century apart, but duplicate imprints of each other.

"Have some lemonade, boys, and then snap a few more whips for me."

"Glad to, Mr. Homer," and Elmer led the other boys to the little table with the lemonade. The younger ones, who had been lazing in the grass, joined them. Then they were back at 'work' for the man who would immortalize them, nameless, on canvas.

This time Elmer leaned back, holding on to Terrence while Wembley/Bill's arms strained to hold onto the other running boys on either side of him, who were likewise straining. The force was so great that Wembley/Bill took a giant leap before the line came apart. It had bent just perfectly, with Wembley at the apex. Wembley felt that rush of dizziness as he also felt a distance from the boys he had known only so briefly.

He saw himself now in that painting, not some other boy -- not Bill. He, Wembley, had been there. It was his face. (Bill's too.) He had seen himself there even before it was, maybe his destiny, that took him to the spot where the painting was painted on that warm summer day in 1872. Now it was a warm summer day in 2011. Wembley was standing in the studio of the painter himself. It was only a print that he had been scrutinizing, but that funny thing had happened again -- that transfer of more than an hour of time compressed into a few seconds of his life.

His parents were still sitting outside, chatting and sipping lemonade. The curator was still at her desk. Wem hadn't moved, yet he had traveled 125 years in time and several hundred miles in space to a Massachusetts farm. Wembley, let out a deep breath. He looked at the painting one last time before he stepped away.

Had he come back to Prouts Neck all these years, had he become so familiar with this painting, only to realize that he had truly been there when it was painted?

"Reminds me of my brothers, that does." The curator had spoken to Wembley.

He had just barely caught her meaning and looked back again at the portrait of himself, seeing also -- in his memory -- the charcoal sketch that Mr. Homer had made of his face, reflected in the face of that boy, himself, on that canvas again. "Yes, Ma'am. My friends and I used to do that, too."

"I'm glad. There's nothin' like the old games."

"No, Ma'am, you're right. Nothing like 'em."

In that reverie, that pleasant state of well-being, Wembley walked outside. His parents watched him come out, without a word to them, and head across the road to the seashore side where he reached down and picked up a few stones, which he threw into the surf as he walked along the rocky beach. His life was no longer a simple one, like the lives of the boys in that painting. It had become so complex. He was glad he was here now. He could think here. It was a spot like the rock in his pasture -- this entire peninsula. The waves helped him concentrate. He focused on his 'DreamTravels'. Everything he 'dreamed' about enriched him in some way. He was certain of that, if he was sure of anything. Maybe they weren't things to be afraid of. What worried him was -- how did it all fit together? He just couldn't come to one single conclusion.

He heard the crunch of rocks behind him and turned to see his Da walking slowly, yet still trying to catch up to him. Wembley arched his arm in a 'come on' gesture and his Da ran to catch up with him. They continued on down the beach together, silent and shoulder to shoulder. Dylan knew that Wem would speak when he had it all ready. Their silent walk took them all the way around the peninsula. Wembley felt complete, somehow, as he walked with his Da. Words, though fun sometimes, were not necessary. It was the knowledge that his Da was there. That was all that was required. He felt lighter than he had a few minutes ago. His Da nudged his shoulder into Wem's as they came around the western tip of the peninsula to see Marged sitting at the little table outside the studio. She was still sipping on her lemonade.

She got up as she saw her men approaching her. She intercepted them and took her place between them, her arms interlinked in theirs. They made off for another tour of the peninsula. This time it wasn't so silent. Wembley began to tell them of all his adventures in the two-mile walk. His Ma was silent, but teary-eyed. She knew that there was some connection to the ancient Tewkes predilection for imagination in Wembley, but she also knew that he would never lie to them. Dylan offered only one comment as they rounded the northern point and headed south again along the Western Shore. "I was never troubled with what you have been, son. But it was me own Da who got the dreams and thoughts just like you're gettin' 'em. I know it's not a comfort now, but when we're there for Christmas you can talk it out with him."

Wembley's heart skipped a beat. The whole month of December in Wales -- with Granda and Gran Tewkes. It would be a good time. Maybe he would find some connections, then. There was always the side trip on New Year's to Gran and Granda Fitzroy, too. Something was happening in his life. He knew that it would take much more than himself to figure it all out.

The bed was so soft. He absolutely sank into its plushness. He had always slept well here on Prouts Neck, and he expected the same thing tonight. He closed his eyes. He didn't remember going to sleep. It had happened so quickly. But he remembered waking up. Was he really awake? Was it another dream? He was in a field of tall grasses and daisies. He had a scythe in his hands and he was working it back and forth. There was Mr. Homer, just a few yards away behind another easel. "Hold it there if you can, Bill -- just a little higher."

Bill/Wembley had a wide-brimmed straw hat on. It was a cloudy day, but it still kept the intermittent sun out of his eyes. His white puffy shirt was tucked into his high-riding blue pants, which were in turn tucked into his boots. He remembered this painting of *The Reaper*, another of his favorites -- he had a copy of it in his room -- as a painting of a boy enjoying the swish of the scythe as it cut through the grass under the power of his own muscles. There were so few activities today that required a boy to use his muscles. Wembley had always tried to do just that -- be a physical youth. America was sometimes a soft place. That was a major difference between here and his home in Wales. They still had hard work to do there. He helped whenever he was 'home'.

Here he was again -- that boy -- Bill! But he wasn't smiling, like the painting he remembered. At least he thought he wasn't. The scythe was not heavy, but it took some effort to hold it steady. Wem felt that he was kind of grimacing. Oh well, the artist could interpret his face any way he wanted to, couldn't he?

"Swing it again."

Wembley did.

"Hold it!"

He was on a back swing and his body was kind of twisted -- how was he supposed to hold this? He did and his shoulders ached a little. It felt like he'd been at this for a long time today already. Bill probably had, but Wembley had just arrived. He felt the ache in Bill's body, but he also felt the lightness of Bill's heart. It became his own lightness. He could do this. It was important.

"Will you put up enough hay this year, Bill?"

"Should oughta."

"I'd say you're a great help to your father."

"I gotta be. I'm all he's got. Can you see my sisters swinging a scythe?"

Mr. Homer chuckled at that one.

Bill/Wembley's body sweat as the sun rose higher. His shirt was damp in places and outright soaked in others. He didn't remember seeing any sweat stains in the painting. It is amazing what an artist can do to alter reality. That was a new thought. Up to this time he had focused on how artists interpreted reality -- especially Winslow Homer. Now, he began to realize that sometimes artists altered reality; manipulated it to suit the overall needs of the work of art, or the artistic vision of the artist.

"That's enough swinging for now, Bill."

Wembley rested, the scythe on the ground, he leaned against its sturdiness. Mr. Homer took his charcoal and paper and sketched Bill/Wembley's face again. The nose, the eyes, the mouth. They were Wembley's. The forehead, the ears, were Bill's, the cut of the hair, Wembley's, but the hair color was all Bill's. Wembley was dark, Bill was lighter.

Winslow Homer finished his sketch and put his materials down. He reached into his pocket and gave Bill a dollar bill and clapped him on the shoulder.

"Thank you, Bill. It's a pleasure having such a man as you for a friend."

"Thank you, Mr. Homer."

Wembley felt light again. He actually felt his body disengage from that of Bill. He felt pulled out of himself, like taffy on a machine; twisted, wrung from himself. He found himself once more surrounded by plush white, soft white. He looked around and found that he was in his bed, in the Black Point Inn, Prout's Neck. He was no longer wherever Winslow Homer had painted *The Reaper*. He was 'home' -- so to speak.

He flopped back against the softness of the pillow and pulled up the coverlet to his chin and placed his arms outside it, across his chest. He wanted to remember every detail of this particular 'DreamTravel'. It had been such a pleasant one. No green eyes. No -- red hair!

Could it be? No, it couldn't be! Evie was not responsible for what was happening to him. She was strange, but not that strange. She was there in most of his 'DreamTravels'! At least the red hair and green eyes had been present. He never really got to see the whole girl. Why did it have to be Evie and not Brindi? Did he feel something for this unusual girl whom no one trusted? No. He was sure that it was nothing romantic. Brindi was all he could think about there. But he did think about Evie once in a while; only with thoughts of pity and curiosity. So why was the image of Evie hanging about his mind? Ever-present? Except that this last time, as *The Reaper*, Evie had not been there. Nor had Brindi, for that matter. As he lay there, green eyes came into his mind again. Eyes that were surmounted by that wonderful light brown hair. The smile that could only be Brindi's spread over him as the morning sun began to peek through the shutters of the inn at Prouts Neck. He felt warmed from without and from within. (Or is that from withInn?)

The wonderful week at Prouts Neck was over. It was, and had always been, exhilarating. This time it was even more wonderful because now Wembley had concrete memories of Winslow Homer himself; of being a part of the immortalizing actions in the man's paintings. He would never look at any painting in the same way again. Especially the ones he was in.

He was content, as well, to have had another vacation where he had his parents all to himself. They had talked a lot. His parents were still worried about him, he knew that. It seemed to the fifteen-year-old that his parents would never be too far away. He felt secure even with the strange things that were happening to him. His Da had mentioned puberty as the cause and Wembley had laughed.

"Da, I'm way passed puberty -- that was years ago."

"It's that Brindi Williams, then?"

"Da!" he paused, an incredulous look on his face -- as if his Da were finding fault with the most perfect girl in the world. "I can't explain it." Dylan softened a little and nodded, knowingly. "I think about her all the time. I see her eyes, her hair, her face. I hear her laugh -- or the laugh of her little brother, Russ. Everything leads back to her. I can't seem to be content without thinking about her."

Dylan Tewkes smiled a warm and now, well-informed smile. It had happened early for him, also. He and Marged had grown up together in the highlands of Wales. Even though her parents now lived back in Dumfries, Scotland, they had for a time, been living in Merthyr Tydfil, where Dylan's parents still lived. He had felt the pangs of love early and he and Marged had married young -- he was just seventeen. Marged had been sixteen. Wembley had been a welcomed by-product of their honeymoon in Cardiff. Yes, Dylan knew well the pangs and difficulties of young love. He now saw them written all over his son's face and body.

"Well, get dressed, son and we'll be on our way home this mornin'."

Dylan sensed that Wembley was more than a physically mature boy -- he had the emotional constitution of a much older, more well-adjusted man. The reasoning power of a Socrates. Yet, his experience in life was sometimes betrayed by his maturity. For maturity is a welcomed attitude, but in one so young, a lack of experience can sometimes work against all the gains that maturity gives because it surprises with twists and turns as eagerness is met with disarming incident after incident. Hills and valleys are run through as emotions rose and fell. It was all a jumble and a tumble for Wembley, just like it had been for Dylan when he was young. While there was still a child-like quality that he felt his son would never outgrow, there was an unsettled age upon Wembley. He was still stretching and yearning and learning. Hopefully that would continue for his whole life long. Dylan was amazed, not really amazed, but most often surprised, at what Wembley came up with or got himself involved in. But as the head on his shoulders was that of a Tewkes, Dylan didn't worry too much. If the boy couldn't figure it out for himself, then he would ask -- someone. It was only that Fitzroy heart (which he loved, dearly -- in two people) and the strange dreams that were the Tewkes legacy, that concerned Dylan Tewkes.

Wembley knew about it only all too well. He knew that his Granda had had some of the same experiences. That it had somehow skipped his Da. He felt chosen, sometimes, but for what? He didn't know.

The trip home was not silent and reflective. Wembley enjoyed the same things on the way back as he had on the way down. He loved the sea and anything to do with it. Ships and sailors and docks and sails. They stopped in Portland, at a favorite restaurant, for lunch. It was a tiny little pub in the waterfront district that served the best food in Maine. It was a tradition with them. Traditions ran deep in the Tewkes family. Wembley held dearly to those traditions for he knew, felt instinctively, that they were not only a part of him and his legacy, but that they helped to feed his need for family, for solidity, for a sense of who he was. His parents enjoyed a glass of Guiness as their son sipped contentedly on his Ginger Ale. Then the feast arrived. Served sizzling hot, the Shepherd's Pie, that all three of them had ordered this time, assailed their nostrils and their palates as they indulged in the rich broth, the fresh vegetables and the tender beef and lamb in the stew. This was home cooking, Wales style. Outside the window that overlooked the busy harbor of Portland, Wem stared at the activity on the docks and the ships, loading and unloading. He thought he heard a bell. He was almost to the point of being there on the ships and being a part of the activity when the bell dinged again and a giant Rum Pudding was laid aflame in front of him. He laughed and 'tucked in' as his countrymen called it. He was not, after all, on some sailing ship, stowing the cargo away in the hold, but he indeed was in Portland, Maine with his parents, enjoying immensely their company and the food of their homeland.

His memories of his early childhood there were dim. It had been over ten years since he had lived there. His Christmas trips every year, and his summer trips every other year, helped to keep some of the memories alive. With each bite of the pudding those rich memories assailed him. He recalled one of his favorite books (and films) "A Child's Christmas In Wales." His mother had read the Dylan Thomas book/poem to him often, until he was old enough to read it for himself. Every time he tasted a pudding made in the Welsh way it took him, in his mind, into the faraway time and place of his ancient home. Maybe his 'Dream Travels' were not so strange, after all.

A tear almost escaped him as he thought of what 'home' meant to him. It was Wales, and Scotland and Maine. It was Ma and Da and his Grans. It was the little brother they had left behind in a well-marked grave. It was the tarn where he had first learned to swim; the Caders he had climbed with his parents. The abers he had boated upon. He was a Welsh boy with American opportunities. He had been gifted with what so many Welshmen over the centuries had longed for: America. He was determined to take advantage of that gift and, at the same time, somehow benefit his homeland. The word 'home' had always held much more for Wembley than it did for others.

CHAPTER SEVEN
Home Again?

Two days after vacation, Wem and Brindi were down at the Dairy King waiting for Sam, Jenny and Bryce to join them. They were all going over to the Middle School field to watch Russel and Asher in a soccer match; to cheer for him and his team. As they walked the few blocks to the school they were interrupted by someone they had hoped not to meet. It was Evie.

"Missed you, Wem. Where ya been?" She was coy and sly. Brindi bristled and just about slapped her, but Wem held her hand firmly and squeezed it gently.

"Been at Prouts Neck with my parents."

"Why would you want to go anywhere with your parents?"

"Maybe because they have what is called a family!" Brindi was agitated beyond belief.

The others looked at her and she regretted her words immediately. She knew, a little, about Evie's situation. It wasn't a good one. Maybe that's why she had said what she did. She knew it would hurt. She didn't like to hurt people, but she could only take so much of this detestable girl who oiled her way around and through the lives of everyone who had the misfortune to come in contact with her.

Evie set her jaw and her eyes became hard, closed. She reached into her backpack. "Have you been missing these?"

Wembley stared open-mouthed at the rumpled and ripped pajama bottoms in Evie's hands.

"Where did you get those?"

"I picked them up on the beach about a week ago."

"You picked them up?" Wembley was not feeling good or easy about this. He looked over at Brindi. She gave him an empty but 'I wanna get out of here' look.

"You had just left them there, so I thought I'd return them to you."

"How did you know they were mine?"

There was no answer. Just a smile. Brindi almost hauled off and hit her.

"When did you find them?"

"Just after you dove into the water."

Wembley recoiled. *They hadn't blown away!* Evie smiled that wicked smile she always seemed to have around Wembley. The smile that said that she knew something that Wembley didn't know she knew. Maybe something that Wembley didn't know himself.

"You didn't ..."

Evie laughed as she walked away from a stricken Wembley.

Daggers could have sailed through the air and down the street after Evie if thoughts could have taken corporeal form. No one in the little group was happy with the girl. Then, they all looked to Wem for an answer to the myriad of questions that were going through their minds.

"I had a rough night, the night before I left for Prouts Neck."

"One of those 'DreamTravel' thingies?"

"Kind of, Sam."

Wembley had confided in more than Brindi. All four of his closest friends knew something about his troubling trips into whatever. What they didn't know, as Brindi knew, was that they were much more real than just dreams. All they knew was that the experiences had upset their best friend.

"It was the middle of the night. I got up and shimmied out the window and ran to the cove. I left my pajamas on the sand and went for a swim out to the sand bar."

"And she saw you ..."

"Yes. I didn't know she was there, or I would never have ..." and he gestured as if removing his clothes. There was a silence. So thick it couldn't have been cut by a knife -- but maybe by a chainsaw!

Brindi tried to think of something that would disarm the entire situation. She was not jealous of Evie, but she disliked the girl even more -- now. "Wish I'd been on the beach instead of her."

All three friends and Wembley stood stock still as their mouths hung open and unmoveable at the thought. Brindi laughed. "I would have told you to put these back on and go straight home!"

They all laughed. Then Brindi fumed a little more. She stopped before her thoughts took her any further. She knew she had been thinking way beyond where she should have been thinking. She closed her mouth, took Wembley's hand and walked on. The little group stayed close. They would not let Evie at him again. They formed a circle around him and soon were laughing and talking about the match.

"Any bets?"

"My money's on Russel. The little beggar is more of an athlete than most of the high school kids I know." At least that was Sam's appraisal. "It'll be the Marlins for sure."

Brindi smiled as the others agreed with Sam's statement of confidence in their little brothers.

They sat there on the bleachers cheering as the Marlins scored their first goal. They were all standing and applauding because it had been Russ who had scored against the other team's goalie, assisted by none other than Asher. As Wem sat down, he felt something, maybe it was a hand, very quickly, touch him. He looked down and there was nothing. Brindi's hands were still in the air clapping. He looked around him. All his friends were still cheering as they began to sit down. Wembley was quiet a moment. The others noticed.

"Another trip?" Brindi was alarmed.

"No." Wem shook his head. The others were now clued into Wem's silence. He leaned over to Sam and whispered, "I think I just got groped."

Sam leaned back with a look of 'how, who, what, why?' The others had heard the careful whisper. They became alarmed.

Wem pointed to the bleachers. Sam took off and made his way to the end of the six-tiered bleachers. He looked under and saw no one, except Evie walking away towards the snack shack. She didn't even turn around to look at him. That's how he knew for sure that it had been her. He could just tell. Unfortunately, he knew her too well, at least from her previous actions.

He returned to the little group. The others looked at him as if they could draw the information out of him with their eyes. It worked. "I saw Evie walking away."

Brindi stood. Wembley pulled her back down. She stood again. Jenny stood with her. The boys sat there helpless against female determination. The girls moved off. The boys got up and followed, slowly. When they caught up with the girls they were haranguing Evie at the Snack Shack. Brindi cocked her arm back as if she were going to strike Evie. Jenny tried to catch the arm, but Brindi swung. It didn't connect with Evie. (That's a good thing because it would have knocked her flat.) It was like she winked, not jumped, to a few feet away. The boys stopped, shocked at the sight. Brindi getting physical? Not just Brindi, but Evie had moved without moving? Her legs had not taken her away from the hit. She had just -- winked away. Wem called to the girls to get back to the match. They came reluctantly, with warning looks back over their shoulders at a smug and defiant Evie.

"What were you thinking?" Wem questioned the heart of his heart.

"I guess I wasn't."

Wem kissed her cheek. He said no more. He grasped Brindi's hand. Sam grasped Jenny's. Bryce just came along. They sat back down in time to see another goal scored, with an assist by Russ. They were on their feet cheering again, trying to put the Evie disturbance away from them.

The Marlins won it, three to two. Russ was the center of adulation as Wembley walked up to him after the match. "Two goals and an assist. Not bad. Not bad at all!" And he hugged his 'little bro.' Russel's smile broadened way past the environs of his face as he hugged his friend tightly. Then his sis. Sam had been busy congratulating his little brother, Asher, about his assist on the first goal. Asher was beaming. Not just because of the praise, but because his new, best friend, Russel, kept his arm hung over his shoulder all the time. Then their friends congratulated them. Both of the boys were being uplifted by the magnanimous actions of the teens that surrounded Russ' idol, Wembley Tewkes. They had been influenced, willingly, by the one person in the town who did not leap first to judgment, but gave careful consideration to every thing that came his way.

They all trooped back to the Dairy King. They all chipped in and got Russel and Asher big banana splits. They got treats, too, and sat there enjoying them and the company. Russel, in his excitement, could't help reliving the match and his role in it. He wasn't boasting, Wem had taught him not to, but he was amazed that he could do what he did.

"How do you do it?" Sam asked.

"I don't know. It's just there," Russ mumbled.

"What did Coach tell you?" Wem asked.

Asher was all ears.

"He told me to be where I think the action is going to be."

"That's right. So, what happens then?"

"The ball just kind of comes to me."

"And?"

"I kick the sucker."

The kids laughed.

"Russ, remember -- right time, right place?"

"Yeah." Russ looked a little worried, disheartened.

"Not that you're not talented, you are, but playing any sport is more than that -- right? Talent is just knowing what to do when the right moment comes."

"So, I can do stuff, and be where the coach told me to be ... and ..."

"... do what the coach told you to do. You remember. Not bad at all, Russ."

Russ smiled. The guys slapped him on the back again.

Sam leaned down to Asher, "Got that?"

"Got it!" and the boy smiled at his big brother as they got up from the table.

They dumped their recyclables in the bins and then the group walked to Brindi's house a few blocks away, where they dropped of the Williams kids and headed their own separate ways. Wembley hopped on his bike. He was particularly reflective as he passed over the bridge to his long road home. The wind whistled in his ears and ruffled his long dark hair. Then she stood up out of the weeds at the side of the road.

Evie! Wem slowed and stopped. He really couldn't believe that he was doing it, but he did it. He stood there silently, facing her, somewhat accusing her. Then he noticed that she was, or had been, crying.

She didn't look at him, at least not in the eyes. She looked down at her own feet, or the dust, or an insect on the gravel of the roadside. She mumbled, "I'm sorry."

"You did do it?"

She nodded.

"Why?"

She shrugged.

"Really?"

She stood there.

"It really bothered me, Evie. I did not like it."

"I know. I don't know why I do what I do, sometimes. It's ..." and she began to cry again.

Wem stood there holding on to his bike as she let the tears flow.

"I don't understand you, Evie. No one around here does. We can't get close to you."

"I know."

"Is there anything you can do about it?"

"No."

"That wasn't the answer that I was looking for."

"What do you mean?"

Wem thought for a moment before he responded. "We want to like you."

"But you can't ..."

"... because of what you do."

"But I ..." and she stopped, she folded her arms. Was she trying to hold Wembley out or keep something else in?

Wembley put the kickstand down on his bike. He reasoned that he might be here for the long haul. Then he got to thinking about how she could have gotten this far out of town by walking. That was a puzzler.

"I want to like you, too, Wembley. But Brindi is always there."

"Evie ... I've known her most of my life -- all of my life since I got to America -- and I, I'm sorry, but I can't imagine my life without her."

"But you could imagine it without me?"

Wembley paused, not willing to tell her that it would be easy to do so. "Sometimes." He smiled.

She had known Wembley longer than anyone. That was something she couldn't tell him; was not allowed to tell him.

Evie looked up at him. "Why don't you hate me?"

"I find that hatred is a waste of time. It's too much work for too little reward."

"Why don't you like me?"

"I want to."

"You do?"

"I think the other kids do, too."

"I don't give them a chance, do I?"

Wembley shook his head, "No, you don't. We know nothing about you."

"You know about my parents."

"Not really -- only what some people have said. But that doesn't mean that it's true."

"I'm an orphan. I'm adopted."

"That we knew."

"Mom and Dad are never home."

"Must be tough."

She looked up to give a tough rebuttal but saw that Wembley was looking at her with great concern, like he really cared about her. She melted in the face of that kind of feeling -- something she hadn't felt since ... "I love you, Wembley."

There it was said!

"I know. And I accept it, but I can't return it. That wouldn't be fair to Brindi."

"Brindi." Evie folded her arms again.

"Don't close yourself off, please."

Evie wrestled with herself and her arms unfolded. Even though there was something that she could never let Wembley know, the prospect of his openness to her was better than her shutting him out and away from her.

"We could be friends, you know. That has to be a lot better for both of us."

"Maybe. But I've wanted you for longer than you can imagine."

"How long?"

"Lifetimes."

Wembley was puzzled at that one. It had to be figurative. She was an older woman -- she was seventeen. Maybe it was something she understood that Wembley couldn't right now.

" I am so sorry for the grope. And the beach."

"I'm glad."

"And all the other stupid things I've done."

"Kind of counter-productive right?"

Evie nodded.

"If you want my friendship, you can have it."

Evie brightened. She began to figure that friendship with the wonderful Wembley Tewkes was better than the enmity she had been unleashing at him. "Really?"

"I don't say things that I don't mean."

"I should know that by now."

"Yes, you should."

"I bet you wish that Brindi had hit me."

He laughed. "No. But how did you do that?"

"It just happens."

"Sounds like the weird stuff that has been happening to me lately. You think it's adolescence?"

"Not likely."

"Hmmm."

"Can I walk you home?"

This question surprised Wembley. "Then how will you get home. It's a long way."

"I have my methods."

Wembley started off on foot, guiding his bike along the road as Evie walked on the other side of his bike, next to him. He could see that she enjoyed his company. So why had she been so downright mean to him and his friends? He couldn't reconcile it. This one was going to take some time. They walked along in silence, mostly, punctuated by a question from one of them that was quickly answered by the other. After a half an hour Wembley was at the end of his long driveway. He shuffled his feet in the gravel there as he looked down, fearing that he might be perceived as being unfaithful to Brindi by having shared this long walk with Evie. Somehow, he knew that Brindi would understand.

"This has been the best hour of my life."

Wem was shocked. "You're kidding."

"No. Thank you."

"It was actually a pleasure. You're so much nicer when you're not screaming at or deriding someone."

"Thanks." There was a half-smile there.

"I'll see you around?"

"Hope so." Evie turned and walked away.

Wem hopped on his bike and rode up the drive to his garage. He turned around and shouted Evie's name, waving. He saw that the roadside was empty. Evie was gone. Not a trace of her. He rode back down the drive and looked in the direction that she would have taken. She was not on either side of the road. He remembered that she had said, "I have my methods." As Wembley put his bike away his thoughts turned to green eyes and red hair. They had been everywhere, in his life and in his dreams and, well, everywhere. There was now even more of a mystery to the girl named Evie Griffith.

CHAPTER EIGHT
God Is Love

He was naked again. He was alone on a beach, thankfully, bright sun, no hair on his head. The Island World. That's what he called it. It was not Eden anymore. Where was his family? His other family? Where were their friends? Shane, Briony and Gerald -- their house was just across the little road! He padded over to it. He knocked on the door. There was no answer. He opened it, just a little and yelled in, "Briony?" There was no reply. He went into the house he had so briefly begun to call home. It was empty. Not a stick of furniture. Not even the 'telly.' He left the house and closed the door. There was no activity on the street. No one was playing on the beach. It had to be close to noon. He walked down the road and peeped into the windows of the other little houses. They were all empty. At least he felt like it was peeping, but he was the one who was naked.

He stopped after the third house. He ran across the road and sat on the warm sand. It felt good as the heat from the sand worked up and the heat from the sun worked down. He was puzzled but at peace. This was a 'DreamTravel' world anyway -- hardly real. Had it ever been really there? Of course it had! He was sitting here -- granted -- alone, but he was here. It was real. He had touched the houses, their doors, felt his feet on the pavement of the road, felt the warmth of sand and sun on his body. It couldn't be anything but real. Alternate in its reality, but still solid and genuine, authentic and identifiable.

There were not even green eyes and red hair here to greet him or stare at him. He was kind of glad of that. Although he felt he had made some progress with Evie, he still felt awkward over the times she had 'seen' him in his uncovered state. Where else had she seen him? When else? Could she just appear at will? She had disappeared suddenly from the road. Who was she, really? The eyes he knew had been on him here in this world felt like the same eyes that had watched him in other wheres, including his own world of Maine -- especially the beach! They felt like Evie's. That was silly. Wasn't it? He had that same sense of uncomfortableness everywhere he remembered her presence. Except for that long walk home. He had felt much more comfortable then. But had she been elsewhere? How long had she been spying on him?

Was she spying? Or was it something else?

Alternate realities. More than one present. More than one where. More than enough to think about in this other where -- this Island World Eden. Was it Eden? Was the world he knew as his home merely the dark and dreary world, the land of Nod -- East of Eden. Steinbeck. Another favorite author. Did he have 'DreamTravels' similar to Wembley's? Was there someone in Steinbeck's life like Evie Griffith? Was she Steinbeck's muse?

Was she Wembley's?

Who was she really? No matter what reality he was in, there was no conclusion he could come to about her. Except that, maybe, Evie and Vivi were somehow the same.

Should he talk to Brindi about it? Why not! She knew everything else about his 'DreamTravels'. He would tell her about this one, and about his suspicions and feelings, and about the pleasant walk home with Evie. Brindi could possibly help to shed some light on what was becoming a very dark area for Wembley Tewkes.

He stood up out of the sand, brushed the grains off his legs and backside and ran to plunge into the beautiful warm water. He swam alone for a long time. Dipping and weaving through the waves, tumbling sometimes with the power of the surf, cutting through the water with his strong body and then diving down to the sandy bottom, not worried about breathing because his gills had returned. Just one of the marvels of this world. He could breathe the air when he was out of it, but he could also breathe underwater. It was magical.

Wembley sat on the bottom of the little bay, thinking about all of the magical things that had entered his life lately. Not just the worlds and times he had visited, but the very fact that he 'visited.' Brindi was a miracle. His parents were miracles. The rest of his friends, yes, even Evie could be considered a miracle.

He pushed off the bottom with his strong legs and shot up to the surface. He breached, again, like a dolphin, and slammed over sideways into an oncoming wave. It tumbled him back to the bottom again, from where he once more shot to the surface. In the embrace of the sunlight he positioned himself to bodysurf into the sandy shore. The wave deposited him, somewhat roughly on the sands -- having bruised a tender area -- and he limped out of the water to sit once again on the sand. He controlled his breathing. He thought the dull ache away. He let the sun dry him. He laid back to bake on the sand.

He awoke to a 'harumph' as he found himself naked on his bed at home, still wet from his shower and his mother standing in the doorway, trying to get his attention. He sat up and covered himself quickly.

"Where to this time?"

"You wouldn't believe me."

"Well, hurry up then or we'll be late for the kids."

"Be down in a second."

His Ma left him and he wiped off the remaining water from his shower -- or was it from the ocean? -- well, he dried himself, jumped into his clothes and just about got downstairs in the second that was promised.

Marged Tewkes was waiting with a smile on her face. "Brindi, is it?"

"Ma!!!"

She laughed as the crimson level rose on her son's face. She bustled him out to the car and they settled in for the drive. That smile was still on her face. "I like Brindi."

"Ma! Please. It's bad enough you saw me -- well, as you saw me. And I do like Brindi, but it wasn't about her! I was somewhere else completely."

Worry passed across his mother's face in a hurry. "One of your 'DreamTravels'?"

Wembley nodded. Then said, "Yeah," because his mother's eyes were still on the road, where they had to be.

"I'll be done with the Ladies Auxillary at Church about three o'clock. I'll come by and pick you up at the Youth Center."

"Okay. Thanks, Ma."

Brindi was there. His mother honked the horn as she drove off. Wembley turned and looked at her but only saw her laughing as she sped away.

"What was all that about?"

"I had another 'DreamTravel' to that Island World. No one was there -- at all. But this time I was naked when I got home. Mom saw me!"

Brindi busted up laughing. "No longer her little baby, eh?"

"Brindi! Not you too?"

"Sorry. Sorry." She spluttered. It was a funny image. She kissed him on the nose and took his hand. His fears and worries were always calmed away when his hand was in hers.

They entered the room to shouts of 'Hi' from their friends. Wem looked around and saw that there were a lot of teens here today. Most of his friends were there to help the kids -- some of the less-fortunate kids of the village -- read, write letters, or just play games. It was 'Big Brother Big Sister Day" at the Youth Center. Even Russel was there with a couple of his friends. They were busy playing blocks, building little forts, with a couple of five year olds. They seemed to be loving every minute of it.

As Wem scanned the room he saw Evie. She was involved with a younger girl, helping her dress a doll in front of a huge doll house. Wem dragged

Brindi over to say hi. He hadn't had the chance to tell Brin about the walk home the other day. But he wanted Brin to see this new side of Evie. He almost -- liked it. They said their hellos and sat down. Evie threw Wembley a doll and he quickly handed it to Brindi. She picked up a dress and put it on the doll. Evie was smiling. Brindi saw it.

"What?"

"You don't believe that I'm here, do you Brindi?"

"Well, it's a little out of character; at least from what I've seen."

Evie nodded. "I can understand that. But Wembley and I had a talk the other day. He straightened me out on a few things."

"Including ...?"

"Probably best not discussed in front of little ears." And she handed another doll to the little girl, Stephanie. "Is this the right dress?"

"Yep!"

The little girl seemed so delighted that Evie smiled. Brindi couldn't believe it, but she saw it so she tried to understand it. Wembley just nodded and tossed her another piece of doll clothing. "I'll leave you two girls to Stephanie. I've got to find Talon."

"Talon Waters? He's such a cutie."

Brindi was startled at those words coming out of Evie's mouth.

"I know, I know. But ... you have a great boyfriend. He helped me a lot."

"He has that effect on people." Brindi didn't believe that she was hearing what she was hearing -- and from Evie.

"Even you?"

"Especially me," Brindi admitted.

Stephanie stood up and took her dolly to the doll house.

"Where did this come from?" Brindi was pointing to the doll house.

"It was just sitting in my attic so I donated it."

"Wow! Really cool, Evie."

Evie beamed. It was a lot easier to like people and be nice than it was to not. The older girls busied themselves with assisting their young charge and having a blast.

Wembley had found Talon. He had just come in and was looking for his anticipated and expected partner for the day. He felt like the luckiest boy in town because he got to spend part of the day with Wembley Tewkes. He was a seven year old, curly blonde, with deep blue eyes who had lost his father in an automobile accident, which he, himself, had survived. He climbed up Wembley as the youth held out his arms to the child. After a hug, and a look from the boy that said, *'are you really here and mine for the day?'* Wembley nodded and placed him again on the floor and took his little hand. He led the child upstairs to where they would be playing shuffleboard, to start with. It was Talon's favorite thing.

As they climbed the stairs Wembley heard strange sounds. Talon's hand remained in his, but the room around them changed. It became dusty, sweltering and noisy. He looked down again to still see Talon's hand in his, but their feet were moving rapidly on some sort of treadbarrel -- like the ones used in the 1800s to grind wheat into flour. They had to keep stepping to maintain their balance. There was a railing for them to hold onto. Talon reached up, fear in his eyes. Wembley looked down at him as he helped to hold the child's hands to the rail.

Wembley knew -- somehow and suddenly -- that he had dragged this little, fragile child into one of his 'DreamTravels'. All he saw were the frightened eyes of his little friend. He spoke to him, "It's all right. I'm here. There's nothing that can hurt you."

Talon nodded, but did not say a word. He had not spoken since the day his father died.

Wembley saw the state of his and Talon's clothes, which was pretty similar to the condition of the rags on the other boys around them. Some were shirtless, like Wembley, others had tatters wrapped around their bodies, both upper and lower, or one or the other, some were trouserless, and all were shoeless.

The two newcomers began to smile as the barrel continued to turn under their footsteps, along with the footsteps of about twenty other boys of varying ages down the line. Despite the clothing, or lack of it, it was almost fun. "This is almost as good as shuffleboard, huh?"

Talon thought for a minute. Then nodded with a big smile on his face.

Then a big bell rang. The treadbarrel slowed as all twenty of the boys who were stepping on the treads along its length stopped walking. An old man came around and snuffed the candles and torches on the walls. Wembley and Talon followed the other boys to a great big dining hall. Talon pointed to a large sign on the wall at the other end of the hall: "God Is Love." Wem's mind started whirring. *This couldn't be* <u>Oliver Twist</u>*, that was fiction! But it could be a workhouse; Victorian London with all its ills and social causes remaining unattended to.*

The boys picked up bowls and marched in a line to a big pot at the end of the hall. There was a thin soup ladled out into the boys' bowls. Wembley actually found a piece of meat in his. Talon didn't. Wembley gave Talon his little scrap of meat. Talon smiled again. Wembley would always take care of him. He knew that.

The hundred or so boys all found a seat at long tables -- just like in one of

Wembley's favorite movies -- and they sat, waiting. A strangely dressed man in a funny hat, called out, "God make you thankful!" and rapped his staff on the floor. The boys began to eat. (But there was no music playing. All was silent except for the scrape of spoon against bowl.) Wembley noticed that the pot was covered up and removed. The room was empty again except for the slurping, hungry boys. When they were finished some old men, in rags themselves, collected the bowls and spoons as the boys left the hall. Talon pointed to his teeth and then pointed to the men. None of them had any teeth in their mouths. Talon didn't smile. He was sad. Wembley patted him on the back and ushered him along to the tall, yet narrow flight of steps that led to an upper floor.

As they started mounting the steps, the boys crowded in between its railings. The prevailing odor was of unwashed boy; uncovered and unwashed boy in many instances, as the boys could barely keep from revealing parts of their bodies that they wished they could keep covered; maybe had grown so numb to it all that they were no longer even aware of, or caring about their unclad condition. Such was the life of a workhouse boy in the time of Charles Dickens. Wembley cried there, in the sea of nameless faces around him. His tears ran copiously when he saw a boy of about nine or ten, just in front of him on the stairs, wearing only a tattered almost too short shirt without leggings of any kind. *How could people do this to children?*

Wembley didn't understand it at all. He looked over into the saddened face of Talon, who seemed to feel the misery of the situation as well. The boys arrived in a big dormitory. There were no beds. Just piles of rags on the stone floor. There were no possessions, no footlockers, no dressers, no candles, no pillows. Six or seven boys crowded onto each pile of rags and huddled together for warmth, for even the summer nights in England were chilly. Wembley gathered the seven nearly naked boys around him into his long, strong arms and kept them close. Talon offered what little warmth he could, just like his older friend. There was a hush that descended on the hall after the light was extinguished. The sound of exhausted, sleeping boys quickly took over the hush of the hall. Wembly, still weeping, held his little charges close to him. He finally fell asleep in the darkness sometime later.

They were awakened by the tolling of a large bell. Some boys wanted to linger, as boys do when sleep has been granted them and they wanted to hold onto it a little longer. Instead, the old men came through and rousted them out of their rags. One boy, at the other end, would not get up. One of the old men kicked at the child. Wembley rushed over to him and lifted the man up and away from the boy. The man weighed almost nothing. Lifting him had been as easy as lifting Talon. The man's eyes got large as saucers as Wembley glared at him, setting him down again. He bowed his head and waited. Wembley leaned down and placed his hand on the child's face. He was cold. He felt of his chest. It was also cold and not moving. He turned the boy over and the child's body remained motionless and somewhat limp. Wembley put his arms under the child and lifted him into his still strong arms. He cradled the child and asked, "Where do I take him?"

The man, who was now weeping himself, snuffled, "I'm sorry, young sir, but I didna know. I'll take him. I'll be good to 'im. It'll be a cold grave in the Pauper's Field for this poor child. I'll be careful. Give 'im 'ere." Wembley handed the child's body to the older man who almost struggled under the weight of the boy who weighed even less that the man did. "I fear I'll be a-joinin' 'im soon, I will." With that he shuffled off with the child. The other men followed him. One looked back at Wembley and smiled. Talon waved and the old man waved back. Wembley kneeled down in front of Talon who was weeping now. He held the boy close to him.

Then he heard, "Pssst! 'urry! She's comin' up to see what's takin' yer so long." and a trouserless boy, only a little younger than Wembley, vanished again into the shadows.

Wembley grabbed Talon's hand and practically dragged him over to the top of the stairs. A fat matron was on her way up, huffing and puffing.

"Wot's goin' on 'ere?"

"A boy died last night, ma'am, and I placed his little body in the arms of one of the servants."

She stopped. Wem could see the sadness in her eyes and face. Her shoulders slumped. "Ah! Not a welcome thing, except for the child. 'e's free of all this now."

Talon cried.

"There, there, now, little'un. Come down and have yer porridge -- make ya feel better, it will."

Wembley placed his hand on Talon's back and guided him down the stairs behind the matron. Talon looked up at him while Wembley nodded and tried to smile.

"Death's a hard thing, but you know that already, don't you?"

"Yes," was the reply that came from Talon's mouth.

Wembley looked at him. Shocked. Startled into inaction. They lingered on the step and Wembley hugged Talon. The boy looked at Wembley and, as they turned to go back down the stairs, they were no longer nearly naked on a narrow, dusty stairway, but fully clothed and warm on the wide stairs of the youth center, on their way down. They stopped.

"No need to talk about this with anyone, eh?"

"No, Wembley. I couldn't."

"But you can talk?" Wembley was all smiles.

"Yes."

"Good. I'll be looking forward to stories about you from your own lips."

Talon smiled, grandly, and Wem took his hand and turned them both around.

"How about that game of shuffleboard?"

Talon practically dragged Wembley back up the stairs. When they reached the top Talon stopped.

"What just happened? Did we really ..."

"It happened. We were there. It's this thing that happens to me. I'm sorry it dragged you with me. It's something that you and I will have plenty of time to talk about -- but just you and I. No one else would understand it. Let's play!"

Then they heard, from out of the gang of boys gathered upstairs, "Hey, Tewkes, about time you got here!"

Talon was breathing hard. It took a lot more effort for him to shuffle the puck to make a point than it did Wembley, or any of the other guys. He was the youngest, by far. When he teamed up with Wembley they never lost a match so, this time as well, Talon's smile just about covered up his face. He hadn't said a word, until he motioned to Wem, who leaned down to him, "This is great, Wembley."

"I think so, too!"

"Hey, Tewkes!" came from one of the guys.

"What, Lanning."

"Come play us sometime without Talon and see if you win!" He winked at Talon.

Talon's smile grew.

"Thanks for the game."

"Yeah, see ya later!"

Talon raced Wembley to the stairs, then hesitated before stepping onto the top step.

"It's okay, Tal. We're safe." He sure hoped so.

Talon rushed down and Wembley caught up with him taking two steps at a leap. They burst into the crafts room to find Brindi, Evie and Stephanie not in the room. One of the girls pointed to the gym. The boys rounded the corner to find the three girls embattled in a dodgeball game. They sat and watched. Brindi was out, on the sidelines, and came over to sit with the boys. Stephanie was hiding behind Evie who was laughing and dodging. They were the only two left on one side. Then Evie caught a ball. The opponent left the court and Evie handed the ball to Stephanie who ran forward and threw it across the line. It hit a girl about her age, who laughed and went to the sidelines. The ball sailed back over and Evie caught it again. Another girl left the court. One girl remained, one of the Big Sisters, who was running all over the court as she gauged her throw; how to hit Evie. She ran up to the line and Evie ran right up to her and confronted her and she bobbled the ball. It rolled across the line and Evie picked it up and threw it, mercilessly, at the girl who ran to the back of the court shrieking, but still getting hit. Stephanie ran up to Evie and gave her a big hug.

"I've never won before!"

Evie leaned down to her and hugged her back. "Neither have I!"

Evie and Stephanie came to the side and their little group congratulated them on their win. Brindi just couldn't get over the change in Evie. She stared at the former nemesis of practically every kid in the town. Evie smiled back at her. Brindi nodded and took Wembley by the arm. She saw Evie bristle and the smile drop, temporarily from her face. Stephanie demanded a 'slap five' from Evie and she got it, and the smile quickly returned. Talon tagged along with Wembley as Stephanie caught up with Brindi, leaving Evie alone.

Wembley called back over his shoulder, "See you later, Evie."

"Count on it, Wembley!"

The little group left the building with Evie standing strangely contemplative, even after her little bristle. Brindi turned to Wem.

"Competition?"

"Never."

"She had fun. She was smiling!" Russ interjected, incredulously.

"Who'd a thunk!" added Brindi.

"Did you have a good time, Tal?" asked Russ.

Talon looked up at Wembley and nodded enthusiastically.

Wembley squeezed his hand. Then looked to Brindi.

"So. You and Evie cool?"

"I wouldn't say that. But I am impressed with her change."

"Friends?"

"Not yet. More of a mutual respect."

"An understanding?"

"Almost."

"I'm glad," was Wem's assessment.

Talon's eyes were full of questions as he looked again up to Wembley.
Wem kneeled down to the child. "Did you notice a change in Evie?"
Tal nodded again, not daring to speak yet in front of others.
"Do you like it?"
Tal nodded again and a tear came to his eye.
"What's wrong?"
Tal pantomimed walking on the treadbarrel. The others looked at him, not understanding. Wem just nodded. Tal pointed up with his thumb and forefinger spread apart, as if indicating something written on a wall. Wem just nodded again.
"Yeah, Tal. God is love."
Russ patted the younger boy on the back. He was part of the gang, the club, the insiders who were beginning to know what Wembley knew. Brindi smiled and kneeled to kiss Tal on his forehead. Tal smiled widely and hugged her back.
The child had known nothing but love from his mother and little brother -- and the others in his life, for that matter. He had just come up against something that he had not been able to deal with. He thought, among all of this love, why had his father been taken away from him? It had happened just over a year ago. Everyone in Yarmouth knew about it. Some had not been kind, but they weren't the people that mattered to Talon Waters. The boy had sensed the sadness in his mother, even at the times when she was trying to cheer him; to make him feel loved and wanted. He was quite perceptive for a seven-year-old. Wem knew it. Russ sensed it, and now Brindi became familiar with it. All without a word spoken by Tal.
Their thoughts were interrupted by the honking of a horn. It startled Talon most of all.
"Anyone need a ride?" came from Marged Tewkes inside the van.
Wembley motioned to the whole group, asking silently for them.
"Hop in!" was the reply from Wem's Ma.
They had all heard him call her that. It was one of Wem's peculiarities retained from his Welsh background.
They piled into the car.
A few blocks away, the van pulled up to the curb in front of a small but well-kept house. Ma honked once and Mrs Waters came out being trailed by her younger son. The van door opened and the little boy ran up to greet his big brother who stepped out and hugged him, then held his hand. Marged's breath was taken away. Mrs. Waters, inspite of her loss, was certainly doing something right!
Wem followed his friend and gave the boy a big hug. "Love you, Tal"

"Love you, Wem."

The two friends then did their intricate handshake as Talon's mother watched with moist eyes, along with the rest of the surprised group.

"What ..." issued from the Mrs. Waters, speaking, in a sense, for everyone present.

Wem just shruged his shoulders.

She whispered, "Thank you."

"No, thank you!" and he hugged Talon again and let the little family head for the house.

As Wem climbed into the van he noticed the silence, especially that of his Ma and Brindi. Russ was smiling, ready with a 'high five' that Wembley was only too glad to return.

Marged managed to speak. "What happened, Wembley?"

Wem was silent for a moment, deciding on whether or not he could share the event. He decided that it would not be a breach of confidence between himself and Talon if he told the people who loved them both all about it. So he did.

Russ, was somber as Wem finished the story. The women were crying. "I thought that only happened in a movie. It was real?"

"More real than you and I sitting here talking, Russ."

"Holy crap!"

"Russel!"

"Sorry, Brin, but that's huge. Not just that it was real, but that Talon experienced it with Wem."

"Yeah. It's a good thing that it was with Wem."

"For sure," Russ agreed.

Brin leaned in and kissed Wem full on the mouth, in front of the others. The kiss was sweet and brief, but Wem clung to her as she did to him. The hug was the expression of a bond. Russ smiled. He knew. It wasn't a giggle smile. It was a smile that came from his toes; one he couldn't talk about.

Marged hadn't said a word. She couldn't. She, only now, began to realize the web of friendships that her son had woven around him. A web that protected and enlivened not only the person at its center, but each and every strand of its structure. She felt humbled to be the mother of such a son. She wasn't sure that she or Dylan had done anything to create the situation, or even if they deserved the son that had been given them. She just knew that, all of a sudden, she was more than grateful.

She was eventually able to pull away from the curb and drive the two blocks to the Williams home. She glanced in her rear-view mirror and saw Brindi and Wembley, huddled close, with Russ cuddled up to Wem's other side. She smiled. She spoke. She was amazed that she could find the words, let alone the courage to express them in this time and place. "I'm glad for the friends that Wembley has made. I couldn't ask for more or better."

There was more silence as the car pulled into the driveway of the Williams home. No one moved. Wem just put his arms around the girl and boy on either side of him and hugged them tighter. Marged sat, the waves of understanding continuing to wash over her grateful soul.

There was a rapping at the window. Mrs. Williams was just staring into the car, smiling and calling out to them, "Come on in! Dinner's about ready! Join us!"

Wem's head perked up, asking the question.

Marged smiled and nodded. "Da can fend for himself. I'll give him a call." She tapped at her cell phone.

No one could really tell who was the most excited as the occupants of the van left its safe confines and came out into the lone and dreary world of Yarmouth, Maine. Russ was beside himself and jumping all over. Brin was hugging and looking and hugging and looking. Even Wem was smiling wide. His Ma was going to know his second favorite family -- and they were going to get to know her.

"We'll be home soon. Thank you, luv!" Marged placed her phone back in her purse. "Looks like it's dinner with the Williamses."

The exultant cheer from Russ was the perfect topper to an afternoon of rich experience. He raced to the door to hold it open for his mother, sister and their guests. Marged was the last one in. She sighed. She knew about the house but had never been inside. It was everything that Wembley had told her -- warm, cozy, full of memories, rich and varied, historical and recent. Photos of the Williams children mingled with chromographs of the ancestors.

Wembley pulled Brindi over to one particular picture. "This is him, Johnny Lathrop."

Mrs Williams stopped. "How did you know?"

"Brin told me all about him. I'd know him anywhere, even if he was standing in front of me." That was close.

Brin and Russ laughed at that one. The mothers only looked a little puzzled and then went into the kitchen where Marged was determined to be of whatever assistance would be needed. Wem pulled Brin and Russ close and whispered, "The other one is me. I mean, I was him. Johnny was a good man. It's so weird that I can say I knew him!"

"Yeah, weird!" agreed Russ.

"But a good weird."

"Yeah."

They settled down on the couch and Wem picked up a game of Boggle. He shook the cube and settled all of the dice. He handed a pencil and paper to Russ and Brin and they were off. The scratch of graphite against paper, a welcome sound to any writer, was both calming and exciting as the three found words and combinations that -- well, boggled -- their imaginations. Brin found twenty-six words! Wem only found twenty-three. They looked to Russ' pad. He hid it. They pulled his hands away and saw a list of ... count 'em ... twenty words! Two of which were not crossed off. "Where did you find stinker?"

Russ leaned into the cube and traced the letters out. Wem, then Brindi, were flabbergasted that they had not seen it. "Thinker?"

Russ traced again. It was there! The older kids had missed it! Wem ruffled his hair. Brin kissed his nose.

"Good job, little bro!"

Russ blushed. He felt like he had won the game. Even though he had missed it by six words. But it was all a part of Wembley's web. They were all caught in it. It was a safety net for anyone who dared to venture in. It wasn't a bite or a sting that was waiting; it was a hug, or a kind word.

Marged entered the room to announce dinner and found the three young people in exactly the same positions they had been taken in the car. She almost hated to announce it but, it was her duty. "Dinner est servi!"

The kids bounced off of each other in their attempts to get up off the comfortable couch. Then they raced for the kitchen. Russ arrived first, then Brindi. Wembley came into the room with his Ma's hand in his own and they all sat down, with Mr. Williams and two littler sisters, for spaghetti and meatballs.

Silverware was clinking on plates as they finished the dinner.

"Mom's meatballs are the best!" bragged Russ.

"You're right there, Russel," was Marged's assessment.

"Have any of you ever had bangers and mash?"

"What's bangers and mash?" If it was food Russ was sure he'd like it.

"Mild sausages roasted in the oven and mashed potatoes topped with butter and sour cream."

"Well, why didn't you say so?" Russ quipped.

"I did. It's what we call them in Wales."

"I'll have to come over sometime and try them." Russ's eyebrows waggled up and down, as if to suggest something to the Tewkes' that they weren't already contemplating.

"Sunday -- dinner at our house!"

"We accept, but only if it's bangers and mash," was one of the few statements issued by silent, smiling Mr. Williams during the evening.

Russel pulled his elbows into his sides and balled his fists in the gesture of victory. "Yes!"

Brin laughed at him.

"Whatcha laughin' for?"

"You're just so cute!"

"Russel, I must say that you are an unusual boy; polite, caring, funny, athletic. Much like I had hoped my little Ioan would be." She caught her breath after saying it. The spirit in the home seemed to just relax her.

"Who's Ioan, Mrs. Tewkes?" Russ asked.

There was a look between mother and son. Wembley nodded.

"I lost him just before he was to be born. We named him anyway." She looked quickly at the Williams family, whose faces fell with her own.

"He's the little brother I never got to know, Russ," said Wembley. "It's why we moved here."

"I'm sure glad ya did! But it would have been cool to know Ioan, too, huh Sis?"

Brindi nodded. She had seen the overwhelming sadness in Marged's eyes at the mention of her other son.

"I'm just sorry that we weren't able to give Wembley any brothers or sisters."

"What? Ma! You gave Ioan to me. We just weren't able to keep him. I don't blame you. I blame the British!"

There was silence for a moment. "I know I'm not your real brother, Wem, but if ya want to, you can think of me that way, can't you?"

"I already do!"

"Forever?"

"Longer than forever!"

Russel ran around the table, for Brindi had gotten the seat on Wem's left and Marged was on his right. He jumped at Wem and Wem took him into his strong arms. It was a long moment. The family had trouble starting a conversation after that one. Brindi was especially grateful that she had chosen, wisely, her companions, and that they included, even centered around, Wembly Tewkes.

CHAPTER NINE
Swift As The Wind

Bryce had almost everyone in the car -- Brindi, Sam, Jenny, Asher and Russel. Only two more to pick up. They were headed to Bar Harbor for the day. Touristy, and a good drive up the coast, but the waterpark and the mini-golf were sensational! They pulled up in front of Talon's home. Talon was pulling his mother who was dragging his little brother behind her.

Talon got out to the curb, where Wembley was waiting and walked up to his older friend and slapped five.

"You're sure this is not too much?" Mrs. Waters said.

"Mo-om." was Talon's reply.

"It's just that you are all so much older."

"We've got Asher and Russel."

"Yes -- brothers. I just don't ..."

"Mrs. Waters," Wem placed his hand on Talon's shoulder. "Talon is like another little brother. We're all like family."

"It's cool, Mrs. Waters," shouted Bryce, the oldest.

"Yeah, way cool," added Russel, the youngest next to Talon.

"Our parents think it's a good thing, too," added Brindi.

"Well, if you're sure ..."

Talon did a little celebratory dance, there on the sidewalk to the laughter of all present.

"What time will you be home?"

"Just after dark," said Bryce.

"The younger ones can fall asleep on the way home."

Mrs. Waters nodded. "What about lunch?"

"I got it covered, Mrs. Waters."

"Have a good time," and Mrs Waters kissed Talon.

"Mo-om!"

But nobody laughed.

It was the last weekend before school and they were all excited to spend it together.

"Bye, Talon," said Trenton, Talon's little bro, waving as Talon got into the van.

"Bye, Trent. See you tomorrow."

The door was shut and they pulled away from the curb. Trenton stayed there, holding his mom captive until the van turned the corner and he couldn't see it anymore.

"I wanna be friends with Wembley when I grow up."

His mother laughed and bundled him close as she walked him in the opposite direction. They were going to the Dairy King for breakfast!

The van trundled along the roadway and crossed the bridge by the falls. They had one more person to pick up: Evie. It was a gamble, or at least that was the thought of Sam and Jenny, maybe even Brindi, but she also, but only recently, thought it was a gamble worth taking. They pulled up in front of the immaculately trimmed lawn and shrubbery of the Griffith's home. They didn't see it until they were all out of the car. It stopped them dead as they turned up the walkway.

"What's that word?" asked Talon.

The slang for a female dog was scrawled across the picture window of the front of the house.

"Never mind, Tal. But it's not a very nice word."

"Why is it on Evie's house?"

"Because some people don't know how much she has changed, like you and I do. Right?"

"Yeah."

Even Jenny and Sam looked sad. They had been on the receiving end of some of Evie's meanest pranks, but they had also heard about the turnaround. They had been hoping ...

Brindi knocked on the door. There was no answer. Wem rang the bell. Silence greeted the ding-dong.

Wem then knocked and called out, "Evie?!"

"Go away!" came from the inside.

"But today's the day for Pirate's Cove," it was Russ's contribution to luring her out.

Then Wem had an idea. He went around to the garage and found a bucket, some sponges and a little powdered soap. Everyone got the idea quickly and they rushed to turn on the water and sprayed the window down, then put water in the bucket. They reached every part of the huge window and scrubbed hard. The paint gradually came off the window. There was only a little part of the hump of the 'h' left on the brick in the corner. Bryce ran to the car.

"I got it!"

He returned with a metal brush that he used for cleaning the battery terminals, and other engine parts. He soaked it in the water, first, and then scrubbed the brick until the paint on it disappeared.

All had been silent inside. There were snickers outside as Wem called to Evie again.

"Come out, please!"

The others echoed the plea.

The door slowly cracked open and everyone outside motioned for Evie to come out. She stepped through the door. They pointed to the window. She did not want to look, she teared up.

"It's okay. We fixed it!" Russel piped up.

Wem reached out and turned her chin, just the littlest bit, until her eyes saw that the hate that had been there had been removed.

"Wha ..." Evie just stood there and cried.

"I thought she'd be happy," opined Talon.

"I am happy," was said through the tears of joy that Evie was beginning to sense in this new-found friendship.

"Girls sure have a funny sort of happy," chirped Russ.

"I was sure you'd see it and drive away."

Bryce offered, "We don't think of you like that. At least, not anymore."

Evie laughed through her blubbering.

"Some of us never did," was Wembley's final statement.

"Hurry and get dressed!" Brindi said.

"I don't know what to wear!" Evie said.

Brin and Jen looked at each other and each took an arm and ushered Evie into her house.

"Be right back!" Jen said.

"Yeah, like that'll happen!" added Sam.

The boys laughed but they sprayed down the outside of the house and window, and the walkway and put all the other stuff away. They only stood back at the front door for about thirty seconds when the girls, all smiles -- all three of them -- bopped through the door. Evie stopped, bringing Jen and Brin up a little short. She looked at everyone around her -- even the little ones. She looked at the window and the wall. All she could say was, "Thanks."

That's all that was needed.

The music blared out of the big bass speakers that Bryce had installed in the back of the van as they pulled out onto Highway 1, heading north to paradise. Lead-foot Bryce assured them that it would only take them a couple of hours. Bar Harbor was not that far away. But all the communities that would be terrorized by Bryce's car along the way ... well, it would be fun, Wembley figured. As usual, he was right.

Music blared, heads bopped to the rhythm, voices sang out -- sometimes on key -- and the first hour was eaten up. Belfast, was a little more than halfway and it was now 9:50. Bryce knew what he was doing. He avoided all the speed traps in and out of the town. He figured that the police would hear the music coming and be ready for the speeders. He went 30 mph all through the town, even though he could have gone 35. One policeman was standing out of his car, staring in unbelief at the noisy car of a teen crawling through his town. Bryce waved. The officer laughed. So did everyone in the car.

Ellsworth was 30 minutes away -- at Bryce's speed -- with nothing of consequence, except the trip around Penobscot Bay, to distract them. As Bryce rounded the bend into Ellsworth he shouted out "Fifteen minutes to Pirate's Cove!"

Everyone woke up. The little ones and the big ones had already taken a nap. But they were ready now. The car bounced along, with the extra help of the youngest three of the group, and Mount Desert Island was achieved. The spectacular mini-golf heaven was just one song away! They pulled into the parking lot and Talon just about crawled through the window to get out.

"Hold on there, Tal! It'll still be there when we get out of the car."

"Sorry, Wem."

"Don't be sorry -- be glad!" Wem extended his hand to the boy. Russel came up on the lad's other side as the boy chatted incessantly about this and that on his way to the ticket window.

All Wem could say at the window was, "Whew! Price has gone up!" But he really didn't care. Two hours here would let them play every hole twice. Then it was on to the water park.

"Wem, I never played before."

"No matter, Tal. Come here. Put your ball on that little spot right there."

"But ..."

"It's a practice green."

Brindi reassured him, "We'll wait. Go on!"

Tal bent over and placed his ball on the little pucker on the mat. Wem stepped up and showed Tal the grip on the club.

"Now you don't need a big swing, except for one or two of the holes, so just try this." Wem swung and Tal watched. "Step up to the ball and try it."

Tal stepped up to the ball. He didn't want to disappoint anyone in the party by not being able to play -- well.

"See that little line on your putter?"

"Yeah."

"Bring it up to the ball, without hitting it, and then take it away in a straight line."

"Okay."

"Now, bring it forward with a little bit of oomph."

Talon did so and the ball rolled off of the mat and onto the grass of the little putting green. It went just to the left of the hole and then stopped. Talon was heartbroken.

"What's the matter?"

"It didn't go in."

"It rarely does. It usually takes more than one stroke to get it to the cup let alone in it."

"Really?"

Everyone nodded in agreement with Wem.

"Now, line that line up with the ball and the hole and then just tap it."

Talon sweat bullets but managed to bring the putter up to the ball with the line aimed at the hole. He hit the ball softly -- like Wem had told him. It traveled about seven inches and dropped over the edge of the cup and into the hole. Everyone applauded. Even Evie, who was so amazed at the tenderness that Wembley Tewkes showed for the smallest among them.

Evie told Talon, "You're gonna beat the socks right offa me!"

"You're joking?"

"Not - at - all!"

Talon smiled and rushed over to the first hole.

"Remember, Tal. Take your time. We'll play from youngest to oldest, 'kay?"

Everyone nodded.

After the first half of the first course they were in the cave, where all four parts of the course intersected. It was cool, water fell in showers and streams all around them. Their voices and putters echoed around. Everyone tried to make the loudest echo, especially Talon. Wem hoped that they weren't annoying those others who had come to play, but everyone around them was smiling.

Each of the players in their group had one stroke to get them into the cave. Now they had to prepare to hit the pipe and go down to the next green.

But the echoes affected Wembley in another way. He lost track of the game. All he could hear was his Granda, Hugh Fitzroy, cautioning him to practice three times before he swung, which was like clockwork to him now. Then -- he was there.

"Granda?"

"Yes, Wembley."

"What's the point of chasing the ball all over the grass just to put it in a tiny hole in the ground?"

"Its a game of stealth and cunning. A game of accuracy. A game of strategy and planning. It helped us beat the British."

"What did you do, club them to death?" The eleven year old Wembley laughed at his own joke.

"No, Wembley. We plotted and planned; we studied the lay of the land. We knew what the British would do -- they always did it -- and we changed our plans. We came at them from different angles, with different weapons. That's why there are so many clubs in the bag. We can choose our tricks depending on what happens. The British just marched. We took steps to get to where we were going. And the significance of the ball in the cup was that we 'put' the British right where we wanted them. In a hole. We 'put' them there."

"Put? Like putting?"

"Put-ing or putting, it's all the same. There has always been more to the Picts and the Celts than barbarism. No matter what the English Historians say. We were sly, cunning. We had to be to survive."

"But it took hundreds of years, didn't it?"

"Yes, it did. Everything pays off in the end. Remember let the ball come to the driver, not the driver to the ball. All it takes is ..."

"... time, yeah, I know Granda."

"Time. Time. Time ... time ... time ..." The echoing memory was fading, but had it been just a memory?

"Your turn, Wem."

"Just in time." Wem laughed at his little joke. No one else got the fact that he had been absent for a while -- at least long enough to go through the playing order to his turn, number four. What seemed to have happened in an afternoon with his Granda Hugh had only taken two minutes of the present time. Wem shook his head and placed his ball. He hit the pipe and it disappeared, down to a lower level, where it came out on the green and rolled right up to the cup and stopped.

"Hmph! British must've found a defense."

"What was that, Wem?"

"Nothing. Nothing."

"Well, hurry and tap out so I can putt." Brin was a little anxious.

Wem did. Brin sounded like she was in a hurry. She was. She lined her ball and struck it, only to have it go too far and bounce around the green to go down the wrong pipe that let her out about six feet from the hole.

"See what hurrying gets you?" He kissed her. Evie bristled again, but it was a short one. Brin just lined up her putter.

"Take your time."

"Is that what your Granda used to tell you?"

"Yes, as a matter of fact."

"Oh, well, I guess he would know -- being a Scot!"

She lined it up. She used her putter as a compass. She was not going to miss, because then she would only be one behind Wembley -- the current leader. She was a competitive little scrapper. She hit her mark and the ball rolled slowly to its destination and eased over the edge of the cup. Brin flounced over to pick it up and Wem gave her a kiss this time.

"See, I told ya."

"No, your Granda told you!"

She laughed as Wem kissed her again and the sound of a ball being hit came from the upper green. Sam's ball throttled down the pipe and spit itself right into the hole.

"Ha!"

"Luck!" and Evie smiled.

"Skill," Jenny countered.

Evie nodded and smiled again. Jenny, Bryce and Evie had all taken three strokes total to get their ball into the hole. Sam was the only one who had made it in two. The younger ones did a respectable job of making par four. Talon was excited. He watched each player; tried to learn their tricks and styles. There seemed to be no sign in him of the tragedy that had struck him a little more than a year ago. Russ was even beginning to see him as a close friend, not just a playmate. Asher felt similarly about the seven year old. Everyone else, including the older boys, just adored him.

Evie, only once, had a problem around Talon. She shed a tear; her emotions ran a little high.

Wem noticed, as he noticed everything. "What's wrong, Evie."

"Nothing."

"Really?"

"Well, no -- but ... well, it's Talon."

"What's wrong with him?"

Evie shook her head. "Everything seems to be right with him."

"I know what you mean."

"I don't think so, but you sure try."

"What?"

"He reminds me of a little boy I knew a long time ago, who's dead now."

"Who?"

"My son."

Wem was knocked for a loop. He hadn't known, hadn't suspected. "I ... I ..."

"Our secret?"

Wem nodded and they went on to the next hole.

As they were walking Wem searched, surreptitiously, the face and demeanor of this girl with the name of Evie Griffith. How old was she, anyway? She had a child, a boy, who was at least seven a 'long time ago'? She definitely looked eighteen, or older, not older than maybe twenty-three or twenty-four -- but way passed senior year in high school. So she had this child anywhere from the time she was eleven-years-old to seventeen-years-old. But she said a long time ago so she had to be closer to eleven when she had him. Wembley's mind was turning in circles. Evie was smiling. He felt a hand on his arm.

"Your turn, Wem." It was Brindi. He quickly looked over to Evie and there was that familiar yet momentary bristle. In a flash it came and went. Wem lined up his putter. He sent his ball over the ramp, around the curve and directly into the hole. Wem was just as surprised as everyone else, especially since he hadn't thought about it at all before he did it.

"How'd you do that!?" was Talon's worshipful question.

"I really don't know, Tal. Luck? I mean, I aimed, but ... I don't know."

"Kewl!" said the boy with the golden curls.

They finished up the first round without more notable incidents and began their second round on the other course. Thirty-six different holes of golf in one facility. Wem loved it. The next surprise, or unusual incident came at the 18th Hole. Each of the younger ones got a hole-in-one, which meant a free game. But then everybody in their party achieved a free game. Wembley looked over at Evie. She seemed to be smiling a lot more than usual on this trip. Was she simply good luck, now, or was there something more to Evie Griffith?

Since it was a ticket that could be used anytime, they all, excitedly, trouped out to the car to drive to Subway, in the center of the town, and get some lunch.

After some five dollar footlongs and drinks Wembley asked the question: "What do ya say? To the waterpark?"

The consensus was unanimous.

"But what about the free games?"

"If we feel like free games after the waterpark, then we'll come back. All right, Tal?"

"Okay."

"But if we don't come back, you still have your ticket -- we all do -- and keeping the ticket will prove that you won a free game!"

Talon thought about that for a minute. "I could frame it and put it on my wall."

"Good idea, bro!" said Russel. "I'm gonna do the same. If we don't go, that is."

They didn't go back. The waterpark was too much fun, and it was a long drive home.

The slides were a blast. They spent hours chasing each other down them. Then they took a relaxing dip in the pool. They even claimed a portion of the pool for themselves and played Marco Polo. Talon was all smiles, because he was in his element. He was quite the fish. He had first met Wembley at the local pool where Wembley worked as a lifeguard and swimming assistant for the little kids. Talon was all set to join the swim team when he turned eight. Then he'd get to be with Wembley all the time.

But for now, Wembley was 'it'. He called out 'marco'. The rest of the group whispered 'polo'. He homed in on Talon, he had to find him first.

What he came up with after several 'marcos' was an armful of Russel. Russel slapped the water, good-naturedly, and moved to the side of the pool. The next catch was Evie, who didn't mind being caught in Wembley's arms. Bryce kind of did! Sam and Jenny were next because they always stayed together, so Wem got a two-for-one when he encircled them. Where was that Talon? Wem reached out and caught Asher, who thought he'd be sneaky and 'polo' right behind Wem, but Wem was too fast for him. He was not only in Wem's arms but in the air and sailing to another spot in the pool, laughing as he flew. Brin and Tal were left. Their voices sounded the same, both soprano, but Brin's was a little deeper. He headed for the higher voice. He realized, without even opening his eyes, what Talon was doing to avoid him. When Wem said 'marco' Talon would reply with his 'polo' and then duck under the water and swim low to the bottom of the pool, like the fish he was. Wem heard Tal's reply and then submerged himself with his arms out and caught Talon by the foot. He hauled the boy up kicking and then wrapped his arms around him and kissed the top of his curly little head.

"You little sneak. That's a pretty good trick!"

"Not good enough, I guess."

"You're the last one to be caught."

"No. You gotta get Brindi," and Talon giggled.

Wembley whispered in his ear, "I always know where Brin is. Watch."

"Marco!"

"Po-"

By the utterance of the second syllable Wem had his arms around Brin and his lips on hers, for a brief peck. Talon laughed, and giggled. So did the rest of their friends.

"What does he know that I don't know?"

"That'll be a secret between Tal and I. Right, Tal?"

"You bet."

There was Evie bristling again. Wembley caught it out of the corner of his eye. Talon approached Wem.

"What is the secret?"

"I like her perfume."

Talon giggled again.

Wembley moved out of the pool. "Who wants to fight me?"

Talon gave Wem a little punch, right in the abs. It didn't hurt but it did surprise."

"Ya little beggar!"

Talon giggled again as Wem picked him up and tossed him about ten feet across the pool. They had done it a hundred times at the pool in Yarmouth. It was one of Talon's favorite things.

"How're we gonna fight you? Bryce and maybe Sam are the only ones big and strong enough to beat you!" was Asher's observation.

"How about a water balloon fight?"

Russel yelled and pretended to throw a hand grenade in Wembley's direction and then made all sorts of explosion noises. He was joined by Asher and Talon, all pretending to 'attack' Wembley.

"Let's see what you can do with a water balloon instead of a pretend grenade!"

"You're on, Tewkes!"

The three younger boys and Bryce clustered together. Sam had a hard time but went over to the boys' side.

"I'll throw in with you, Wembley," offered Brindi.

"So will I," said Evie.

"I'll help the losers," said Jenny.

"Big surprise there," said Russel.

Asher puckered up his lips and said, "Oh, Sam, Sam, Sam!"

The younger boys cracked up. So did Sam. But Jenny stood by his side and the noisy boys quieted down.

"I bought six buckets of balloons. Each team gets three."

Well, the war was on -- in a special place in the park reserved for water balloon fights. It even had a small plexiglass shield for one member of each team to hide behind and get their breath. Bryce assigned each one of the younger boys to be with one of the olders. Teams on the team. Each team got a bucket. Jenny got Talon, if she couldn't have Sam, Talon is the one she would have chosen, anyway. Bryce pulled his brother Asher to his side. That left Russel to be with Sam.

Good choice, Sam thought.

Yelling, screaming, the sound of a balloons bursting against the shield or on a person filled the next thirty miutes with mayhem. It was a riot. They were all wet anyway. Even Evie didn't mind getting plastered with a balloon. She saw her opportunity and she took it. She hid behind the shield for a moment to focus her concentration. Then she took Wembley away. Oh, their bodies were still there, but they were absent for a second, or two.

Wembley was in the middle of throwing a balloon. It had just left his hand when he saw blue all around him. Turquoise type of blue.

The Island world -- again!

He stood up out of the water and Vivi was on the beach, staring at him. He looked up and down and saw the same emptiness as on his previous trip. They were alone.

"Where is everyone?"

"Gone."

"The last time I was here, they were also gone."

"I know."

"How do you know?"

"Because this whole world was my invention."

Wembley almost swore. Instead, he just stood there stammering. "How?" finally emerged from his throat.

"Let's just say that I have certain abilities; things I've been able to do since I was born."

"When were you born?"

"AD 481."

"You're joking!"

Vivi just smiled and her green eyes flashed.

"Were you born here?"

"No."

"Where?"

"I'd rather not say -- yet."

"Were you born to a world without clothing?"

"No, it was cold there, sometimes. I like it warm." Her eyes flashed again.

"Then why ..." Wembley stopped. He covered himself and turned away. *Could it be?* His back was to her and his shoulders slumped forward. "Evie?"

"It's about time you noticed."

"Why the Vivi thing?"

"I have many names."

He stood there facing away from her. Then he heard sloshing through the water and she was standing in front of him. He pressed his hands more tightly together.

"You're embarrassed?"

"Evie, this is an invasion of privacy. My privacy. You may feel at home naked but, I don't appreciate it. If this is your doing, you've got to stop."

"You don't like me anymore, do you?"

"That's the problem, I want to like you. I want the other kids to like you, but this really gets in the way. It's not right. I ... it makes me very uncomfortable. I don't know what these powers are that you seem to have, or why these things are happening, but if it's you, I need you to stop it."

Evie couldn't tell him too much; like the fact that they had been married in another life; that they had a son who looked like Talon. Wembley would never accept it with what little he knew, now. She would have to wait. She began to see the situation through Wembley's eyes. The reason he had been chosen in the first place was because of who he was; his goodness, his innocence. Not who she wanted him to be. Her interference here could change that.

"So it is you?"

Evie nodded.

"How?"

"I ... can't tell you."

"Then why did you do this?"

"I thought you'd like me better."

"Evie ..."

"I just want you to like me."

"I like both of us better with clothes on. When it was everybody, Briony and Shane and everyone, it wasn't so bad, so invasive. But when it's just the two of us, I just don't feel ... right. It's just ... wrong."

She couldn't tell him of the years they spent together, just like this, in another life. She couldn't express her full love and longing for him and their past life together. It is not that she didn't want to, she just couldn't. It was forbidden, for now. All she could say was, "I will not bring you here again."

"Promise?"

Evie nodded and their naked bodies began to transform to bodies wearing the swimwear at the waterpark, in the middle of a water balloon fight. But during the dissolve back to real life Evie's hands pressed against Wembley's unbalding head. As they formed, she remembered the curls that she had held hundreds of times in that other life and it was even harder for her to take away this memory, but she knew she must. She removed only the memory of this particular 'DreamTravel'. His earthly self could not know that she had such powers. She realized that now. She was impetuous and eternally selfish, in some ways. The girl with no hair and green eyes would have to remain a mystery until the proper moment.

Upon arrival, Evie stomped out of the pool, angry at herself for what she had done. *Stupid! Stupid! Stupid!* was repeated over and over to herself in her mind.

"Evie, where're you going?"

"I'll be back."

"What if we win and you're not here?"

"Then you win and I'm not there."

She went off towards the dressing rooms. Wembley thought to follow her, but decided that she needed some time for herself. Besides, he couldn't leave Brin alone to fight the other team. He stood and chucked another water balloon at Talon. It hit him on the forehead and splattered all over his curly blonde hair and in his eyes. He spluttered a moment and then laughed as he threw three balloons in succession at Wem, who ducked two of them but got hit square in the chest with the third.

It wasn't like dodgeball, there were no outs. Just points per hit, kept track of by two officials whose job was made easier at Evie's departure.

The other team took the remaining balloons in their hands, some had two, others with bigger hands, had three. Brin and Wem had three total balloons left. Wem gave Brin two and he took one. He pointed to the left and Brin went out. Wem went to the right. Fifteen balloons sailed in two directions. Only one balloon hit Brindi. Wem remained untouched. Wem nodded and three balloons launched themselves at the unarmed team. It happened so fast, that all three balloons hit. Sam got it in the face. Asher got it on the leg and Bryce got it, well you know where.

"Tewkes! I'm gonna kill you!" And he ran forward and managed to get the only slightly smaller Wembley in a cradle hold. He carried his friend and nemesis to the pool and threw him in. He then jumped in after him and they laughed. The rest of the gang joined them.

"That was a blast!"

"But we lost, Ash!"

"So. It was more fun than I ever had."

Jenny had to agree. "It sure was fun!"

"Where'd Evie go, anyway?"

"She said she didn't feel well," Wem explained.

"That's too bad, she's a pretty good shot!"

"She got me twice!" admitted Sam.

"Do you know where she went?" asked Brindi.

"I think so. I'll go see. Don't have too much fun without me."

Talon smiled his wicked little smile and said, "We won't!"

Wembley walked over to the dressing room area where he found Evie sitting on a bench, crying.

"Evie, what's wrong?"

Evie startled, then just sobbed and shook her head. Wembley stood there waiting for an answer to his question. He put his hands on her shoulders. One of her hands came up to touch one of his. He gently pulled his hands away and turned her to face him, leaving about a foot or two between them, he sat near to her.

"Evie?"

Evie calmed to the point where she could speak. "I love you, Wembley."

"I know. I think I've known it for a while, now."

"Do you love me?"

"I like you. That's as far as it can go."

"But you're only fourteen."

"Fifteen."

"Oh, that's right, you had a birthday I wasn't invited to."

"Well, we weren't exactly friends, yet, were we?"

"I guess not."

"Don't ruin what we have. It's all I can offer."

"I'm sorry. I want more."

"I know. It's silly, to me, for someone to want all or nothing."

"I guess you're right."

She reached out and placed her palm on his muscular chest, right over his heart. He took it in his hand and held it for a minute.

"We better get back."

She nodded.

They stood and walked towards the pool.

"Who won?"

"We did!"

"How?"

"Total luck!"

She laughed. It was that laugh that Brindi saw as they rounded the corner of the pool house.

"Feeling better?" Brindi's question was almost confrontational.

"I'm sorry. I have my moments. Mood swings."

Brindi wanted to object, to press the issue, but she realized that Evie was a lot like her. She had her good days and bad days. Sometimes those days changed from moment to moment. She wanted to dislike her, but she couldn't. She had been influenced too much by Wembley Tewkes. "I think I know what you mean."

She didn't, but Evie couldn't tell her that. Wem and the other boys were a little perplexed.

"Girl stuff." Evie explained. It was something universal that any boy over thirteen should understand. It only made girls more mysterious to the three youngest among them.

"What time is it?"

Wem pulled his watch out of his boardshorts pocket. "5:30."

"Anyone for dinner before we head home? There's a McDonalds in Ellsworth."

"Mickey D's, please," yelled Talon. Asher, Russel and Sam echoed his sentiments.

Jenny poked Sam.

"What?"

"I always knew you operated on a lower cultural plane."

"What's wrong with Mickey D's?"

"Nothing, if you're 10." She looked at the boys.

"What about the Spicy McChicken?"

"Oooh, well, you've got me, there. Mickey D's it is."

On their way to the dressing rooms Bryce asked a simple question. "What's wrong with McDonalds?"

Evie answered it. "Nothing, I guess."

They laughed all the way into their separate dressing rooms.

$$\boxed{10\text{:}00}$$

The halls at Yarmouth High School were terribly boring and noisy after the fun of their last escapade at Bar Harbor. Brin, Wem, Sam and Jenny were Sophomores, Bryce was a Junior and Evie was a Senior. With pledge week, they settled into the rhythms of school life and the activities that came with it. The Thespians announced the production of *Les Miserables* and Wembley ached to play Marius. He wished that Brin would try out to be Cosette, but she would never do it. Evie surprised them all by getting the part. Wembley had a tough decision to make. Brin told him to go for it. She would support him.

"It doesn't bother you?"

"No. It's acting right?"

No answer from Wem.

"Right?"

"Yeah, right. Sorry. Okay, I'll go ahead."

He had to balance rehearsals with his other club duties as well as with the Cross Country team. Bryce was his support there. XC practiced after school. The arts practiced in the evenings. It was a full schedule, but Wem handled it.

He trained hard, which only served to help his singing and stamina onstage.

On a Saturday in mid-September he had a home meet. He stood at the starting line and shook his hands and fingers, he flexed his knees working through his foot. Bryce was right next to him. They wanted to make it a one-two finish. Their friends as well as 'little brothers' were in the crowd. He heard the report of the gun and was on his way. The course lay across dirt and grass, amid tall brush and trees. He settled into his rhythm and plodded on. He got to thinking that he hadn't noticed Evie before the race started. It was kind of hard to miss her red hair, but he figured that he just hadn't seen her. There was a little jostling for position that brought his attention back to his running.

He was kind of on auto-pilot until the halfway mark was passed. When he came back to himself he saw things that he hadn't expected to see. There was only one other runner, he was bare-chested and wearing a sort of loincloth as his legs pumped his feet on and off the ground. The other youth seemed close to Wembley's age and had long, dark beaded hair. There was a stripe of red across his cheek, but it didn't look like blood. Wembley was also bare-chested and loin-clothed.

"Aluwalamae!"

"What?"

The other runner pointed ahead and Wembley took off. The other youth was right on his heels. It didn't seem like they were in competition with each other, but that they were running together for some reason. The youth glanced behind them, Wembley did too. They were running away from something, or someone. He could hear the crashes through the underbrush behind them. The low-hanging branches of the forest whipped against his and his fellow's skin leaving little welts and cuts on their torsos.

He turned to the front again just in time to see two green eyes, disembodied, but watching him. He pushed himself and sprang forward. The other runner shouted again.

"Aluwalamae!"

Wembley only heard a voice whisper loudly, "Hurry!"

He didn't know where the voice had come from, just that he had heard it. Is that what 'aluwalamae' meant -- hurry? He was hurrying. He broke through the edge of the forest into a large meadow. As he looked around he found that it was completely ringed with trees and he would soon be back in the brush. He heard yelping and his fellow runner screamed and stumbled. The fallen youth shouted again, "Aluwalamae!"

What, Wembley thought, *is there only one word in this language and it means everything?*

Wembley stopped and turned around to help his fellow to his feet. The youth screamed back at him. "Ahn! Ahn! Talahwalumae!"

The yelping sounded closer. Just as Wem helped the youth to his feet the creatures broke through the brush on their backtrail. Wembley's jaw dropped to the ground. There were two -- dogs, wolves, coyotes -- somethings! Their fur was a dull green and they had intermittent red spots. They were growling and snarling and drooling. The other youth withdrew his long-knife from the sheath in his boot. Wembley reached down and found that he also had one. It was in his hand in a flash. The two beasts lunged at the two youths and all four went down. Wembley had held his knife straight out and felt the full weight of the thing on his right arm and then it hit his chest. The other youth was screaming.

Wembley quickly pushed the dead weight off of him and yanked his knife out of the chest of the beast. He then leaped onto the back of the other beast and repeatedly rammed his knife into the thing's ribcage until it stopped snarling. He rolled the creature off of the other youth. He noticed that the youth was a little younger than he, maybe twelve or thirteen, with long, strong legs but an almost child-like build. He also noticed the other youth's knife imbedded under the chin of the dog that had attacked him.

Wembley discovered a large gash across the boy's left side. He pressed his hands against the wound, holding the blood back. He checked. The boy's chest was rising and falling only slightly. He was still alive -- but just barely. With one hand pressing against the boy's side, he took his other hand and removed one of the long leggings that the boy was wearing. He, himself, also had a pair, protecting his legs. He then removed the other legging and tied them together with their laces. He then wrapped them around the boy's chest, slit their ends with his knife, and tied them in a knot over the gash.

He sat back on his haunches, almost breathless and looked up at the ... yellow sky with three red suns arching across it. He sighed, then took a closer look at the grass, which he had assumed was green, but was actually blue. The trees had blue leaves, too, not green.

Where am I this time?

He had assumed that he was in the past of his own America among a noble tribe like the Chippewa or Cherokee, or even the Mic-Mac. But this was nowhere near America, in the present day or at any time in its past. This was a new world, a 'DreamTravel'. Not a memory.

He looked at the boy, Wembley was the older of the two. *The kid was sure fast!* His eyes fluttered open.

"Waantu?" was weakly uttered.

Wembley just shook his head.

"Een tah walas to melah?"

"I don't understand."

The boy shrank back at the strange words of his older companion. He spoke again.

"How did you save me?"

Wembley just about fell over. "You speak English?"

"I do not know 'engleesh' I speak what you speak, brother."

I have a brother?

"How did you save me, Waantu?"

"It was our knives that defeated both creatures."

"Dirty talanks!" He spit at the bodies of the wolf-like talanks.

"I thought we were dead."

"I, too, though we would never see our family again."

"I am grateful, Waantu."

"Me too, brother. Does it hurt?"

The boy nodded.

"Then just lay there for a while. We are in no hurry, now that we are not pursued by man-eating beasts."

The boy fell back against the cool, blue grass with a short laugh. His darkly tanned upper body was covered in the hide that Wembley (Waantu) had wrapped around him and the leather cloth that was tied around his hips. His calf length leather boots hugged his lower legs. Wembley reached over to the beast and retrieved the boy's knife. He handed it to him, hilt first. The boy took it and reached down to put it in his boot but grimaced at the pain.

"Here, let me."

Wembley slipped it into the sheath he found inside his brother's boot.

"Mother will be looking for us."

"Can you move?"

"I think so."

"Can you walk with my help?"

"I can do anything with your help."

The boy smiled gamely as Wembley assisted him to his feet and pulled the boy's right arm across his ample shoulders.

"I did not know you could run so fast, Waantu."

"Nor I you."

"It is a good thing our father is fast, or we would both be dead."

Wembley couldn't wait to meet his mother and father. His brother limped along. They passed into the forest again and Wembley realized that he did not know which way to go. Except that there was a path that they were on. He decided just to follow it; maybe let his brother lead them on. They reached a fork in the path and his brother naturally wound to the left. Wembley just kind of followed. Before a half an hour was up the smell of cooking fires hit Wembley's nostrils.

"Smells good!"

"We must send the others back for the talanks. They will feed many."

"You're right."

The village came into view on a little rise in the forest. Smoke curled up into the treetops and played with the light coming down from the three suns. The rays were multi-radial and cool as anything, each refraction having three centers; each shadow being a triplet. As the brothers topped the rise the children of the village came around them, all voicing their questions.

"What happened Taanal?"

"Waantu saved me from the talanks."

"Taanal was brave. We fought the talanks together and won."

Taanal smiled. Their mother made her way from one of the huts to where her sons were standing.

"More tales of bravery, I hear, Waantu?"

"Not tales, Mother. He saved my life."

"You honor your entire family, Waantu."

"I only did what had to be done."

"Go, children, bring the talanks to us so that we may feast."

There were no older warriors? Just this woman and these children. How would they carry the talanks? "Where is Father?" asked an overanxious Waantu.

"You must know that he will not be back until the next moon. He is with your older brothers on the hunt."

Wembley decided to play a part. "Why am I always here?"

"Because someone must protect the village, like you always manage to do!" yelled Taanal.

"And your betrothal is tomorrow night, just as the moon disappears."

"Yes?" Wembley was suddenly more than nervous. "I ... remember."

"Killing two talanks has overtaxed you, my son. You must both go and rest. I will send Uhumai to tend to your wounds, Taanal."

Taanal smiled and led his brother to their shared hut. When they arrived there were two other boys inside, resting. Both had poultices of some kind on their necks. Both wore only loincloths.

"What happened to you two?"

"We ran into a nest of tumalas. Uhumai is healing us."

"She will heal me, also. I was gored by a talank. Waantu saved me."

"We are honored to share your hut, brothers."

"It is our hut -- all of us -- brothers."

The flap of a door parted and a young girl, well, a girl of near Wembley's age, maybe a little older, came in with cloths and wooden bowls filled with a pasty mixture.

"Lay down, Taanal, so I can heal you."

He did. She unwrapped his chest and laid the leggings by. "Who wrapped you?"

"Waantu!"

"You did a good job, brother."

"Thank you, Uhumai."

"Where did you learn it? I did not teach you."

"It seemed like the right thing to do." Wembley was flying by the seat of his ... loincloth on this one.

"Luckily the gash is not very deep. But the claws of a talank have a poison ..."

"I know, sister."

"Yes, Taanal, well, these hides drew out that poison. They are the hides of the talank, itself."

Taanal gave his older brother a look of 'how did you know?'

Wembley shrugged his shoulders.

It seemed that the women in this culture were the healers. The men provided, and sometimes just obeyed.

Uhumai soaked the cloths in the pasty mix and began applying them to Taanal's side in layers, cloth crossed across cloth. Wembley watched. Once the poultice was finished she took a remaining cloth, dipped it in her bowl of clean water, and washed the boy's face, neck, chest and legs. She got terribly close to what Wembley considered personal space, but this was a new world, different from his. These were a simple and intelligent people. He went with it. Uhumai watched Waantu as she finished up with Taanal.

"Your turn."

"What?"

"Remove your leggings."

He stood there. So, she, very business like, untied the laces of his leggings and washed his face, neck, chest and legs in a perfunctory way. "It is too hot for leggings inside, anyway."

She put everything into her bowls and stood up and left.

"You are a lucky man, Waantu," was Taanal's assessment.

"How is that?"

"Uhumai will make you a wonderful wife."

Wembley blanched as the other boys in the hut laughed. But the laughter sent Taanal into a coughing fit. Wembley leaned over him and pressed his bandages back into place, trying to get him to stop laughing.

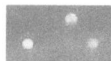

The chittering of some animal brought Wembley to consciousness the following morning. He didn't believe it could happen, but he had actually gotten a good night's sleep -- in a 'DreamTravel' -- without his mattress. The mat, and the leaves under it, seemed to provide all the comfort he needed. He stretched and stood, securely retying the laces of his loincloth at the hips. The mats of the other boys were empty. He left the hut and found them all seated on a log around the fire. The two boys just younger than Taanal had no poultices this morning. Their necks were red, but no wounds showed. Taanal was still bandaged. Still tender, but he sat up straight and tall. Wembley marveled at the strength of the boy, who could almost outrun him.

Uhumai was there to redo the bandage on Taanal. Just the bandage this time. As she finished she turned passed Waantu and her eyes flashed. Wembley reacted visibly as she entered a hut down the row.

"What is the matter, Waantu?"

"She has green eyes."

"We all have green eyes."

"Ye-es, I know, but hers are very green."

The boys laughed with a little too much innuendo behind it. They knew that tonight was the night. It would happen for them within a year or so -- their own betrothal. Tonight was the night for Uhumai and Waantu. He was a strange brother, this Waantu. He had become so unlike himself lately. Ever since the talank attack.

Suddenly -- without a warning of any kind -- there was a noise coming from the edge of the camp. A scream. An arrow zinged passed Waantu and stuck in the side of their hut. It was on fire in seconds. Another flaming arrow lodged in the chest of one of the younger boys seated on the log. He fell over backwards, lifeless, and on fire. Waantu gathered the other boy and Taanal and ushered them into the hut. It was on fire, but so what -- their weapons were in there. They emerged again fully armed and hiding behind the flap and the one open window of the hut. They loosed arrow after arrow as dark-haired naked warriors from what must have been another tribe swarmed through the camp.

"The Intanobi!"

They took out warrior after warrior. They were the oldest boys left in camp and had been trained since they were very little to shoot straight and fast. They saw arrows flying out of the windows of other huts.

"Must be the older girls and some of the young boys. They always come through."

Flaming arrows were lodging in the walls of every hut in the circle. But then as arrows flew from the huts, Intanobi warriors fell into the clearing. Three warriors appeared and released a string of arrows into the hut where Uhumai had been. There were screams and Waantu doubled his efforts and the arrows flew from his bow and downed those three. They were only to be replaced by five more. The village was totally aflame. They would have to vacate the huts soon and fight in the open.

Wembley grabbed a spear and surged into the central area. He swung his spear like a quarterstaff and two warriors went down. He then thrust and skewered another. He pulled that out and thrust and swung his way around the camp. The younger boy, Tuumal, followed Waantu's example. He took out three warriors in a row before he was hit with three flaming arrows and went down. Taanal ran to his younger friend and pulled the arrows from his flesh. A warrior appeared with a spear and Taanal screamed.

"Waantu!"

Wembley turned, after staving in the heads of two warriors, only in time to see the spear enter the body of his younger brother and pierce all the way through his back. Tuumal, grabbed his spear and thrust it into the warrior's back. He did it with enough force that it protruded from the man's chest and he keeled over.

Tuumal went to Taanal and cradled him against his body, against the wounds of the arrows that had burned and torn his own flesh but not taken his life.

Wembley swung his staff and batted a line of warriors, who could only look at him with the wide eyes of fear. They had never witnessed such a warrior -- especially in a boy! With either end he pierced the bodies of the Intanobi.

He was finished and the clearing was empty. The huts were burning, some were already ash and cinders. He rushed to Taanal. Tuumal just shook his head. But Taanal's eyes opened.

"I love you, brother."

"I love you, Taanal."

And Taanal's eyes closed for the last time.

War cries of more warriors came at the two remaining boys. Wembley grabbed Tuumal and they ran. Tuumal was almost as fast as Taanal. They raced into the woods, towards the place where Wembley had killed the talanks the other day. They ran out into the meadow. The warriors were in pursuit, screaming and brandishing their spears. They passed over the blood-stained grass where the talanks had died. They raced on. A spear flew by them. Then another. Then one grazed Wembley in the shoulder, but it was a glancing blow that tore a little flesh and slowed him for only a moment. Tuumal passed him and then he caught up with the boy again just as a spear took the boy down. No scream, just silence on the trail. Wembley saw two green eyes ahead of him. He raced through them. He felt strange and saw green leaves in front of him, green grass, he heard the pounding of feet on the grass and saw the bright colors of XC uniforms all around him. He stumbled, but caught himself. He saw the flags ahead, he lurched forward. He crossed the finish line to fall onto his back and sob.

He awoke later, in his bedroom. Ma and Da were there, along with Brindi and Russ, Asher, Bryce, Sam and Jenny, Talon ... and Evie? He came to consciousness slowly, before he realized the number of people in the room with him. He did not feel well.

"Who's Uhumai?"

Wembley saw Evie smile.

"A girl in a 'DreamTravel' I had."

"And Taanal?"

"My brother."

"Who are the Intanobi?"

"Murdering savages who killed my family and chased me back here!"

Wembley looked down at his shoulder. There was no wound. He was still in his XC uniform.

"If it's any consolation, you won," said Bryce.

"And you?"

"Right behind ya, buddy!"

There was a chuff from Wembley, then silence. "It was horrible."

Marged sat on the bed next to her son. "Another 'DreamTravel'."

Wembley nodded.

"Then it wasn't real."

"It felt real. I almost died three times!"

The whole room seemed to lurch at that one. Talon came running up to Wembley.

"Don't die, Wembley. Please, don't die!"

"I won't, Tal. It was just a dream."

Sam tried to divert them from this talk of death. "I've never seen anyone break away from the pack like that at the last minute."

"Yeah," Bryce added, "you left me in the dust."

"Well, nobody in any XC race has ever been running from spear-wielding Intanobi!"

"You're as fast as the wind," gave Russ an entry into the conversation.

Wembley laughed. "It's all that kept me alive." He saw the smile erased from Evie's face. He looked at her, almost as if he could kill her.

CHAPTER TEN
Artifice and Artifacts

He had felt challenged and threatened before, but never afraid for his life. He remembered every moment of every 'DreamTravel', but this newest one, haunted him; hung about him like a shroud. He had seen green eyes before, but this time he possessed an inkling as to whom they belonged.

He didn't understand his feelings at all; couldn't fathom his thoughts. How could Evie be connected to it all? She was an orphan! No ties! No past!

Brindi had green eyes, too. That was dumb! How could Brindi cause these warps in time and space? For that matter, how could Evie?

The bus jolted him back to reality as it lurched to a stop in front of the school. He picked up his backpack and joined the line of students exiting. As he hit the pavement his favorite green eyes were standing in front of him, inside a head this time, with a face that was smiling at him. No disembodiment here. For which his lips were grateful.

"Sleep?"

Wembley shrugged. Brindi's green eyes tried to see into him, to know what he knew, to sense how he felt. That was something she had never been able to do -- successfully. She knew that something was wrong, when something was troubling him, but not what it was or how to ease the pain that antagonized her favorite person.

They walked hand in hand, passed the sculpture of the old Schooner near the front door of the school where Wem stopped and looked at the ship. He judged it as if he were seeing it through the eyes of Winslow Homer -- did it measure up? He decided that, for a piece of metal, it had almost as much movement as many of the boats in the seascapes of the master. It held a heritage of hard work and industry, of life lived and lost; of hope with the rising of each new sun. It was fitting that his school adopted it as a mascot, of sorts.

Tradition was good. Wembley knew that. His Welsh heritage suited him, supported him, purposed him, as the Schooner propelled the dreams and lives of the students at Yarmouth High. When the first bell rang, he pulled himself out of his reverie.

"Where were you?"

"Not far." He imparted to her his considerably heavy thoughts of the last few minutes as they entered the school for their first class of the day -- Chemistry!

The day progressed, as school days do, and lunch was in full swing. Wem and Brin sat together in the corner. Bryce, Sam and Jenny joined them. Then Evie sat down across the table from Wem. Wem stared at her. She laughed, uncomfortably. Right there, with the others of his closest friends present, he accused her.

"You were the green eyes!"

He didn't know why he said it. It was impossible! His closest friends knew that he frequently saw green eyes in his 'DreamTravels'. They just thought that it was a tribute to Brindi; a confirmation that they were the 'right' couple.

"Don't be silly! I was here," protested a very nervous Evie; if you could judge by the face that contained and surrounded that particular pair of green eyes.

"I guess so. Silly, huh?"

"Totally."

Wem's other friends looked at him a little askance. Was he letting her off or had he tested the waters of confrontation? Where was this new friendship with their old enemy going to take them; him? The little coterie of lifelong friends were very protective of their capable poster-child-for-all-that-was-possible. He was so able. But that didn't make him infallible. They questioned this new relationship; went along with it for Wembley's sake, because it seemed to be what he wanted them to do.

The various leftovers from trays and sack lunches were scraped and tossed into the garbage cans and everyone made their way to fifth period. The one class of the day that not one of them shared with each other. It was going to be like separation anxiety every day of the fall semester -- at least for Jenny and Sam, and maybe Wem and Brin.

The rest of the day flew by. Wem was just about to board the bus, he was holding Brin's hand a little too long; but he needed the strength that it gave him. He had to get home and take care of his sheep, clean the pens, do the masses of homework! Why did every teacher at school think that they were the only ones who gave homework? It was a conspiriacy! That was Wem's conclusion. His backpack weighed more than any of his sheep.

As their fingers left contact with each other and the bus doors soughed together behind him, he heard a few snickers from the Middle School kids already on the bus. They weren't laughing at him. No one laughed at Wembley Tewkes. They all liked him too much. They laughed, like all Middle School kids did, at what they didn't undertand; hadn't experienced yet. A solid relationship was something that was still outside of them. They were just beginning to test those waters and maybe they were a little envious because they knew Wembley Tewkes, and Brindi Williams fit. Even inexperience can see that. They all wished for what seemed to come so easily to Wembley Tewkes.

Wembley sat with his pack on his lap, alone, in the middle of the bus. Everything about him right now said, 'Don't talk to me. I need some space.' The kids honored what they sensed, because they knew Wembley.

Amid the chatter and noise of his surroundings, Wembley was lost in a sea of thoughts. The waves of contemplation roiled around him like the waters of his favorite paintings. The principal wave tips touched on why he could read others so well, help them, guide them, love them -- and yet not be able to read or guide himself, at times. We rarely see what is reflected back to us in the mirror with any clarity at all. It is far easier to diagnose and assist others. After all, what stake do we really have in their lives? We <u>are</u> our lives. How directly do we connect with and to them? In Wembley's case those directions were clear. His friends didn't have all of his talents; couldn't make those connections as strongly as he could, except maybe for Brindi. It's the principal reason they fit. She filled the one need in him that he could not fill for himself. She completed him, as he hoped he completed her.

Wem was interrupted as the bus stopped again.

"Mr. Tewkes?"

Wem jolted to awareness. It was his stop. "See ya, Wem" was offered from several dozen throats as he made his way quietly off the bus. He nodded and waved and galumphed down the steps onto the gravel of the road in front of his house. As he walked up the drive, the crunch beneath his feet somehow comforted him. As he crossed to the barn, the crunch disappeared, to be replaced by the suck of mud on boots. It wasn't a backpack in his hands, it was a feed bag. The barn was grey. The house was brick. His place, but maybe not his time -- again. He was getting used to reading the immediate signals around him as realities changed.

A voice came at him from the direction of the house.

"Mercer, Pa's been stuck in the fields all day. Could you see to the cows, sheep and horses?"

"Sure ma! But I wanted to go to the town meeting tonight. They're talking about the war!"

"That's fine! Just help yer Pa. I'm sure the meetin'll be no problem."

Mercer, huh? The only Mercer he knew of was Brindi's great-grandfather -- the one who died in the Civil War.

"Mary's not up yet. That little one tires her out so."

Wem had forgotten that Mercer was married at fifteen and had a child by the age of sixteen. That he attended school, worked at the hay and feed in town and then came home to do the chores around the farm. Luckily, there were also younger brothers, and an older sister, to help out and the entire burden didn't fall on Mercer. Wembley thought about that and considered himself lucky. He couldn't bear the thought of not being with Brindi. How would Mary manage after Mercer didn't return from the war? She must have done, mustn't she? Because Brindi was here and the Fletcher line was there, too.

Feeding and watering all the animals wasn't so hard. What took the time was mucking. By that time all his brothers were home and they did it together. There were times when they got more muck on each other than in the wheelbarrow, but they were brothers; the muck was a shared badge of honor among the Fletcher boys. Even nine-year-old Samuel took it with the best of them. Albert, 11, was the instigator of nearly every questionable act the brothers participated in. Thirteen-year-old David, and fourteen-year-old Thomas were followers who loved a good time. Fifteen-year-old Eustace and sixteen-year-old Mercer, were the calming and leveling influences, who didn't mind having a good time, if the work was done. It was seventeen-year-old Julia who didn't understand her younger brothers -- at all. But she sure was grateful for the 'sister' that had been brought into the family in Mary. They fussed together over the baby and the housework.

Six strong boys always made short work of the barn. They had to if they wanted dinner on time. Their mother met them at the door, every time and they shucked their animal stained clothing right there, down to their longjohns, pounded their boots until the soles were clean, and still had to leave them on the back porch while they trooped in to the kitchen to receive their nightly washing before dinner. Six naked boys in the kitchen kept the women folk busy with the meal and the soap, and the hot water, while the boys washed themselves and each other in the three large basins their father had managed to provide for them. It was almost timed to perfection as the boys finished, Pa would come in and splash in the tub. He had walked the one-hundred-sixty acres by himself today and all was shipshape. He had no complaints and he was proud of his sons. The wheat and the corn and the future were growing nicely. The harvest would happen next week.

It was Samuel's duty to wash Pa's back. The child enjoyed every minute of it. His time -- every day -- with Pa. Each of the boys had gone through it. It was a time -- as it had been for every one of them -- to talk and laugh and learn. Seven naked males then traipsed up the back stairs to their rooms and got dressed for dinner -- not in Sunday clothes -- but still in clean clothes; shirts, pants and shoes. How Ma did it, none of them knew, but they loved her for it.

Wembley took a moment to reconnoiter. He stepped out of Mercer for a second as the boys dressed. He felt a little strange, doing it, like he was being false to the 'DreamTravel'. They were in his room, after all. Why hadn't it been this full of things the last time he was here? Why had it been empty? There were six beds here now! It was the biggest room in the house. Mercer didn't sleep here anymore! He slept with Mary and the baby, across from Julia's room. Ma and Pa slept at the other end of the hall, away from all the noise.

He looked closely at the walls. No torn paper. No empty windows. Shelves and pegracks held mementoes and clothes for a family of boys. The room was loud, as it should have been. Wembley laughed as he searched. A glass ball stood on a little pedestal on one of the shelves. It was clear, plain, no insect or toy pressed inside of it. It kind of had a glow as he picked it up. It resonated in his hand. He found himself, distracted and still naked, examining it.

"Better hurry, Mercer! We're hungry!"

Several of the boys stood there waiting for him, others were nearly ready. Mercer/Wembley replaced the glass ball and flew into his clothes. He finished tying his shoes and the boys pitched out of the room together, while Wembly managed to look back at the glass ball; so out of place, it seemed.

As the boys tumbled down the stairs to supper, Wembley/Mercer felt a shift. He never made it to the table.

He was in town -- with Eustace -- to learn about the War. The room was hot and stuffy and smelled of cigarettes and cigars; pipes, too. This was the first 'DreamTravel' where Wembley had this awkward type of shift -- like in a real dream -- where the end of the previous episode didn't fit together with the beginning of the next.

There was a lot of talk -- hyperbole, was what his teacher at school had called it the other day. Mercer recognized it. So did Wembley. Embellishment, overstatement. Wembley wondered how they ever got recruits with such obvious fabrications.

You had to be sixteen to sign up. Eustace couldn't wait for the day! Mercer was a little less enthusiastic about leaving a wife and a new baby. But they'd take him if he volunteered. Wembley felt the pull and tear of two opposing feelings tugging at Mercer; the romantic notions of the hyperbole dragging him first one way, then the reality of his responsibilities pushing him in the other direction. He made no decision that night. Wembley thought that he might just stay home.

Mercer was a romantic -- a hard-working one, but a romantic none-the-less. The war won out. Mary was in tears.

Wembley went through another clumsy shift. He was on an operating table. His body ached. Blood was everywhere. The doctor, covered in crimson, stood over him. He looked down -- he was naked again but he saw why. There was a huge festering wound just below his belly button. The doctor handed him a bottle. He drank. The scalpel flashed. The pain seared. Then a hot iron cauterized the wound. He passed out.

He awoke, groggy. He pressed his hand against the pain. His left leg was missing, along with his manhood. His right leg was heavily bandaged and there was a large sear mark just below his belly button. He pounded his fists against the cot. He screamed. A nurse came into his sight. She smiled, the kind of smile that says, *'you poor devil.'* She gave him a sip of water, he took it, and then another. She draped several wet cloths over his missing anatomy to keep what was left of the skin moist.

Time shifted again.

Wembley/Mercer looked down again. Everything left below his waist was green and swollen. He cried. Wembley didn't know whether it was him or Mercer, but he figured it was himself. Mercer was too far gone to cry.

Suddenly Wembley was looking down on what was left of Mercer's body. It was as if he was floating in the air. Then the bloody tent winked away.

Wembley, in his own self, with all of his parts, was standing outside his house. But it wasn't his house. He saw Mercer's brothers, sister, wife [crying again], baby and parents, through the window. Everyone was there except for Eustace and Mercer himself. Had the war taken them both?

He turned away. It had all happened in what had seemed like a flash -- to him -- as well as to those he knew about and had come to care about in such a short amount of time. He turned around and walked down the drive toward the road. His chest heaved. He suddenly heard the crunch of gravel take over and his sneakers returned to his feet. He turned around again and headed back toward the house. The van was parked near the back door. He knew he was home, this time.

Several days later, Friday, after school, Wembley was walking with Brindi to her house. Evie flounced by on the sidewalk on her way home.

"Hi, guys!"

"Hi, Evie."

"Hi."

"You're awfully bright today."

"I got an 'A' on that Spanish quiz."

"Congrats. I got a B+," moaned Wembley.

"I got an 'A' too," and she slapped five with Evie.

"You always get an 'A', Brin." Wem was proud of her.

"Why didn't you?"

"Too much on my mind."

"You mean you didn't study?"

Wembley shook his head.

Evie was aghast. "How do you get a B+ without studying?"

"I kind of have a knack for languages."

"A knack? Is that what you call it? Well, I gotta get home."

"Where to, Evie?"

"My parents are taking me to Portland, to see a show."

"Cool!"

Parents? Doing something with her? What was going on here?

"What show?"

"Portland Stage is doing Camelot."

"Ahhh!"

"I can't wait until Nimue pegs Merlin in that oak tree!"

"Why doesn't that surprise me?"

"Now, be nice."

"Isn't it supposed to be an Alder tree?"

"Dramatic license. He was a meddler anyway!"

They both looked at Evie like she was totally foreign.

"She had to stop him from spilling the beans. Arthur just couldn't know about Lancelot and Guinevere! He just couldn't! It would spoil a perfectly depressing story."

"Reality sucks, sometimes Evie."

"Yeah, well, it's all we really have, isn't it?"

Brin and Wem exchanged looks.

"Have a good time?"

"I will. Thanks!"

Evie flounced off. Brin and Wem watched, silently, until she was about a block away.

"Rooting for Nimue?" was Wem's concern.

"Which one was Nimue again?"

"Elaine. The Lady of the lake. She's the Sorceress who stole Merlin away so he could not warn Arthur of Guinevere or Lancelot. It was her price for returning the sword to him. She was kind of Merlin's foil; his nemesis. Her sister, Morgause, was the one who bewitched Arthur into conceiving Mordred. And Morgan Le Fay, the third sister, was an outright witch! They were all half-sisters to Arthur."

"That's freaky."

"Without Nimue, Eden might have had a chance."

"Even the real Eden didn't have a chance, Wem."

"What do you mean?"

"If Adam and Eve had stayed innocent in the garden, kind of like Arthur and Guinevere before their marriage, you and I would not be here talking to each other."

"So, you're saying that Camelot was supposed to fail?"

"Man isn't capable of that level of perfection, Wem. At least not here on Earth. That's what I got from the Arthur myth."

"Myth?"

"Okay, legend. Sorry. You believe it, too?"

Wem nodded. "I think it was more than a fantasy. I've studied it since I was little."

"Guess we still have some work to do with Evie?"

"Of course. We still have some work to do with us!"

Brin laughed and kissed him on the nose. She grabbed his hand and pulled him along to her house. Wem had kind of invited himself over, but Brin didn't mind. He had to talk. She sensed that. He also had to check something out; investigate. He somehow had to tell Brin that he knew exactly how her great-grandfather died.

As they jounced and jostled through the front door -- Wem was tickling Brin at the time -- they were both laughing.

"That you, Brindi?"

"Yes, Mom. Wem's with me."

"I have some lemonade. Would you like some?"

Wem licked his lips and nodded.

"You know Wembley!"

"Yes, I do," came from a voice in the kitchen.

As the friends settled on the couch Mrs. Williams came in with two tall glasses of ice-cold lemonade -- fresh squeezed.

"Thanks, Mrs. Williams," as he began to not sip, but gulp.

"Slow down there."

"Sorry. Didn't know how thirsty I was."

"You're always thirsty."

"For your Mom's lemonade? Yeah!"

Mrs. Williams went out knowing that she had been intentionally buttered up. She didn't mind, because it was Wembley.

"You mom's lemonade is good, too."

"Yeah, but not as sweet as your mom's."

"It's all fresh squeezed."

"Yeah -- none of that powder stuff!"

"Eew! Yuck!"

They looked at each other over their glasses as they took another sip.

Brin was not one to beat around the bush. "So, why did you need to come over? Not that you're not welcome -- anytime, but ..."

Wem put his glass down and got up. Brin put her glass down as her eyes did nothing but follow him while he strode to the other side of the room. He was suddenly a little uneasy; fidgety. He ran his fingers across the photo of Johnny Lathrop and Mercer Fletcher. He had known Johnny. He had been Mercer -- twice.

"I know how he died."

"Who?"

"Your great-great-grandfather."

"Mercer?"

Wem nodded.

Brin went to call her mom.

"No! She doesn't know about my dreams! How could I explain it to her?"

"Brin already has." Mrs. Williams came around the corner from the kitchen. "You live in their house. How could you not be touched by them?"

"What do you mean?"

There was a pointed look, a kind of *'should we tell him'* that passed between mother and daughter.

"He died in the Civil War, didn't he?"

"That is the information we have."

"I had this, well, I call them 'DreamTravels' ..."

"Yes, I know." Mrs. Williams was suddenly not the Mrs. Williams he had known.

"I was ... there ... was him ... when he died."

"You died?"

Wem nodded.

"But you're alive now."

"Yeah. Everything that happens in my 'DreamTravels' kind of stays there; the experience, the memory comes with me, but the reality of it always stays in that other world."

"I'm sorry it has touched you."

Wem paused, trying to understand that comment. "I come from a long line of Welsh, Pict and Celt, Mrs. Williams. My family has been 'blessed' with these 'DreamTravels', in one way or another, for centuries -- or so my Da says."

"Does he have them?"

"Not one. Ever. It's Granda Gwyllym. It seems to skip every other generation. His Granda had them. He said that he had found ... discovered ... uncovered some really magical things. He's going to show them to me at Christmas."

"So you have your own magic?"

"Me? No! Just the dreams."

"Living in that house can't but enhance those dreams."

"What do you mean?"

"Captain Horatio Fletcher built that house. The Fletcher's lived in it until ... just after the Civil War."

"And the William's, well, the Lathrops, lived here?"

"Yes."

"Mercer Fletcher married Mary Lathrop, Johnny's older sister."

"Mercer lost everything below his waist but his right leg when he was hit by that canonball. He lived for days afterward, until gangrene took him."

"And you experienced that?"

Wembley nodded. "I've never felt that kind of pain. There was schrapnel in my abdomen, nothing left of my left leg ... or my manhood."

Brin gasped. Wem looked into her eyes. There was such sorrow there. She reached out and held his hand. Mrs Williams saw it, but did nothing to prevent it.

"You said there was magic, Mrs. Williams -- that I had been touched by it in that house."

Mrs. Williams pursed her lips together, looked at Brindi and began. "It seems that you do have magic of your own and are only beginning to have contact with it. Magic goes a long way back in our family. Do you know who Cretian DeTroyes and Thomas Mallory were?"

"Yes. Shapers of the Arthur legend."

"We are descended from both of them."

"So, if you knew, why did you ask me about Nimue, today Brin?"

"She has chosen not to know what I know. Which, I think, has been a blessing in her life."

"Did they know?"

"Who?"

"De Troyes and Mallory."

"I have confirmed an old legend in our family -- that they are both descendants of Mordred and also of Galahad, Lancelot's son with Elayne. The story, the lore, the magic was passed down to those two writers, and through them, to us. And I guess to the world. It's also been said that Tennyson is descended from the same line."

Wembley just about fell off the couch. "You tie right to Morgan LeFey?"

"No, to her sister, Morgana, or Morgause."

"All I know is that the Tewkes family centers around Wales and Cornwall, Ireland and Scotland."

"Prominent places in Arthur's story."

"Yeah. I've always dreamed about it -- even before the beginning of these 'DreamTravels' last year. I've read everything I could about Arthur since I was little."

"It's been a burden to this family. But I thought you ought to know about it, since we seem to be tied together." She looked directly at Brin, who smiled.

Wembley squeezed Brin's hand and smiled. "I love Brin, Mrs. Williams."

"I know. I've always thought that fourteen or fifteen was too young. But I see the two of you together and I know ... it's not. Guinevere was only thirteen when she married an eighteen-year-old Arthur. At least that's one of the legends. Arthur was only fourteen when he conceived Mordred; sixteen when he was crowned King of the Britons."

"Excuse me, Mrs. Williams, but what is magic about my house?"

"It wasn't the house itself. It was something that was in the house."

"The glass ball," was said almost to himself.

"You've seen it?"

"In a 'DreamTravel' -- the last one."

"Where?"

"I don't know if it was his, or not; Mercer's. It wasn't in the room he shared with his wife and son. It was in the boys' room. Six boys in one room! My room, now. It was all alone on a shelf on the wall. It was on this little wooden pedestal; just a plain glass ball."

"It was Horatio who placed it there. It stayed there until the family left the house."

"What is it?"

"It is rumored to be an Orb of Power."

"Magic?"

"Ancient. Some in the family have called it evil. Did it glow?"

"Only when I picked it up."

"You touched it?"

Wembley was frightened by her reaction.

"Mother, please!"

"I'm sorry, Wembley. I didn't mean to scare you." She placed her hands on either side of his face, in a comforting gesture. Then she hugged him to her. "You need to know that whatever magic you possess may now have been amplified by that orb."

"I ... I ... how ..."

"I didn't know, for sure, until Brindi told me about your experiences. She was worried. I'm worried. Ever since Horatio died, mysteriously, no one in the family has really known what the Orb was for or what it could do. All the work I've done is maybe only guesswork, but there is something to that orb. The legend in the family is that no one has ever been able to destroy it or to even get rid of it."

"Where is it now?"

"That's the mystery. No one knows. It's like it just vanished. But it cannot be gone if you are feeling the effects of its power."

"Are you sure it's the orb?"

"What else could it be?"

"Mom, are you saying that it could still be in the house, somewhere?"

"It is not here. Mary did not bring it with her when she moved back home with Mercer Junior."

"What if I found it?"

"It could do more harm than good. It could do you harm. But I have thought that someone outside the family -- maybe not you, as you seem to be tied to it -- but someone else, could possibly destroy it."

"Mom!"

"Then it all would just end."

"Is it supposed to?"

"I'd like to think so."

Wem's mind was awhirl with new information. Who would have thought that someone here in Yarmouth, Maine, might have the answers, or at least some of the explanations, to Wembley's 'gift'? Wembley couldn't wrap his mind around it -- yet. He just sat there with Brin holding his hand. He lifted her hand to his lips and kissed it. She sidled over to him and they cuddled close together as Mrs. Williams went into the kitchen with empty glasses.

When she poked her head around the corner, the two were still leaning on each other and holding hands. She nodded, smiled and left the room.

Wembley was standing outside his house again. It was a quiet evening.

The sun was down and the stars were beginning to blink. He walked around the house, feeling the light from the windows on his face as he searched for a secret room, some space that didn't appear to be there from the outside. But every inch inside was accounted for by Wembley's walk that evening. No unexpected closets, no unknown cubbies. That left the attic -- or the cellar. Wembley went outside to his thinking rock, where he had a good view of the house.

"Wembley, what are you doing out there?" came wafting in his mother's voice from the other side of the house.

"Just walking and thinking, Ma."

"You comin' in?"

"In a few minutes, Ma."

"Aren't you cold?"

"Ma, I'm okay. This isn't Wales, it's warm here in September."

"All right."

He sat on the rock and looked back at the house, again. Nothing winked. Nothing shifted. He saw it from it's roofline to the cellar windows. He had explored it all a hundred times in the ten years he had lived here. There must've been something he had missed. He was sure of it. The cupola, with the chimneys on either side of it. Someone said that there was an old widow's walk up there, for the wives of the sea captains to watch for their husbands to come home, but he had never found that, either. Yet, he could see it from the ground!

He dashed from the rock and flew into the front door. He dashed up the main stairs and tripped down the hallway in front of his room. He picked himself up, entered his room and grabbed a flashlight from his closet and tore out into the hallway again.

He stood in front of the attic door, breathing hard and hoping. He reached out and wrapped his fingers around the doorknob. He turned the piece of crystal and heard the click as the door came free. He flipped the light switch and began to mount the steps, searching the walls on the way up. He got to the top, it was all one big, somewhat cluttered, room with two chimneys back to back in the center. The cupola above them? It had to be between them! Why had he never thought of it before?

He stepped over and around old toys, trunks, boxes and pieces of furniture until he reached the center. He knocked on the brick with his flashlight. It sounded like brick and mortar, to him. Whatever brick and mortar was supposed to sound like. He walked along, tapping the brick and the sound changed from a thick, dull thud to a hollow boom. He walked all the way around both chimneys. There was nothing between them. Just 'brick.' He pushed along the hollow parts of the brick wall, searching for a trigger, a knob, a clasp, a hinge -- something! He took the flashlight and kneeled down and ran it along the floor where the hollow brick met the floorboards. He couldn't see anything. He left his light on the floor, pointed toward the jointure of brick and board. He walked around to the other side. He just about choked when he saw a thin beam of light trying to peek out between the brick and wood on this side of the chimney. He found a piece of cardboard, not the corrugated kind, and began trying to jab it into the space where the light was escaping. He crawled around the whole thing again.

There was a four foot space between the two chimneys! But how to get in? He couldn't just destroy it. His Da would never understand. There had to be a way. A door. A latch. The ends and sides of each chimney were solid. Not a crevice or a nook or any space at all to hide some sort of mechanism. That left the hollow walls or the floor. He went over them again.

Suddenly he heard something at the end of the attic. He turned to see his Da.

"What're ya lookin' for up here?"

"Did you ever notice that there was a space between these two chimneys?"

"Yep."

"Why?"

"The stairs to the widow's walk."

"It's been here all the time and you knew about it?"

"When I bought the house, I checked it out before we moved in."

"But you never told me!"

"Just what I needed; a five year old climbing those stairs and falling off the widow's walk to his death. Explain that one to yer Ma!"

"I see. So, you do know how to get to the stairs?"

"O'course."

Dylan walked toward Wembley, looking up toward the rafters. He went to the north side, where a thin, short chain hung from the superstructure of the house. He held onto it and pulled. Wembley heard a click and turned around, in keen anticipation. The wall of brick swung open revealing that it was only an inch thick. It was dark in the passage but he could see the outlines of a circular stairway, shadowed in the dim light of the single bulb from the east end of the attic and from the light of his flashlight shining across the floorboards.

"Da! Why didn't you tell me?"

"I forgot it was there until you asked about it."

"Ten years?"

"Been there longer than that."

Wembley ran around and retrieved his flashlight. "You wanna come up with me?"

"Sure. Only been up there the once."

Wembley ran the flashlight over the interior walls of the secret room. Solid brick on the two ends, wooden lathe and faux-brick on each side. He placed his foot on the first of the triangular shaped steps. He motioned to his Da, who ascended right behind him. Everything was dusty. Cobwebs crossed and interlaced as Wembley's face and hands tore them from their decade long perches. The flashlight roamed, along with Wem's eyes. Wem counted -- twenty-two steps. His head was above another floor. There were louvered shutters on two sides of him. His Da arrived, flipped some interior window-lock type things and pulled on a knob on the inside of one of the shutters and it folded inward -- a door opened up from the floor to the lentel.

Moonlight flooded into the little structure. Wem stepped out and his father stepped beside him. The boards of the walkway were made of cedar and there was an iron railing that Wem leaned on as he looked out over his favorite site -- Broad Cove about a half a mile distant. The beach, the swim, the pajamas came flooding back to him and he laughed. His Da looked over at him.

"Just remembered something."

Wem was exhilarated. He hadn't found the orb, but this secret was almost treasure enough. He stayed there for a long time. Dylan placed his arm across the still broadening shoulders of his son. It was a good time.

"I'm glad you showed me."

"I'm glad I remembered. What you are seeing is one of the reasons I bought this house."

"What?"

"What direction do we face?"

Wembley looked around. "East."

"Yes. Wales. Beyond that sea is home."

"Do you miss it, Da?"

"It's in here," as Da pointed to his breastbone.

The teen touched his own chest. "Can you wait for Christmas?"

"No. Can you?"

"I couldn't wait if Christmas was tomorrow!"

"You love it that much?"

"Maybe every bit as much as you do."

"Why did I take us away?"

"Because you thought you had to. Britain -- Ioan -- Ma's health. We've had the best of America and the best of Wales. It would have been a shame to just have one or the other."

"It was the right decision, then?"

"How can you ask that, Da? Of course it was."

Dylan's hand went and wiped something out of his eye and then fumbled at his nose.

"What more could I ask for, Da?"

It was a rhetorical question that didn't demand an answer. Dylan hugged his son to him. They shared a few more minutes of the night on the widow's walk on the roof of their home in America, and looked forward to seeing the land beyond the ocean once more: their first home and family.

CHAPTER ELEVEN
The Art Of War

"I have to. Please?"

"Wembley ... Oh, all right. Where are you taking me?"

"You'll find out when we get there."

Wem finished tying a blindfold around Brin's eyes.

"Can you see anything?"

"No, that's why they call it a blind-fold."

He took her hand gently in his and led her down the long hallway that bisected the second floor of his house. He opened the attic door again and led her up the stairs.

"Smells funny. I know we're in the attic."

"Very smart. Now shhh!"

He guided her to one of the brick facings of the chimney closet. He positioned her there, facing the wall, then he loosened her blindfold.

"Don't take it off yet. Wait 'til I say to."

Her hands held the ends of the cloth. "All right."

Wem moved over to the pull chain. "Ready? Now."

When he pulled on the chain, her blindfold came down and she saw a brick wall swinging out as if to hit her in the face. She turned to Wem with an incredulous look. "Wem ..."

"I found it!"

"The orb?"

"No, the secret place in the house."

"Is the orb in there?"

"I don't think so, there's no place to hide it."

Wem was back at her side. "Come on up."

He led her up the narrow circular stairs. When they got to the top he faced her to the opening louver and pulled on the knob. Just like it had happened to him, her breath was taken away as the vista of land and sea assailed her eyes.

There was silence for a while, until Brin could no longer keep quiet. "It's ... breathtaking. How did you find it?"

"I just took a good look at the house. I saw something that nobody remembered was there. Then, when I asked Da about it, he remembered and pulled the chain in the attic and the wall opened up."

"And the orb?"

"Nothing yet."

"Let's look!"

"It's a bright, sunny day. Might be different without a flashlight!"

They remained up top for a while taking in the beauty of the Yarmouth area from their third floor aerie. They both wanted to locate the 'magic' of the house; solve the mystery. Their hands felt every corner, crevice and surface of the stairwell. They combed each face of the cupola itself, inside and out, for the widow's walk went all the way around the cupola. They pulled and pushed at each brick inside the closet. They spent hours, only to end disappointed and maybe a little frustrated when they reached the bottom of the stairs empty-handed for the fifth time.

Wem closed it all up and the brick wall shut behind them.

"What's all this?"

"Just stuff."

"Where'd it come from?"

"We brought it over from Wales."

"All of it?"

"No. Some of it was here when we moved in."

Wem's and Brins eyes alit with the same idea at the same time.

"I'm calling Sam and Bryce. They can help us look."

"What about Jenny?"

"If I call Sam ..."

"Yeah. Right!" and Wem laughed.

Bryce and Sam, with Jenny, showed up in minutes. They started sorting through the piles stuff. If Wembley recognized it, it probably came from Wales, so Wales was moved to the other side of the attic. It was the stuff that the families of this house had left behind that began to fascinate five eager teens, all anxious to help Wembley solve his mystery and maybe end the more-terrifying-with-each-new-day 'DreamTravels'. It took a little over an hour of a warm Fall Saturday to separate all the junk. The last item was an old desk that Sam and Bryce were shifting to the 'non-Wales' stack.

Jenny came alive as she saw them moving it. "The Resolute Desk!"

"What?"

"Remember in that movie the desk had all sorts of secret compartments that hid the main clue to the mystery?"

"But that was only a movie!"

Jenny remained resolute.

So, the desk was set down and ten hands were roaming and pressing and pulling. The panels of the desk turned out to be solid. The drawers were pulled out, their cubbies were all empty, and the insides of the desk were searched. Nothing! Sam picked his drawer up to replace it and stopped. It had a weight to it.

"Hey! It looks like this one, well, it's not as deep inside as it is outside."

"A false bottom?" was Jenny's question.

"My thoughts exactly!"

Their hands cascaded over the drawer, inside and out but there was no latch. There was a little handle, the drawer pull itself, that was fastened to the drawer through a tiny, ornate brass backplate. Jenny played with it and the handle turned. She twisted it as far to the right as she could and they all heard a click and the bottom of the drawer inside popped up. Jenny got two of her slender fingers in and pulled the bottom out of the way. There was a small wooden box sitting under the false bottom. Wembley lifted the box out of the drawer.

It was clean. No dust on it at all. There was a small hasp that he rotated out of a loop and then carefully lifted the lid. The box was lined in deep blue velvet. There was an indentation in the center of the box that held ... nothing. The box was empty. The indentation was about the size of a ping-pong ball; maybe just a little bigger.

"Must've been the lucky ball of a professional ping-pong player," Bryce quipped.

"How big was the orb when you held it, Wem?"

"About that size."

"Do you think it could have been kept here?"

"Definitely!"

"Kind of looks like a Snitch!"

"Well, somebody snitched the snitch!"

"It's a cool desk anyway. Help me take it down to my room."

They put the drawers back in.

Brin asked the next question. "Is there a false bottom in that box?"

Sam's hands were on it this time, but he couldn't pry anything apart, and there was no button. He even took the hasp and loop off, but they were just screwed in to the wood; just a simple closure.

"Nada."

"Well, it was worth a try."

Wem and Bryce muscled the fairly large desk over to the top of the stairs. Sam got on the downside with Wem, and Bryce leaned back as the desk began to slide down between the bead-boarded walls of the attic steps. Stair by stair the massive desk disappeared into the maw of the stairwell. The girls brought the drawers and the box.

When they got it into Wem's room, without mishap, he pointed and they placed it against the south wall.

"Why here?"

"This is the wall that held the shelf that the orb was on in my dream."

"Good a reason as any."

The box was returned to the drawer, the drawers fit back into their slots and the group just stood there looking at it.

"Who's was it?"

"Don't know."

"Horatio's?"

"Could have been."

"You should have it appraised. They could tell you how old it is."

"Good idea, Jen."

Just at that moment, Marged came into the room. "What's all the noise up here?" She saw the desk. "Where'd that come from?"

"I ... we ... found it in the attic."

"Beautiful piece of furniture, that's sure."

"Why didn't you bring it down earlier?" asked Wembley.

"I didn't know it was there; never been up in the attic."

"Never?"

"No -- never needed to go up."

"Looks real old."

"How old, Ma?"

"I'd say 'bout 200 years old -- early 1800s."

"Think it was Captain Horatio's?" was Wem's eager question.

"Coulda been."

"You know about Captain Horatio?"

"Just that he built the house," Marged admitted.

"Why didn't I know?"

"I don't know. His name's over the fireplace."

Marged's eyes twinkled. She loved it when she could put one over on her son, because it didn't happen very often. "You kids hungry?"

Are teenagers ever hungry after noon on a Saturday?

Marged laughed as they jostled passed her and into the hall. "Sandwiches are ready!"

Wembley stayed behind. "Ma, do you think that this house could have anything to do with the weird stuff that's been happening to me?"

"Could be, but I'd bet that it's your Granda's peculiarities that's got hold of you. Come eat."

Wem put his arm around his Ma and they went down to the kitchen where his friends were immersed in sandwiches and chips.

"Hey, save some for me!" Wem exclaimed as he came through the door.

"That's yours over there!"

Bryce pointed to a small paper plate with half a sandwich and one chip on it.

"You've got to be kidding!"

They all busted up laughing, including Marged. Another plate was pulled out from under the table and pushed at Wembley as he sat and began to chow down.

"You guys are nuts!" Wembley quipped through a mouth full of PBJ.

"Takes one to know one," came from another full mouth.

Marged smacked her son playfully on the shoulder, "Manners! And slow down! You'll all make yourselves sick!" Then she sat down and joined them for a sandwich, laughing at the antics of her son's friends; enjoying it; appreciating the fact that his friends were always there for him. From what Granda Gwyllym had said to her over the phone, Wem might be in for a rough ride.

$$10:00$$

After lunch, they drove over to the pool for a few hours. Wembley stayed close by his friends, hopefully allowing no side-trips or distractions to be foisted upon him. In typical fashion, they lost track of the time and they were going to be late -- for their own internet game of OrcLand. They'd been planning it for weeks.

Each from their own homes, which they rushed to, they were joining to play the ultimate battle -- everyone on his or her own computer. Plus, Asher, Russel and Talon were scheduled to be joining them. An eight player Human squad dedicated to the annihilation of Orcs!

On each computer in each house of each participant they watched the screen intently as a digital version of a clock counted backwards to zero. When the four zeros appeared they launched into the mission of Orc hunting. They had communities to build, soldiers to train, peasants to put to work and a legion of magical humans to create and unleash on the invading enemy. The enemy had broken through the forests and mountains off their screens -- somewhere -- eight communities were all that existed to save their world from being overrun and annihilated by the numerous and seemingly unending hosts of the enemy. There was a portal, somewhere, and they had to find it, also, and close it!

They each had their identities -- their virtual doppelgangers -- some were mayors, generals, mages, footsoldiers, horsemen, -- or even a king (Russell drew that card). Eight friends became eight allies in this ever-changing virtual world.

Somehow the computer knew to hit the king first.

No one knew where the other encampments or forces were, to begin with. They all had to be discovered and then unite against the Orcs. Eight scouts were roaming, searching, needing to discover where the sounds of battle were coming from.

"We're under attack" rang from Russel's computer. Brin was right across the room on her laptop and she sent a message to all the players to hurry their explorations so that they all could join together in a massive force to repel the invaders.

Russel reacted in shock to something on his screen. Brin saw it and worked harder to finish her defenses and build her forces to send help. Then Russel screamed as his character, the king, was attacked by a massive Orc. "It's got red hair!"

Brin sent the message

This massive red-haired Orc was everywhere. Reports about it came in from every player. Wem ruminated about how the same big Orc could hit everyone at once. Then he saw it. It was standing right in front of his mage. Then Wem was hit. The hit was more than just an image on a computer. Wem was no longer pushing buttons on a controller or keyboard. He, himself, was reeling from a physical blow that could have killed him if he wasn't virtual. The Orc hit him again. He felt the pain of the blow. He extended his arms and attacked the Orc with everything in his body. The Orc reeled, this time. Wem got close, but not close enough to be hit by its massive scimitar. He sent wave after wave of power at the being and drove it back. It swung its huge weapon and missed the mage but hit a building, which crumbled in front of Wembley's eyes. It swung again to fend off another wave of energy and took out several of Wem's forces. He saw the bodies fall to the ground and the blood drain out of them. Amid the arcs of energy leaving his fingers, Wem had another thought, *Who had programmed this thing? It certainly wasn't one of the players. It had to be a new computer based scenario. There had to be a weakness.*

He called to every person in his army to focus on this giant. He saw his forces turn from the fights they were in to focus on the red-haired monster. They hit the Orc with everything at once. He lost a few forces of his hundreds due to his one-pronged attack, but the life-line of the Orc was rapidly decreasing. It was kind of funny, but the life-line appeared above the head of the Orc. He looked up, over his own head, for a moment and saw his own life-line slowly decreasing. Just before the Orc's life-line winked out, a massive face took over the battlefield in front of him -- kind of like a hologram. Green eyes under that red hair flashed at him as a scream that seemed not to be computer generated washed over his ears as the giant died a spectacular death on the ground and faded through its own skin and bones to disappear into the virtual earth.

Wem stopped and pressed the amulet on his wrist to send the message. *'Throw everything you have at it. No other Orc matters.'*

Soon all eight players had sent return messages of victory over the gargantuan. Still, they all had to find each other, unite their forces and close the portal.

Wem was more than unsettled about what had happened. Even though his unease disturbed him he marshaled his forces and moved forward, leaving a small garrison behind to protect his community, as he advanced out into the surrounding countryside. He wondered if this was another 'DreamTravel', or if the others were experiencing the game like he was. He'd have to wait to find out. Something about that Orc still haunted him.

He found the location of Russel's army, then Brin came in, followed shortly by the remainder of the human allies. Then they sent out forces in a series of concentric circles to kill whatever Orcs they could find. Bryce sent the word. Wem heard it, he wasn't reading it on his screen any longer: *'Portal discovered. Northeast behind the mountains.'* Because of their preplanning half of every force headed off to the northeast to help Bryce destroy the portal and the huge Orc force that would be guarding it. Those that remained behind scoured the rest of the gameboard dispatching every Orc they came across. The human color of blue began to visually dominate the map of each player's screen but Wembley's -- because he had no screen -- and the color of red diminished everywhere. All Wem had to do was look at the amulet on his wrist. It told him many of the same things that his screen had, after he figured out how to read it. He was the mage, after all!

Wem heard another scream. It sounded like Brin's. Then he heard the message, *'Russel disappeared from his chair!'*

Wembley sent a message, *'I think I have, too. I'm in the game. I think that's where Russel went!'*

Then the voice of Russel came to Wembley's ears, "You guys are ... right. I'm here ... fighting these ... Orcs."

The battle at the portal was fierce. The Human forces were able to entirely surround the gateway and wear it and its protectors down. When Wembley arrived, his mage powers helped immensely. He suddenly felt like a lone human standing on the battlefield before Minas Tirith in <u>The Return of the King</u>. There was not an inch of space that wasn't covered by an Orc. But he saw light and color flashing from every side. Somehow the others had been able to summon the powers of the mage by building one of their own. They weren't as powerful as Wembley was, because his light encompassed the Orc forces and they were trapped. They couldn't move as their army was encircled by humans. The edges died and the center pressed outward. Humans fell, Orcs fell, but with the powers of the mages, the Orcs dwindled faster.

Wembley was tired. As his game seemed no longer really virtual -- he had expended the energy of his own body, not just his mind, in this extermination of Orcs -- his spirits flagged a little under the strain. He found, strangely, that with each Orc he killed, his energy was renewed, just like in the game. He surged forward, ducking and weaving under the weapons of the enemy. A blade caught him on the shoulder and he winced and turned and blew the sucker apart!

His shoulder ached. There was blood streaming down it. He touched the amulet on his wrist and felt the healing power surge through him. The blood stopped. He thought, *that would never happen in reality. I am a virtual character!* It kind of set his mind into a panic. He created a ball of energy around him and walked forward. Weapons crashed down on him but he pressed on and rolled over his enemies. That made him even more tired than the fighting, it demanded more of his energy to maintain the ball, so he collapsed his ball of death and began to shoot light from his fingers again at everything in front of him.

Soon there was no one in front of him. He had cut a deep swath -- a gouge -- into the forces of the enemy. He met Russel, standing there face to face. He knew it was him. The form was human; no pixels stood there. They smiled at each other and turned to cut down Orcs coming at them from their flanks. Was this really Russel? Or was it his virtual representative? After the annihilation of the Orc forces, Russel walked forward and extended his hand to his best friend and Wembley took it! They had both been called into the game physically. It was the weirdest feeling to not just be watching it, but living it. Russel was scarred and covered in Orc blood. Wem poured his magic into Russel's body. Russel was held immobile for a minute as he felt the energy surge through him, searching for damage to repair. When the energy left him he felt wonderful. None of his own blood was leaking out anymore. All his cuts had been sealed and even his bruises were gone. Nothing was sore! He looked over at Wem and he looked great -- except for the gash in his clothing at his left shoulder, but the only blood there, was on the cloth. The flesh beneath it was all right.

Soon the six remaining friends showed up, but they all looked a little funny. They were made up of little squares of light, not the rounded forms that Wembley and Russel had become. There was a great reunion and the music that played was loud and almost hurt the real ears of Wembley and Russel as they winced. The Portal had fallen to Bryce and Asher, working in tandem, as the remainder of the generals had destroyed the forces of the Orcs. Their strategy, decided on before the game, had paid off. What they hadn't counted on was losing Wembley and Russel into the game. Their celebration and reunion didn't last long because the pixellated players began to wink away leaving Russ and Wem standing there in their more corporeal forms.

The two victors heard Brin's voice, "It's time to come out!" It must've been typed into the keyboard of her laptop, but was sounding too much like her.

Then the most disturbing voice he had heard came blasting at him as if from the direction of the doomed portal, "You won this time, Tewkes, but your little friends might not be there the next time!"

Russel looked at Wembley as if asking *'did you hear that?'*

Wembley nodded.

Russel said, "That wasn't an Orc voice. It sounded like a girl!"

"Anyone we know?"

"Evie?"

"I think so -- somehow she crashed our game -- at the programming level."

That sobered them up a bit. Then Russel started to shimmer and disappeared from in front of Wem's eyes. Then Wem felt a little queasy, like he was going to throw up. The decimated countryside around him began to shake, its pixels falling away from him, then elongating like a starship going into warp drive. He found himself sitting in his chair, in front of his computer with his cell phone ringing.

Groggily, he answered it. "Hello, Brin!"

"Russel's back!"

"So am I -- I guess." He stood and felt more than a little woozy, so he sat back down. "You call the girls. I'll call the boys. Meeting here -- in the attic -- in half an hour."

Wem greeted each of his friends at the door in silence. Nothing could be spoken until they got into the protection of the attic. Some of the uninitiated tried to say something, but Wem just hushed them, politely. It only served to raise their suspicions about why they had been called here. They even began to look a little fearful.

Sam and Jenny huddled close to the chimney. Bryce and Asher stood resolutely at the head of the stairs. Brindi stood close to Wembley with an arm around Talon and Russel.

"Some of you may not know it but Russel and I got sucked right into the game."

"But we were all there. It was awesome!" Bryce added.

"Yes, we were, and it was. But Russ and I were really there."

"Russ disappeared from his chair during the game. He was there one minute and not there the next." Brin hugged her little brother closer to her.

"You're kidding?" was Sam's question.

"No. Somehow Russ and I were taken into the virtual world of the game. It's a good thing I was a mage or I wouldn't have been able to heal us. We were both bloody."

There was an audible gasp. Talon hugged Brin. Wembley noticed.

"It was a lot different from the time you and I went to the workhouse, Tal. We weren't in danger there. But Russ and I were in danger during the game."

"Why?" asked Jenny.

"I'm not sure. Someone programmed the game or changed the programming while we were fighting it -- up until one point. Were you guys threatened by a big, red-haired Orc?"

There was a silence that seemed to give assent to that question as everyone looked at everyone else.

"I thought so. Did you notice that the Orc had green eyes?"

More silence at the uncomfortable memory.

"Did you each kill it?"

Heads nodded and a few voices said, "yes."

"Did you notice that after you killed that Orc you were able to move forward?"

"You mean," said Bryce, "that someone was that Orc?"

"Not one of us. Someone else. I think it is the same someone that is causing most, if not all, of my 'DreamTravels'. Russ and I had a kind of a 'DreamTravel' into that game. Bryce, can we use your van to go to Evie's house?"

"Sure. But how could she...?"

"I don't know. That's what I want to find out."

They all piled into the van and Bryce hauled out of the drive heading back to town. They crossed the bridge and drove up in front of the ranch house built of white brick. They went up to the door and it was open. They went inside and stood gaping in the living room.

There on the couch were two adults that none of the kids had ever seen before. The two figures sat there motionless, eyes dull, sort of slumped together. The young ones backed up to the door and stepped out, just beyond the threshold. Sam and Jenny looked behind them, saw the little ones and stood just in front of the threshold, as if in a protective stance. Bryce, Wem and Brin crept forward toward the figures on the couch. Wem reached out and Brin caught his hand.

"Don't!"

"I have to, Brin."

He touched the faces of the two 'dead' adults. Brin and Jenny squealed a little. So did the three younger boys. This was just way too weird.

"They're cold. Stone cold. And their skin doesn't feel like skin. It's more like leather -- no -- plastic. Like a Barbie doll!"

"You're kidding, right?" was voiced by Bryce.

Wem shook his head.

Bryce crept forward. Asher called out, "Don't, bro!"

"It'll be okay, Ash."

Bryce touched the faces of the -- whatever-they-weres -- and nodded. "Dead!"

"No -- never alive," countered Wembley.

Then the two heads of the bodies on the couch turned and looked at Wem and Bryce. Their hollow eyes bored into those of the two youths. Then the figures stood, looked again at the boys and walked away, awkwardly, down the hall and disappeared into one of the bedrooms. Bryce and Wem followed.

"Let's get out of here -- please!!" came from Russel.

Wem firmly stated, "You young ones go to the van!"

"Not without you!" shouted Russel and Talon simultaneously.

"Then stay here. We'll be right back."

Wem and Bryce inched down the hallway. Wem was shaking. He was frightened. He looked into Bryce's eyes. Bryce shrugged his shoulders. But they kept walking, well, inching. They gained the door where the two whatsis had entered and stood there. It was now closed. Wem reached out and turned the knob slowly. Once he felt the bolt slide out of the jamb he threw the door open. It rebounded off the wall. The room was noticeably pink.

"Evie's room?"

"Has to be."

It was empty of any figures. The two -- things -- had disappeared. There was a bed and a desk. A dressing table and a chair. A closet. The doors to it were shut. Wem and Bryce walked toward it.

"Don't," was whispered at them.

They turned to see Brin at the door, along with the faces of all of the others crowding in behind her. Wem motioned them to stay still and silent. He put his finger into the little depressed ring of the closet door and pulled it to the side. He jumped back at what he saw there. Bryce came up next to him. They saw the two beings standing in the closet with their eyes shut, arms lifeless at their sides. Wem motioned for the others to come in. They came forward cautiously and looked into the closet.

Russel asked the next question. "Robots?"

"This is way too weird!" was Sam's appraisal.

"Are these Evie's parents?" asked Jenny.

"She is an orphan!"

"She made them up!"

"Literally!"

That thought silenced all of them until Talon asked, "How? This isn't a movie."

"We traveled to a workhouse, Tal. It did happen. Just like this is happening. Only it is here and now -- not then. I can't explain it. I don't know how or why. I just know that it is not any dream. Dreams can't be shared."

The two robots in the closet opened their eyes and shock was registered on their faces. They panicked and turned around. Wem saw the wall behind them slide away as the two ran into the darkness.

"What the..."

The friends hadn't even had time to react. The two bodies were just gone! The wall was open.

"Not again," said Asher.

Wem went through the opening in the wall before anyone could stop him. His fingers fumbled in the dark but it seemed like another hallway. Then there was nothing below his feet. He lurched forward but caught himself on a railing of some sort and pushed himself upright. He searched out in front of him and down and his foot found something solid. He stood on it. It did not move. He heard the sounds of distant crashing of glass and breaking of wood. He felt bodies press up behind his.

"It's us."

"All of you?"

"Yes. No one wanted to stay behind."

"I think I'm at the top of some stairs. I'm going down. Come along or stay here, but do it together."

He took another step forward clinging to the railing -- hoping there would be another place for his foot to land. There was. He stole down the stairs and soon he heard the others following. He got to the bottom and waited for them. They then crept forward again toward the sounds of smashing and crashing. There was a light around a corner up ahead. They slipped around the corner and saw a door, partially open. They caught up with the door and entered. The two robots were in the middle of tearing the place apart. It looked like a laboratory full of beakers and retorts, vials and other equipment. The friends stood there totally bewildered as the two figures finished their destruction. Everything was smashed to little pieces. Nothing -- not even the tables -- was left. Then the two figures looked at the little group of their discoverers and burst into flame. They melted. No bones. No flesh. No gears. No wires or cables. Just two pools: one of silver metal and another of fleshy colored plastic.

Wem picked up a table leg and stirred one of the pools.

"Simulacrums."

"What?"

"Simulacrums. I read about them in a SciFi book. No moving parts just metal and plastic."

Jenny didn't believe she was saying it again but, "You're kidding," came from her lips.

"No. This is no joke. Somehow -- and we're all involved in it -- we've found something that we have to stop."

CHAPTER TWELVE
History Can Be Dangerous

"It's pretty cold out."

"But I wanna see it, please?"

Wembley turned to Brindi, and Russel was looking like a boy who had just asked for a puppy.

"OK, Russ."

"Maybe we should wear our coats?"

Wem nodded and they jammed their arms through the sleeves of their winter jackets. Soon they were upstairs in front of the attic door.

"This is gonna be so kewl!" Nobody ever knew when Russ was excited.

Russ was all eyes as they passed up the attic stairs, just the beginning, but still an adventure. Wem almost chuckled, because he remembered being ten-years-old. It wasn't that long ago. Everyday life was an adventure, a risk, a quest, a game; some fun to be discovered in the plainest of everyday things. Russ loved his own attic. Someone else's just had to be cooler.

As the eyes of Russel Williams cleared the floor of the attic, gazing to the right, they opened even wider than they had been while climbing the stairs. "Whoa, this is huge!"

The two piles were still there; all sorted as Wem and his friends had done last month.

"Let's see if you can find the trigger."

"What's it look like?"

"Wouldn't that be cheating?"

Wem leaned against a stack of boxes and pulled Brindi close to him as they watched her little brother search through the attic. He looked at the floorboards, scanned the rafters and finally stood in front of the brick chimney. His fingers touched the crevices.

"Cold, Russ." Wembley was shaking his head.

"Would you tell me if I was warm?"

"Of course. But you're not."

"What?"

"Warm."

Russ walked around the north end of the chimney.

"Freezing!"

"You cold?" asked Russ.

"No, you are!"

Russ turned around and walked back passed the chimneys into the little 'L' made by the master bedroom below.

"Mucho calor, Senor."

"What?"

"A lot warmer."

Russ went to the outside wall.

"Frigidaire, mon frere."

Russ turned and faced the north end of the attic while standing at the very southern part of it. He looked at the wall of the 'L,' he eyed each side of the chimneys, he scanned the 'L' again, he stepped along the floorboards, looking for a trip.

"Mucho frio."

"English?"

"Coooo-ooold!" Wem laughed a little as he shivered. So did Brin.

"A little help?"

"Not in the floor."

"What -- in the air?!"

Wem just shrugged.

Then the boy saw it. He ran over to it -- a chain hanging down at the front of the 'L' -- but he found that he couldn't reach it.

"Caliente, muchacho!"

"I'm not tall enough."

Wem walked calmly over to his 'little brother' and placed his hands on the boy's hips and lifted him up, like a dancer in a musical, until Russ' hands found the pull on the chain and yanked on it. He heard a click, but was still, himself, dangling in mid-air.

"Well, put me down, Samson!"

Wem set his charge on the floorboards and he ran to the chimneys, the north wall of which had pushed out at an angle from the rest of the structure. He placed his fingers into the crack and pulled.

"Whoah!" and Russ looked back to Wem, as if for approval.

"Go on!"

"You coming?"

"Right behind you."

Russ slowly climbed the circular set of stairs that he found behind the wall. He touched the walls and the railing, his fingers came away blackened with soot from the chimneys. With each step some new exclamation burst forth from the enchanted boy. Wem remembered that he had felt the same way when he went up for the first time. The louvers normally let in the light but the grey day outside provided little illumination. Russ stopped and Wem and Brin soon joined him on the little platform inside the cupola.

"Now what?"

"Gotta have a door to get out."

"Well, where is it?"

"What do doors have?"

"Hinges."

Wem raised his eyebrows.

"Knobs!"

Wem's eyebrows waggled.

Russ searched the dimness of the interior and his hands found a smooth protrusion. He wrapped his fingers around it and pulled. Nothing. He pulled again.

"Stuck."

"Let me try."

Wem started to yank on the knob but the door wouldn't budge even to his strength. "Hey, it was easy the last time. Right, Brin."

"Yeah."

The wetness of the coming Maine winter must have swollen the wood to the point where the door would not open out onto the widow's walk. Wem put both hands around the knob and his knee against the jamb and yanked. He succeeded only in pulling the knob from the door.

"Dumb thing broke."

"The bolt was probably rusty."

Russ picked up the bolt from the floor and handed it to Wem, who was staring at the knob in his hands because, through the grime of years, there seemed to be a glow coming from under the century of dirt. Wem started wiping the grime away with his coatsleeve. It became brighter by bits in the little cupola of Captain Horatio Fletcher's house.

Wem's eyes were highlighted by the glow. He was all smiles and wonder.

"The Orb?" was Brin's question.

"Has to be."

"But ..."

"Russ, give me the bolt."

Russ handed it over. Wem pushed it through the slot made for it in the glass ball. Once it was all the way through, the orb dimmed to nothing again.

Wem pulled the bolt out and examined it. "This thing is iron. I read -- somewhere -- that solid iron dampens the properties of magical objects."

"Magical ..." Russ was stupefied. He stared at the bright, round, little globe in his friend's hand and the shaft of iron in the other. "Maybe we were better off when it didn't glow." Russ was just a little worried. "You can always put the bolt back in? Keep it there?"

Wem did and the orb went back to it's glass self. "I'm not ready for magic in my life."

"But if that bolt neutralizes the power of the orb, how could it ever have affected you all these months?" Brin was the keen and inquiring mind, this time.

"I touched it."

"But that wasn't 'til a long time after your 'DreamTravels' started."

"You're right!"

"So, the orb isn't the answer?" Russ asked.

"Or maybe it's only a part of the puzzle?"

"Can I see?"

"What?"

Russ nodded his head to the outside.

Wem grabbed a hold of the louvers in their sturdy frames and pulled. The door snapped inward, wobbling on its hinges and the view to the east, although quite grey, was revealed. Russ went out and leaned on the railing.

"This is awesome!"

"Yeah. It is. I wonder how the Captain knew to build here?"

"It's the only hill for miles."

Wem thought for a moment. "This farm is the highest point in this part of the county."

"Sure is pretty, even without the sun."

The two teens were surprised at this remark coming from a ten-year-old.

"What?" was the defensive comment that came from Russ.

"Nothing." Wembley smiled and ruffled Russel's hair. "You're right."

Russ held his hand out and wiggled his fingers. Wem placed the orb, no bigger than a ping-pong ball, into the palm of the ten-year-old's hand. Russ looked at it and then held it up to the sky. He pulled the iron bolt out. The orb began to glow. "That's so cool!" Russ wrapped his fingers all the way around the ball, closing his fist as tightly as he could. The glow spread from his hand, up his arm and across his body in a matter of seconds.

"Russel!" Wem reached out and grabbed a hold of the glowing boy. Brin had a hold of Wembley already and as the strange glow spread across the three of them, they all winked out.

When the flash faded from their eyes, they couldn't believe what it was that their eyes were telling them. They were hovering in the air forty feet above the ground. There was no house below them. Just a hill. Their feet were standing on the air.

"This is awesome!"

"No, Russ, this is scary."

"Why?"

"Where's my house?"

Russ looked around him. "Ummm ..." Fear began to wash over him.

"We haven't moved anywhere, but the house is not here." As he looked around him he saw that the roads were different -- almost non-existent. There were a lot more trees. No lights at all. Wembley felt like he'd been here before -- whenever here was -- but that he had felt much safer at that previous time because his feet were on the ground then. This was terribly unsetting; this hovering.

"Is this another 'DreamTravel'?" squeaked out of the frightened boy.

"Seems like it."

"So it was the orb!"

"How could it have been, Brin? The shaft neutralizes it! And the shaft's been in it for a hundred years or more."

"Holy ..."

"Russel!"

"Where are we?" Russ was worried.

"When."

"When?"

"When." Wembley nodded. "Before the house was even built, looks like. You see any lights, cars, roads?" Wembley had become a keen observer of the past.

As they looked down, still not comfortable at the height, a man was walking, below them, around the base of the small rise of ground that passed for a hill in southern Maine. He was pacing as if counting off some sort of measurement and jotting notes on a little pad of paper. The man disappeared. The clouds had whirled away and the sun was going down and then coming up again.

The sun flashed by three times, and in between, each time, the man paced off and marked the ground with stakes and string. Days passed by in seconds as wagons arrived, first with stone and the foundation of the house was dug deep and the rocks were piled and cemented. More exchanges of sun and moon and the wagons had dropped off lumber, fresh cut and waiting. It was like they were viewing the whole scene through a time-lapse camera. Months of construction flashed by in minutes. It almost made Wembley sick, all that fast movement.

Floors and walls went up. Siding and shingles went on. There was the cupola, sitting right where it should be -- under their feet. The Captain -- it must've been him because he was wearing a uniform of some kind -- was fiddling at the louvers with a bolt and the orb; wearing gloves. The orb was not glowing. As the Captain drew the door shut Wembley, Brindi and Russel were catapulted to the opening and managed to squeeze through it just before it closed. They were inside the cupola as the Captain wound his way down the stairs. They were drawn after him and found themselves in a completely empty attic. The Captain stood at the head of the stairs to the second floor -- there was no dust -- the wood looked new. He shook his head as if he had seen something he shouldn't have. The little trio of time-travelers whooshed after the Captain and escaped the attic to the second floor. The Captain stood at the window by the attic door for a while. His hands were behind his back. He seemed to be thinking about something. Wem and friends just hung there, suspended; their feet not yet on the floor. This was not like his 'DreamTravels' -- where he became a part of the action -- he, they, were merely observers, here.

The Captain turned and walked right through the feet of the unseen watchers. It felt weird to be walked through; even if it was just your feet. Then, along they went, compelled to follow the Captain. He turned in to what would eventually become Wembley's room. It was full of books and maps and charts. A large table in the center contained unrolled maps, compasses and a few more books; but the charts weren't charts of the sea. It looked like different views of England, Wales, Ireland and Scotland. Marks had been made. Notes were piled high in sheaves of paper and parchment. A quill pen sat next to an ink well amid the clutter of geographia.

Wem was hovering just behind the table and looked to his right. He directed the other's attention to a little shelf on the wall. It held a small black pedestal and a little glass ball. The trio was astonished for they had thought that the orb had been placed on the door of the louvers. Wem whispered, "I held it. It couldn't have been the doorknob when the house was built or it wouldn't have been neutralized until sometime after my visit!"

"So that's just a piece of glass upstairs?"

"I guess."

"But it glowed!"

The Captain was sitting now, reading from a book. Wembley wanted so much to see what was being read that the little trio floated over to take a look. His wish, and they were in motion. Odd! *Whose wish had brought them here? Must've been Russel's!*

The Captain was scratching ink onto the pages of the open book. He was taking notes and asking questions. The margins were scrawled with them. Wembley leaned in and saw the following upon the printed page:

Then Sir Arthur looked on the sword, and liked it passing well. Whether liketh you better, said Merlin, the sword or the scabbard? Me liketh better the sword, said Arthur. Ye are more unwise, said Merlin, for the scabbard is worth ten of the swords, for whiles ye have the scabbard upon you, ye shall never lose no blood, be ye never so sore wounded; therefore keep well the scabbard always with you.

Wembley turned to Brindi, "I thought that Excalibur was wrung from the stone?"

"Me, too."

"But the Lady of the Lake also gave Arthur a sword. Same sword?"

Brin nodded towards what the Captain was writing.

"I have discovered that the sword from the stone and the blade from the Lady of the Lake were one in the same."

"Well, that answers that!"

Wem said, "But all he found was the sword. I don't remember a scabbard ever mentioned."

The Captain stopped scribbling. He looked around, as if he had heard something. Finding nothing, he went back to scribbling.

"I need that book!"

"What book is it?" asked Russel.

"Le Morte D'Arthur, by Sir Thomas Mallory."

"How do you know that?"

"I've read it."

"You can understand all the 'ye' and 'likeths' and 'whiles'?"

"Yes. It's not that hard, Russ," and Wem chuckled.

"There's a copy at the library," Brin offered.

"I have a copy. I need that copy!" And he pointed to the one that the Captain was writing in. "We've got to get home!"

As he said it, he was drawn backwards, with his friends, through the door of the room, down the hallway, up the attic stairs, to the chimneys, up and out the cupola to hang in the air as years started flying by until there was a flash of light again and they hovered over his house and settled again to the boards of the widow's walk.

It had all happened so fast that they hadn't had the opportunity, or even ability, to speak -- just whoosh! Now that they were on firm footing, they could talk again. They began to make their way down the cupola stairs.

"That's the second time I been magicked away, Wem. It's not my favorite thing."

"Sorry, Russ. Do you think that that book could still be in the house? Where did all the Captain's things go?"

"I don't think they came to our house with Mary. They could still be here -- or somewhere else."

"Or nowhere," inserted Russ.

"That's a lot of help! Ask your mom?"

"Sure?"

"Should we look in these boxes?" Russ was determined to be of more help.

"Russ, that's not a bad idea."

Russ smiled and they each started pawing through one of the endless numbers of boxes. After about twenty boxes had been searched, Wem made an assumption.

"No books. Just clothes and stuff. Doesn't even look like this belonged to the Captain."

Brin sat back on her haunches. "Yeah. You're right. Doesn't seem old enough."

"Yep. How 'bout those trunks?"

"When'd you get so smart, little bro?"

The piles of stuff were no longer very distinct, just masses of stuff; maybe even messes of stuff. Russ smiled as they pulled four large trunks out into the open. Wem's eyes lit up because, to him, the trunks looked old enough. Then the smile left him. "They're locked!"

"All of 'em?"

Wem jiggled two locks and Brin and Russ each pulled on the hasps of locks bearing the shape of a keyhole in their faces. None of them opened.

Russ sat up straight; "I found a bag of old keys in that box, over there."

"Brilliant!"

Wem rummaged through the box until he came up with the bag in his hands. He poured out a pile of clattering and clinking keys on top of one of the trunks.

"That's a lot of keys!"

They each took a key and made the rounds of the trunks. Each key proved more stubborn, and much more of a stranger to the locks, than the previous ones. After a while the trunks were still locked and the bag was once again full of keys.

"Break 'em open?"

Wem shrugged. Could the orb help them? He pulled it out of his pocket. It began to glow immediately.

Russ piped up. "I don't wanna go to any two-hundred year old locksmith.

Just get a hammer and smash the suckers!"

"Maybe you're right." Wem thought about it and pocketed the orb.

Brin spoke. "Even though we can only watch, it might be helpful. If these trunks belonged to the Captain, or at least if the stuff in them did ..."

"Russ, I don't think that we'll have a trip like before. I think we'll stay right here. I just wanna see who brings these trunks up into the attic."

"Think it'll work?'

"I think it's worth a try. What about you, Russ?"

"Okay -- go ahead." Russ, although in apparent agreement, looked none too sure about it.

Wem pulled the orb out and it started glowing again. It was already disturbing and unsettling but Wem thought about seeing the trunks being brought up. The shifts happened in front of their eyes. Then another flash and they were standing in the same place, but this time the attic had furniture and some crates. They heard some bumping coming up the stairs. As they looked over they saw the Captain, greyer and more haggard than before, emerging from the stairwell carrying what looked like one of the trunks. He set it down. Wem peered at the hasp. It was already locked.

"Sorry guys, but I gotta do this."

They began to move again, following the Captain down the stairs and into Wem's bedroom. Close inspection revealed that the table was now clear. All the maps and papers were missing. They saw the Captain packing up another trunk with all of the other stuff in the room. He picked up the orb, like it was an old and dear friend. He brought it to his lips and placed it into a small, velvet lined chest which was then carefully set in the corner of the open trunk. More books and papers came from the shelves, covering the chest, and the trunk was full, the lid closed and then locked with an iron padlock. Russ pointed to the Captain's belt. There were four keys on a ring.

"Can we go back now?" was Russ's question.

"Will staying here teach us anything more?"

"I don't know, Wem. It seems that we can always come back."

"Yeah. I guess."

They were whisked back up to the attic and then flashed through time. They were soon standing near the piles of stuff with the trunks a tantalizing few feet away.

Russ spoke up, "Like I said before, got a hammer?"

"In the basement or the barn."

"I'll go!"

"Why?"

"Cause I can walk on my own two feet to get there!" Russ was gone, in a kind of a flash.

"He really doesn't like all that ... whatever it is."

"I don't blame him."

There was a silence, pregnant with the rushing thoughts of their recent discoveries.

"Wem, I don't get it."

"What?"

"The orb in your hand ..."

"... is some kind of time travel device."

"That I do get. But you took it off the door in the cupola. We saw the Captain place it there when he moved in here, or soon after. Yet, the orb was also in your bedroom, before it was your bedroom. You touched it there decades after the house was built. How can one orb be in two places?"

"It's magic?"

"It is, but ..."

They were stymied. Russ came bounding up the stairs with three hammers. "Got 'em!"

He gave the hammers to Wem and Brin but kept the two pound sledge for himself. Wem gave him a look.

"I need a little more oomph 'cause I'm not as strong as you two."

They laughed and each moved to a trunk. They swung down on the hasp and the lock. Their hammers practically bounced off -- not like rubber, but they were diverted from even touching the metal.

"An enchantment?"

"That would be cool," Russ said.

"But inconvenient."

They tried again. Same result.

"Looks like we need a key after all."

Russ, dejected, slammed down on the top of the trunk with his sledge. It ripped right through the wood.

"Why'd you do that?"

"I don't wanna go on another travel thing." He hit the trunk lid again.

"Russ, hold it! What if you break something inside?"

Russ stopped the sledge in mid-swing. "Sorry. But I did get us in!"

"Yes, you did." Wembley peered in through the two-hit hole in the lid and saw books and papers. "These are the trunks that the Captain had! We've got to get them open!"

"What about the hinges?"

"What?"

"The hinges in the back. Smash them off or ... pry them open."

"Brin, you're brilliant!"

Wem started beating on one of the hinges with his hammer. It was taking it but there was damage. Dents. Then the hinge was bent out of shape. "Russ, can I use your sledge?"

"Your sledge, you mean."

"Well, yeah, but ..." and he took the sledge and hit a hinge on the holey chest. It shattered. He did the same to the other hinge. After a few whacks it, too, shattered. Wem lifted the lid, straining against the press of the hasp and lock, reached in and began pulling papers out. The other two kneeled down and took items from his hands as fast as they came out of the trunk and started piling them up. Sheaves of papers, stacks of books and a simple wooden chest were all on the floor of the attic.

"Is that the ... orb?"

"It sure looks like the chest the Captain put it in." Wem held the chest. There was no lock. "This chest has a twin."

"That's just what I was thinking. There have to be two, because you already found one in the desk."

Wem just held the chest.

"Open it!" Russ cried.

Wem eased the latch to the side and opened the lid. There was the glass ball, with no holes, and it began to glow.

"Two orbs?"

"Looks like it."

"Think they're different?" asked Brin.

"I don't know. But I bet we'd find out if we read through these papers and books." Wem suddenly handed the orb to Brin, who wasn't sure if she should touch it, but had no choice in the matter as Wem was already down the stairs. He sprinted back up with the other chest in his hands.

"Two chests. Two orbs."

He opened the second chest and Brin placed the orb/knob in it. They put the chests down on the attic floor, side by side.

"They are different!"

"How?" Russ asked.

"Only one has a hole drilled through it."

"The Time Travel orb."

"Yes."

"So what's the other one?"

"That we are going to have to read about," as he pointed to all of the books and papers on the floor.

A big frown crossed Russ' face. "Read? I can't read!"

"You love to read!" countered Brin.

"Not that! Look at it! All those loops and swirls and thees and therefores ... that's not English!"

"Um, Russ, I hate to inform you that it was English before what we read now was English."

Russ' face screwed up into the biggest consternation of his young life.

Wem came up with a solution, pointing to the stack of books, "These are printed books. You read in them and Brin and I will handle all the 'loopy' papers."

Russ picked up a book and leafed through the pages. "There aren't any loops and swirls, but there are some funny words. Look at this!"

He tilted the book toward Wembley and pointed to a word: 'Magicked.'

"Means the same thing but spelled differently, that's all. You'll get the hang of it."

Wembley had an unanticipated thought. "The book!"

"What book? There's lots of books already!"

"Le Morte D'Arthur! Three other trunks!"

They all put down their reading material and picked up a hammer. The chests were beaten open, the contents sifted through, sorted and stacked. When they were done it was quite a daunting pile of material.

"It's not here! The one book I need."

"But what about all this other cool stuff?"

There were daggers and swords, pens, compasses, trinkets as yet unidentified, several flintlock pistols, a mirror, a whole tree's worth of paper and books. But no Le Morte D'Arthur.

"Think your mom would know?" asked Wem.

"What could mom know?" Russ responded.

"You're descended from the Captain. She knows a lot more about The Captain and Mercer and Mary than she has told us about."

"It wouldn't hurt to ask."

"Why do you need to know all this stuff, Wem?"

"Because I love Arthurian history."

"You said history. Arthur was a myth -- that's what my teacher said."

"Russ, everything I've read points to history that was kind of muddied and obscured by legend and myth, by some of your ancestors."

"So?"

"So ... I want to know the truth about Arthur and Merlin."

"Merlin was a fake. Magic isn't real."

Wem pointed to the orbs. "Isn't it?"

Russ' face came alive. "You mean ..."

"I mean that there's more to all of it than has been written about in the published stories. I think the Captain was well-acquainted with the real Arthurian lore; the secrets handed down in your family. If what your mother told us was true, then the Captain might have known more than anyone else -- ever."

"How?"

"I don't know, yet. Let's go!"

Wem grabbed Brin's hand and they made for the stairs. Then they stopped. "You coming?"

Russ got up and trudged over to the stairs. Brin grabbed his hand and they ran through the house.

"Mom, can you take us to Brin's house? It's really important. It won't take long."

She'd heard that before, and the accounting could always wait.

"Let's go."

The kids were out the door and waiting in the van before Marged exited the door of the house.

"You found what?"

"Four trunks full of stuff from Captain Fletcher."

"You're sure?"

"Has to be, Mrs. Williams. But we need to know if anything came down to you through Mercer or Mary."

"There were a couple of books ..."

"Le Morte D'Arthur?!"

"No. That wasn't one of them. I remember The Mabinogion."

"Anything handwritten in it?"

"No."

"You're sure?"

"I cut my teeth on it when I was very young. The Idylls of the King was there, too."

"No. It has to be Mallory's book."

"Why?" came from a very worried mother.

"Because we saw him writing notes in it."

"All of you?"

"Yes ..."

"How?"

"We all ... time-traveled there."

"Orbs."

"So they're real?" There was an expression on Mrs. William's face that betrayed her confusion.

Wembley nodded.

"And you have them?"

Wembley nodded again.

"And you took my children ..."

"It was me, Mom. I did it first. I was holding the orb and I just wished, in my mind, to see the Captain and whoosh! The orb took us there."

They all looked to Mrs. Williams for a reaction. She was trying not to over-react; the kids could tell. She was trying hard!

"We have everything we saw the Captain with, Mrs. Williams, except for Mallory's book. It was all in locked trunks buried in my attic."

Mrs.Williams ran her hands through her hair and mumbled, "The Wheels Of Time are real."

"The Wheels of Time?" Wem was puzzled.

"Yes. They suppose that they are the devices that allowed Merlin to work his magic."

"Who's 'they'?"

"The Keepers of the true lore. I know they wrote many things, but not always the truth. They had to keep secrets; hide; obscure facts and places; protect the Wheels at all cost. The Captain was the last of the Keepers. He was a Guardian and a Compiler as well."

Wem was thunderstruck. Many of his suppositions had just been legitimized.

"But he had children."

"None of them wanted the burden. That's why he packed it all up. To hide it until a new Keeper could be found. Tennyson brilliantly wrote down what was given to him, with necessary alterations, but he refused the job of Keeper." And she looked at Russel.

"What?"

Then she looked at Wembley. "You're tied to this, too, somehow."

"I think so. More than just living in the house."

Brin edged into the exchange. "So either Wem or Russ is supposed to be the new Keeper?"

"I don't think so. Wembley might have another mission -- and I don't know what that is -- no idea -- but Russel seems to be destined for the job."

"Why?"

"Because the orb responded to your wish first. And you are a blood descendant."

"But I'm the one who wished us home!" replied Wem.

"It has been said that only those who are connected to the orb can wield it's power."

"Then we're both connected to it."

"Why haven't we known about this, Mom?"

She chewed on her lip, stalling, but their eager stares called the answer from her. "I was hoping that it would spare you -- skip you children like it did my brother and I."

"Why am I not the one?" Brin was almost hurt.

"The Keepers have all been men. I don't know why. The Orb chooses its Keeper. It hasn't spoken up since the Civil War."

"Mercer?"

"He refused."

"And he died?" Russ' face blanched at the thought.

"He died. He wasn't killed by the Orb," was Mrs. William's calm reply.

"He was killed in the war, Russel."

"The Wheels do not exact retribution for any decision made. The mantle of Keeper must be accepted by, not forced upon someone. But once accepted it cannot be given away. Since Mercer, no one has died anything but a natural death."

"How do you know all this stuff, Mom?"

"I have a book."

"Where?"

"It's in the attic." She smiled. "In a trunk."

Russ ran off. He knew exactly where it was. "Come on, Wem!"

Wem followed, shrugging his shoulders at Brindi. She tagged along. Mrs.Williams brought up the rear.

Russ had found and opened the trunk with Wembley at his side. The trunk was otherwise empty. The ladies arrived.

"It's empty," observed Wembley.

"It's all I was bequeathed -- just the book."

"And the trunk. It's just like the ones in Wem's attic."

"Really?"

Wem nodded. "Yes, Mrs. Williams. That makes five. But Russ, I thought you said you knew everything in this attic?"

"I do. I just didn't know what it was for. It's just an old book with funny words in handwriting that I can't read."

"It's a journal -- centuries old. I am not a Keeper, but it was all left to me to hold on to. If no one of your generation claims it, Brin, I'm afraid that you will be entrusted to hold onto it until someone does claim it."

"I think ... I ... want it," came almost whispered from Russel. "But I can't read it all. I tried before -- before I knew anything -- but none of it made sense."

"Brin and I can read it with you -- together. Maybe it has some of the things that the Captain discovered, too."

"It does mention that there was another book -- one he kept the deepest secrets in."

"Le Morte D'Arthur?"

Mrs. Williams nodded.

"How many times have you read it, Mom?"

"I've read it every year since you were born, Brin."

The children looked at her, perplexed.

"I may not have been a Keeper. But I needed to remind myself as to how to confirm who was to be Keeper."

"How?"

"It's all in the book."

"Do you think that the copy of Mallory still exists?"

"The Wheels of Time do not let anything vital to it be destroyed, so I am sure it exists."

"It has to be at my house, then."

"It could be, because it is not here."

"Did any of the Captain's stuff get sold off?"

"The journal mentions crates of books being sold and a lot of furniture."

"Antique stores? Bookstores?"

Mrs. Williams smirked at that statement. "There are two antique stores and a bookstore that have been here since before the 1900s."

"Do you remember ..."

"Read the book."

Russ handed it to Wem.

"No, bro. If you are going to be the Keeper, you need to know it all just as much as I do."

Russ looked at the book. He opened it and flipped through some of the pages. He found he could decipher about one in twenty words. He flipped to the first page and showed Brin and Wem. The words there were written in a very neat hand -- but the spelling was atrocious.

"They spell worse than I do!"

They all giggled at that one. Russ began to pronounce the words that he found there, haltingly and with great difficulty, in some cases.

"The journeye fromme mortal to Keeper is one fraught

withe the caprices of the Wheels. What does that mean?"

"It seems that the orbs are indeed in control, once someone agrees to their charge. Read on."

"Once accepted, it is not poffible for one to recant or renounce."

"What's poffible?"

"Old English spelling of possible."

"Funny esses."

"A true heart and willing mynde shall the succeffful Keeper poffeff."

"I'm kind of getting the hang of this."

"Once chosen he should read and learne, should add unto the pages of thysse booke. It being his solemne dutye."

"Then it's signed."

"By whom?"

"Look closely," urged Mrs. Williams.

They all peered at the signature at the bottom of the page.

"Myrd-dyn-ap-Em-rys."

"Who was he, Mom?" asked Russ.

Wem's mouth was open, he looked like he had just been struck with a mallet and he was the gong.

"Wembley, you know a lot about this time period -- I know that -- who was Myrddyn?"

"Merlin!"

"Yes. The very hand of the Wizard -- the High Druid -- began this book."

"Why haven't you shown it to anybody?"

"Because I was entrusted by the Keepers <u>not</u> to do so."

"But this would prove he existed!"

"Many would say it was a forgery, or merely a fiction. It would be discounted. The secrets would then be un-Kept. And my role as Protector would be compromised."

"No wonder the Captain was so miserable. He knew all this stuff that he couldn't tell anyone."

"So how come Wem and I could share this with Russ -- if he chooses to ..."

"You are my daughter and destined to protect. Wembley seems foreordained to help in other ways. He is prepared, right now, to help the Keeper. That seems clear. What better Protectors for the Keeper than a big brother and a big sister."

"My 'DreamTravels'?"

"Yes. And your vast knowledge of the times and legends of Arthur."

"Not really legends, are they?"

"What the public -- and even some scholars, perhaps -- know of is a mixture of myth, legend, truth and mis-information, carefully sculpted and crafted over the centuries to hide the most important things."

True to the form of the ever perceptive ten-year-old, "So if I say, 'yes' then I get to be a professional liar?"

They laughed and Wem punched him in the arm.

"No. Consider yourself an author of historical fiction," Ms. Williams advised.

"You're only ten!" Brin blurted.

"The Wheels will make everything possible."

"Don't you mean, poffible, Mom?"

The next day, the trio of Keeper-Protectors visited the two antique stores in town. The old barns were chocked full of stuff. At the second location the first and second floors and the loft were packed with treasures mixed with some trash. But hey, not everything was a real antique. The three youths poked around finding all sorts of things they thought interesting or funny. The owner came up to them, almost with a sneer on his face.

"Can I help you find anything?" He didn't really expect them to be looking. He just wanted to put pressure on them to leave his store before they were tempted to steal something.

"Do you know about all this stuff?"

The old man was taken aback. "Pert near."

"Do you have anything that might have come from Captain Horatio Fletcher's house?"

"Well, well, my, my, my ... what gets you interested in that old swindler?"

"I live in his house."

"You the Tewkes boy?"

"Yes, sir."

"Ayuh. Well, this table was supposed to have belonged to him."

"It looks like it's off of a ship."

It was carved with nautical signs and filigree.

"Twas. The Captain's table off his own ship, the *Lady Of The Lake*."

Wembley almost choked. "I never knew the name of the ship, before. Anything smaller?"

"Ship's bell, off the same ship."

"No, thanks."

"Set of silver from the Captain's house. Full set."

Wembley picked up the price tag. It was marked with $15000.00. "A bit pricey, don't you think."

"Nope. Real silver. The genuine article."

"How do you know?"

"My grandfather got it from the Captain himself. My father gave it to me."

Wem looked at the price tag again. His eyes just about bugged out of his head. He called the tag to the attention of Russ and Brin. He pointed to the name, above the price, on the tag, "Fletcher's Antiques."

"You a descendant of the Captain?" Wembley asked.

"He was my great-grandfather."

"He was our great-great-grandfather," replied Brin.

"You the William's kids?"

"Yes."

"Knew your mother since she was born. There's a couple o' knick-knacks and knives -- a sword, too --"

"Sword?" asked Russ.

"His ceremonial cutlass."

"Kewl."

"Any books?"

"Nope. Sold all of them to the bookstore."

"The one in town?"

"The only one from Bucksport to Portland on Route 1."

The kids moved toward the door.

"Any of this interest you?"

"It just might, but I can't spend that much money without asking mom and dad first."

"It'll be here."

"I'm sure of that. Thanks, Mr. Fletcher."

When they got back to the car, Brin confronted her mom. "Why didn't you tell us that he was related to us?"

"We've never really gotten along. I think it's part of the Wheels of Time and their influence. The family has been kind of fractured. With us apart, secrets are better kept; notes not so easily compared."

"I see."

"Anything?"

"Yeah, furniture and knick-knacks, but no books."

"Bookstore?"

"The one and only."

A smile crossed the face of Mrs. Williams as she shifted out of park.

It was cool and musty -- even a little damp -- in the oldest standing building in the town of Yarmouth. Once they had entered they saw more books than Fletcher had antiques. Thousands of used, rare and collectible volumes lined the rickety, overflowing shelves of *Friends of the Book* bookstore. Wem had been in here many times before, but he had been browsing in the dollar book sections at the front of the store. He now ventured, with his friends, into the heart of the labyrinth -- the Rare Books section. Wem looked at some of the prices. He leaned over to Brin, and whispered, "You'd think that nobody was in business to sell anything in Yarmouth -- at least not the old duffers. Who could afford these prices?"

"Sell one book and this guy's good for a month."

"Excuse me, Sir, but do you have a copy of <u>Le Morte D'Arthur</u>?"

"Yep," and the man's handlebar moustache puffed out at the edges.

"Can I see one?"

"Got three." Another puff.

"Okay, uh, where would I find them."

"Up front, seventh row on the left, under the 'M' for Mallory."

"Thank you."

The man harrumphed. Then Wem heard him mumble something like, "what's that kid want with Mallory, for Arthur's sake!"

The three removed themselves to the shelves indicated and searched there. Two volumes were found. This place may look crowded and disorganized but it was only crowded. One of the books was almost new and still had the book jacket on it. The other was older, but not old enough. Still Wembley pulled it off the shelf and fingered through the pages.

"Nothing written in the margins."

"He said there were three."

They shuffled back to the pouty old poop behind the counter. Wem spoke.

"You said there were three. We only found two on the shelf."

"Hmph. I thought that the third one would be out of yer price range."

"You never know."

The old man raised his considerable eyebrows and puffed out another breath across his bushy moustache. "You been in here before, ain't cha?"

"Yes, sir. If you had a frequent flier list, I'd be on it."

"Tewkes, ain't it?"

"Yes, sir."

"Growed a bit."

"Yes, sir."

"It's here in the glass case. You can see it -- on the bottom shelf."

Wembley almost couldn't look. He saw the old, worn, engraved cover, no longer bright with the colors of its youth. It was a dull green with a faded brown leather binding, still embossed with flaking gold leaf, that was beginning to wear away. It sat there all alone and separated from its brother-books; its sister-books too. It seemed an orphan, cast off and careless in its loneliness.

"Could I see it?"

"Sure you don't want that brand new copy?"

"No, sir, I like the old books best." Wembley smiled such a warm smile that the man almost relented. Almost.

"Yer hands clean?"

Wembley was almost tempted to tell the man that his hands were dirty from the dust of the man's own shelves, but he didn't. He looked at them, turning them over and over. Then the man produced a plastic container of baby wipes and handed one to Wembley, he wiped. The man unlocked the case and reached in and cradled the book in his fingers. He handed the book to Wembley, and Wembley was in awe. He just ran his palm over the cover. It looked so familiar.

"Where did you get it, Mr ...?" In all the times he had been in here he had never asked the man's name!

"Lathrop. Bill Lathrop." Lathrop, himself, had grown immensely in the last few seconds in the respect that he had for this kid who seemed to treat books like old friends.

"You related, by any chance, to Johnny or Mary Lathrop?"

"Johnny was my grandfather."

"How old are you?"

Bill laughed. "I'm eighty-seven. How do you know about Johnny?"

"He's my great-great-grandfather. So is Mercer Fletcher." Brin admitted.

Bill was quiet for a moment. "I heard rumors about this book. You wouldn't know anything about that, would ya?"

"Just possibly."

"Then open it."

A huge breath was expelled from Wembley's lungs as the pages inside the green and brown volume revealed the scratchings of a nib style inkpen. "This was the Captain's."

The man's eyes narrowed. "Are you the Keeper?"

The trio's eyes rounded out as if they had seen the Captain standing right next to Bill Lathrop. Wembley managed to maintain as Russel and Brin seemed to shake in their shoes. It was all quite unsettling. "Russel here, will be the first Keeper since the Captain himself."

The old man reached out and gently took the book from Wembley's hands. He removed the little price tag. "You won't be needing to pay this, then." He then stuck the price tag on Russel's forehead, and smiled. Brin leaned in to her brother.

"$25,000.00!"

"For the Keeper, it's free. Couldn't have just anyone buying it, now could I?"

Wembley butted in on the conversation. "Just how many of you people are there around here? How many know but don't say anything?"

"There is a Keeper and there are Protectors. I assume that you two are Mary Williams' children?"

"Yes, Sir."

"And yer the boy from Wales, aren't'cha?"

"What does that have to do with ..."

"Yer familiar with the stories in this book?"

"Yes. Very. I already own a copy."

"Then you know that any Welshman has direct ties to these tales."

"My family goes back to the Picts and the Celts. I know that. My Grans still live there."

"Then take the book and go!" The three could see the conflict in the man's eyes and face. "I said go! And don't come back here. It'll be too dangerous."

There was panic in three young faces and horror overcoming the eyes of a fourth, older face.

"Be safe. Keep it safe! There are powers and persons after it -- and anything that might be connected to it." He juggled imaginary balls in the air. "Leave! Now!"

The Keeper and his Protectors ran out of the shop. They jumped in the car and Mrs. Williams sped away.

"Where're we going, Mom?"

"To Wembley's house."

"Why?"

"While you were in the store I was reading in the journal. We have to get the journal and everything else into that attic."

"Why?"

"Because it was built by the Captain to protect and shield anything connected with the Wheels and the books ... from anyone who was searching for it."

"Is that why I could only find out about it once I was up there?"

"Precisely."

"Two books and two orbs."

"What about everything else?" asked Mrs. Williams.

"It's all in my room."

Mrs.Williams stomped her foot on the accellerator and the car screamed toward Wembley's house. After a few seconds they heard a big explosion. They looked behind them and saw a plume of flame reaching skyward.

"What the ..."

The car sped up the gravel driveway and the kids got out and ran for the house. Wembley stopped still as he noticed that the windows to his room were open. He also looked behind him at the plume of flame. It seemed to be changing direction, blown by a stiff wind directly toward him. He and the other kids raced inside and up the stairs. Wem threw open the door and discovered an absolute mess. Papers, parchments and artifacts were strewn everywhere. Wem closed and latched the windows.

They searched in panic and found that the desk had been overturned, the drawers opened. Brin, Russ and Mrs. Williams filled their arms with the detritus on the floor. Wembley reached into the drawer and turned the latch. The bottom popped up and there were two small chests stashed securely inside. He grabbed them both and ran to the hall, lifting up a stack of books from the corner. The others followed with their arms full of stuff and they raced down the hall and up the attic stairs. Wem held the door, which he slammed and locked as soon as the others were heading up the stairs. There was a scream outside the house as soon as the attic door closed behind them. They placed everything in the trunks, papers in one, books in another, artifacts in the third and the two small chests in the last one. They sat down on the chests, breathing hard.

"Well Russ," Wembley hacked, "you wanted an adventure. I think you've got one!"

"Does this mean I've been chosen?"

"It seems that we all have."

"I want to do it."

"Be the Keeper?"

"Yeah."

Wembley stood off the trunk he was sitting on and extracted the copy of Mallory. He kneeled on the floor and placed the book, open, in front of him. Brindi, Russel and their mom joined Wembley.

"What are we doing?" asked Russ.

"There's a ceremony that has to be performed."

"You gonna do it, Wem?"

"Not me. But I read about it this morning. Just wait."

Soon the room began to whirl. The words on the opened page of the book began to enlarge in front of them, they felt their feet leave the floor and then they were sucked into the open book, without so much as an invitation, or a 'come with me, if you please!' Sooner than Wem expected they felt their knees again on solid ground, they saw an old man with a long, grey beard standing above them, by a familiar looking table, which they were leaning on. Wembley saw the man's eyes grow big, as if in recognition, but Wem didn't know what he had recognized, so he dismissed it. No one in their little party could possibly know this man. But the man was looking directly at Wembley.

"Are you the new Keeper?"

"Me? No. It's Russel."

"And the others?"

"His sister, and mother."

"Then you are?"

"A friend -- I guess the book calls me and the two ladies here, Protectors."

"Remarkable. It's about time." The man laughed as if he had made a joke that only he understood.

Wembley stood. "Who are you?"

The man looked astonished. He blustered and puffed and finally said, "Myrddyn ap Emrys."

"Merlin?"

"A crude appellation. Now, then," he dismissed Wembley with a wave of his hand, "Russel, is it?"

"Yes, your majesty."

Myrddyn laughed. "I am no King, but I am here to induct you into the order of the Knights of the Round Table. All of you."

Brin grinned.

The little group hadn't noticed but they were indeed leaning on a familiar round table. "Protectors and Keeper. Anointed in this time to serve in your own time. Protection is afforded you all through the power of the Wheels." He shook a wand at them that had some sort of liquid on it. It sprayed them, lightly.

"Do we get to fight with the Knights?" asked an eager Russel.

"No. They no longer fight, unless it is to protect. You must return to your time and be faithful."

"To what?" asked Wembley.

"To the principles and instructions and covenants laid down in the books you have gathered. You do have the Wheels, don't you?"

"Yes."

"Good, keep them safe."

"They are."

The room began to swirl again. As they arrived they heard a crashing against the walls of the outside of the house, and against the roof. Thunder rumbled. Lightning flashed. The circular stairs let the storm outside be seen from the inside, but the protection of the last Keeper was still in place, and the storm stayed outside, where there were shapes and shadows chasing through the clouds.

"We and the items are safe here." Mrs. Williams mentioned.

"What if we leave?"

"The items will be safe as long as they stay here. So will we."

"You mean we gotta move in with Wembley?"

"No. Sorry. We, too, will be safe as long as the items are safe here."

"Wem? You said that history could be dangerous." Russel was a little defiant.

"Yeah. I did."

"Not as dangerous as the present."

CHAPTER THIRTEEN
Storms Coming

The storms continued, even on clear days, to rage around Wembley's house. One of the worst low pressure cells had settled right over this particular area of Yarmouth, Maine, isolating the Captain's old house. The clouds and the winds were not the only storms to buffet the Tewkes' family home. A storm of emotion blanketed Wembley with a keen sense of danger since Mary Williams had come to the door the day after their flight from the bookstore.

"I need to see Wembley."

"Certainly, Mary. Come in. Is something wrong?"

Mary handed Marged the newspaper, which was almost blown from her hand before she could shut the door. On the front page was a picture of what was left of a building and the headline, 'Lifelong Resident Dies In Fire.'

"We were there just yesterday."

"Wembley, would you come down here please? Mrs. Williams is here to see you."

Soon the pound of rapid footsteps was heard, then Wembley leaped down the last run of stairs and into the room. Mary and Marged were seated on the couch.

"What's wrong? Is it Brin?"

"No, Wembley. Brin and Russel are fine. You need to read this and then we need to talk."

Wem walked over to the couch and took the paper from his mother, looking all the time at Mrs. Williams. The two women watched as Wem's anxious eyes clouded over with amazement, hurt and grief.

"Mr. Lathrop ... I ..."

"It was the explosion we heard as we left. That plume of flame behind us came from Mr. Lathrop's store."

Wem stood there, he let his arm fall to his side, paper still clutched between his fingers. "But everything is safe -- right?"

"Yes, for the new generation. But someone was angry at the old one."

"Is that why he told us to get out?"

Mrs. Williams nodded. "I'm sure that he knew what was coming. He had fulfilled his responsibilities."

"Are you all right, Wembley?" was certainly his mother's concern.

"I ... yeah. Mr. Lathrop ... and all his books..."

"I'll get you a glass of water," and Marged left the room.

Wembley looked over his shoulder at his departing Ma.

"What about Fletcher and you?"

"Our enemy seems focused here, now."

"That's them, outside, then, hunh?"

Mary nodded. "But the protection the Captain left seems unbreakable. The work of the Keeper is supreme."

"I can't leave the house, though, can I? And we're going to Wales for Christmas."

"I don't think that will be a problem. You are not the center, and there will be a Keeper and two Protectors left to guard, even though the enchantment is impregnable."

"You're sure?"

"Quite. Read the books."

"I will, today."

There was a second of silence. "Was Lathrop a Protector?"

Mary nodded.

"And Fletcher?"

"Yes."

"Is he alive?"

"Yes, he possessed nothing vital. He is more of a lookout."

"Why didn't Fletcher and Lathrop get found earlier?"

"The Captain was a master Keeper. He wove too many myths and that force, whatever it is, knew nothing about that book until you, Brin and Russel knew it."

"So we caused..."

"No," was a stern remonstrance from Mary Williams.

"What about you?"

Mary shook her head and put a finger to her lips.

Marged re-entered the room. "Here's your water, Wembley."

"Thanks, Ma." Wembley downed the glass in several large gulps.

"I'd better go."

"Thanks, Mrs. Williams. Will Brin and Russ be over today?"

"Later this afternoon."

Wem held the door for the mother of his friends. The Protector of the Wheels. He closed it slowly even though the wind howled, screaming at him, hoping to reach in and grab him. He listened and thought he had heard his name amid the screams.

It was his Ma. "Wembley? Wembley, what's the matter? Are you in trouble?"

"It's nothing like that, Ma. But I can't tell you about it -- yet."

Marged went to object.

"Neither can Mrs. Williams. I wish I could, but it's really complicated."

"Does it have something to do with your 'DreamTravels'?"

"I think it might. But it's Russ and Brin and Mrs. Williams that are kind of at the center of it all. I'm just on the edges."

"And poor Mr. Lathrop?"

"He was closer to the center than all of us." He hoped he hadn't lied to his Ma, but he could see the worry that creased her pretty face.

"Granda Gwyllym faced similar things, until you were born. Then it all kind of eased up on him."

"Maybe."

"Maybe what?"

"Maybe he faced similar things."

"I thought you meant maybe it eased up on him."

"That, too."

"Can he help you?"

"I think he can, but I don't know if he faced what I'm facing."

"Do you want to call him?"

"No. I have to be with him. I ..."

"Two weeks and we'll be there."

"I'll make it, Ma."

On November 21st the storms outside the Tewkes home died out a little as the first snowfall of the year crystallized the area. Sheets and blankets and garlands of white glittered in the sun of a new and colder day. It seemed to also still the disturbance of whatever it was, like a deep snow quiets the ambient sound of any environment. Wembley ventured outside. He had to. The animals needed to be fed. The crunch under his feet this time was not the gravel of the drive. He loved it as his boots sunk passed his ankles in the new fallen snow. He reclaimed the snow-blower from it's drift and tarp and made a path from the back door to the front door and from the back door to the barn. He returned to the kitchen for the bucket of leavings. His pigs loved them. He fed his sheep and spent time currying his two horses, spreading fresh straw and piling new oats in the troughs. The work pleased him. It felt good to help those who, at that moment, could not do for themselves.

Besides the sheep were cute as they 'baahed' while the pigs and horses snorted and nickered in response. The barn was alive and safe; nothing out of the ordinary; nothing menacing. He was able to focus on all the things that had happened; everywhen he had been; each place and how it related to him, or not. What he could not figure out was why him in the first place? Brin and Mrs. Williams had not been plagued by these distortions of reality -- at least not like he had. Russel had only come along through the Wheels lately. What was particular or special about Wembley Tewkes? *'Nothing!'* was his dismissive answer. Then he pulled himself up short. He could not dismiss it any more. He was tied to Russel, Brin, Mrs. Williams -- to Mr Lathrop and Mr Fletcher -- to Captain Fletcher; to the strange green eyes that reminded him of Brindi every place he traveled. That might mean that somehow he was tied to Evie. That was not the most settling of thoughts. Two and two may add up to four, but as far as he was concerned, he hadn't even learned the numbers of his new reality, yet. If it was a reality? Nothing added up.

It all seemed so real while he was there. He knew it wasn't a dream. Dreams were too nebulous, ethereal. There was nothing hazy about almost dying, or saving someone from a death, or about people so like him, yet so dissimilar. That naked world was the most uncomfortable of all his visitations. Then there was Liam and Willem -- his own family.

He wasn't just a watcher there. He was a participant. His latest experiences with the orbs had let him see things. What was it that allowed him to be in the moment and live the experience? Why did he sometimes feel like two people -- the person he was inhabiting and himself? He was conscious of the duality inherent in the 'DreamTravels' while he was there. At least his Wembley/Self was. Did that other person sense Wembley like he sensed them? He didn't know.

One of the horses kicked the stall and brought him out of his contemplation. It wasn't his horse that had kicked. The horse was in this barn. But this wasn't his barn. He looked at his hands. They were smaller, dirtier, calloused with work and toil. His jeans had been replaced by a tweed of some kind, well-worn and patched. Braces held his trousers up. His plain linen shirt was stained with dirt, honest farm dirt. (Hmm. Not so different from that at home!) But he was older this time. He was no longer seven.

"Liam! Liam! Come quic ... Ahhh!"

The voice was interrupted by the report of a musket. Liam/Wembley burst forth from the barn and raced to his brother, who's body was lying on the turf, outside the enclosure of the family's farm. Before he got to Willem he saw another ball enter the body of his brother. The body just jumped a little at the impact. The shot had come from the right. Liam raced out the gate and saw a

184

man in a red uniform, reloading. The man's eyes panicked at the sight of Liam, only a boy, only twelve, but still the enemy. Memories of family legacies of long ago flooded into the mind of Wembley/Liam.

Liam charged the man as the soldier tried desperately to pack the wadding. Wembley/Liam ripped the musket from the hands of a surprised soldier, who began to scramble backwards, crablike, away from the boy. Wembley reared back and thrust the musket forward. He saw the soldier's eyes widen in surprise and pain as the bayonet invaded his body. Liam could not see for the tears that blinded him. He pulled his arms back and thrust them forward again, overpowering the Wembley inside him. The soldier folded in half and fell to the ground. Wembley/Liam looked down on him and stabbed again. A third red mouth opened and dribbled blood across the man's uniform. Then Wembley saw a fourth, fifth and a sixth mouth open up. It was not easy but he was able to stop the forward movement, leaving Liam just holding the gun.

Wembley/Liam felt restrained. Arms reached around him; held him as he began to sob. The weapon dropped from his hands as he sank to his knees. The arms that held him sank with him. They were strong arms. The wail of a woman's voice split the air and Wembley/Liam reacted. He pulled away from his father and lunged for the weapon. He swung it at the red uniformed corpse on the ground. The soldier's face disappeared in the pulp of battery. The musket was taken from the boy. Who ran to join his mother over the body of his brother.

Willem was dead. Wembley/Liam once again pulled the comforting arms from around him to look at his brother's prostrate form, splayed in such an unnatural position. He reached down and straightened the body's legs. He pulled the right arm from underneath and placed it on his brother's chest, then joined it with the left one, hands clasped together. His father tried to help him, but Liam pushed the man away. His mother tried to hold him but he shrugged her off. He placed one of his hands under his fifteen year old brother's knees and another just under his shoulders. He prepared and yanked up and struggled to his feet. His father again tried to assist, but all Wembley could hear was a sharp "No!" that came out in Liam's voice. Mother got the gate, Father followed behind his sons. Liam/Wembley surged through the door and lifted his older brother to the table.

What had happened? His brother had just been with him, mucking the stalls. Then he left to go to the house. Now Liam/Wembley was collapsed over the body of his only brother; his only sibling. His body heaved, racked with the sobs of loss and pain that a twelve year old grandfather shed. And hate. He hated the British. He heard voices as he hugged his brother's body to him.

"Hide the body!'
"Sink 'im in the bog."
"Cut 'is head off first."
"Throw the musket in too."

There were more voices than just his parents. The McPhees were there -- helping as they always had. The bog next door was the best place to dispose of the British intruders. Liam knew it. He reined in his sobs and went to help.

His father carried a headless body. His mother had a heavy basket -- the head. The McPhees were gathering up anything else that was on the road. Where there was one Red Devil there would soon be others. Liam/Wembley followed his father. As the man's body and head hit the bog, his father pushed them down with a stick. Liam spat. Wembley did, too. He felt the embrace of his parents. Others joined them.

"Ye've got ta flee!"
"To where?"
"Wales!"
"Aye. The only place."
"How?"
"Take our coracle."
"What about Willem?"
"We'll bury him as one of our own."

It was Billy's voice. A strong seventeen he was now and still the best friend that Liam or Willem could ever have.

"What happened, Billy?"
"Not sure, Ma. Didn't see it happen. But Willem had no weapon; that's sure. The soldier just shot him."
"And Liam?"
"Stabbed the Limey six times with his own bayonet. I never seen the like."
"Here!" Mrs. McPhee thrust a filled basket into Mary's hands.
"What's this?"
"Food and provisions."
"But ..."
"Ye'll need 'em."
"Take the cart and the coracle. We'll pick the cart up later."
"The estuary?"
"Roight! Now go!"

Liam/Wembley felt numb. He had killed a man! It sank deeply into both of his consciousnesses. The 'man' was nothing but a Limey pig; not a man at all! That is what Liam was feeling. He was right. Wembley felt a little differently -- mostly -- because he hadn't lived solely in this time, nor under the oppression of the British for very long in his own time; but he thought he understood Liam. He was right.

A still numb Liam was led to a place next to his mother in the cart. She cradled the basket of provisions and another bag as well as Liam. The bag contained the family Bible and a few sheets and blankets; small items of remembrance were also tucked away in the folds of its contents. The coracle was tied over them. Pa got into the seat and hitched the reins. That was the night that the shattered Connell family left Ireland forever. Wembley had read about it over and over in the journal that Mary had brought, with the Bible.

They couldn't let their twelve-year-old son be marked for death by the British Patrols who were running rampant through the countryside. No one may ever find out, but they couldn't take that chance. Wem realized something, even while in the body of his younger forebear -- a shared epiphany: death comes to us all, when least expected, sometimes at the hands of the most innocent of us all; but life is a choice we make every minute we breathe.

Then he felt ripped up and out; he saw the bottom of the coracle on the back of the cart, briefly, before he saw nothing more than the floor of his own barn beneath his feet and a spilled handful of feed amid the straw. Wembley stood and pounded his fist against the posts of the stall. The horses startled and whinnied. Wembley hung on to the post, reliving the 'DreamTravel' over and over again, as he cried. He was crying for Willem, and for Liam. He was crying for himself. Because a new fear had crept into his consciousness: could he kill? If he had to; was forced to -- could he end another man's life? He had killed the Intanobi, but they were not even real. This was his family! Liam and Willem hated the British. Wembley himself disliked the British Government to distraction for all the wrongs it had done to the Welsh and the Irish, and, for that matter, the Scots. But he didn't hate. He didn't want to hate. He couldn't hate. So why did it feel like hate was overwhelming him at the moment?

The barn door opened and the light of the outside refracted around the barn, illuminating Wembley's tear-stained face. It was his father, who rushed to his son and let the boy collapse in his arms as he cried the cry he didn't get to finish in Ireland. It became a cry that had only just begun for him here and now.

Thanksgiving came and went, without much, if any, notoriety. Except for the fuss that Wembley made over the delicious turkey, mash and green beans, that his mother had made, with a huge slice of pumpkin pie. Wembley's most favorite of all American meals.

December 2nd was his last day of school for him. He received an assignment in his Drama class that both excited and challenged him. It was due in January, upon his return. His teacher handed him a copy of *Henry V* and told him that his report would be on the play, as Shakespeare wrote it, and how the character of The Boy was a small but vital part of the entire play's structure. His major question, the one to answer in the report, was; why did Shakespeare include the character of 'the boy'? He would also have to memorize and present the monologue of The Boy upon his return.

"That's really cool!"

"So, who did you get?" came from a guarded Wembley.

"Helena, from *A Midsummer Night's Dream*."

"At least she's important!"

"Mrs. Linney wouldn't ask it of you if she didn't think you could do it."

"Yeah, yeah!"

"Well, see ya, Wem. Have a good trip!"

"You, too, Evie. Happy … Christmas."

"Yes. Thanks. Hap ... You too!"

Wembley boarded the bus, to find Brin already on board.

"What are you doing here?"

"Russ and I have to talk to you!"

"Kay, but ..."

"Russ will get on at the Elementary School."

It hit him square in the face; nothing that was momentously important, but something that connected another parallel in his life. If he was Liam, each time he went back to Ireland, Liam's older brother was Willem. They were five years apart. So his relationship there was very much like Russ's relationship with Wembley here. Five years apart and 'brothers.' Except that he was the younger there, and the older here. He supposed that there were connections everywhere. Then he began to understand that he was just responsible for finding and making them. A new mission! Maybe a little more clarity than just the 'not knowing' of it. Each place or time he visited had to have some meaning he could take from that world and use in this world. For this world was his primary reality; which realisation came flooding home to him until the moment that Brin kissed him. He left his thoughts behind him and kissed her back.

It wasn't a peck, and it wasn't a messy, sloppy one either and lasted a good long time. Wem figured that Brin wanted to get it in before the Middle School students boarded the bus. No good getting any of them too overheated. So Wem played along until it wasn't play, it was serious. When the kiss was broken -- the Middle School was looming in front of the bus -- there was a happy contentment as Brin cuddled close and the thoughts that had been preoccupying Wembley's mind were somehow chased away, unable to be recalled at the moment -- a kind of euphoria remaining in their place. They would come back to him, as soon as his mind could focus on them, that is.

The chatty, newly hormone driven 7th and 8th graders almost filled the bus with bodies and noise. The bus pulled away amid the clamor of who was doing what to whom and what should be done about it. One more block to the Elementary, then the bus was overflowing. Russ squeezed into the seat by his sister and 'brother.'

"So, what's this all about?"

"Keeper-ing it a secret!"

"Huh?" Russ got it. "Oh!" He drew an imaginary zipper across his lips.

As usual Wembley was peppered with questions about everything from history to the upcoming swim meet to taunts and teases about Brindi Williams. Brindi just smiled for most of those talking about her hadn't even met her and didn't know she was sitting right there; although there were a few snickers among the younger crowd, probably because they knew Russ.

One 7th grade girl, bold as brass but terribly uninformed for a person who had lived in Yarmouth all her young life, asked Brindi, "Who are you?"

Brindi smiled before she responded. "Brindi ... Williams."

The bus took on the hush of a funeral parlor in mid-embalming mode. Except for Wembley's and Russel's laughter.

Most of the kids turned beet-red and sat there hunched over in embarrassment. However, when Wem and Brin and 'that little kid' got off the bus and the door closed, the inside of the bus exploded like a stadium hosting a touchdown.

Brin and Russ couldn't move as the bus drove away. They were laughing too hard. Wembley was thinking again. He gathered his friends and they trooped up the driveway to the house. Wembley checked around, anxiously, for signs that anything might be changing or about to change. But all was quiet on the Wembley Front. They made it to the door and Marged greeted them. The stairs didn't shift. Wembley's furniture was still in his room. Their bookbags went on the desk, relocated to its spot on the south wall after it's unceremonious upending of a few weeks prior.

They sat there, staring at each other. Wembley spoke first. "I think you'll have an easier time of it after I'm gone."

Brin whimpered.

"No worries, Brin. I'll be here," confirmed Russ.

"Yes, but as I won't be, I think that the 'disturbances' of the last few weeks will also go away. It will be easier to keep the house protected. And you will be able to read everything in those books. You must read it all! I finished the journal this morning. It's amazing. I photocopied the other book and am taking it with me on the plane. You'll have the original to read -- and keep safe. I figured that whoever it is wouldn't care about or even be able to sense -- if that's what they do -- the photocopy. I made some notes from the journal that will go with me, too."

"And the Wheels?"

"In their chests in the attic, Russ. No using them while I'm gone. Keep your feet on the floor of the attic in this house."

Russ agreed, if a little reluctantly. He had lost his apprehension about the travels that he had taken with his friends. He was looking forward to more, but Wembley had said no. He needed to do what Wembley asked. Wembley was the Protector.

The room erupted into silence as Brin and Wem sensed something unasked in Russ. They waited, expectation written on their own faces.

"Wem -- what's it all for? Why is there a Keeper and why am I him?"

It's something that Wembley had been pondering over for almost a year, now: why him? Why any of them? He had no answers for his younger and close friend because he had none for himself -- yet. He was sad that such was the case. He had felt a burden on his shoulders, but he couldn't imagine the burden that young Russ was facing.

"Our families are tied together. It seems that we have been for a long time; even before I moved here. There's something that we have to do -- I just don't know what it is yet."

Russ looked at Brin, "Does Mom?"

Brin shook her head. "She's just like Wem. She knows there's a purpose, but she doesn't know <u>what</u> it is. Maybe the books will help?"

"Maybe," was said by Russ and Wem at the same time.

The conundrum just kept rebounding within each of them. Captain Fletcher. 'DreamTravels'. Time travel. Wheels. Green eyes. Books, papers, screaming! Nakedness, hairlessness, paintings, ancestors, imaginary people, Merlin; well, at least, Myrddyn ap Emrys. Were they to meet Arthur, too? Guinevere? Lancelot? Why? How did it all connect? What was it for? What did they have to do with it all?

Wembley was certain of one thing: that some of the 'DreamTravels' were harmless; just things he was interested in, and he had been blessed with a way to learn something about them -- first hand. Then, there were others that were terribly disturbing. Unfathomable with the present lack of information. It was like staring at a computer image without all the pixels in place; just a mess of dots.

CHAPTER FOURTEEN
An American's Christmas In Wales

Even with Christmas coming early for the Tewkes family, the trip back home was the best present of all. Wembley had a difficult time saying goodbye to his friends; especially Brin and Russ, for the William's kids had made him a solemn promise. They would care for Captain Fletcher's house. They would read and learn. They would know everything they could by the time Wembley came back.

The family drove the few hours to Boston in a light fall of snow; just enough to keep the wipers on the van moving in intermittent mode. Passports and tickets checked, TSA endured -- Wembley almost felt like slapping the man's hands -- they had boarded their flight to Cardiff International Airport. Wembley was aglow, alive with anticipation. He was going home! Yes, Yarmouth, Maine, USA had been, and was, where he lived -- and he thought of it as a home. But Wales is where his 'home' was: family, people, lineage, traditions, history -- roots. He loved his Gran Bronwyn, and his Granda Gwyllym. They were two of his most favorite people in the world.

Wembley got a real kick out of his Da, who hated to fly. He and his Ma giggled over it every year. Da had no sooner sat down and buckled up and he was asleep. Ma read -- some biography of great importance. Wembley slipped his photocopies out of his carry on. The six-and-a-half hour flight would be the perfect time to get ahead on this 'Keeper-Protector' thing.

The journal of Myrddyn ap Emrys had been a quirky thing to read. He didn't understand it all. In fact, he understood very little of it. Someone had been stolen away from modern times -- decades ago -- and sent back to Arthurian Britain, just as T.H. White had postulated in his treatment of the legend; The Once and Future King, written over fifty years ago, which Wembley had also devoured, by the age of ten. Myrddyn was an Ancient-Modern; or a Modern-Ancient. A dichotomy, a contradiction, and a complement in and of himself. He was wise, but had come from the future only to have lived since the dawn of man -- or so it was supposed. He was part of the land and yet a citizen of nowhere; he lived through all time yet had a foothold in none. He was someone who lived in all times and yet had no time of his own. Wembley had almost 'met' him; had been anointed by his wand.

Was it a dream or was it fact? It had to be fact.

Wembley was on a mission, and he was going home.

He opened the copy of the book written in by one of Brindi's ancestors; one of the Keepers of the Myth. Even the crisp new white pages of the photocopy felt well-worn. The title page had scrawls of ink all over it. Wembley assumed that it was the Captain's hand, as it was all the same style of handwriting. There were names added under the name of Thomas Mallory. Crétien DeTroyes, was one that he recognized. Next to this name was the note: *'So close, that it is almost scary.'*

Another name, Wolfram von Eschenbach, bore the note: *"Fancy, that, all fancy. Good job, enemy mine."* What did the Captain mean by that? Could his enemies be into distorting the myths as well? What were they enemies over?

There were other names he couldn't read, but he would come back to decipher them later. He wanted to start with the first chapter. He had read all forty-four chapters before -- but not with the notes of Keeper Fletcher etched into the pages.

> *CHAPTER I. How Uther Pendragon sent for the duke of Cornwall and Igraine his wife, and of their departing suddenly again.*
>
> *It befell in the days of Uther Pendragon[1], when he was king of all England, and so reigned, that there was a mighty duke in Cornwall[2] that held war against him long time. And the duke was called the Duke of Tintagil. And so by means King Uther sent for this duke, charging him to bring his wife with him, for she was called a fair lady, and a passing wise, and her name was called Igraine.*
>
> *So when the duke and his wife were come unto the king, by the means of great lords they were accorded both. The king liked and loved this lady well, and he made them great cheer out of measure, and desired to have lain by her. But she was a passing good woman, and would not assent unto the king. And then she told the duke her husband, and said, 'I suppose that we were sent for that I should be dishonoured; wherefore, husband, I counsel you, that we depart from hence suddenly, that we may ride all night unto our own castle.' And in like*

---

[1] these NOTES, by Captain Fletcher, were scribbled across the page: 'also know as Romulus Augustus, last Emperor of Rome.'

[2] 'Gorlois, King of Cornwall -- Kings were of every corner of the island -- large kings, lesser kings -- no Dukes yet.'

wise as she said so they departed, that neither the king nor none of his council were ware of their departing. All so soon as King Uther knew of their departing so suddenly, he was wonderly wroth. Then he called to him his privy council[3],

After reading the note, Wembley sat up. Fletcher had talked to Merlin? He traced his finger across the hand-written notes and read the passage again. That seemed to be what the note said!

and told them of the sudden departing of the duke and his wife.

Then they advised the king to send for the duke and his wife by a great charge; and if he will not come at your summons, then may ye do your best, then have ye cause to make mighty war upon him. So that was done, and the messengers had their answers; and that was this shortly, that neither he nor his wife would not come at him.

Then was the king wonderly wroth. And then the king sent him plain word again, and bade him be ready and stuff him and garnish him, for within forty days he would fetch him out of the biggest castle that he hath.

When the duke had this warning, anon he went and furnished and garnished two strong castles of his, of the which the one hight Tintagil, and the other castle hight Terrabil. So his wife Dame Igraine he put in the castle of Tintagil, and himself he put in the castle of Terrabil, the which had many issues and posterns out.[4] Then in all haste came Uther with a great host, and laid a siege about the castle of Terrabil. And there he pight many pavilions, and there was great war made on both parties, and much people slain. Then for pure anger and for great love of fair Igraine the king Uther fell sick. So came to the king Uther Sir Ulfius, a noble knight, and asked the king why he was sick. 'I shall tell thee,' said the king, 'I am sick for anger and for love of fair Igraine, that I may not be whole.' 'Well, my lord,' said Sir Ulfius, 'I shall seek Merlin, and he shall do you remedy, that your heart

---

[3] 'Uther sent straight for Merlin, by a messenger -- the rest is a clever fiction -- or so Merlin told me!'

[4] 'No one else but Merlin knew of every in and out of that castle.'

shall be pleased.' So Ulfius departed, and by adventure he met Merlin in a beggar's array, and there Merlin asked Ulfius whom he sought. And he said he had little ado to tell him. 'Well,' said Merlin, 'I know whom thou seekest, for thou seekest Merlin; therefore seek no farther, for I am he; and if King Uther will well reward me[5]*,*

Wembley stopped reading again, and re-read the note. It was so clearly and carefully written in the margin that you would think it important, as if having been slowly and particularly scribed. He flipped the pages with his thumb. The notes throughout the book were mostly hurriedly scratched onto the paper. But occasionally, there were notes like this one about Merlin. Wembley figured that he needed to pay attention to the legible ones and only mark the existence of the less legible ones.

and be sworn unto me to fulfil my desire, that shall be his honour and profit more than mine; for I shall cause him to have all his desire.' 'All this will I undertake,' said Ulfius, 'that there shall be nothing reasonable but thou shalt have thy desire.' 'Well,' said Merlin, 'he shall have his intent and desire. And therefore,' said Merlin, 'ride on your way, for I will not be long behind.'

Wembley knew this -- that Merlin was indeed not far behind. He was waiting for Uther at Tintagel with a plan; an impersonation. Then the siege began.

As Wem leaned back in his chair, pondering the note, again, there was a howl outside his window. The clouds had gathered and the sky had gone dark around the airplane. The plane lurched -- just a little, normal turbulence -- but it happened so closely in conjunction with the darkness appearing that Wembley thought it more than just coincidence. He peered out over the wing behind him and saw swirls of ... shapes -- like he had seen outside his own house. The rain started to batter against the windows as lightning flashed. He was drawn to look at the wing again where he saw two green eyes, not lights on the wing at all, but two distinct human eyes blinking. He imagined a sneer

---

[5] 'Merlin asked for no reward. He knew that he must help Arthur to be born. Igraine had to be Arthur's mother, because of who her daughters were. But this is what a good Keeper/Protector does, occludes the truth. I am the 9th Keeper -- there shall be only one more and our job will be to clarify for him who comes after us. The enemy already knows.'

just below them. He tried to put the eyes and the sneer to a face, but it would not materialize for him.

Then he was wet. The rain was pelting him as the winds buffeted his face and long dark hair. His slicker was flailing behind him like a magician's cape. He grabbed the edges and pulled it tight around him. As he clued in to his surroundings he found a ship's rail underneath his hands. He looked aft and saw a lone pilot at the wheel, and then he noticed a carved name just above the hatches of the quarterdeck, yellow letters against a darker, brown background: *The Lady Of The Lake*.

Just then the hatches from the quarter deck flapped up into the wind and almost closed themselves on the person trying to gain the upper deck. Coat collar high and hat pulled down against the gale the man was blown along the deck until he reached the stairs to the poop. He slid along the upper deck until he had his hands on the wheel. Wembley could not hear what was being said, but he knew that a conversation was happening for the pilot turned the wheel two points to port and the ship faced the gale straight on. The man -- Wembley could only assume it was the Captain of the ship ... The captain! He was on the Lady Of The Lake -- Captain Fletcher!

The Captain passed near to Wembley. As they came abreast of each other he said, "Get below, son, or ye'll blow overboard!"

Wembley heard himself saying, "But Father ..."

"Best do it, Reggie. We're almost home. I'd hate to lose you now!" and Horatio disappeared through the hatch.

Reggie? Reginald Fletcher! Horatio's son and only heir. The refuser of the duty of Keeper. Did he know Merlin before he was asked? That would tend to bias one's decision.

Wembley almost hit himself before he slid to the ladderway and below decks. Then Wembley thought he might as well have helped Reggie to jump overboard! He repented of that thought and was glad that he, and Reggie, were safely stowed. Wembley followed the wet footprints to his father's cabin. He heard voices within. He opened the door, or was that Reggie's action? What he saw flabbergasted Wembley, which fought with the smile that was fast encroaching on Reggie's face.

An older man with a long grey beard and long, scraggly grey hair, stood conversing with Horatio. He wore little half-moon spectacles and his hands were very animated.

"Well, we have an intruder!"

The Captain looked at his son. "Reggie! I've told you not to interrupt me. Especially when Merlin is here."

"But father ..."

Merlin laid a hand on the Captain's arm. "I sense that this is not only Reggie. Wembley, are you there?"

Wembley couldn't speak. Neither could Reggie. Reggie started to shake his head in the negative but Wembley managed to turn that into a nod of acknowledgment.

"I see. Another one of your 'DreamTravels'?"

"I don't think so, Sir," was all that Wembley could manage.

"Not yours? Well, it's not mine."

Wembley was staring at Merlin. "You have green eyes."

"Yes, I do." Merlin narrowed them at the boy.

"I am always seeing green eyes everywhere I go; especially in the 'DreamTravels'."

Merlin nodded and smiled.

"Were they yours, Myrddyn?"

"It's possible -- maybe -- some of them."

"If they're not yours, then whose are they?"

"I am not sure."

"Is this where you told the Captain everything I'm reading about?"

"This is one of the times I have visited him."

"Who is this strapping young lad, Merlin? He looks like my son, but he doesn't talk like him."

"He is a Protector from the future. He protects the final Keeper, your great-great-grandson, Russel Williams."

"Ah! I see. So it is best that he not hear too much?"

"That would be beneficial -- for him to not hear too much."

"Can you tell me one thing?" Wembley paused until he had the attention of both of the men in the room. "Why me?"

"It is your destiny."

"But I am not the Keeper," Wembley protested.

"You have another task."

"You can't tell me?"

"Foreknowledge of any task or possibility in one's life may preclude the attainment of that particular objective."

"In English?" Wembley was a little too stressed to sort that phrasing out.

"You can't know because it might affect the outcome."

"Why didn't you say so?"

"I thought I did."

"May I shake your hand?"

"Best not."

Wembley wasn't getting anywhere with Merlin and his cryptic answers, so he faced the Captain. "I live in your house, Captain. I really like it."

"I'm glad."

"I have everything that you packed away in your trunks safely stowed in the attic."

"Even the books," Merlin interposed.

"What books?" was the Captain's question.

"The volumes you have begun to write."

There was a look of incredulity on the Captain's face -- as well as on Wembley's.

"You know?" was Wembley's query.

"Yes. I see all. Well, this has turned into quite a report. But the Captain and I must continue and you -- both of you -- must leave us."

The room began to spin as Reggie/Wembley turned to go to the door. Then they turned again.

"Wait! You said Russel was to be the final Keeper! Why?"

But the rain was splattering against the glass of the window and Wembley was dry and firmly buckled into his seat and the copy of the book itself was on his lap. He flinched and almost spoke aloud.

"What is it, dear?"

Wembley took a breath and let his energies escape into the seat cushions, "Nothing."

Ma was more perceptive than that. "Another 'DreamTravel'?"

Wembley could only nod and run his fingers along the pages of the photocopy. Then he thought about it. He should not be depressed! He had just met Merlin! Hadn't he? Merlin knew him! He still wasn't entirely certain as to how all these things worked. He remembered everything, but did they really happen? Yes! They were not shadows of his imagination. They were alternate but corporeal realities. Or maybe historical realities within the spheres of his influence; but he could touch every single place while he was there. Hold the people or talk to them, [except shake hands with Merlin], feel the environment with his soul as well as his hands. It had to be something more solid than ethereal; more fact than fiction; more real than imaginary.

He didn't want to go to sleep, he had so much to read, but his eyes grew heavy quickly and he dozed. He felt a hand on his shoulder. He opened his eyes and saw his mother pointing to the tray in front of him. It had little squares and piles of something all over it. It was dinner. Food! But was it? He remembered a Charleton Heston movie he had seen once, during a long night where he couldn't sleep. The memory of that movie almost spoiled his appetite for whatever it was that was on that tray. It looked eerily familiar. A favorite comic lyric from one of his favorite musicals popped into his head. It ended with the words, "anything that is grey -- don't eat!" He surveyed the tray in front of him. There was nothing grey, so he picked up a plastic fork.

It wasn't as bad as the last time. In fact, it was quite edible. It even had taste to it. He longed to travel in a flying restaurant, like the old Pan Am Clippers that had traveled from the east coast to London over forty years ago. He'd heard about that from his Geography teacher. Fine food, well-prepared -- even a little wine if you were lucky -- and your parents agreed to it. He had tasted wine at a family gathering in Wales -- just last Christmas. It was good, but nothing to go and get drunk over!

The cake or torte was a little dry and he pushed his tray away. He wasn't tired anymore and he needed to read. He had about five hours left and he figured that he could finish the book before they landed. He dove in. He found almost as many words in the notes as in the original manuscript. Mallory had really done some inventing and the Captain called him on it. He heard the voice of the pilot announcing their arrival and he heard the landing gear going down. He looked down at the book. He was only half way through it. Too many notes. So many things to think about. He raced to read the last few verses of the section on Merlin and Vivien; he had not even remotely finished the book.

> *Then, in one moment, she put forth the charm*
> *Of woven paces and of waving hands,*
> *And in the hollow oak he lay as dead,*
> *And lost to life and use and name and fame.*
>
> *Then crying 'I have made his glory mine,* [6]
> *And shrieking out 'O fool!' the harlot leapt*
> *Adown the forest, and the thicket closed*
> *Behind her, and the forest echoed 'fool.* [7]

He heard the screech of the tires against the runway, felt the lurch of the mechanical bird touching down, and slipped the pages in his carryon. He laughed a little as he thought about Vivien, kind of like Russel thought about Evie at first, *What a ho!* It wasn't true, at least not about Evie. Evie had turned out to be very different from the person that she had portrayed herself to be. She was almost likeable. Thoughts of Evie led to thoughts of Brindi. He'd only been away from her for less than ten hours, and still he felt the pangs of absence.

---

[6] 'not a chance that any of the master's glory had touched this student.'

[7] 'because she did not conceive of what was in store for her for her betrayal.'

Everyone was unbuckling so he had to move or lose his parents in the mass of departing passengers. He bustled and jostled through customs. No problems there, except for the question of the Custom's Agent over the contents of Wembley's carryon. "What's an American bairn doing reading Mallory?"

"I was born here, in Wales, Sir, in Merthyr Tydfil."

"Better then: read Geoffrey of Monmouth."

"I have." Wembley walked through the gate with a smile on his face.

The agent nodded, knowingly and smiled back.

The family finally gained the car hire desks: Europcar, and its American invaders. Dylan Tewkes always chose Europcar. He didn't want to hire an American car. Back home he drove a Chrysler! He presented his ID and they were soon in their 4-door Jaguar coupe and driving to the Port Road, then to the A48. After fifteen minutes they were on the A470 and headed for Merthyr Tydfil. Wembley was jumping around in the back seat. Another half hour and he'd be home!

He still bounced but watched the countryside through the window. It was a little like Maine, but more rocky and hilly, all covered in snow at the moment. Another roundabout and the A4 was passed. As he looked to the southwest he saw storm clouds gathering. They looked angry.

"Da, I don't remember thunderheads in Wales. Do you?"

"Where, son?"

"To the left and behind us."

"They happen, but not very often. Better get there soon, eh?"

They zoomed along, barely feeling the road in their once-a-year luxury car. Wembley didn't fear about the price. He wasn't going to have to stop eating for the month of January, or anything. Da had a great job and they could afford it. Besides, why drive American when you don't have to?

The villages and hamlets of southern Wales flew by them as they wound up the valley of the River Taff. Remnants of the coal mining industry were all around and in the distance. The few still in operation were stark reminders of a proud and prosperous history as they pointed to the sky like steel and masonwork fingers asking God for a helping hand. Wembley looked below them and saw the River Taff beginning to ice over in places. Then the valley widened and the outskirts of the city of Merthyr Tydfill greeted them.

The exit from the high speed carriageway came quickly. The A4060 took them to another roundabout in the suburb of Abercanaid. Wembley loved roundabouts and he wondered why there were not that many of them back in the US. He was just about jumping through the roof as they drove up in front of the large white detached house with plenty of lawn and gardens off to the side. Dylan honked as they pulled into the drive and Gwyllym and Bronwyn appeared through the door while Wembley exploded from the car and ran to embrace his Grans.

The clouds, still angry in the southwest, pulsed and thrust themselves directly towards the house on the hill, unnoticed by any of the people below.

After endless hugs and kisses the family entered the pleasant cottage where Wembley again raced up the stairs -- two flights -- to his attic room. He had slept here for part of every Christmas and Summer vacation since he could remember. Everything was in its place. The soft, downy bed, the gable-ended window, his armoire and plenty of photos on the walls. It was warm and cozy as he settled into the bed's softness. His parents and Grans entered the room laughing. They had known right where to find him.

Then the sky darkened outside the attic gables and the screams hit as the little community of Abercanaid was shrouded in the storm that was far more than a disturbance of weather.

They were not able to leave the house for two days. It bothered Wembley, but at the same time it didn't disturb him. There was plenty to do, to talk about, to discover, in the house of his Grans -- even though he knew every inch of it. There were copies of the complete Dickens, Dumas and Defoe, Shakespeare, Shelley, and Swift on the bookshelves. He had read every word of every book -- more than once. He laid on his bed, feet pointed towards his windowed gable, winds fussing about outside, keeping him a prisoner. He looked up from his copy of Henry V at a noise from the darkness beyond the panes of glass. He dropped the book. What he saw was two green eyes staring in at him; like someone was seated on the roof outside. He scrabbled around and threw open the sash and screamed "Leave me alone!" He pulled the window back down and stood there, on his bed, fuming. The howling started again.

A head poked in the door, "Y'all right, Wembley?"

"Yes, Granda."

"Yer sure now?"

"Yes."

"But yer all wet!"

"I know."

"You opened the window in this gale?"

"I been in worse."

Gwyllym was not sure how to ease his grandson's humour at the moment. His mind clicked and clacked with a thousand thoughts at once. All he came up with was, "Best to not anger the fates."

"That's not who's out there!"

Gwyllym reacted to the strength of the response. Wembley had said, 'who.'

"Who, is it?"

"I'm not sure, but I've seen them almost every day for the last year!"

Wem threw Henry in the corner and paced across the room. Gwyllym came in and sat on the corner of the bed, placed his elbows on his knees and folded his hands together.

"I seen such a storm as this."

Wembley stood still and listened.

"I was just sixteen and in this very house. 1955 it was and it scared the bejeepers outta me." He paused, waiting for a response from Wembley, but there was none. He knew that the boy was scared, uneasy, confused. He had been, himself, all those years ago. "It only happened the oncet. But I've never forgot what I saw."

Wembley turned around and wiped a tear from his eye. He looked at his Granda, asking the question without words.

"Green eyes." The word fell like a hammer from his Granda's lips.

The answer hit him like another storm. Wembley wordlessly strode to the door. He ran down the stairs, then through the hall and down another flight of stairs. He screamed through the house all the way to the back door. He threw it open and ran out into the deluge of rain that almost drowned the path into the gardens. He headed for the center where there was a bench under a little wooden awning. He sat. He stood. He screamed, "Go away!"

He heard the crunch of booted feet on the gravel pathway. Granda, with a slicker and an umbrella, emerged through the curtain of rain to sit next to him on the bench.

The winds and wet continued to rage and howl around them. They sat there. Wembley couldn't even look at his Granda. He managed only to stare at his own shoes. He stood and flew out into the clamor of the elements.

"What do you want from me? Go away! Leave us alone!" He pounded his fists repeatedly against his thighs. He dropped down and picked up some gravel and stood again to throw it into the air. "Yer bloody awful. Damn you! Go away!"

Wembley collapsed into a heap as the cataclysm intensified around him. Lightning. Thunder. Rain. Howling, almost vocal winds. He felt two arms encircle him. They calmed him, even with the rage outside of their influence, they eased his fear in the moment. They didn't remove it. He felt that nothing could ever do that. He was able to stop adding to the flood dripping off of his face and onto the gravel. He wiped his eyes. He sat there, with the loving arms of his Granda -- the only one who could possibly know, anything about what he faced -- around him; keeping him safe.

Suddenly there was no rain. He and his Granda were still huddled together as if there were. They were dripping but the ground around them was dry. There was no snow, but green grass. Rocks were strewn about, growing out of the ground. Wales grew a bumper-crop of rocks. Wembley stood and found an outwork of stone piled in an ordered manner, not unlike an upthrust of rock, but this was man-made. He pressed his fingers against the stones.

"What's this, Granda?"

"Morlais."

"The castle?"

"What's left of it."

"We came here two summers ago."

"This is two summers ago."

"Wha ... How?"

"Yer Ma has told me everythin'. I figured that I could get us here in one of yer 'DreamTravels'."

"How would this help?"

"There's more to Morlais than the stones you saw ... see. Follow."

Wembley stood up and followed Gwyllym around the breastwork of wall and down into a steep ravine on the south side.

"The stones are from the 13th Century, but what is underneath is much older."

They rounded a curve in the ravine and a wall with an arched opening presented itself.

"We're going in?"

"Certainly."

"But you wouldn't let me before."

"You were just thirteen. Not ready for this."

"You said it was dangerous."

"It was -- then."

They ducked under the pointed archway and almost tumbled down a flight of uneven stone steps, and into what looked like a cathedral. The sunlight flooded through to parts of the underground crypt. There were pillars that extended up and out and across the ceiling in beautiful radiated patterns. The floor seemed higher than it would have been when the place was built. The columns had been taller, once. Now the heads of the two explorers almost touched the ceiling in places. They continued onward, Wembley awestruck at the intricate simplicity of the design, amazed at the fact that it was even still standing; hadn't been destroyed, ducked under another arch and Gwyllym shone his flashlight in a corner. Wembley moved over and saw that the floor had fallen away. Gwyllym motioned for him to descend.

"Really?"

"Go on."

Wembley lowered himself into the hole. His head was below the floor as he finally dropped to stand upright. He was surprised as his Granda, aged 72, dropped in next to him; then pointed the light down a tunnel -- much older and plainer than that through which they had just come -- Wembley figured that they must be deep under the center of the hill on which the castle was built, even though the entry arch was right under the former location of the southernmost tower.

"Who built this place?"

"Romans."

It was a barrel vault -- Wembley could see that plainly now as the flashlight illuminated it's length. He looked over to his Granda, whose eyes twinkled in the dim light of the torch. Wembley's smile spread from ear to ear. He walked down the corridor with Gwyllym, stopping at the end, waiting for his Granda to shine the torch into the darkness.

"You won't believe what you see, but it's true."

Wembley's eyes bugged out. Gwyllym laughed.

"You're serious!"

"I'm always serious when I laugh."

As the torch shone into the huge underground chamber, it was found to be empty except for a small altar in its center. The light was reflected and refracted around the cave by the shiny rocks on its walls. Gwyllym walked in and then over to the altar. Wembley followed, spellbound by the crystals. His fingers touched their glittering surfaces. No glyphs, no paintings or mosaics. Just crystals. He didn't know what he had expected but it wasn't this. Gwyllym harumphed. He stood by the altar and pointed. It wasn't really an altar, it was too short -- it only came up to mid-thigh. Wembley reluctantly left the shining walls and looked down at the top of the small stone. It had a narrow diamond-shape cut into the top of it. Gwyllym knelt at one side of it and shined the light of his torch on an inscription.

"Read it with me."

The words were carved simply, in a blocky, Roman type of script. It was difficult to read, but Wem gave it a try.

"He who ... pulleth thysse ... sworde from thysse stone ..."

He didn't have to finish reading, he knew this by heart!

"is borne to be rightful King of Llogres. Granda, what? How? When?"

"The stone. The famous one!"

"Yeah, I see."

"By magic and ox cart, I think."

"Okay."

"Just after Arthur was crowned."

"But it was at Winchester!"

"Yes, it was."

"But ..."

"Merlin brought it here."

"How did you ..."

"I've never had a 'DreamTravel', until today, but I've been given visions; I saw things happen, but I was never a part of them like you have been; more of a peeping Tym.

'You mean a peeping Gwyllym." They laughed. "Why haven't you shown this to everyone? It would prove the story!"

"That's just the problem. Everything is safer if there's a mystery to it. We're all safer. Besides the crystals would have been stolen."

"You're not a Keeper."

"No."

"You're a Protector?"

"A lot like you."

"But ... "

"I couldn't say or do anything until I was certain that it would touch you."

Wembley kneeled down and ran his hands over the stone. "Whoah! This is the coolest thing you've ever shown me!"

"It's the rightest secret I've ever kept."

"This is amazing. Everything I've ever read -- and it all gets straightened out by this one ... artifact."

"Not all, but it gets us in the right track."

"What do you mean?"

"I had another vision."

"And?"

"We have a Quest to go on."

"Like the Knights of the Round Table?"

"Just like."

Then Wembley felt that he had to make a revelation. "I am a member of the Knights of the Round Table. I was inducted last month."

"By whom?"

"Merlin himself."

"A 'DreamTravel'?"

"Yes. Along with Russel, Brindi and Mary Williams. We were officially made Protectors."

"Was that when Russel accepted the position of Keeper?"

"Yes."

"Do you wish it was you?"

"Not really. My life is strange enough without having to be a Keeper."

"Good choice."

"What do we do now?"

"I brought you here not only to see the stone, and the crystals…"

"Is this the Crystal Cave?" It was a revelation to Wembley.

Gwyllym nodded, then continued, "…but to tell you of our Quests. There is a magic that enchants and protects this place. We cannot be overheard here. Merlin's magic is stronger because of the crystals."

"So no one else knows about that hole in the floor?"

Gwyllym shook his head. "Only a Protector can see it. To all others it's a closed door."

"Where are we going?"

"I don't know it all yet. I get it a piece at a time."

"Where to, first then?"

"We'll find something at Caerleon."

"Why?"

"It was Camelot, you know."

"Geoffrey of Monmouth was right? He let out the secret?"

"He was denounced for the idea; ridiculed and reviled. He knew when to let the truth out and when to keep it hidden. Truth is stranger than fiction, sometimes, especially when you want to keep a secret."

"What will we find there?"

"It will be the first of five quests; that much I know."

"When?"

"I have been told that we must wait -- until you are sixteen -- to begin."

"Next summer? That's forever away!"

"But you will be ready, then -- stronger, more powerful!"

"Powerful?"

"I can't say anymore. But know that it will come -- and soon."

Wembley looked down at the stone. "I don't believe this. I mean, I believe it, but…I don't believe it."

His Granda laughed. "Most of what Protectors and Keepers do is unbelievable."

"What did it look like?"

"What did what look like?"

"Excalibur."

"I only saw it through a hazy vision, but it was the most wonderful object I ever observed. It was all encrusted with grime and vine before Arthur placed his hand on the hilt. Then it lit up and it shone with the magic of a million years as he slid it out of this mouth, here, with the greatest of ease, and raised it to the sky. No other could have budged it from the stone! It looked like it weighed less than a feather -- and Arthur was only twelve. Either he was strong beyond his years, or it was all magic."

"Maybe both?"

"Could be. Then the vision shifted to a cart with a wrapped object being drawn by two oxen. Then the cart stopped here and Merlin enshrouded the stone with some sort of magic warding and levitated it into this room through the tunnel, which went all the way out to the bottom of the hill in those days. Then the vision closed and I was alone in my room."

"Which room?"

"Yours."

"You slept in the attic, too?"

"Never anywhere else."

Wembley threw his arms around his Granda, who welcomed his embrace. The crypt around them began to shimmer and disappear. Wembley suddenly felt wet. His Granda put up the umbrella and rushed the two of them into the house. Gran Bronwyn and Ma Marged ushered their separate charges to their own rooms and told them to get out of their wet clothes. No talk. No excuses. No nuthin' but business was what the female Welsh demeanor demanded of the two wet males who must have been out of their minds!

Dylan chuckled at the predicament of his father and his son. He remembered many a time when his Ma would strip him naked in the kitchen because he came in wet to the bone, rub him down with a big towel, then set him by the fire to warm with a cup of cocoa or tea. No public nakedness today! *Thank heavens!*

Wembley, still wet in his room, chuckled to himself over the antics of his 'women' and the memory of the stories that his Da and Granda had told him. As he dropped his soaked clothes and picked up the towel that his Ma had thrown at him before she left the room, he looked at the storm outside, still scraping and clawing at the window. Then he saw those two green eyes. He imagined that he saw a smile below them. He raged to the window, naked as a jaybird, and drew the curtains shut. Then he picked up his towel and dried himself quickly, slid into his pajamas, slippers and housecoat -- his Grans insisted on a housecoat -- and went downstairs to join Granda and Da -- in similar attire -- and the women, and cocoa and tea by the fire.

"I had a dream last night, Granda!"

"Another 'DreamTravel'?"

"No. Just a dream."

"I had one, too."

"Tell me yours, Granda!"

"Merlin gave me the words to protect the entire town, or wherever it is that we go, so this storm stays away."

Wembley was openmouthed at his Granda. "Me too!"

"We'd better get at it!"

Wembley scrambled to the car -- Granda's Mini-Cooper. His Grans were so cool! "Can I drive?"

"You have to be seventeen, here, son."

"I know."

Granda stopped. Looked Wembley in the eye. Wembley could not look back. "You're not even sixteen. You know that the more correct decisions you make, the more powerful your magic can grow?"

"No. I didn't know that."

"Well, now you do."

"Sorry, Granda. But you told me you drove at sixteen."

"Ah! Sorry! They changed the law. Too many accidents. Not me, of course. Never had one. I'd hate to be killed by my own Grandson."

"I'd never do that. I guess the British Government is braver than the Americans, though."

"How's that?"

"Too many teens back home would revolt and pull everything down around their ears if they took our cars away."

Gwyllym chuckled as they buckled in. They pulled out into the roadway and headed for the outskirts of the village. They drove as best they could all the way around the outer limits of town. They muttered the incantation each and every meter of the way.

"*Spell of magic protect this place. Let no dark magic pass.*"

They heard howls of anger raised at them but the storm receded and eventually disappeared.

As Wembley settled back down through the sunroof of the car, even the dampness of the interior seemed to have disappeared. "Whoa! The meteorologists back home would kill for a spell like that one."

"I'm sure it doesn't work on real storms, just the magical kind."

"You're probably right. Are you sure that's all this was?"

Gwyllym looked around them. "With the clear skies now -- yes."

"How long?"

"Who knows."

"Merlin does!"

Grandfather and grandson cracked up at Wembley's little joke.

"Up for a little drive?"

"How little?"

"To the seacoast."

"West?"

"No. We're goin' to the Baltic! Of course, west."

"Sure."

They cut through the Breton Beacons, where Wembley had spent part of many a summer hiking, climbing, biking and loving Wales, and then headed northwest -- out across the wide wastes of western Wales. Aberystwyth was Granda's destination, but he left Wembley to guess about it. Wembley didn't even bother guessing because he was so enraptured by the passing, but snow-laden scenery. The road climbed up a small mountain ridge and down into the valleys of Cardiganshire -- known as Ceredigion during the 6th Century. That all important century; the time of their first known ancestor -- Gwyllym Gryffudd. To Wembley the two hour drive felt like it had taken fifteen minutes. He had seen a lot of Wales but not this part. Motoring along the seaside for several miles they saw the crags and towers of the small seaport rise in the near distance.

"Where, Granda, Where?"

"There's two sites. The first is Aberystwyth itself. The castle here is not ours, it was built much later. But the land belonged to Gwyddno Garanhir, who was probably the grand-father of Gwyllym.

"Gwyllym Gryffudd?"

"The very one."

"You're named after him?"

"That I am."

"Who am I named after?"

"You're an original."

Whatever it was that Wembley was thinking, or was about to say, was stopped by the view of the tower of Castle Aberystwyth. Wembley started bouncing.

They pulled up into the car park of the castle environs. Incomplete, some of it just piles of rubble, it was still majestic, especially as it bordered the sea directly. They walked the ruins and Wembley was once again enchanted. The spray of the sea occasionally came up and over the breakwater, misting them with its icy cold.

"The story goes that Gwyddno was being visited by the son of the King of Dyfed. A huge feast, lasting for days was underway. A monstrous storm -- a surge from the sea -- came upon them and began to sweep the castle over the cliffs. Gwyddno and his people fled. The Prince was lost with most of his company. Sixteen seaside castles, all across the land, were destroyed by that wave -- so it is said. And it drove Gwyddno from his beloved Cantref y Gwaelod; the land given him by the King of Dyfed."

"Tsunami?"

"Maybe. Or maybe the beginnings of the same types of storms that follow you."

"You mean this spray?"

"You never know."

"Cantref y Gwaelod, you said?"

"Yes."

"Never heard of it."

"It's been known by many names, Llanbadarn-Vawr, Llan-Badarn Gaerog, Tan-y-Castell, Aberrheidol even before ..."

"Aberystwyth?"

"From what is known, yes."

"But because of the Keepers we don't really know what is known, do we?"

"It's all shadow, mist, and mystery, son."

"This place is huge, Granda."

"One of the largest in Wales."

"How come this tower is still standing? It's almost complete."

"Must've been built better than the rest, eh? This way."

"Where're we going?"

"Cliffs."

"Why? I want to explore the castle."

"It's not the castle that's important -- at least not to us."

"But it's cool."

"That it is." Gwyllym just couldn't deny Wembley the right to explore. "Fine, then. We finish the castle and then the cliffs?"

"Thanks, Granda."

After wandering about the ruins and poking and questioning, Wembley stopped. He was standing next to a strange configuration of stones. There was a central stone, with others surrounding it in courses of concentric circles. "This looks like something magical."

"It is. But few know of it. It is a circle for a Gorsedd."

"A festival of Bards?"

"Yes. Some think it was laid there after the castle was built. Others think it was there from the times of Taliesin."

"The one who sang in Arthur's court? Sang of Urien and Dyfed and Maelegwyn?"

"That's him!"

"What do you think about it?"

"I think that it is the very reason the castle was built! To protect and hide these stones."

A cold wind whipped in off the sea and chilled Wembley and Gwyllym. Wembley shivered and then tensed. He looked up and saw that there were clear skies and no green eyes, so he relaxed.

"So why did we come here, Granda?"

"There were five castles in this town on various spots. And a most important one, to us, further inland."

"So?"

"Someone must've thought this an important place." He pointed to the circle of stones. "A magical place."

Wembley did not want to think about what his Granda was getting at. But there was no other conclusion. He'd read the journal and the annotated Mallory. It hadn't all made sense at the time, but some of the information was coming back to him. "Everything ties to Myrddyn?"

"Everything important."

"What about the cliffs?"

"We finished here?"

"For now, Granda. Thanks."

Gwyllym walked away and Wembley followed. They strolled down the bulwark holding the town in against the sea and soon passed from the man-made cliffs to those of the natural dark slate of the region -- sharp and jagged; picturesque. They found a stairway down to the beach -- the pebble kind of beach, not much sand at all -- and walked for about half a mile. Wembley didn't care about their destination, he was by the sea. He was so intent upon the water that he didn't notice that his Granda had stopped.

"Wembley?"

"Yeah, Granda?"

Gwyllym pointed to the cliffs. Wembley looked. They were pockmarked with indentations.

"Caves?"

Gwyllym smiled and nodded.

Wembley started to run.

"Ah! Wait!" Wembley stopped and turned around. Gwyllym pointed. "I think you'll find that one to be of particular interest."

Wembley followed the direction indicated and was soon standing in the opening of a cave that was not much taller than he was. He stepped in and Gwyllym went past him into the darkness. The light of a torch preceded them as they crept along.

"How far in does it go?"

'No one knows for sure."

"You're kidding?"

Gwyllym raised his eyebrows.

"I guess you're not."

They walked for about five minutes, dodging and ducking the occasional sharp downthrusts of slate. The floor was wet. The sea was the master in this tunnel.

"When does the tide come in?"

"Not for hours yet."

More walking. Not much to see but Wembley maintained his patience. Granda had never disappointed him before. Then the passageway opened up. Wembley noticed that the floor was dry here.

"Tide can't come up this far. We're under a hill."

"What's its name?"

"Brygraven Dioddau."

"The Mount of Suffering?"

"Yer Welsh has not suffered."

"I try. Who suffered?"

"It was a place of dark magic. Still is."

Wembley's eyes enlarged in the torchlight. Then Gwyllym stepped into the cavern. A moan issued from the darkness ahead, giving rise to a green glow that illuminated the entire cave. Wembley watched intently as the figure of a woman emerged from the floor at the center of the cave that was filling with the greenish aura. The only thing she was wearing was that green light. Her noticeable attributes captivated Wembley immediately, until he saw that her eyes were green and her hair was red. Then he looked away, puzzled, but was soon drawn back to the vision. She hovered in the air, not moving, but wailing.

"She's harmless. She has no power over Protectors or Keepers. But she does manage to scare the locals away."

"She's beautiful."

"Aye, she is that. But dark."

"Scary ... but hot."

"Spoken like a Tewkes!"

Gwyllym laughed as he strode past Wembley again.

"Where to now?"

"Come along."

Wembley managed, somehow, to take his eyes off that captivating figure and follow his Granda into the gloom of another tunnel. She screamed as they proceeded. She writhed and flew at them but could not touch them. The light behind them was extinguished, along with the noise, as they stepped out of the cave and into the corridor; one that had changed from slate to limestone. The walls were chalky, the ceiling blackened with the scorch marks of fire. Soon they were into a smaller chamber. Gwyllym stopped and pointed the light at an object sitting on a rock shelf across the room.

Wembley looked and didn't believe what he was seeing. It was a quarter-staff, but not a plain one. It was white and carven with filigree and runes. It shone like a long beacon as its whiteness reflected the light of the torch.

Wembley didn't know what to say. He looked at the staff, then at Gwyllym and back at the staff. "Are you kidding?"

Gwyllym remained silent.

"The Erwydd ap Emrys?"

Gwyllym only smiled. Wembley reached out.

"Don't touch it!" Wembley looked at him. "You'll be shocked right into the next life. There's more power in that staff than in all the wands ever wielded in the world."

"Why are we here? This is really cool Granda, but why?"

"You need to know what exists and where it is located. You may need it sometime."

"I may need this staff?"

"It's a possibility."

"Where to now?"

Gwyllym nodded to the tunnel behind them.

"Nothing more here?"

"Just the Erwydd."

"Then, I guess its back to Bodicea?"

"Who?"

"The scary naked lady."

"Naked ladies scare ya, son?"

"Well, that one does." That's all Wembley would commit to.

They were greeted at the end of the tunnel by Bodicea, screaming and ranting at them about having defiled the shrine. It was in Welsh and Wembley didn't catch all of it, mostly just the curse words and the rude words, which seemed not to have changed much from whatever era it was in which she had lived. They exited the cavern of suffering, as Wembley thought of it. Then it hit him. It wasn't a cave to make others suffer. It was a cave to make her, Bodicea, suffer. He laughed as he walked into the entrance tunnel and the light and noise winked out. It's funny how names come about!

"Who was she, Granda?"

"You don't know?"

"Not really."

"That was Nimue. This was her punishment."

"But didn't she cure Arthur at Lyonesse, or Avalon?"

"Yes, she did. But she did a lot of other things later that angered the powers of the Erwydd."

"So she is imprisoned in that cave?"

"Her spirit is. No one knows where her body is. Maybe rotting with Arthur at Avalon."

Their course turned downward, noticeably and a small point of light appeared in front of them. Gwyllym switched off the flashlight. They were greeted by the cold spray off the waves of an incoming tide. They stayed close to the cliffs and trotted up the first set of stairs that presented themselves.

"I thought you said that it would be hours until the tide came in!"

"I did."

"Well?"

"Time alters around the staff of Myrddyn. Minutes can stretch into hours, or days compress into seconds."

"Oh. What time is it?"

He glanced at his watch. "Noon! Hungry?"

"Starved!"

They hopped in the Cooper and stopped at a local pub. The best food in any town or village was not in any 'restaurant,' but in the pubs. The savoury Welsh stew called Tatws Pum Munud (five minute potatoes) was more than filling. It warmed even the capillaries of Wembley's body, like nothing else could. His favorite part was the bacon! He sopped up the liquid with a crusty piece of tasty bread. His mom had tried for years to make the dishes he loved from his homeland -- and she did very well with inferior American ingredients -- but Wembley was in heaven here.

Finished and ready for the drive -- about 20 minutes at the most -- they sprang onto the B4340 to be greeted by a never plowed road. The ruts in the snow gave enough purchase for the tires and they crept along. About a half an hour later they pulled into the tiny village of Ystrad Meurig. They parked in front of the school and walked up the lane and turned to the south. Within a minute they were standing on the slope of a hill that had a large motte on its west side. It did not look like a totally natural depression in the ground. It wasn't. It was part of the defensive mechanism of the 6th century fort of Ystrad Meurig. The snow matted down the grass and revealed a little more than just the rounded hill. There were places where rock foundations showed through. One of the outlines was square, another was rounded, or better, curved.

"You know Taliesin?"

"Not personally, Granda." A stern look from the man prompted another response. "But I have read his poems and songs in the Mabinogion."

"There was a square tower here. It was three stories high and known as Henblas, the home of Elffin ap Gwyddno."

"He's the one who found Taliesin and named him."

"Yes."

"How does that apply to us?"

"Taliesin was the name given the boy by Elffin, when he was found at Lake Tegid. But his real name was Gwyllym Gryffudd."

"You're sure?"

"Yes, and so is Captain Fletcher."

"Oh! Yeah!" The light dawned. Now what he had read about that all made sense. Mallory had speculated a lot, on purpose, and covered the tracks of Taliesin well with that story of Ceridwen, Tegid Foel and Gwion Bach. It was a fun story -- but only another mis-direction.

"So who was Gwyllym's father?"

"We don't really know that, for sure. But Taliesin was Gwyllym. That I know. And Henblas is where it was discovered that he could sing."

"So, this is where he grew up?"

Before Gwyllym could nod they both heard a click behind them.

"Got offa my land'r there'll be less o' ya for the next one to shoot."

Wembley and Gwyllym said nothing but turned and walked off. Once on the laneway, Wembley opened up. "The locals aren't very friendly, Granda."

"I guess not."

"Anything hidden here?"

"No magical staves or stones, no."

They hurried to their car and Gwyllym drove around to the point where the road touched near the bottom of the hill. The man with the shotgun was gone. They stayed there and looked back on the property.

"Our family owned it before his did."

"That may be true -- but possession is nine-tenths of the law -- at least for some people. Elffin was King here, but Taliesin left at the age of thirteen, to sing for Maelegwyn, and never returned home, at least not to live."

"Didn't he end up at Arthur's Court?"

"In Caerleon, yes."

"Why lions, Granda? There aren't any lions in England."

"Nor are there dragons, yet look at the flag of Wales -- a red dragon on a green and white field. A lion has been on the crests of the most noble families and of the Kings of Britain for centuries; most of England, or Llogres, in the 6th Century was Welsh; from Yorkshire to Cornwall -- even London. Before the incursion of the Saxons. The crest of the Pendragon family also contained a Red Lion, not a dragon."

"Where did the dragon come from?"

"The Dragon Legion of the late Romans was stationed near Hadrian's Wall. Uther was Romulus Augustus."

"Yes. So Arthur was son of both the dragon and the lion, and his Caerleon was the Castle of The Lion?"

"Exactly."

They heard a shot -- the report of a rifle -- and Gwyllym slipped the car into gear and they drove off.

"The English Lion, Leon ap Prydain: Henry V; Richard; Arthur, The Lion of Summer; all lions. And Camelot was the Kingdom of Summer."

"Wish it was summer now!"

"Don't wish too hard or, with your abilities and history, you could go back there."

"Good point."

They drove in silence. Gwyllym kept his eyes successfully on the road but Wembley let his eyelids close. He dreamed of lions and dragons. He dreamed of both of them fighting on the same side against their enemies. He saw battles, bloody and raw. He heard the wondrous words spoken by Henry on the battlefield.

"Once more unto the breach, dear friends, once more; Or close the wall up with our English dead!"

At least that was Shakespeare's retelling of it, that Wembley had recently read. Time and place were shifting. Images blurring in and out of each other like a collage in constant movement. The play came alive in front of him.

"For he today that sheds his blood with me shall be my brother; be he ne'er so vile, this day shall gentle his condition: and gentlemen in England now abed shall think themselves accurst they were not here; And hold their

manhoods cheap whiles any speaks that fought with us upon Saint Crispin's day."

Suddenly he was not on a battlefield but on a stage. It was no longer a dream. He was, himself, standing on a stage.

"Alexander!"

Wembley looked around.

"Master Cooke -- come hither."

Wembley walked toward the voice. Obviously, this time, he was Alexander Cooke. Whoever that was!

"You little knave!" and the older man with longish hair wrestled with Wembley/Alexander for a few seconds. Alexander seemed to take over the conversation, so Wembley followed along.

"What part this time, William?"

"You'll not be playing Katherine -- you're voice is too low."

"But they loved my Juliet and my Helena. Is there a part for me at all?"

Wembley could tell, from the feelings inside of him, that the -- boy -- was fake pouting. What a little actor!

Shakespeare gently chided the boy. "Fear not, gentle Alexander. I have written a role expressly for you. No one else could assay it."

Wembley felt a smile spread across their face. "No one?" he heard himself say.

Wembley thought, *No one? Of course, no one else could play it. No one else in the company was fourteen!* The two other 'boys' were twelve and the next youngest actor to Alexander was 20. Now he remembered! English class and their study of Shakespeare's Company and the way the play was staged in 1600.

"No one, you little devil!"

"Who is it?"

"I call him simply, The Boy."

"Sounds like a bit part."

"He is the foil of the comics, the very conscience of the play. He calls all things into question and we see people through him much more clearly. He is in four major scenes with two major soliloquies. Do this for me and your next role will be Romeo himself."

"I'll do the role if you promise me Romeo in the fall."

"You shall have it!"

"Who will be my Juliet?"

"How about Nathan? Young Master Field would be perfect opposite you."

"I agree."

Alexander liked Nathan. They were the best of friends, even though they had, until recently, competed for the women's roles. One role that Nathan had never played was Puck. That role had belonged to Alexander since he was ten.

"In ten years I could do Henry himself!"

"Maybe fifteen?" countered Shakespeare.

"A promise?"

"A promise!"

Alexander grabbed at the sheaves of paper that William was holding. He shuffled through them and began to read.

> *As young as I am, I have observed these three swashers. I am boy to them all three:*

Then he began to voice the words and strut the stage.

> *"but all they three, though they would serve me, could not be man to me; for, indeed, three such antics do not amount to a man."*

Alexander laughed. "I like this!"

"I thought you might!" was the playwright's reply.

> *"For Bardolph -- he is white-liver'd and red-faced; by the means whereof a' faces it out, but fights not. For Pistol -- he hath a killing tongue and a quiet sword;"*

Alexander and Wembley snickered at the double meaning of the line.

> *"by the means whereof a' breaks words, and keeps whole weapons. For Nym -- he hath heard that men of few words are the best men; and therefore he scorns to say his prayers, lest a' should be thought a coward: but his few bad words are match'd with as few good deeds; for a' never broke any man's head but his own, and that was against a post when he was drunk."*

"This is wondrous good, William. Every word has its opposite and I can play those. The jokes will have the groundlings rolling on the floor." After reading silently for a few seconds, Alexander then began to mince across the stage like a thief.

> *"They will steal any thing, and call it purchase. Bardolph stole a lute-case, bore it twelve leagues, and sold it for three-half-pence. Nym and Bardolph are sworn brothers in filching; and in Calais they stole a fire-shovel: I knew by that piece of service the men would carry coals."*

"I'm a regular insult, I am!" and Wembley giggled at Alexander's delight in the role. He saw it all now, through the unbelievably perceptive mind of this boy actor of five hundred years ago. The role was a commentary on the world, really. A social commentary, written for the groundlings who would know about men of the world, and for those in the seats for they were such-like gentlepersons and engaged in similar activities as these that The Boy criticized. He leaned on one of the posts of the outer below, and looked around as if picking the dirt out from under his fingernails with a knife. He continued reading and picking.

> *"They would have me as familiar with men's pockets as*
> *their gloves or their handkerchers: which makes much against*
> *my manhood, if I should take from another's pocket to put into*
> *mine; for it is plain pocketing-up of wrongs."*

"So, I, as a boy, am more of a man than them all?" This was a pleasant thought for a boy who had just recently graduated from playing the parts of girls in the theatre. Wembley sensed the boy's joy.

"More of a man than any but Henry himself."

"I will rail on the winds with this role and give James trouble as Henry!" He looked down at the page. There was one more line. He walked calmly to the front of the stage and kneeled down as if talking to someone in the audience.

> *"I must leave them, and seek some better service: their*
> *villainy goes against my weak stomach, and therefore I must*
> *cast it up."*

Alexander pretended to wretch and heave and William was laughing and cheering. Applause came from others in the theatre who had been practicing their roles, but stopped at the masterful improvisation of the youth. They bowed to the Young Master and he returned their courtesies.

"That was ever so wise and funny," came from a very young voice. "You will be brilliant!"

"Thank you, Nat. I can't wait to hear your French and watch you woo James!"

Both boys busted up at that mental picture. Wembley, still trapped in another's body, but still learning -- soaking it all up like a sponge -- saw that there was just as much talent and contemplation in the preparation of a role, and that maybe even more skill was necessary for an actor in the 1600s, than was necessary in today's players. We, as moderns, tend to think we are superior in every way to those who came before us. Wembley was beginning to see that this was not the case. He would take what Alexander had demonstrated for him and see if he could not add to it for his own presentation. However, if he couldn't bring anything new, what he had learned would provide a solid performance, anyway. Talk about research! How could he explain it to his teacher?

William came forward and embraced both of his boys and complimented them. The boys, including Wembley, scampered off the stage. They almost bumped into James Burbage, one of the greatest actors of the day, and part owner with Shakespeare in the company. He would be playing Henry and Nat would have to woo him as Katherine!

"Hello, James!

"Hello, boys!"

The boys giggled as they crossed to the seats. Wembley sat in one of the stalls, still in Alexander's body, reading over and over the lines he was given. He heard the booming voice of James Burbage and looked up to the stage. He heard the words, *"... that fought with us upon Saint Crispin's day."* He was almost sorry that he had been reading his own lines when he should have been watching. It wasn't often that you got to see the Morgan Freeman or the Dustin Hoffman of another day preparing for a role. Those words made him feel queasy. He held his stomach, leaned to the right and fell against the small body of his friend ... Gwyllym Tewkes, still driving and now swerving across the road because of Wembley's added weight on his arm.

"Sit up, son!"

"Sorry, Granda. I ..." He exhaled and sat back watching the headlights come at him on the other side. It was dark.

"Another travel?"

"Yeah."

"Where to this time?"

"The Globe Theatre."

"Met the man?"

"You could say that. Where are we?"

"Just turning up the hill into Abercanaid."

"I missed it!"

"Missed what?"

"Wales!"

"You saw it on the way out! Wales in the light is much better than Wales in the dark!"

"You're funny, Granda." Wembley laughed.

Christmas in Merthyr Tydfil. Everything else that happened, before or after, was icing on that sweet cake. The anticipation of Christmas Eve; as if that anticipation had not been building since even before they left Maine, was keenest on that night before Christmas. Not because of the gifts that the morning would bring, but because of the feelings that Wembley had always felt -- that maybe had been inculcated in him since he was very small -- that family meant everything. The fire and the cocoa on Christmas Eve had been a tradition since before they left Wales. They gathered together in their pajamas and housecoats and sang "Adeste Fidelis" in Latin, while Ma played the piano and sang with them. Then they read the chapters from the Bible -- from Luke -- each taking a turn, each apportioned so many verses, from oldest to youngest. Wembley always read of the angels and the birth. Then there was staring into the flames and recounting the stories and joys of Christmases past.

The morning dawned bright and white with a twinkling in the dusting of new-fallen snow. Breakfast must be had -- before anything -- the most important meal, in many Welsh houses, it was the tradition, Christmas or not. With eggs and bacon and potatoes and hotcakes, the day began, and then came alive.

Like one of his favorite books, <u>A Child's Christmas In Wales</u>, he too loved the snow and the music and the fires and the ghost stories and the sleeping adults and the blazing pudding, just like he had enjoyed for every Christmas he could remember. The book was more than a remembrance by another. It was a revelation about all Welsh boys and their families. And it was true! His favorite book had always helped him to relish the time his family spent together. It taught him that things were meant to have meaning and a feeling associated with them. Memories are good things; whether they're of exploring castles and caves or seasides, or sitting in front of a roaring fire and tearing open your presents so that you could hear the crackle that the paper made in the flames, or just listening to your mother singing her favorite Christmas songs as the dinner was prepared. Memories were a huge part of the life of Wembley Tewkes. What he was finding was that there were many kinds of memories available to him.

He was only just beginning to appreciate them all when the doorbell rang.

CHAPTER FIFTEEN
A Fluke of Magic

"Evie. What are you doing here?"

"Just like you. I'm Welsh."

"Griffiths. I should have known. But you don't have parents."

"I told you they died, not that I didn't know who they were!"

"My bad. Sorry. So, you just happen to be from Merthyr Tydfil -- the place where I was born?"

"No, actually my Grandparents are from near Casnewyedd."

"Newport?" She nodded. "Then, why are you here?"

"Because you said you were coming here."

"Why aren't you with your grandparents?"

"Because they're dead, too!"

It came out a little too forcefully, and Evie was sorry for that, but nothing could be done about it now. They both stood there in silence.

"I'm sorry, Evie. But this is a little too much of a coincidence. I ... it's difficult."

"And Brin wouldn't approve."

"Maybe, maybe not. You're traveling alone?"

"I'm older than I look."

"You look eighteen or nineteen."

"Well, then I look just the right age."

Evie looked at Wembley, who stood there fumbling with his fingers. She leaned in and quickly kissed him -- on the lips.

"I love you, Wembley."

Wembley was silent; felt a little angry, a little betrayed? "I know."

"Well?"

"My heart, my mind and my soul are with Brindi."

Evie was ... well, she looked like someone had kicked her dog. "You don't like me?"

"You're my friend ... *I hope*." The last two words were an unvoiced thought. "Look, Evie, I'm flattered and all that you wanted to see me ..."

"But ..."

"But, I -- I don't feel comfortable with you ... like this. And that kiss was somewhat out of line."

"Can I see you again, before you leave?"

"Maybe. I have a lot of things to do and ..." he hated to say this next one "... a family to do them with."

Evie's eyes were tearing up.

"I don't want to hurt you, Evie."

"Then don't."

"Christmas is my time with my Grans. We do lots of things together and I want those memories to be just of my Ma and Da, my Grans and me."

"Secret?"

"No. Private. I have a life and much of my life doesn't concern you." He could tell that he had really hurt her. "Part of it does."

"Which part?"

"School. Friends. But you're not family."

Evie bristled. The brush was stiff and harsh. "And Brindi is?"

"More than you can know."

"More private stuff?"

"No, this time it is a secret!" And Wembley smiled. "A secret I have to keep, or people could get hurt."

"Who?'

"You, for one."

"Oh." She began to see just how complicated Wembley's life was; she was, unknown to him, a part of that complication and she thought that there was nothing she could do about that; it was as it had to be. "See you at home?"

"This is my home." He had never admitted that to anyone before.

"Well, then see you in Yarmouth?"

"Count on it," he said with a smile.

She brightened a little. If only she could tell Wembley the secrets she knew! Not a possibility, for she was certain that they would conflict with Wembley's secrets, which could be disastrous. For both of them.

As the outer door closed behind Evie, Wembley felt a little more secure -- he breathed a sigh of relief -- but he wasn't relieved, he felt threatened. His shoulders slumped. How did she get here and why? That anger that rankles and rises under the skin began to inflame the body of Wembley Tewkes. He suddenly burst through the house and ran up the stairs, two at a time, to his attic room. The still calmness of Christmas was even more stilled as the grown-ups looked at each other, wondering what could have set Wembley off like that. Wembley hadn't let Evie in the parlor, they had talked in the vestibule, so no one else knew that she had even been there. Which suited Evie's purposes just fine.

Wembley rose up off the bed. He was still asleep, but hovering. The comforter and sheet were torn away as if by an invisible hand. The room was full of an unnatural light. It wrapped around Wembley and dissolved his pajamas, leaving him naked. There was a wicked laugh and a flash of green from outside the window. Wembley found himself submerged in a bright turquoise world and suddenly awake and gasping for breath as his gills slowly took over. He was alone again.

Wembley tried to remember how he got here. He had been asleep. But then, without really waking up, he remembered feeling very cold just before feeling very wet. Had he been naked before he got here? That was a disturbing thought! His nakedness now seemed like nothing to him. Just as he was accustoming himself to the surroundings, not as difficult as it was at first, his lack of attire seemed insignificant.

Until Briony and Shane appeared in the water from above -- as if they had dived in. They settled to the bottom to find Wembley. His hands went to fig leaf position. They smiled and waved at him and he waved back -- really glad to see that they were real and alive. Briony made the gesture, 'come on' and Wembley pushed off the bottom and they swam away together around the reef.

Wembley loved it that he never had to go to the surface, or depend on a tank and mouthpiece, or anything, not even a snorkel. He could stay down forever, if he wanted to. He followed the bubbles and flipping feet ahead of him. They led him to a sort of coral cave. They swam inside. He expected to see visions; which did not materialize, to his relief. It was only three friends in the beauty of a natural wonder. They watched the fish and other aquatic wildlife come and go. Wembley reached out his hand as a large multi-colored fish swam by. He felt the rough scales and the fish didn't even lurch away. It just swam on, undisturbed.

When they swam out of the cave another splash from above clouded their vision. It was Vivi. She touched bottom and Wembley saw her and just about choked to death on seawater. Right in front of him her legs disappeared -- well, they didn't vanish, but they transformed -- and were replaced by a fish's tail -- a fluke. Wembley's face screwed up into one big question mark. Briony and Shane pulled him off the bottom and the four swam along, Vivi in the lead, of course, out towards open water.

Something seemed to have changed -- other than Vivi's legs -- there seemed to be a closer friendship between Briony, Shane and Vivi. At least that's the impression that Wembley got. He couldn't trace the relationship because no one had been here the last two times he visited except Vivi and himself. He felt much more comfortable with others around, but not as pleasant as if Vivi were missing.

On their swim, the marvels of the island never disappointed Wembley. There was enough to see as they rounded point of each cove. They weren't quite back to their home beach when they felt the sun going down. They surfaced, saw the orb touching the horizon and raced for the shore. Vivi took a little longer to un-fluke herself -- Wembley was astonished -- but soon her feet carried her, racing across the beach to the trees. As the sun sank completely, the sand began popping just as the four friends each climbed their own trunk and held on as the feeding started, crested with the arrival of the whales and faded away as all were satisfied. No one had spoken.

"How do you do that with your legs, Vivi?"

"It happens as we each change into adults. You three are too young yet, but it will happen."

They were extricating themselves from the trees and came to sit on the beach.

"Is that why I didn't see the adults playing in the water?"

"Exactly. Most people here prefer their legs. I prefer my fluke."

"So how long does it take?"

"For what?"

"For you to be able to change."

"Not long. One day you are walking and the next day you are walking and fluking." That was Shane's assessment.

"Sounds better than were I come from. It takes years for a child to change to an adult. It's slow and painful."

"That makes me even more glad that I live here."

"Don't you like it here better, Wembley?" was Vivi's sultry question.

"I'll take my world -- with the sudden change of this world -- if I can swing it!"

"What do you call it?"

"We call it puberty."

"What a strange name."

"Yes. For a strange change." Wembley giggled and spoke a thought aloud. "Flukerty."

"What?"

"If I could name it I'd call it 'flukerty'."

The three companions laughed. "That is funny," Shane remarked. But the girls did not laugh again.

Vivi looked down her nose at Wembley, making sure that she made him as uncomfortable as possible with where she was staring. "We simply call it 'the change'."

Wembley closed his knees and wrapped his arms around them as they sat on the sand.

"How far is it to home?" Wembley tried to divert their attention.

"It's a short walk down the beach."

"Is it safe?"

"Now? Yes."

The three set off as the darkness enveloped them completely. Then after a minute the moons rose on the far horizon and the beach and the trees -- even the ocean -- were flooded with a soft blue. The white of the little houses was soon in sight and they walked to the doors of two houses, the first let Vivi enter with a goodnight stare at Wembley. The other three walked two doors down and disappeared into the next house together. Wembley felt at home here -- somewhat. Safe -- mostly. Home -- not quite. The telly was blaring and Gerald, Stella and Ralph were laughing at a program that was on. It was the one set in that department store, but a different episode than the one he had seen before.

After a brief reunion, which felt a little awkward to Wembley he asked them all a question. "How long have I been gone?"

"You left this morning, Wembley. You haven't been gone. We just went around the island today."

Wembley felt a little weak. What was going on here? He couldn't tell them that he had been here twice since he left and there was no one here. Even these people would think he was crazy! So he just excused himself and went to lie down. As he settled on his soft mattress, it enveloped him and eased him quickly into sleep.

Images came and went. He was soon in the water again, still flukeless, but not alone. Hands that weren't his ran over his skin. He saw Vivi's face come around in front of him and try to kiss him. He backed away and swam into a wall -- a wall of solid glass. He felt different and Vivi was not in the water with him, she was outside the ... tank he was in. He looked towards his feet and found that he was clothed but his hands were tied behind his back and his feet were in some kind of restraint. He was upside down! Soon a curtain was placed over the tank. It was dark. A dim, but useable light, came on at the bottom of the tank. He fumbled with his hands and they came undone. He reached for his feet and pulled a lever. The locks released and he was standing in the tank. Then the light went off, the tank drained and he slipped out the bottom while the tank refilled.

He crawled in the dark and found a ladder that went up. He sped up the ladder and stood atop a platform that was also curtained. He did not know why or how he was doing what he was doing; but he was doing it. With the removal of the curtain he saw that the tank, down below him, was empty. There was thunderous applause and he threw his arms wide. He grabbed onto a pole and slid to the stage floor.

Vivi was there (with clothes on, although not many) to embrace him. As they bowed to the audience he felt a hand on his rear end. He intercepted it and held it tightly. Then they both disappeared in a puff of smoke. The applause was thunderous. They were under the stage and the trap door was closing, blocking out most of the roar. Vivi held him close. He pushed her away. She kissed him. He pushed her hard. She fell.

"Vivi -- I'm sorry -- but that was totally unacceptable!"

Her eyes flashed. She was soon in the air, flying around him, ripping at his hair, his wet tuxedo and his shirt. He ran but she kept after him. It was like spell after spell came at him and he could do nothing to stop it. He was down to his underwear before he was able to duck into a doorway and slam the door shut. He found a lock and turned it. He turned around into a wet mop. He was in a janitor's closet! He saw mist coming in under the door.

He opened it and ran down the hall in his unders. He felt himself lifted off the floor, he saw swirls of color and light, mist and shadow enveloping him as the hallway disappeared and he was hovering over his bed. He was dropped, upside down onto his mattress and groaned as he heard his arm snap under him. Out of blurry eyes, powerless to get up or do anything, he saw the photocopy of Mallory rise into the air off of his desk and vanish. The room felt like a vacuum for a moment as everything that was not supposed to be there was sucked away, all the light and shadow and mist, out the open window it went and he was left to cradle his arm on his bed.

"Dislocated, but nothing broken."

"You sure?"

"Yes, Mr. Tewkes. You think us Cumry don't know what we're talkin' about?"

"I'm sure you do, but it really hurts."

"Dislocations are sometimes more painful than breaks. You're entire elbow joint was out of place, that involves tendons, ligaments and muscles as well as the bones. Lots of pain."

"You can say that again."

"Lots of pain."

"How long, Dr. Hinds?" was Marged's fear.

"Could be a month or two before he'll have full use of that arm. He'll need PT and lots of it. You have that available?"

Wembley piped up, good-naturedly, "We're not the Colonies, anymore, no matter how much you think we are."

The Doctor gave Wembley a look that could have broken his right arm, and then smiled. "And we're not England. I hope you know that."

"I do. I sometimes get called a Brit but I tell them I'm not British, I'm Welsh."

"Then it's true to the Land ya'are!"

There was a laugh all around and the Doctor handed a few papers to Gwyllym. "Follow these instructions and he'll be good as new soon."

"Thanks, Doctor." The little group of parents, Grans, and injured party trooped out of the office and down to the car.

"I hope this means that we're not going to stop going places?"

"Ya can walk can't ya?"

Wembley smiled. After all, he and Granda had a quest.

"Son," said Dylan, "you lied to the Doctor."

"What was I going to tell him? That I was injured in a 'DreamTravel'?"

"I guess not. But those didn't used to be so dangerous."

"Well, it looks like they are now." Wembley was a little miffed -- but not at his family. "What do I do? I can't fight them off!"

"Or can ya?" asked Gwyllym.

"You think I might be able to decide not to go somewhere?"

"It's worth a try."

"Or Granda could go with you!" was Marged's contribution.

"That's right, Da, you are one of those Protectors, aren't you?" asked Dylan.

"But I don't have any real powers."

"Maybe just your presence could dissuade this Vivi from hurting him again."

Wembley looked like he had something to say, but didn't know how to, or couldn't bring himself to say it.

"What is it, Son?"

"She seems to be after ... my ... virginity." There he had said it. "She wants me with her, if you know what I mean."

"How do you figure?"

"She's always putting me in situations where she can get her hands ... or her lips on me. Flaunting herself, teasing me. Testing me. Touching me."

The room was quiet. No adults like to hear about the abuse of a young person in their care or within their influence. Wembley was almost a man, but it was still abuse, because it wasn't what he wanted. It wasn't what his family wanted for him. It was just plain dangerous.

Dylan spoke up. "Are ya sure, Da, that you have to do this Quest?"

"Pretty sure."

"It seems like she's trying to stop you -- at all costs. What does that include? The life of my son?"

Wembley answered. "Da, I'm scared -- and you know I don't scare easily -- but it seems that there is something that has been leading all of us to this for a long time. I'm real glad it didn't touch you, but it has touched Granda and I. I think it's something I can't NOT do."

All Dylan could do was shake his head. He'd grown up with the 'curse', as he called it, all around him, only touching him indirectly through his Da. He had been in denial that it was anything but lunacy. Until now. It was brought home to him because it had caught his son in its mysterious grip.

"I'm puttin' shutters up inside and outside yer window. No sick, spectral, peeping Thomasina is going to bother you!"

"That will make me feel better, Granda. Those eyes are freaky. And I know they're not Merlin's, or else he'd be nothing but a dirty old man."

"Merlin?"

"Yes. Ma. I've met him in my travels. And he told me he had taken me a few places -- so I could learn and experience things."

"Like he supposedly did to Arthur."

"I think so, Ma. Vivi just gets in the way. He's helping to prepare me for something. But I don't know what."

"I guess we find that out when you turn sixteen," had Gwyllym letting that proverbial cat out of the bag.

"What happens at sixteen?" was Marged's panicked response.

"We don't know yet."

"That's why we ... why I need to see everything I can. Maybe I can get a sense of it before I turn sixteen. That way I'll be prepared for whatever it is."

"How can you prepare for this?"

"I've got to try, Ma! If I meet this knowing nothing, it won't be good."

There was silence again. They were all frightened. The possibilities were numerous and mostly negative in consequence. Gwyllym and Wembley together seemed to be the best solution, for the moment.

"I'll break the cot out and sleep up here with you, if you don't mind, Wembley."

"Why should I mind?"

Gwyllym chuffed a sort of laugh, but there was not much to be happy about. "I think it's back to the Cavern of Suffering."

"Really, Granda?"

"To me, Nimue's a key -- maybe the key."

"How? I thought it was Vivi?"

"You finished Mallory again?"

"Yes."

"I did, too. Who was in the chapter with Merlin?"

"Viviene." Then the light dawned. "Vivi?"

"Has to be! One and the same! But I thought you'd already made that connection."

"No. I was focused on Vivi, not Nimue as Vivi. But that's why her appearance in the cavern seemed so familiar. I see that now."

"But she was naked there."

"I've never seen her in clothes. Except for once."

Gwyllym laughed.

"Granda!" and Wembley gave him an elbow with his good arm.

"Sorry," but Gwyllym was not entirely contrite.

"It's not funny!" With the way his Granda was looking at him, it made Wembley laugh.

"Can we 'DreamTravel' to the cave?'

"You got us to Morlais, didn't you?"

"I think that was me."

"You think?"

"It wasn't Vivi, that's sure. She doesn't know about the place. Even if she did know, she couldn't get in. Her magic would help to bar her."

"Merlin?"

Gwyllym nodded, "Or us, the combination of two Protectors."

"Or all three."

"Yes. You and I have to confront her there. We need some answers."

"Will she cooperate?"

"We'll see."

They had a good night's sleep, even Gwyllym's snoring didn't keep Wembley awake. He did wake several times with his arm throbbing, but he lulled himself back into a -- thankfully -- dreamless sleep. At least he didn't remember any dreams after he woke up in the morning. No messages from Merlin. No advances from Vivi, Evie. Evie! It made him sad. After all the trust, all the convincing of his closest friends to accept her. It began to make Wembley a little angry.

He tried to stretch out -- that early morning feel-good type of yawning release, but his arm pained him when he lifted it incorrectly. He barked at the stab in his elbow and it woke up his Granda. They dressed and went down for breakfast.

Eggs and potatoes and cheese and big glasses of milk. Everything was silent in the house that morning. Apprehension filled the air with its own electricity. All that was unspoken seemed to be fully understood by each member of the household. If it wasn't total understanding, it was at least awareness.

"Ready to beard the lioness in her den?"

"How do we do this?"

"If I'm right, like this!"

Bronwyn, Marged and Dylan saw the two wink away. They were there and then they weren't.

"Something's happened," cried Marged, after a few seconds.

"Already?"

"Before, when Wembley traveled he came back instantly. They're not back."

Then the phone rang.

The screams as they touched down on the pebble beach were ear-piercing. Wem and his Granda scurried into the cave from the seaside, not sure if they really wanted to face this gale head on, but knowing that they had to. The passageway was more difficult to traverse this time because of the wisps and wafts of energy that pushed at them from out of the Cavern of Suffering.

"She must really be in pain to cause this much disturbance."

Wembley winced. He had struck his bandage-wrapped and slung elbow against a pokey rock. "Blast!"

"All right?" Gwyllym was surprised, he had rarely heard Wembley curse. He knew better than to correct him.

Wembley cradled his injured arm, trying to push the pain away. "Hit my elbow dodging that last wisp of whatever."

Laughter rang down the corridor as if it was making fun of Wembley's pain. He set his jaw and moved ahead. Gwyllym followed. More energy streamed toward them but they pushed against it. It was only delaying the inevitable. It was clear that she couldn't leave the cavern, but her energies could. Sooner than expected the floor of the cavern sloped up. They just about ran forward in their eagerness as the tunnel opened up and gave access to the cavern.

It was alive with light; colors that Wembley hadn't even imagined were swirling and weaving -- filling the space -- and at the center of it all was Nimue, red hair blowing and green eyes flashing. Wembley pointed to the left and Gwyllym started that way. Wembley went to the right.

"I thought I could get you back here."

"We needed to return," countered Wembley. "That's all!"

"I brought you here!"

"We decided to come, nothing you did physically transported us!" offered Gwyllym.

"Granda Protector. How quaint!"

"You have no power over us." Wembley hoped he was not bluffing.

"Not until you voluntarily placed yourselves here!" And she reached out and slammed Wembley into the wall of the cavern, followed by a blast at Gwyllym that sent him not quite to the walls, but to the floor.

Then the spectral image began to solidify. At least Wembley couldn't see through her anymore. A flesh and blood Vivi/Nimue stood in the center of the cavern -- attractive as ever.

"What is it you want, Vivi?" Wembley spat at her.

"Just you." She slammed Gwyllym to the floor again with a wave of her hands. Wembley backed up and placed his hands against the wall so he could not be slammed into it. He wanted to go to Gwyllym but his Granda held out his hands and shook his head, as if telling the boy not to move. Vivi turned to Wembley and Gwyllym went to work.

"I want you Wembley. I want your mind, your body" and she paused and looked at him, making him feel like he was filthy already, "and your soul."

"You can't have me -- not one part of me -- because I belong to another."

"Poor Brindi. She and Russel are not doing well at home."

"Don't listen to her, Son. She's always dealt in lies." Gwyllym was holding his hands out in front of him. Vivi/Nimue turned and blasted a spell in his direction but it bounced off of his hands, or maybe off of what was in front of his hands.

"So -- the Protector has learned a trick."

"How'd you do that, Granda?"

Vivi smiled and turned back to Wembley and sprayed energy at him that held him against the wall, tearing at his clothes and skin.

"You have it!" Gwyllym yelled, "Use what you have -- just imagine it."

Wembleys jacket and shirt had disappeared but he held his right hand, he couldn't use his left, out in front of him. He saw particles of energy leave his fingers. He didn't know what he was doing, just that he was doing something. At least he didn't lose any more layers of clothing. But he was bleeding from little cuts and tears in his skin. Then Vivi was right in front of him -- in a flash

-- she pressed against whatever it was that his hand had created.

"Impressive. You have it too. It's not half as impressive as your body."

Wembley's anger started to rise; he felt abused again, it wasn't through her touch -- she couldn't get to him -- it was her thoughts that were abusing and assailing him. He felt them catapulting themselves around the barrier he had erected; felt them washing over the skin of his torso; defiling him. Then he pushed the wall he had built and she was moved back. He shoved at the wall and she flew off her feet and landed on her backside. She was up in an instant and raging, but not before Wembley had the idea to wrap himself up in his -- warding! That's what it had to be.

He looked across the room, his muscles straining to keep the energy intact, as Gwyllym moved towards them. He, too, was encased in a warding of energy.

How did you know I could do this?

Because I found out how to draw the power through you. I did it before at Morlais.

They weren't speaking but they could hear each other. Vivi/Nimue looked confused as she diverted her gaze alternately between the two. Confident that she could crush them at any minute, she circled. She had the upper hand, the advantage. She flung her arms out to her sides, flashes of lightning left her fingertips, yet bounced harmlessly off the barriers of the Tewkes. Then she waved her hands -- and the cavern disappeared!

They were on a hilltop and Vivi raised her hands to the sky and bolts of energy connected her to the clouds. She rebounded that energy towards the two Tewkes but it, too, merely bounced off their protection. She waved her arms again and they were in the clearing of a forest.

Granda?

Broceliande. Her place of power.

Granda waved his arms and the surroundings changed again before she got off another shot. They were on a hilltop fort. There were no lights but he could see lots of trees outside the walls.

Vivi voiced her astonishment. "How can you do this?"

"We're Protectors. Much more than you anticipated us to be."

"I can kill you."

"No. You can't. You won't, because you need Wembley."

"But I don't need you, old man!" and she threw everything she had at Gwyllym. He was forced backwards but not toppled over. Vivi screamed, baffled at the sudden impotence of her powers. Then, just as suddenly, another figure appeared between the two. Wembley's eyes grew huge. So did Gwyllym's.

"Granda Hugh! What ..."

No time. Box her in!

With what?

Your wardings. Turn them from you to her.

Gwyllym's wall moved first. Then Wembley's, then Hugh closed off the two shields to form a triangle. A forth form shimmered into being on the hilltop and closed off the top of the warding.

"Gran Adelaide?"

Good to see you, too, Wembley, Gwyllym.

Gwyllym smiled.

Push! Smaller and smaller! came the thought from Hugh.

The wardings closed in on Nimue as she screamed in her weakness; the weakness that she had counted as a strength. The weakness that she had never learned to control or counteract or cleanse from her psyche -- what came from deep inside her. What <u>she</u> wanted was always more important than what the powers that controlled the Earth, Sky, Air and Water wanted; what they required of her. She had always gotten into trouble following her own ends. This was not the first time she had been imprisoned by lesser beings.

The four Protectors, for that is what they were, compressed the walls of the warding until they were touching the naked body of Nimue. Holding her to the ground, keeping her from them. She was trapped in a space no bigger than her own body's space. Then, dirt and rocks, from Hugh's and Adelaide's hands began to heap themselves on top of the warding, immediately followed by the grass growing over the little mound so that you couldn't tell that it was not anything but a natural and always-been-present part of the hill.

Wembley -- sweat, dirt and blood streaking his shirtless chest -- was kneeling and breathing heavily; exhausted. But the power of the eternities still seemed to radiate from him. Gwyllym was panting with difficultly and dropped to sit on the verdant grass, near his grandson. Hugh and Adelaide walked over to them as if this was nothing; was something that they did every hour of every day. Wembley stood and hugged them. Gwyllym shook their hands.

"When did you ..."

"We have always been Protectors -- since we were sixteen. Just like you, Gwyllym."

"Our powers are only activated when she threatens someone physically."

"Yes," said Hugh. "We are chosen to defend others, besides ourselves, but mostly Wembley."

"I didn't know," sighed Wembley.

"It wasn't allowed. No one could know, until they are ready for the information and secrets we carry. Even you Gwyllym, I'm sorry."

"I fully understand. Wait 'til Marged hears about it all. Both sides of the family ..."

"We are all here for Wembley. We have not been told what he will do, only that he will do something important."

"But how could you protect me when you're over here and I'm in America?"

"We created talismans. Your rug. Your afghan. Even the pictures of us you keep on your walls and dresser."

"How do you know where I keep them?"

"We are watching," was said by Adelaide with a smile.

"You mean you can see me ..." Wembley's blush rose quickly.

"Not all the time. We don't spy on you. Only when we are prompted to by the power that motivates all of us. We respect your right to your privacy -- and your secrets." Gran Adelaide smiled.

"Well, I'm glad of that!" and his blush diminished, but only slightly. "Where are we?"

"Better ask when."

"Okay, when are we?"

"6th Century Carlisle, about an hour from our Dumfries home."

"How did we get here, Gwyllym?"

"When she started taking us outta that cave I had to do something. So I started changing the 'DreamTravels'. I took us to one of the sights of Arthur's greatest battles. I thought that would help us defeat her."

"You can do that?"

"Apparently."

"You thought correctly, Gwyllym."

"So how do we get home?"

"Just like any other 'DreamTravel'."

They appeared at the Fitzroy's home in Carlisle, Cumbria. Before they cleaned up, or even did anything else, Wembley, dancing around, had to do one thing. He ran to the telephone.

"I've got to call Da!"

CHAPTER SIXTEEN
A Clue Is Only The Beginning

After the phone call the party of Protectors arrived by mysterious means and scared the living daylights out of Bronwyn and Marged. Dylan just took it as an extension of the insanity that had been brewing since before his own birth. Stories were told and minds were opened, but fears were not eased, at least not all the way.

The Fitzroys and the Tewkes together in Merthyr Tydfil! It had never happened. The Protectors had had to keep themselves separated, without knowing why. The comfy little cottage was full to bursting, but no one cared. Days passed and the New Year approached. This year, all of the family would be together, as was tradition for Wembley and his parents, in Dumfries. They were complete, but they had work to do before New Year's Day.

The Protectors had a meeting. Dylan and Marged were only too happy to go shopping for a few hours. It was all a little too much for them. They figured that whatever they needed to know would be explained to them. They didn't have the constitution to help make the suggestions or the decisions. They would leave that to those trained and foreordained for the purpose.

Gwyllym was the first to speak. "Have you heard of The Five Prophecies?"

Wembley nodded, but the Fitzroys shook their heads in bewilderment.

"Nennius only helped to muddy it all up giving us just the twelve battles of Arthur and thirty-three cities of Prydain. Wembley's quest starts in Caerleon."

"I knew that would come into play."

"Still chasing the Round Table?"

"No, not really."

"Why, then?"

"I have a feeling that Wembley and I will find the first clue to the first prophecy there at Caerleon."

"How? There is nothing left of the castle but a crumbling tower."

"The Wheels will provide."

"You have them?"

"Yes, but not here."

"They're safe at our house in Maine."

"Safe?"

"Captain Horatio Fletcher."

"Safe."

"And the prophecies lead to?"

"Wembley's destiny. I have a feeling that they will tell us all about everything that has built up in our family since the first Gwyllym, who was renamed Taliesin -- The First Keeper."

The Fitzroy's looked shocked.

"You're serious?"

"Absolutely."

"Taliesin?"

"Really?"

"Yes."

"Well, I guess that we're both good at keeping secrets."

"We have to be."

"Up for a drive?"

"What? Right now?"

"Of course, now."

"We can come?"

"For some reason we have been joined together in this fight -- and it's about time."

"Yes -- its always been about time." Adelaide chuckled a little.

"So why not save time through a 'DreamTravel'?" Wembley, terribly anxious and concerned, was hoping for a quick trip.

"I think that would open us up to the influence of Nimue."

"But she's ... in prison, isn't she?"

"Yes. But for how long? She has always managed to escape her prisons."

Wembley's head was in his hands. "But ..."

"It's all right, son. But I do agree that a car trip is safer. Will yer Da let us take the Jaguar? We'll never fit in the Cooper."

"We can ask them. They just pulled up."

Within thirty minutes the four Protectors were on their way to Caerleon, just outside of Casenewydd, modernly called Newport, in a Jaguar. The roads were clear, it was a bright, sunny day and the ice had disappeared. No snow -- not even a threat of it -- was possible out of a blue sky. The hour was eaten up by talk and chatter. All four were seriously concerned with the outcome of their drive. Gwyllym impressed upon them that the quest was Wembley's; that the three Grans were there for protection -- and moral support.

They pulled into the car park at the hotel that now occupied the old castle grounds, right on the River Usk. They walked to the old stone tower at the corner of the hotel. They stood, waiting to feel something.

"What am I supposed to feel?"

"What's right."

"That's not much help."

"It's all I can give."

"The only thing I am feeling is that it is not here."

"Not right here?"

"No. But somewhere close by." Wembley faced west. "Over there." He pointed.

"Do you know what's over there?'

"No, just that we have to go in that direction." Wembley was kind of mystified at what he was sensing.

"When I show you, you won't believe it." Gwyllym was all smiles.

They walked across the car park from the remaining tower and traversed the road, which led them into a field as they kept pursuing their course due west. After crossing the field they came upon an area with some mounds and rock work. They walked between two of the mounds, upon Gwyllym's suggestion, and stood in a large open area less than a thousand feet from the castle tower.

"What is this place? It looks like a theatre."

"It is. The great Roman amphitheatre of Isca Silurum. The Tabyll Mound. Or just maybe: The Tabyll Round."

"It's almost a circle."

"Imagine Arthur, standing right here where our feet are, looking around him at his legions of knights, pennants flapping in the breezes of the Kingdom of Summer. The best of them and the most well-known, sitting right in the front row. They not only talked about bravery and chivalry, they practiced it on this field in mock battles to hone their skills. This was a place where each hopeful seeking Knighthood, could prove himself in mock combat."

"But what about a table?" was Wembley's question.

"It is handed down that a table was given to Guinevere by her father Leodegrance, King in Eirinn ..."

"Ireland?"

"Yes, as a part of her dowry. It is mentioned that that table was large and round."

"So there are two round tables?"

"What do you say to that, Hugh?"

"I'd say that there might be three. There's a circular shrine not far from the Castle at Carlisle that many consider The Round Table. One of Arthur's

Twelve battles was fought near it. But I'm beginning to think that good things come in threes. Why not? Anything is possible with the magic surrounding Arthur."

"Maybe there was more magic than anyone supposed. It was all turned to romance by the Keepers. But the facts are plain and staring us in the face."

Wembley ran over to one of the rock structures. It was kind of on the northeast side of the circle of seats. "This is so cool!"

Gwyllym yelled to his grandson, "Sense anything?"

Wembley ran back over to the little group. "There's more than what we see. Those piles of rock used to be stairways -- down."

"That's what I have thought."

"How do we get there?"

"Time for a travel without much of a dream to it?" Gwyllym suggested.

"Give me your hands!" Wembley screeched as he held his out.

Everyone grabbed a hold. They expected to go somewhere. But stayed right there in the center of the arena. As they grasped each other they heard a twinkling, tinkling, sound. Wembley looked up from his closed-eyed circle of family to see a shaft of light coming up from the very rock structure he had run over to. He spoke softly.

"I think we have to go back over there."

They all looked and were dumbfounded at the shaft of light. Wembley led them to the former stairway only to find that stairs had indeed appeared. Wembley stepped down into the light and his foot took to the first step. It was solid so he took another. He turned, still holding Gwyllym's hand and pulled him after him. Adelaide and Hugh followed. They couldn't help themselves; they were too anxious to be able let go of the hand in front of them.

As they descended they felt that the light was withdrawing before them. They looked behind them and all was dark. The light was pulling them to where they had to be. It wasn't a captive feeling but an enticing one -- one which is filled with promise.

It led them through the catacombs under the circle above them. It was a maze! But Wembley figured that they were supposed to be here; that there was no danger, since they were all Protectors. This was an enchantment not by anyone like Nimue -- it was a first class Merlin work of art! There were so many turns that they could not count them and lost track, trusting in the light. They rounded the corner of one of the walls and found themselves in a small chamber.

There was a door -- beckoning them -- from across the room. Wembley ran to it. He placed his hands against it, willing it to open. It did not. Gwyllym joined him. The door still did not budge, unwilling to give its secrets up so easily. Then Hugh and Adelaide added their hands to the face of the door and it clicked, shifted and withdrew itself into the depths of the room before them, out of which, once again, the light was streaming. It took all four -- Four Protectors was the key to this room.

They walked into the room to find it lined with shelves. The only contents of the shelves was dust and a few small pieces of parchment. A great library had been here once, that was certain to all of the Protectors.

"This is it?" was Wembley's complaint.

Gwyllym handed his grandson one of the small pieces of parchment. Adelaide handed him the other. He looked closely and saw that there was writing on them. It was in Cymraeg. Wembley got some of the words but it didn't make sense -- he didn't have the whole picture. But Gwyllym was fluent in Welsh and he translated:

Bourne from the bloode of Cuchulain and Glam;
Riche in the lore of Morgan and Isolde;
Torne fromme his tyme by threads of olde;
Woven in tapestry baleful and bolde;

Gwyllym almost cried. He had been searching for this since the first phone call from Dylan alerted him to Wembley's predicament.

"What's it mean, Granda?"

"Don't know yet. But I'm feeling that it's a part of somethin' bigger. Somethin' that has plagued our family since the time of Arthur. It's about Merlin -- 'that torne fromme his tyme' part. Somethin' that concerns you more than it did any of the rest of us, or yer friends back home."

"It sounds like its about Merlin."

"It does at that."

"Do I have to help him?"

"In some way -- it seems."

"But there's only four lines. It seems incomplete to me. It's a quatrain where only three of the lines rhyme."

"Something's missing, alright. The outer edges on the two sides are cut and even. But the top and bottom as well as between the two bits are torn."

"There has to be more."

"Granda, while we were DreamTraveling with 'her' you said that one of the places that we stopped was Broceliande."

"Yes."

"But that's in France."

"Broceliande is not in Brittany."

"What? All the scholars say so," came from Hugh.

"They say so because they have been cleverly mis-led by the other

Protector-Scholars, Keeper-Scholars."

"Everything I've read is a lie?"

"Remember your annotated Mallory. It was fascinating! And terribly accurate from what I have read. Fact and fiction have been mixed. There are many magical forests in England. Birnham Wood did actually come to Dunsinane, you know, Sherwood Forest hid the enchanted Robyn of Locksley. Then there's the great forest of Caldeonia."

"Yes, Ceilidon, just north of us in Carlisle."

"So where's Broceliande?"

Gwyllym waited until he had them all guessing, "Just over the mountain from Caerleon. What's left of it, at least. We humans have never seen the magic in forests. That is why they are disappearing all over the world."

"Men only believe what they want to believe."

"They only believe what they see."

"Yes, that's right. That is why the Keepers were so successful at hiding the secrets concerning Arthur. They confused them and then infused them with romance. That is why the true legends of Arthur, Lancelot, Guinevere and Merlin have been safe for a long time. They had to be. The first Eden failed. So a second Eden was tried -- but it, too, failed, because of the frailties of men."

"Why not tell that to the world?"

"Most don't believe in the first Eden, anyway!"

"But what does Eden have to do with these pieces of parchment?"

"It is not Eden itself, but the belief -- the very concept. Who besides us would believe what these bits are telling us?"

They looked around the cell for an answer. Nothing was forthcoming.

"So do we go to Ceilidon? Broceliende?"

"I don't think we will know until you turn sixteen."

A warm wind blew through the room. They felt like they were standing still but they were being blown through the maze without having to move. Soon they were standing on the grass by the pile of rock that became a stairway, then closed. The magic was gone. Again.

CHAPTER SEVENTEEN
Home Again Again?

It was a sombre New Years. A tearful goodbye. A solemn drive to the airport. A downright boring, long and uneventful plane ride across the Atlantic. After what Wembley had been through anything would seem tame. Dull. Finally, his eyes lit up as the headlights of the car bounced off Captain Fletcher's home in Yarmouth, Maine.

He rushed inside -- for he had one of those feelings -- that something good was waiting for him. The lights were on as the family came trudging through the door to find Mary and Brindi and Russel, who could only laugh at the reunion of his sister and his best friend, right where they promised that they would be.

"Boy, Wem -- the storms started after you left and I've never seen so much rain."

"Then they just quit a few days before New Years."

Dylan, Marged and Wembley shared a guilty look. Wembley nodded. They all sat down and told their friends and Protectors about their trip. It took most of the night, but school didn't start for several days yet, so what the heck! Brin looked like she had something to add to the information.

"What is it, Brin?"

"I ... don't know if it's related, but the day after you left, we went over to pick up Evie for a Christmas party. She wasn't home."

"That's not so unusual."

"She's not back yet."

"She ... um ... she was ... she was in Wales." Wembley admitted. "I didn't tell anyone, not even you Ma, Pa."

"Why did she go to Wales?"

"I don't really know. She said that her roots -- Griffith -- were Welsh; from Caerleon."

"And she just happened to go when you were there?"

Marged asked, "Was she the one you talked to at the door for so long -- Christmas morning?"

"Yes, Ma." Wem was really struggling over this.

"What's wrong, Wem?" Russel climbed into his big brother's lap and laid his arm around his brother's neck.

"I've been fighting this connection but I can't get it out of my head. It won't go away."

"What?"

"Vivi and Nimue are the same. My 'DreamTravel' and the legend. I don't know how, but we're pretty sure about that. Nimue had many other names -- one of them was Ninieve."

Brin's and Russel's faces went ashen.

"Evie?"

Wem nodded. "I hope not, but what if?"

"What if your job is to keep Merlin away from Nimue?"

"Yeah -- what if?"

Characters (this novel as it is now written is set in the year 2011)

Wembley Tewkes -- long, dark, curly hair and blue eyes; an average successful 14 year old; (turning 15 in 2011) good at just about everything he puts his hand to -- athlete, scholar, socialite, humanitarian; prone to visions and dreams called by him 'DreamTravels'; is touched by magic; born in Wales on August 29, 1996, lives now in the area of Yarmouth, Maine. The Tewkes family emigrated to Maine in 2001 just before Wem turned 5.

Dylan Tewkes -- his father; magic has, fortunately, missed him; born in Merthyr Tydfil, Wales in 1978

Marged Fitzroy Tewkes -- his mother, born in Dumfries, Scotland in 1979, lost a son, Ioan, in 2000,

Ioan Tewkes -- the little brother who did not get to live.

Evie Griffith -- striking red hair and green eyes, an 'adopted' orphan, parents could be made up, or non-existent as no one has ever seen them; the puzzle of Wembley's existence; jealous of Brindi because of her own desire for Wembley. She appears 17-18. She possesses a mystery and a magic. Claims to have been born in January of 1994

Brindi Williams -- also 15, Wembley's girlfriend and long-time friend, green eyes, light brown hair, b. 1996

Russel Williams -- her little brother, age 9-10, worships Wembley, b. Sept 2001

Gwyllym Tewkes -- Wembley's grandfather, he has been touched lightly by the family quirk, enough to aid his grandson who has a bad case of it; Dylan's father, lives in Merthyr Tydfil, Wales, b. 1949

Bronwyn Gryffudd Tewkes -- Wembley's Grandmother, Dylan's Mother, lives in Merthyr Tydfil, Wales, b. 1946

Hugh Fitzroy -- Wembley's grandfather, from Dumfries, Scotland, Marged's father, b. 1945

Adelaide McShane Fitzroy -- Wembley's Grandmother, from Dumfries, Scotland, Marged Tewke's mother, b. 1946

Ivor Tewkes -- Wembley's great-great-grandfather, born in 1889 in Glamorgan, Wales

Sam Tupper -- 15, a tennis friend, b. June 1996

Jenny Copeau -- 15, another tennis friend, Sam's girlfriend, b. April 1996

Bryce Hauer -- 16, dark hair; taller than Wem, longer legs and quite a fast runner; on the track team with Wem; slender but wiry-strong. b. March 1995

Talon Waters -- a seven year old, mute because of the death of his father, which he witnessed. Wem tutors him at Big Brothers-Big Sisters. He is the first to travel with Wem on a 'DreamTravel'

Mrs. Waters -- Talon's widowed mother

Trenton Waters -- Talon's little brother, aged 5

Stephanie -- a girl at the Youth Center to be 'Big-Sistered.'

Mrs. Mary Williams -- Brindi's and Russel's mom (Protector)

Mr. Williams -- Brindi's and Russel's dad

Thaddeus Fletcher -- Antique Dealer (Protector)

Bill Lathrop -- Bookstore Owner (Protector)
Asher Tupper -- Sam's 10 year old brother
> *Civil War Dream Friends*
>> Johnny Lathrop, b. 1847, Sheriff of Lynnfield, MA, Sergeant, A boy, age 12 or 13; later, Mercer Fletcher (the other grand-father, the one who died.)
> *Island Dream Friends* -- Fiona, Allison, Jared, Elisha, Lisa, Peter, Colin, Sharon, Vivi (teens) & Shane, Briony(teens), Gerald (about 7 or 8), Stella and Ralph (parental adults).
> *The Herriott Dream* -- Reilly Johnson, James Herriott, Will/Wembley
> *The Potato Dream #1* -- Liam Connell(7)b.1845/Wembley, Willem Connell (10)b. 1842, Billy McPhee (12)b. 1840, [Liam (and Willem) are actually Wembley's Irish ancestors.], Ma Connell (Mary McGill), their mother.
> *The Winslow Homer Dream* -- Winslow Homer, Bill/Wembley, Elmer, Jimmy, several boys,
> *The Workhouse Dream* -- a hundred boys, boy in shadows, Matron, Old Servant
> *Captain Horatio Fletcher Dreams* -- Captain Horatio Fletcher (The Ninth Keeper); Reginald 'Reggie' Fletcher, his son; Myrddyn Emrys or Merlin;
> *The Potato Dream #2* -- Liam Connell(12)b.1845/Wembley; Willem Connell (15)b.1842; Billy McPhee (17)b. 1840; [Liam (and Willem) are actually Wembley's Irish ancestors], Mary McGill Connell their mother; Collin Connell, Pa; Mrs. McPhee; Mr. McPhee;

C. Michael Perry, Author, Composer and Lyricist, is a graduate of Brigham Young University. He is the composer of more than thirty musicals including <u>Cinderrabbit</u> for PBS, which won an Emmy Award and a "Best Of The West" Public Television award. He spent nearly a decade in television assisting in over 300 weekly episodes and commercials for ABC and PBS, Hasbro Toys and Toyota. He has performed in front of over 2000 live audiences from Utah to Italy in various plays and musicals. He has received acting awards for his many leading and supporting roles, won awards for lighting and scenic designs, more than forty shows have seen his directorial hand, and he has choreographed over fifty productions in is career, including <u>Big River</u> at the Sundance Summer Resort during the summer of 2010. Also a playwright and lyricist, he has written more than twenty plays and award winning musicals that have been published and produced across the nation and around the world. His ENCHANTED APRIL A MUSICAL, written with Elizabeth Hansen, has premiered in Provo, Utah and now has other production prospects popping up around the country. He is the founder and former President of Encore Performance Publishing, a publisher of plays and musicals for amateur, educational and professional markets, now owned by Eldridge Plays and Musicals of Lancaster, Pennsylvania. This is his third novel. He currently works as a freelance writer for Scottsdale MultiMedia, of Scottsdale Arizona. He resides in the Maine with his wife of over 30 years. His son, Jon-Christopher and daughters, Jessica, Janalynn and Joelle are out on their own; married and such.